TALES OF THE LOREKEEPERS
TOME III

THE LAST PRINCE OF TROY

MARTIN ROUILLARD

THE LAST PRINCE OF TROY
Tales of the Lorekeepers, Tome III

Copyright © 2014 Martin Rouillard
Cover painting by Danny O'Leary

Legal Deposit - September 2014
National Library of Quebec
National Library of Canada

ISBN : 978-0-9919627-7-8

Tales of the Lorekeepers:

1. Rise of the red Dragon
2. The Giants of Albion
3. The Last Prince of Troy

This book dedicated to my family: Thérèse, Jocelyn, and Geneviève.

ACKNOWLEDGEMENTS

Well, I can't believe we've made it to this point, halfway through the Tales of the Lorekeepers series. When I first imagined the world of Metverold, back in 2011, I believed I had a strong idea, on which I could build a great story. And I knew this story was mine to tell. I certainly did not think it would be easy, nor that it would be done overnight, and yet, it almost seems like it was yesterday that I anxiously typed the first words of Rise of the Red Dragon.

What a journey it has been, and I cannot wait to see what comes next.

Of course, I would never have made it this far without the talented (and patient) Keith Miller to edit my books and make it look like I actually know what I'm doing. He is a very talented author and a real teacher of the craft. You can get to know him at his website : www.millerworlds.com.

The cover for this book is a painting from Danny O'Leary, an artist that you can discover here : www.dannyoleary.com

I would also like to thank the following people for donating a little of their precious time and helping me polish all three books: Geneviève Laurier, Jocelyn Rouillard, Thérèse Gagné and Geneviève Rouillard. I appreciate everything you are doing for me and I love you all very much!

www.martinrouillard.com

"The depth of darkness to which you can descend and still live is an exact measure of the height to which you can aspire to reach."

- *Pliny the Elder (Gaius Plinius Secundus)*

1

Samuel rose from the depths of sleep with the remnants of a dream still seeking to drag him back into Morpheus's kingdom. Ethereal beings called out, asking him to join them so they could carry on their nocturnal dance—a waltz whose steps only the dream people knew. Samuel tried to resist, but the wheedling voices only grew stronger. For just a heartbeat, he allowed the mesmerizing chants to lift him up, and almost fluttered away into seductive fantasies.

Then his senses tore him fully away from his dreaming, and he remembered what had awakened him a few moments earlier: a sinister noise that did not belong to his imagination.

He chased away the clouds dividing the world of the living from that of the shadows, and finally opened his eyes. Above him, the ceiling fan spun hypnotically, creaking with each revolution. The fan was not strong enough to dissipate the room's suffocating heat, but he relished the slight breeze. Samuel laboriously pulled himself up onto his elbows, the thin cotton sheet sticking to his sweaty skin. He turned his head toward the bedroom window and pricked up his ears. The noise that had pulled him out of his sleep was still present outside. It taunted him, challenging him to get up and peek out at the street.

He swung his legs over the side of the mattress and slipped out of bed. It had been almost a week now since the nightly noises began pulling him out of sleep, and he was still not used to the strange routine.

Samuel took a deep breath and went to the bedroom door. He made sure the door was still locked. His father did not appreciate it when Samuel locked himself in his room, but Samuel preferred not to take any chances. He shuddered to think what would happen if one of his parents barged into his room in the middle of the night and heard the gloomy sound as well.

Chasing away the horrible images trying to slip into his mind, Samuel turned his back to the door. On the other side of the room, on his desk and next to his laptop, dozens of papers were piled: the notes he had written down in the two months that had passed since his last adventure on Metverold. They were printed excerpts from research he had carried out, as well as special quotes regarding certain legends. There were also detailed profiles of some of the most important characters of different mythologies, as well as many maps of mythical lands. Samuel had thought about transferring it all to a digital document on his computer, but had not found the time yet. These last few days, almost all of his free time was occupied with more important research, which took precedence over everything else—even his quest to find the sorcerer's identity. It pertained to the creature standing outside his house at this very moment.

Samuel walked to his closet and slowly opened the door, clenching his teeth when the hinges complained. Blindly feeling around, he found what he was looking for fixed to the wall inside the closet with a couple of hooks. Being careful not to make a single noise, he took out the sword he had kept since his journey on Albion. As soon as he felt the leather hilt between his fingers, Samuel's courage coursed through his veins again. He may not have the same fighting abilities in this world as he had on Metverold, but holding a weapon in his hands brought back self-confidence and subdued the fear that sought to get hold of him. Quietly he shut the closet door and turned to the window again. As he did so, he glanced at the alarm clock on his nightstand. Two-twenty in the morning.

He's early, thought Samuel. Cautiously he walked to the window. He moved with such vigilance to avoid alerting his nocturnal visitor, but also to prevent his parents from waking up and knocking on his door. He had no intention of explaining why he was strolling around in the middle of the night, wearing only his briefs, and carrying a three-thousand-year-old sword. Not to mention that he had no idea how the creature would react if it saw his parents. So far, Samuel believed he had successfully spied on his spooky visitor without being spotted, but should his parents get up and make noises, the situation could deteriorate in a heartbeat, and the consequences would be terrible.

The thought that the creature standing outside at this very moment could slip into the house and attack his family made Samuel's hair stand on end.

He paused for a moment and pricked up his ears again. The eerie noise was still there, barely perceptible among the rustling of the leaves, but impossible to mistake. It had nothing to do with the usual sound that occupied a warm summer night. It was a breathy whistle, like the sound of a viper weaving through desert sand, or the icy northern wind squeezing between two forgotten mountains. It was the sound of Death blowing into the neck of its next victim, right before it reaped its soul.

It was the sound of a monster that did not belong in this world.

Samuel hugged the bedroom wall until he reached the window. On each side of the opening, the damp breeze lifted the blue-and-yellow checked curtains. Samuel tightened his fingers around the hilt, summoned his courage and slowly moved his head forward to peek outside.

The ghostly rays of the moon painted the front lawn with spectral light. The trees standing along the street swayed hesitantly under the summer wind, and the houses' shadows pressed against each other like a protective rampart surrounding the neighborhood. In the street below, Shantel's car stood guard in front of the house: his sister was in town for the Fourth of July weekend. Across the street, Mr. Thompson's hundred-year-old oak stretched its branches toward the stars.

To anyone looking at the scene, the neighborhood would have looked perfectly safe, without the slightest danger in sight. But to the eyes of a Lorekeeper, the world was rarely what it seemed. In the course of his adventures on Metverold, Samuel had acquired the ability to detect traps and threats. It was almost like an instinct that set his entire body on alert as soon as his enemies were about to attack.

Enemies like the forces of Yfel.

Samuel scanned the houses across the street, meticulously examining every dark corner and shadowed space. He let his eyes linger on the cedar hedge between two neighboring houses, then on the back of a minivan parked a little farther down the street. He saw no sign of the creature standing outside. He still heard its disturbing whistling, but it was impossible to know for sure where it came from. It was as if the wind carried the baleful noise from every corner of the area.

"Where the heck are you hiding?" whispered Samuel.

But even as he said the words, he spotted a movement right behind Mr. Thompson's centennial oak. Samuel's heart nearly jumped out of his throat, and he fell to his knees.

Even though their little game had been going on for a few nights now, Samuel always surprised himself by thinking he had imagined it all; that the memories he had in the morning were only the result of Metverold's influence on his mind. But every time he spotted the monster's outline, reality rushed in to shatter his naivety. The dangers were no longer limited to his adventures on Metverold. Someone—or something—had found him here, on Earth, and threatened Samuel and his family.

Samuel tightened his grip on the sword until his knuckles turned white. He squinted and slid his head a few inches toward the window. The creature was still there, a black shadow barely visible against the tree, perfectly camouflaged in the night.

When the creature took a step forward, its face suddenly revealed by the moon's white light, Samuel lowered his head once more. Had the monster noticed him? Did it know the young man was awake, spying on it from his bedroom window?

The first time Samuel saw the creature, he had believed the intruder was nothing more than an ordinary man. Of course, he had found it rather peculiar that a strange man would be watching his house in the middle of the night, but he had concluded the man was most likely the Yfel sorcerer, searching for the Lorekeeper. Angeline had frequently mentioned that his sworn enemy was someone from his home world. She had also added he could be anyone, even someone close to Samuel. However, she had always hinted that the sorcerer was human, and the creature standing across the street was not human— that much he knew for sure.

For starters, its black eyes were like two curved lines, angled toward the slits of its nostrils, from which whistled the distinctive sound that had awakened Samuel for the past few nights. On each side of its hairless head stood two pointy ears. The foul creature's lipless mouth was forced slightly open, the teeth piling up inside. Samuel could not distinguish more details from where he was, but he was certain the creature's mouth was the last thing he wanted to see up close.

During the creature's first visit, Samuel had dived back into bed, and had remained hidden under the sheets. After a while, he had found the courage to go back to the window, but the creature had disappeared. At that moment, Samuel thought his imagination had played a trick on him. After all, it had been over two months since he had been called to Metverold, and the wait for a sign from the dice was almost turning into an obsession. It would be plausible that his mind had invented an enemy to satisfy his growing need for adventure.

However, when the creature had come back in the wee hours of the following night, Samuel understood that it was real. He had spent the night observing it from the corner of his window, hoping to learn what it was and what it wanted. For almost an hour, the monster had remained still, standing close to Mr. Thompson's house, looking at every home across the street in turn. Samuel had concluded that the creature was looking for something, and was waiting for a sign from its prey to go on the attack.

And Samuel had immediately understood what prey this frightening hunter was looking for: himself, the Lorekeeper.

The creature had then come back a third time, just before sunset. That time, it had appeared closer to the street, hidden in the shadow of Mr. Thompson's house. Once more, Samuel had observed it for almost an hour, but that time he had kept paper and pen close by and taken notes about his enemy. He had also attempted to take a picture of it with his cell phone, but the picture had produced inconclusive results, since he had avoided the use of a flash. The picture was dark and almost impossible to make out, not to mention that the spot where the creature should have been was empty.

This last detail had offered the first lead in Samuel's quest for the creature's identity. In the following days, he had conducted a more thorough investigation to follow up on this clue. He had consulted countless obscure websites, studied hundreds of images of ancient paintings, and read dozens of dusty reference books at the local library. He had even sent emails to a few authors and university professors, to which some of them had politely replied, but without being able to hide their bewilderment at Samuel's strange questions.

In the end, he had been forced to accept the truth. The nature of the creature spying on him for the past few nights was beyond doubt.

It was a vampire.

More precisely, it was a strigoi, a kind of vampire originating from Romanian mythology, somewhere in the Carpathian region. The distinctive physical appearance of the creature, as well as its strange behavior, made any other conclusion impossible to even consider. The ancient stories he had uncovered, as well as the answers from the experts he had contacted, all inclined toward this hypothesis. When he had recognized the creature in an anonymous carving of Hungarian origin, dating from the fourteenth century, the last lingering doubts vanished from his mind. He was the prey of a strigoi.

Samuel had then steered his investigation toward the means to get rid of such an infernal creature. Of course, most of the sources he had consulted merely repeated the usual techniques to kill a vampire: a wooden stake through the heart, followed by a clean decapitation and, finally, the torching of the body's remains. Nothing too complicated!

However, this method had to be performed on the vampire while the sun was shining in the sky. In order to do so, it was necessary to know the identity of the vampire, and the place where it rested in the day. Samuel had no idea who the strigoi had been before its death, and he had no way of knowing where it was hiding during the day. What's more, some legends claimed the strigoi were no ordinary undead, walking around at night to suck the blood of their victims, but rather that they were eternal demons, created by other strigoi. Some stories even suggested that they were impossible to kill, no matter how one would go about trying to do so.

Samuel focused once again on the sinister creature standing across the street. As it usually did, the strigoi looked at the nearby houses, observing them one by one. Slowly, the dark eyes moved from one window to another, while its eerie whistling disturbed the quietness of the night. Samuel did not understand how the vampire knew the Lorekeeper was around here somewhere, but it was now clear the creature had no intention of leaving the area before it found its prey. Was it his scent that told the vampire where Samuel was? Or had someone pointed it in his direction?

The vampire took a step toward Samuel and raised its eyes to him. Samuel dropped to the ground, holding his breath and clinging to his sword.

The strigoi had seen him; he was sure of it. He had let his thoughts distract him and must have raised his head too high, revealing his presence to the creature. Right now, the vampire was certainly walking toward the house. Any second now, it would try to get inside.

Samuel's heart was pounding at his ribs. His blood pumped in his ears, and the air he held in his lungs turned to stone. He had to lift his head and see what was happening, if only to get ready for a terrifying attack by a creature straight out of Hell.

Slowly, Samuel stretched his neck, until he could see the street again.

The strigoi was on the sidewalk, illuminated by the rays of the full moon over its head. Its eyes were now turned to the house beside Samuel's.

He didn't see me, thought Samuel with a sigh of relief.

Then a new noise caught his attention. It was the humming of a car approaching. The strigoi turned and frenetically sniffed the night air. Two headlights appeared on the horizon, like a couple of will-o'-the-wisps dancing under the stars. The car sped toward the vampire, its occupants unaware of the looming danger.

Samuel looked again at the dark creature across the street. The strigoi sniffed the air a few more times, and then it slowly backed into the shadow of the centennial oak and hid behind the trunk once more. A second later, its silhouette merged with the shadow of the tree, and it disappeared completely.

The car slowed down, passed before Samuel, and stopped in front of the house. Horrified, Samuel saw the occupants were none other than his sister Shantel and Patrick, a young man with whom she went out every time she spent the weekend with her folks, which was becoming more frequent these last few months.

Samuel's heart began to race and sweat beaded on his forehead. His sister was only a few meters away from the terrifying creature. He glanced at the oak, but the strigoi remained invisible. Still, he was convinced the creature was there, waiting for its chance to strike.

Should Samuel rush outside? Should he warn his sister and Patrick? He did not have the slightest idea what to do.

The strigoi had certainly been sent by the Yfel to find him, and Samuel did not think the monster knew exactly where he was. It had a general idea of where to look, but the fact it had not attacked the house yet indicated it still had not discovered in which house Samuel lived. If he were to come out now, the strigoi would know exactly where he was hiding, which would put the rest of the family even more at risk.

What's more, since the vampire was taking such precautions to remain unseen, it could mean that it had no intention of making a fuss and announcing its presence. Samuel wanted to believe it was because of him and his role as the Lorekeeper. Maybe the creature was not entirely sure that Samuel was vulnerable in this world.

Now that he thought about it, maybe staying hidden and keeping the illusion going was the best chance of keeping him and his family out of danger. Still, sooner or later, he would have to find another solution.

The slamming of a car door pulled Samuel away from his thoughts. Shantel was out of the car and walking around the back. On the other side, Patrick was standing by the car, a smile on his face.

"You're sure you don't want me to come up and tuck you in?" he asked without any regard for the open windows around them. "You never know, there could be a monster under your bed, or in the closet. You need me to protect you. Or even to—"

Shantel smothered her laugh with her hand and threw herself into his arms.

"Shut up," she said. "My parents' window is probably open. I'll be lucky if they aren't already up with the racket your car is making."

Samuel looked again at the oak across the street. The strigoi was still invisible, hiding in the tree's shadow.

"All right, I have to go now," Shantel said.

Before Patrick had a chance to find another excuse to hold her back, she pressed her lips against his. Without hesitation, Patrick took her in his arms and kissed her back.

"Don't forget that tomorrow you must—"

"Yes, yes," answered Patrick, "but don't forget you promised not to leave me alone with them!"

"I promise! But you'll see, they aren't that bad."

Shantel planted one last kiss on Patrick's cheek and quietly made her way to the front door. Samuel kept his eyes on her until she was safe inside, and then looked at Patrick again. He did not like him very much, and did not entirely trust him. Ever since he had met Shantel, following the larping weekend he and Lucien had attended, Patrick and his sister had been out almost every weekend. He did not know much about him, but something about Patrick made his skin crawl.

Patrick climbed back into his car and, without any consideration for people sleeping, he floored the accelerator and drove off in a cloud of dust.

Knowing that his sister was now safe inside the house, Samuel relaxed a bit and breathed normally again. For the moment, the danger was over. He looked up again at the spot where the creature had been hiding.

Samuel had to call upon all his willpower to strangle a scream of terror. Across the street, under the branches of the centennial tree, the vampire's silhouette was visible again, its dark eyes now locked on his.

The predator had found its prey.

2

Samuel sprang up in his bed, covered in sweat and out of breath. Outside, the sun was shining brightly, its rays dimmed by the curtains pulled over the bedroom window. The air in the small, closed room was heavy and warm, even with the fan still spinning under the ceiling. Outside, a lawnmower buzzed.

As he was slowly catching his breath, Samuel tried to organize the memories of the previous night, so he could make sure he had not imagined it all. He remembered the whistling breathing that had pulled him out of his sleep, the silhouette of the vampire under Mr. Thompson's oak, and the arrival of Patrick and Shantel. He remembered the eyes of the strigoi locked on his from the shadow of the oak tree. They were dark, evil eyes, full of anger and boundless grudge. He also recalled the grin on the mouth of the vampire, satisfied that it had finally located its prey's hiding place. Samuel had closed the curtains in a hurry, before diving to the floor and lying still on the wood. In his hurry to hide, he had come within a hairsbreadth of impaling himself on the sword. He could not say how long he had remained in the dark, petrified, as he waited for what would follow, but after a while he had finally summoned the courage to lift his head again. There was no trace of the strigoi.

Without knowing what the vampire was plotting, without the slightest clue as to where it was hiding, or how it would attack the house, Samuel had closed the window in a hurry, pulled the curtains shut, and crawled back to his bed. He had remained seated on the sheets, his sword on his knees, watching the hours slip away and waiting for a horrible attack, which never came.

At least for now.

He must have fallen asleep as the sun was coming up, his body too weak to stand guard any longer. Now his sword was lying on the floor next to his bed. Samuel quickly put it back in its hiding spot, before his parents insisted he open his door to them.

Samuel walked to the window and pulled the curtains apart. Outside, Mr. Thompson was slowly mowing his lawn beneath the oak. In the street, a couple of kids were decorating the street with chalk, and others were racing their bikes. There was not a trace of the strigoi. Not the slightest sign that the vampire had attacked anyone. Nothing even suggested that such a monster had been standing in front of the Osmonds' house a few hours earlier.

Still, Samuel could not shake the image of the infernal creature. He knew his imagination was not playing tricks on him. For the past few nights, an immortal vampire had been stalking him, and now the creature knew exactly where its prey slept.

A shiver ran along Samuel's body. He had to get out of his room and clear his mind. At least he was safe while the sun was in the sky. Samuel grabbed a black t-shirt from his desk and a pair of jean shorts from the chair. Why had the vampire postponed its attack? he wondered as he dressed. Did it fear the Lorekeeper so much that it preferred to wait for the perfect moment to strike? Maybe it was only here to find the Lorekeeper, and reveal his identity to its superiors. If that was the case, Samuel did not dare imagine what sort of diabolical monster the Yfel would send to deal with him.

One thing was for sure: a vampire—or any other creature sent by the Yfel—would be back in the area tonight, and

Samuel had no idea how to defend himself and his family against it.

Before joining his parents downstairs, he took a few steps toward the closet and grabbed the Trojan armor he had brought back from his last adventure on Metverold. With some difficulty, he had convinced his parents it was a particularly realistic costume for his role-playing games. Every time he laid his eyes on the bronze chest plate, he recalled his friends on Albion: Arkadios, Brutus and Corineus, as well was the beautiful Ignoge. What would they do if they were in the situation he was in? Brutus would most likely take control of things and find out where the creature was hiding, so he could kill it. Corineus would probably challenge the entire vampire race to a barehanded fight.

However, Samuel was neither Brutus nor Corineus. He was a simple young man from Massachusetts, tracked by a creature straight out of the most dreadful nightmares.

With a hint of nostalgia in his heart, he put the armor back in the closet and closed the door. He looked at the alarm clock, and saw it was already nine-thirty. It was time for him to go downstairs and do his best to hide the fear coursing in his veins. In the kitchen, his mother was sitting at the table, a cup of coffee in her hand. She was reading the paper's classified ads, looking for a used fridge to buy for a charity she devoted most of her time to. It was a soup kitchen, located in the most poverty-stricken area of town. When she heard Samuel come into the kitchen, she raised her head and welcomed him with a smile.

"Good morning," she said.

Samuel answered with a nod and made his way to the coffee maker on the counter, next to the sink. It had been a few weeks now since he had discovered the virtues of caffeine, and today he especially needed it.

"Still having trouble sleeping?" asked his mother.

"Yeah."

"Is there something on your mind, Samuel? Do you have problems? You know we can talk about it if you want to."

"No, I'm good. There's nothing bothering me," answered Samuel. "It's just the heat keeping me awake."

Mrs. Osmond put the paper down.

"You should help me persuade your father to install the air conditioning," she said. "He's starting to run out of excuses. If we work together, I believe we can make him yield."

Samuel replied with a smile and sipped his coffee.

"Tell me, did you hear your sister come in last night?"

Samuel's coffee went down the wrong way and he nearly choked.

"No. I guess she came back after I fell asleep."

"Do you know this boy she's seeing? Patrick?"

Samuel shook his head and swallowed another gulp of coffee.

"I am not particularly fond of him taking away my daughter like that every night," she said. "Your father and I still have not met him, and we don't know anything about him. At the very least, I'd like to know who his parents are and what they do for a living."

"Well then, you'll be happy to learn that I invited him for dinner tonight," came a sleepy voice from the kitchen's entrance.

Shantel stretched her arms with a yawn that lasted nearly a full minute, and then walked in the kitchen. She was wearing a Boston University Terriers shirt that hung just above her knees. With her eyes still shut, she fumbled her way to the coffee maker, gently pushing Samuel aside. With mechanical gestures, she grabbed a mug and poured herself some coffee.

"You invited your new boyfriend for dinner *tonight*?" asked Mrs. Osmond.

Shantel took a long swallow of coffee, closed her eyes and nodded. She staggered to a chair and sat facing her mother.

"Is there a problem?" she asked.

"No, no problem at all," answered Mrs. Osmond. "I would have appreciated it if you'd told me about it, that's all."

"Well, there you go. Now you know."

Shantel turned to Samuel, while she tried to rub the remnants of sleep from under her eyelids.

"You could invite your girlfriend too," she said. "What's her name again? Clara?"

"She's not my girlfriend. We're friends, that's all."

He noticed the mocking smile Shantel tried to hide behind the coffee mug as she swallowed some more coffee.

"All right, no need to get upset," she said, "but you should learn to lie with more conviction, Samuel. It's obvious you like this girl. Are you afraid she won't want anything to do with you? You want me to give you some pointers in the art of seduction?"

"Shantel, leave him alone," cut in Mrs. Osmond. "Samuel, why don't you go see your dad outside? He'll need your help cleaning the pool and trimming the hedge."

Samuel had completely forgotten he had promised his dad to lend a hand around the house today. He hated to disappoint him, but more urgent matters required his immediate attention: the imminent attack of a strigoi. Samuel was sure the vampire would be back tonight, and this time he might not be content with watching the house from under Mr. Thompson's tree. There was no doubt that the monster would attack, and Samuel had to be ready for it.

"Mom, I'm really sorry, but I promised Lucien I'd meet up with him this morning," he said. "There are some craftsmen who set their tents in the park, and we wanted to go check out their goods."

"But you promised . . ."

"I know and I'm terribly sorry, but the craftsmen only come once a year. I'll try to be quick. Tell him I owe him one, okay?"

Without waiting for an answer, Samuel kissed his mother on the forehead, grabbed an apple from the fruit basket on the table and ran for the front door.

"Samuel, wait!" his mother called, but Samuel closed the door behind him.

He had to find a way to kill a vampire before sundown.

Of course, Samuel had never promised Lucien to meet him for an afternoon of shopping among friends. In truth, he had run from home to get to the public library. He sat in front of a computer. He had very little time to find a solution, and every minute mattered. Household chores would have to wait a few more days.

For almost two hours, he typed words and sentences into various search engines, without finding an answer to his questions. He tried to reword his queries in a thousand different ways, but could not find a single clue regarding a method to get rid of a strigoi, other than the traditional solutions he had already learned, and for which he had to know the identity of the vampire. Samuel carefully read dozens of tales about the hunt for vampires, but they all ended in the same way: the decapitation of the vampire's cadaver, which was something he could not do.

He did find several clues regarding different methods to protect oneself against a vampire attack, like hanging garlic across the house, or refraining from inviting them inside, but he would have preferred to gather information that did not strictly come from superstition. He had a hard time picturing himself throwing bulbs of garlic from his bedroom window, like a low-budget horror movie, and he doubted that politeness was going to influence this vampire.

In the end, his stomach insisted that he eat something other than a single apple, and he left the library to go to a small restaurant across the street, the Brigantine. At a table on the patio, he dialed Lucien's number on his cell phone. Half an hour later, the two young men were enjoying a couple of tasty burgers.

"You look tired, Sam," said Lucien.

Samuel shrugged. "I haven't been sleeping very well lately."

"Something's bothering you?"

"You could say that."

"Anything I can help you with?"

"It depends. Do you know how to kill a vampire?"

Lucien almost choked on his burger, and then looked at Samuel doubtfully, sure that his friend was mocking him.

"It's just a joke," Samuel said, pretending to laugh. "The heat keeps me from sleeping."

"I know what you mean. Let's hope this heat wave won't last more than a few days."

Lucien bit down on his burger and some ketchup spilled on the table. Samuel watched his friend. He wanted to tell him he had been serious. He felt so alone before the danger that lurked around him, so powerless before a monster that he had no hope of vanquishing.

"Would you look at these two shitty dumbasses enjoying a sweet romantic meal," a voice from the sidewalk suddenly called.

Lucien raised his eyes to Samuel, who stared back at him. Both boys knew exactly who was calling out to them. They slowly turned their heads to the street and saw Danny, who looked at them with his hands on his heart, miming that he was moved by what he was seeing.

"Don't you have anything better to do than bother us all the time?" asked Lucien.

"No, not really," answered Danny. "To be honest, there's nothing I enjoy more than seeing the love between you two dumbasses."

"Dumbass, dumbass, dumbass!" called out Lucien. "Is that all you can say? You do realize only my great-grandfather and you still use that stupid expression, right?"

Samuel let a tiny laugh slip between his lips. Lucien would never change. Even with all the punches he had received and all the insults he had endured, he still held his own against the bullies, and against Danny in particular. The latter did not seem to appreciate how Lucien was talking to him, and walked toward the two boys.

"You're nothing but a pathetic dumbass, your great-grandfather is a dumbass, and your mother is also a dumbass," said Danny to Lucien.

"I'm impressed," answered Lucien. "It looks like you can use the one word you know in different contexts. Congratulations. Are you taking summer classes?"

Without warning, Danny grabbed Lucien's wrist and made him drop his burger. Samuel immediately sprang to his feet and pushed the bully away with a punch on the shoulder. Danny let go of Lucien, but quickly turned to Samuel and aimed for his face. Samuel barely had time to pull back and avoid the blow. He bumped into a customer sitting behind him, who spilled her beer all over the table.

"What's going on out there?" called out a voice from inside the restaurant.

The owner came out on the terrace and quickly made his way toward Lucien and Samuel. According to what was embroidered on his shirt, his name was Momo.

"What's all the ruckus about?" he asked. He looked at Danny. "Are you messing with my customers?"

Danny looked at him defiantly, and then replied with indifferent laughter. Without adding anything else, he took a few steps back before turning to Lucien again. "One of these days there won't be anyone to save your ass, and then you and I will have some real fun, dumbass!" he said. He turned to Samuel. "As for you, we still have a fight to finish."

"Whenever you want, wherever you want," answered Samuel.

"Come on, get *out* of here!" yelled Momo, waving a white tablecloth at the bully as if he was trying to get rid of a fly.

Danny gave one last venomous glance at Lucien and Samuel, and then disappeared down the street.

"As for you two," said Momo to the two boys, "you can finish your meal, but at the slightest sign of trouble, I'm throwing you out. Understood?"

"Yes sir," they answered in unison.

"Good."

Then Momo leaned in closer.

"Between us, don't let bullies like this guy get to you. Keep holding your own against those idiots, okay?"

"Yes sir."

"Good. Your meal's on the house."

"Thank you, sir."

Momo smiled at them, and went back inside the restaurant.

Lucien grabbed his burger again and took a bite out of it.

"I thought we would be rid of Danny during the summer vacation," Samuel said, "but it seems he has nothing better to do than annoy everyone around him."

"And we're not the only ones," said Lucien, his mouth half full. "Carl, Simon and Jessica told me he had also messed with them in the past two weeks, whenever they crossed paths."

"Sooner or later, someone will have to put him back in his place."

"I couldn't agree more."

Samuel sipped his Coke.

"Are we still meeting later for the fireworks at the park?" asked Lucien. "We should get there before sunset."

"Yeah, I'll meet you there, but I don't know when I'll be able to go. My sister invited her new boyfriend for dinner at our place, and my mom will surely pull all the stunts to make a meal worthy of a prince. Every time someone comes over for dinner, it's as if we're welcoming the president."

"Your sister has a new boyfriend?"

"Patrick, the guy she was talking to after the larping event a couple of months back."

"Simon Underwood's brother, right? You know, the little boy who stutters all the time."

"I think so. I'll try to get out of there as early as I can, but I'm not making any promises."

Lucien nodded and took another bite of his burger, followed by a handful of fries.

"I also asked Clara to join us," added Samuel.

Lucien rolled his eyes. "Did you really have to invite her?"

"It's the Fourth of July, Lucien, and she has no one to hang out with tonight. I told her she was welcome to join us if she wanted to watch the fireworks."

"I really don't know what you see in that girl, Sam."

Samuel took another bite of his burger. "I don't know what you mean," he said.

"Something's not right with her," said Lucien.

"Don't you think you're overreacting a bit?"

"Her story about moving here doesn't make a lick of sense," replied Lucien. "And did you notice how she has a knack for always showing up exactly where we are? We'd be chilling somewhere, just chatting about nothing and *bam!*—there she is. Just thinking about it gives me goose bumps."

"Really? That's your whole reason for not liking Clara? Because she finds herself in our path from time to time? We live in a small town, Lucien. We always run into the same people, on every street corner."

"Maybe, but this girl is weird, I'm telling you."

After lunch, Samuel returned to the library to resume his research. His best friend's company had allowed him to take a step back from all the horror, but the fact remained that time was running out. He had to find a solution before the sun came down, or else, he would be a nightmarish creature's meal.

Unfortunately, after three long hours, all he managed to get were dry eyes and writer's cramp. Before the library closed its doors and the staff threw him out, Samuel left and went back home.

His mother was in the kitchen, preparing a meal that would make any European chef red with envy. To take his mind off his impending doom, Samuel decided to give her a hand. He set up at the table, and started peeling carrots and potatoes. A few minutes later, the fragrance of roasting meat and maple cake filled the house, which did wonders to warm Samuel's heart.

Patrick knocked on the door and Shantel quickly opened it, throwing herself on his neck. She introduced him to the rest of the family. Mrs. Osmond put on her most polite and friendly smile, but her husband did not seem that impressed with his daughter's new boyfriend. Patrick was most likely very nice, and he probably made an effort to wear a clean t-shirt, but the holes in his jeans and the ring in his eyebrow did not fail to make Mr. Osmond frown.

Once everyone was seated at the table for dinner, Patrick did not help his image with Mr. Osmond when he told him he played lead guitar in a rock band, that he wanted to record an album, and that he dreamed of touring the United States. Samuel could not help but wonder what was worrying his father the most: that his daughter would have to stay home while her boyfriend partied in a different town every night, or that she would join him on those adventures.

Samuel had to smile thinking about what his dad would say if he knew his son risked his life in every adventure he had on Metverold.

Fortunately for everyone around the table, as time passed, Patrick managed to convince Samuel and Shantel's parents he was not such a bad boy after all. Among other things, he talked about his involvement with kids through larping events. He told several funny stories, including one about Samuel and how he had been killed only a few minutes into the battle, a little while ago.

"It was the other two players with me who couldn't stop making noise," protested Samuel.

"Yes, that goes without saying," answered Patrick, laughing. "It's probably also their fault that you got struck down by an archer who was participating for the first time, and had never fired an arrow before."

Samuel's retort was lost in the laughter of his parents and Shantel.

When dinner was over, Mr. Osmond went as far as to invite the young man into the living room with him. But Patrick decided to score a few more points with the family, and offered to lend Samuel a hand with the dishes instead.

As Samuel was wiping a plate, he nervously peeked through the window. Dinner had lasted a little over two hours, and outside the sun was approaching the horizon. Another thirty minutes and darkness would cover the town. Then the creatures of the night would come out of hiding, among them a famished vampire.

A shiver slid down Samuel's back and he excused himself and went up to his room. He still had a few minutes before he had to meet Lucien and Clara, and he wanted to check on some things before nightfall.

Once in his room, Samuel walked over to the closet. He took out the Trojan armor. Would it be a good idea to wear it tonight? It was not the best idea he'd ever had, and he did not know how he would conceal the armor under his shirt, but it was the only idea he could think of. Maybe with the bronze armor and a lot of luck, he could fight back the vampire. The monster seemed to be reluctant to take any risk in attacking a Lorekeeper. Maybe a warrior's attire would be sufficient to scare him away for good.

"Scare a vampire with three-thousand-year-old armor?" whispered Samuel. "Might as well wield a cardboard sword while I'm at it."

He threw the armor back in the closet and shut the door.

He suddenly thought of Angeline and Cathasach. He would have given anything to have them with him right now. They would surely have an idea to get rid of the strigoi, and if not, Cathasach could have handled the monster by himself.

Samuel sat down at his work desk and pulled back the bottom drawer. He grabbed a small leather pouch hidden inside, and emptied it into the palm of his left hand. The ivory dice fell out and rolled between his fingers.

Don't you have any suggestions for me? he asked.

Samuel rolled the dice in his hand. Had he learned anything in the course of his adventure that he could use now? Maybe he could repeat the moves he had made with his sword when he was on Metverold, but he doubted it. At best, he would avoid slicing off one of his legs while trying to strike his foe.

"You know, I have dice exactly like those," a voice behind him announced suddenly.

Samuel's blood froze in his veins and he had to put a hand on his desk to keep from falling out of his chair. Slowly, as if Death itself had just tapped his shoulder, he swivelled the chair around. Patrick was standing in the doorway, arms crossed over his chest.

"You … you have dice like these?" asked Samuel.

"Yeah. Well, almost exactly like those. But mine are black."

3

The air in Samuel's chest turned to stone, and the room around him swirled.

His enemy was here, a few feet from him. He had discovered the sorcerer's identity. Or rather, the sorcerer had found out his. Had the vampire told Patrick who the Lorekeeper was after he had seen him the night before? Did it mean there would be no attack later tonight? Samuel somehow doubted it. If anything, the Yfel's attack would take place much earlier than he had expected.

"You don't mind if I sit here for a minute?" asked Patrick. "Your sister is in the shower and—don't take this the wrong way—your parents, they're … let's just say I'll owe you one if you let me hide in here until Shantel is ready."

Without waiting for an answer, Patrick walked to the bed, where he let himself fall heavily. He glanced at the nightstand and grabbed the comic book he saw there.

"Ah cool! *Cain the Ogre Eater*! Is it the latest issue? I love this comic."

Samuel could hardly believe what was happening before his eyes. Since Patrick had come into his room, Samuel had not dared to move a muscle. He was petrified by shock and fear. The Yfel sorcerer was right there, on his bed, reading his comic book, and he acted as if the two young men were the best friends in the entire world.

"What are you doing here?" Samuel finally managed to ask.

"I told you, I need to hide from your parents while Shantel is getting ready," answered Patrick, without raising his eyes from the comic book. "You'll see when you're older; you'll understand what I mean. Your folks aren't mean or anything, but they're pretty boring."

"Don't you even dare touch a single hair on their head," said Samuel, recovering a little bit of his senses.

Patrick immediately raised his head toward him, his eyes goggling.

"Oh, chill, dude," he said. "Who do you think I am? They're not *that* dull! Good God, what a twisted mind you got there." Patrick put the comic book back on the nightstand and swept Samuel's room with his eyes. "Needs more posters in here," he said.

"Stop acting like an idiot," Samuel cut in.

Patrick fixed his gaze on Samuel again. This time, his eyes were showing a certain apprehension, and even a hint of animosity. "What the hell is your problem?" he said. "If you don't want me to touch your things, it's cool. You just have to say it, that's all. For God's sake, are you guys all morons in this family or what?"

The last words from Patrick were said with such contempt that it pushed Samuel over the edge. He lurched to the closet, grabbed the bronze sword from behind the door and pointed it at Patrick.

"Son of a bitch!" yelled Patrick, jumping to his feet. "Is that a freaking sword? Are you out of your mind?"

"You're the one with the black dice," shouted Samuel. "I know you're the Yfel's sorcerer. I don't know what kind of sick games you're playing, but you come into my house as if nothing was going on, you announce that you have the black dice, and then you call me a moron? Who the hell do you think you are?"

"Samuel!" a third voice suddenly yelled.

Shantel was standing at the bedroom door. She still had a wet towel wrapped around herself and water was dripping on the hardwood floor. Her eyes were glued to the bloodstained sword Samuel was holding.

"Samuel! What are you doing?" she asked with a trembling voice. "Where did you get this?"

"Shantel, stay where you are," said Samuel. "He has lied to you. He's not who you think he is."

"What on earth are you talking about?" asked Shantel, her voice edged with hysteria.

A few seconds later, Samuel's parents appeared behind her, alarmed by all the commotion upstairs. Mrs. Osmond screamed when she saw the scene, and Samuel's dad moved in front of Shantel, his eyes wide open in bewilderment.

"What's going on in here?" he said. "Samuel, what are you doing with that weapon?"

"He said he has the black dice," yelled Samuel, unable to control his voice. "It's him. He's the Yfel's sorcerer!"

"Sorcerer?" asked his father. "Have you lost your mind? Is this a bad joke you're pulling on us?"

"I swear, Mr. Osmond, I didn't do anything," said Patrick, his hands high in the air. "I don't have the slightest clue what's going on. I only wanted to get to know him a bit and chat for a while, and he jumped at me with this sword."

"You said you have the black dice," screamed Samuel. "Stop acting like an idiot! You're the sorcerer!"

"A sorcerer?" asked Mr. Osmond again. "Is this another of your role-playing games, Samuel?"

At that moment, Patrick's face cracked a smile and he slowly lowered his hands.

"Wait a minute," he said. "I think I know what's going on. That's it, right? It's a new kind of role-playing game that goes on twenty-four seven, right?"

Samuel did not know what to answer. Was the sorcerer trying to deceive them? Maybe he was only hoping to get rid of

Samuel's parents so they could have a little chat, just the two of them.

"Yeah, I think I got it now," added Patrick, before turning to Samuel and Shantel's parents. "Samuel probably belongs to a group of players who take their roles pretty seriously. It's a new trend in the world of role-playing games. The match isn't limited to the evenings or weekends. In fact, it never really ends."

Samuel wanted to say it was all nonsense, that it had nothing to do with role-playing games, but the words got stuck in his throat. Something in Patrick's attitude led him to believe the young man was not acting or lying.

"Now I understand why my little brother hung on to those weird black dice like they were the pupils of his eyes," added Patrick.

"Your little brother?" asked Samuel, lowering his blade a few inches. "You said it was you who had the black dice?"

"That's what I said, but if you had asked me where they were instead of shoving a sword in my face, I would have told you I gave them to my brother a few days after I bought them."

A doubt crept into Samuel's mind. Had he acted too quickly? Was Patrick telling the truth? Was it really his little brother who now had the dice, making him the real sorcerer?

"Could somebody please tell me what the heck is going on?" asked Shantel.

"Your little brother is acting out a role. Right, Samuel?" Patrick said. "The goal of the game is probably to find the player who has the black dice, the so-called sorcerer, and eliminate him from the game. When I said I had the dice, he thought the sorcerer was me."

"Is this true, Samuel?" asked Mr. Osmond.

Samuel lowered his sword until the tip of the blade rested on the floor. Something in Patrick's voice made him believe the young man was telling the truth, and that he had given the black dice to his little brother. Samuel remembered that Lucien had mentioned earlier that his name was Simon. If Patrick was not the sorcerer, then it had to be his little brother.

Samuel looked at Patrick, his parents and Shantel in turn. He then realized he had almost given his mother a heart attack, and that he must seem completely insane to everyone looking at him at this moment. Whether Patrick was telling the truth or not, he had no other choice than to pretend he was, if only to break the tension.

"I ... yes, Dad," he said. "It's nothing more than a game, and I was wrong. I thought Patrick was one of the players, like his little brother. I'm really sorry."

"It's cool, don't worry about it," said Patrick. "It's not the first time ..."

Mr. Osmond raised a hand to quiet him.

"Samuel, give me that sword," he said.

Samuel turned the sword in his hand, grabbed the weapon by the blade and presented the hilt to his father. Mr. Osmond took it, not hiding his surprise when he noticed the weight of the weapon.

"It's only a replica," said Samuel. "Lucien and I, we have—"

"Not another word," his father cut in with a tone that did not leave room for negotiation. "We'll talk about this tomorrow morning. Until then, you will not leave this room."

"What?" said Samuel. "But I have to meet Clara in less than an hour!"

"You should have thought about that before," replied his father. "You threatened this young man with a sword that is much more realistic than it ought to be for a boy your age. You almost made your sister cry and gave your mother an ulcer, and you scared the heck out of me. You will stay in this room until we talk it out tomorrow."

Samuel opened his mouth to protest, but his father turned and stormed out of the room, quickly followed by Mrs. Osmond. She looked at her son with tearful eyes, and then disappeared into the hallway. A second later, Shantel rushed to

Patrick and pulled him out of the bedroom, looking daggers at Samuel as she passed by him.

"Don't you think it's about time you grew up, Samuel?" she said in a voice trembling with rage. "We're all sick of your stupid games."

Patrick followed her, but just before he disappeared as well, he turned to Samuel again.

"Don't worry, Samuel, I won't tell my brother you know he's the sorcerer."

Shantel slammed the door shut behind them.

Samuel let himself fall back on his bed. He had really outdone himself this time. His parents and sister now thought he was completely insane, he could not spend the night with Clara and he was grounded until further notice. And to top it all, he now had no sword to defend himself against a vampire that was about to attack.

When the sun disappeared over the horizon, Samuel watched his parents walk out of the house, followed a few moments later by Shantel and Patrick. They were on their way to the public park, about a fifteen-minute walk from the house, to watch the Fourth of July fireworks. As she passed in front of Samuel's bedroom window, his sister shot him an angry look, while Patrick mimed zipping his lips shut to indicate he would not say a word to his little brother. As for Samuel's parents, they kept staring straight in front of them, studiously avoiding their son at the window. Evidently they were still mad at Samuel.

When they turned the corner, Samuel checked the time. The alarm clock showed nine-fifty. It was still early for the vampire to come around, but Samuel did not want to take any chances. Fearing the monster was already in position, he went back to the window and meticulously scanned the surrounding area, carefully examining every dark corner he saw. After a few minutes, he concluded the strigoi had not arrived yet, and sighed in relief. The only commotion in the street was from the neighbors making their way to the park to witness the fireworks.

Trying to create an illusion of safety, Samuel pulled the curtains shut and then went to sit on the bed. He grabbed the cell phone from his nightstand and punched in a text message for Clara, to let her know he would not be able to meet her at the park. He waited a few minutes for a reply, which never came. He hesitated for a moment, thought about sending the message once more, but opted to text Lucien instead. A few seconds later, his friend replied:

Is everything all right?

I'm grounded, replied Samuel.

Why?

Nothing, texted Samuel. Then he added: *I drew a sword on Shantel's boyfriend.*

He looked at the screen for a couple of minutes, imagining the face Lucien was making as he read his answer. Since his friend was not answering, Samuel quickly typed that it was only a joke.

Are you at the park? asked Samuel to switch subjects.

Yes, replied Lucien.

Is Clara there?

No.

It had been a few minutes now since Samuel had sent a message to Clara's cell phone, and she still had not replied. She was probably busy, or maybe had forgotten to bring her phone with her, but Samuel could not help feeling a little pinch in his heart. In the past few weeks, he had spent more time with Clara, and he had been looking forward to spending the Fourth of July evening by her side. He thought the festive atmosphere in the park, as well as the fireworks' magic, might have given him the courage to finally tell Clara how he really felt about her.

31

Unfortunately, his role as the Lorekeeper had spoiled his plans once again.

Can you tell her I'm truly sorry? typed Samuel.

Sure, Lucien answered.

Lucien had never really liked Clara, and every time she would join them, or whenever her name passed Samuel's lips, Lucien immediately changed his attitude. For reasons that remained unknown to Samuel, Lucien seemed to carry a grudge against the young woman. Samuel had thought that after a while, Lucien would have gotten to know Clara, and that they would all become good friends, but unfortunately the situation only seemed to get worse.

You guys have fun, Samuel wrote.

You too, replied his friend.

Samuel thought about sending a new text to Clara, if only to know if she had received the first one. In truth, what he wanted to know was if she was as disappointed as he was that they could not spend the evening together, but since he could not find a way to formulate his question without looking like a perfect idiot, he let it go. Romance did not seem like Clara's strong suit anyway. She was more the kind of person to get straight to the point. If she had any feelings toward Samuel, she would have let him know already. Since she had done no such thing, he preferred to keep his own feelings for her to himself. It was pointless to create uneasiness between them for no reason.

Samuel put the phone back on the nightstand. The idea of sitting down at his computer to resume his research on the strigoi passed through his mind, but he quickly waved it off. He'd had just about enough of investigating vampires. For a week now, it was all he could think about. He had spent countless hours before a screen, scrutinizing every result, and had still found nothing useful. Even today, he had spent the majority of his time reading all kinds of ridiculous information about the creatures of the night, and had not made any progress.

After all, everything was still calm. Maybe the vampire had decided to postpone its attack for another night.

Samuel got up and went to the closet. He did not have his sword, but he was not completely defenseless. He reached for one of his old t-shirts, hanging at the end of the pole. Inside, he found a little knife, stored in a small leather scabbard with a metal tip. He had brought back the dagger with his armor from his last adventure on Albion. Samuel slid the weapon into the waistband of his shorts and shut the closet door.

He sat down in front of his computer. The ivory dice were still on the desk, next to the leather pouch in which he usually kept them. With all the commotion he had created when he believed he was facing the sorcerer, he had completely forgotten to put them back in the drawer.

He picked up the dice and rolled them between his fingers.

"When are you going to send me back to Metverold?" he asked, but, the dice remained silent.

Samuel had often reflected on the nature of the dice. Angeline had told him that beings of supreme power, the Parcae, walked in our world and left the dice in specific places. The little fata had also revealed it was the Parcae who were in charge of Virtus, but Samuel had a bit of a hard time believing that both these facts were true. If the Parcae were responsible for the dice and Virtus, then why would they also leave a pair of black dice with the white ones? If there were no black dice, then there would be no sorcerer, and therefore no problems. Of course, trying to understand the gods' shenanigans was like trying to understand the rules of a cricket game, and Samuel quickly let it go.

Still, some bitterness persisted in his mind. No more than a week had passed between his first adventure and the next one, and Samuel had thought he would not have to wait long this time. However, it had now been almost two months since he came back to Earth, and he had to admit he was starting to miss Metverold and the legendary friends he had made there.

Once or twice, he had even cast the dice, hoping to provoke a journey to the land of heroes and legends. After all, his first adventure had started like that, after he had thrown the dice on his desk. Alas, his few tries had been in vain, and so he had been compelled to be patient and wait for a sign.

Samuel looked at the alarm clock once more. It was a little after ten. Was the vampire outside, waiting for him to fall asleep before jumping through the window? Maybe it was searching around the house to find a way to sneak inside? There was only one way to find out.

Grabbing his courage with both hands, Samuel pulled the curtains a few inches apart, sat on the hardwood floor and peeked outside. Once again, he saw nothing out of the ordinary, only more neighbors making their way to the park. Samuel decided that if he was going to spend the whole night keeping watch by his window, he might as well do it on a full stomach. Although he was grounded, he was the only one in the house at the moment, and no one would know he had left his bedroom. After all, he wasn't ten anymore!

He got back up and went to the bedroom door. Without really knowing why, he opened the door with caution, making sure he was truly alone. It was stupid, but he almost thought the vampire could have been roaming down the hall. Of course, there was no one else in the house. Relieved, Samuel quietly went down the stairs.

He walked to the kitchen and turned on the light. His heart calmed down a little when he realized there were no gloomy figures hiding in the room and waiting to jump at his throat. Thinking himself a little ridiculous, he lowered his eyes to the table. On it was the most magnificent sandwich Samuel had ever seen, along with a bag of BBQ chips. A note was leaning against the plate:

Hurry and eat it before your father and I come back home, Samuel, and have a lovely evening!

"Thanks, Mom," whispered Samuel with a smile.

He grabbed the plate and walked out of the kitchen. Since he was all by himself for a few hours, he might as well enjoy it. He walked past the stairs and went into the living room, where he sat down in the recliner. He grabbed the television remote and raised his eyes to the black screen.

As soon as he saw his reflection in the television, his heart nearly jumped out of his chest and he yelped in horror. He immediately dropped his plate, and it shattered on the wooden floor. On the black screen before him he saw his own silhouette, outlined by the light in the kitchen. Behind him was the silhouette of the vampire, slowly creeping toward him.

Samuel jumped out of his seat and swiftly turned around. He fumbled to find the knife with trembling fingers, but then remained perfectly still. Before him were only the kitchen and the empty vestibule. There was no sign of a strigoi; nothing to indicate that the monster had been standing only a few meters from Samuel just a second before.

Samuel carefully walked to the stairs and glanced up them, but again he saw nothing out of the ordinary. He went back into the kitchen, looking under the table and behind the counter, but once more, everything was perfectly normal. There was no trace of the hideous vampire.

It's probably my mind playing tricks on me, thought Samuel.

After all, he had not slept very much lately, and the vampire occupied his thoughts almost constantly. It was easy to imagine that if he thought he had seen the monster, it was not truly there.

Still covered in goose bumps, Samuel went back to the living room. When he saw the shattered plate on the ground, he sighed heavily and went to get a broom. As he was cleaning up his mess, he heard strange sounds coming from the second floor, and his blood ran cold in his veins. The noises were like quick, muffled steps, as if a child was running. Without daring to move a muscle, Samuel remained perfectly still, hunched next to the recliner.

Was it his imagination playing tricks on his mind again? Samuel did not know what to think anymore. The noise had lasted just a few seconds, and silence had now fallen in the house, but he could have sworn someone had walked above him a few moments earlier.

With great care, Samuel got back to his feet and took out the knife at his waist. This time, he would not take any chances. Before he let fear petrify him on the spot, he climbed up the stairs. With each step, he paused and turned his head to keep an eye on his back. Finally, after what seemed like an eternity, he reached the top of the stairs and scanned the dim hallway.

Everything was quiet, without a trace of an intruder, and no sign of a vampire.

Samuel's gaze came to rest on his bedroom's closed door. Had he shut it himself after he had come out earlier? He didn't recall doing so.

On tiptoe, clenching his teeth with each creaking of the wooden floor under his weight, he walked to the door. When he put his fingers on the doorknob, he held his breath for a second, and then opened the door quickly, unable keep a scream from getting out.

In his room, everything was in its place. Once again, there was no sign of a strigoi. Had he imagined it all? Maybe he was going mad.

Still with the dagger in his hands, Samuel examined the bedroom, making sure to check under his bed. Cautiously, he made his way over to the closet, his ears pricked, ready to warn him at the slightest sound. Once more, he held his breath when he put a hand on the knob, then yanked the closet door open. Inside, there were only his clothes, an old piece of armor, and a few articles for role-playing games. With a sigh of relief, Samuel shut the door and turned on his heel. Ignoring the mocking voice at the back of his mind, he knelt on the floor and checked under his bed again. Nothing.

Relieved, but still apprehensive, Samuel slowly got back to his feet. His eyes wandered to the window and the curtains hanging over it. The voice inside was not mocking him anymore. Instead, it was whispering frightening ideas, and scenarios he preferred not to think of. And the voice only grew more insistent. Samuel knew it would be impossible to resist much longer.

He had to know.

He had to make sure that everything was still normal outside; that the vampire was not there, waiting for him to go to bed.

With his fingers wrapped around the knife so tightly his knuckles turned white, his jaw clenched so hard his teeth ached, and his breath shortened by the fear growing in his stomach, Samuel slowly walked to the window. With his heart beating like a drum, he slid a finger between the curtains and pulled them apart in one quick move.

Outside, he saw Shantel's car, Mr. Thompson's tree, the neighbor's hedge … and a shadow standing right in the middle of the street, its eyes locked on him.

The strigoi was there, looking straight at its prey.

Even worse, it was flanked by two more vampires, their dark eyes also directed at Samuel. When they saw him at the window, an eerie grin appeared on their horrible faces, and all three figures took a step toward the house.

Samuel flattened himself against his bedroom wall, unable to catch his breath.

The vampires were here, and they were attacking.

4

Samuel clenched the Trojan dagger against his chest, the dull blade flat on his black t-shirt. Cold droplets of sweat slowly rolled down his spine. His eyes were wide open and looking straight in front of him, his muscles paralyzed by fear, and his mouth suddenly as dry as sand.

He could hardly believe what he had just seen.

All day long, Samuel had feared the moment when the vampire would appear in front of his house, but he had never imagined it would be accompanied by two of its fellow creatures. Had they always been there, hiding in the shadows? Had they led similar searches in other neighborhoods of the city to find the Lorekeeper? Were there other vampires that would join them in the next few minutes?

All these questions did not matter anymore.

The vampires were there, and they were walking toward the house.

Samuel's neck stiffened when he tried to raise his head to the window, as if it was imploring him to stay still, but he knew the vampires would not leave the area. After all, they had seen him at the window. Besides, waiting in ignorance was unbearable. The monsters were probably very close to the house now. Maybe they were even climbing the walls at this very moment. There was only one way to find out: he had to look outside again and be ready to face his enemies. Of course, that was easier said than done.

Drawing on every drop of courage he could summon, Samuel finally raised his hand and slid a finger under the curtains. Moving cautiously, he pulled the curtains slightly apart and peeked outside.

The street was empty. There was no sign of the vampires. However, Samuel was convinced he had seen them a few minutes earlier. He was sure his imagination had not played any tricks on him this time, and the strigois were outside, hiding in the darkness.

Suddenly he heard a series of quick steps in the ceiling.

They're on the roof, he thought.

Instinctively, he bent his knees and hunched his back, as if the ceiling was weighing on his shoulders. The vampires must be trying to get in through the attic. If they succeeded, they would sneak into his parents' bedroom, using the trapdoor in the closet. Samuel had to find a way to prevent them from doing so. He had to do something before it was too late.

Without thinking twice, he stormed out of the bedroom and flew across the corridor toward the master bedroom at the end of the hall. Images of the vampires sneaking in through the closet tried to compel him to turn around, but he quickly discarded them. Every second mattered and he could not have any doubts. He had to barricade the closet door with the bed, the furniture, and anything else he could get his hands on.

He rushed into his parents' bedroom, half expecting to see the three vampires already in the house, but the sound of more footsteps greeted him. This time they were moving toward the front of the house, though much more slowly than before.

Then someone knocked on the front door. The three knocks echoed throughout the house, and Samuel froze.

Was it the vampires having fun at his expense? Maybe the neighbor across the street, Mr. Thompson, had seen the strange shadows lurking around the area. Maybe he just wanted to warn the Osmonds, like any good neighbor would, without thinking for a second that his life could be in danger. Samuel imagined the vampires pouncing on the old man and tearing him apart without mercy, while the poor man raised his hands to the sky and pleaded for help.

Samuel chased away these horrifying thoughts. Mr. Thompson was probably at the park anyway, along with the rest of the neighborhood.

Three more knocks echoed again through the house from the ground floor, with even more emphasis this time.

Tock.

Tock!

TOCK!

Samuel backed out of the bedroom and walked to the top of the stairs. When he saw the lower half of the front door a chill tickled the back of his neck. Since the visitor was not a neighbor, then it certainly was one of the vampires. But why were the vampires knocking on the door, rather than forcing their way in? After all, it seemed unlikely that the simple door lock prevented such monsters from invading the house. Did they only want to toy with him, before sucking all his blood? Were they amused by this kind of torture?

Samuel put a foot on the first step with extreme caution, then slid the other foot onto the following step. A flicker of hope suddenly appeared in his mind. Maybe the legends were true, after all. Maybe the vampires could not enter unless they were invited in. The monsters were probably knocking in the hopes that Samuel would answer the door and make a fatal mistake. Therefore, if Samuel was cautious and kept a cool head, maybe he would survive until dawn.

The strigois knocked on the door once more, this time with such force that Samuel heard the hinges creak from where he stood. With his knife still in his hand, he carefully made his way down the stairs, until he was standing by the front door. For endless minutes, he remained still, waiting for what was to come. On the other side of the door, he heard the whistling of a vampire, the noise that had awakened him every night for the past week. The whistling seemed louder and faster now, and Samuel smiled, thinking the vampire was probably frustrated by his silence.

The legends were true, thought Samuel. *They can't get in.*

Another series of knocks shattered the silence inside the house, but this time they were coming from the living room. Samuel quickly turned his head to his right and saw a gloomy shadow looking at him through the window, an evil grin on its face. One of the strigois was standing there, both of its hands flat on the glass, staring at Samuel with its dead eyes. Its skull was misshapen and devoid of hair, its pointy ears seemed glued to its head at different heights, and its nose was nothing more than two holes in the middle of its face. It was wearing a dark, dirty, moth-eaten coat, which came to below its knees. At the end of its bony fingers, Samuel saw yellow nails as sharp as a jackal's claws.

The vampire slowly opened its mouth, revealing a pair of bone-chilling fangs, still bloodied from its last victim. It knocked on the window again, slowly and softly. Without taking its eyes off Samuel, it stuck out its black tongue and lazily licked the glass. Then, without warning, the strigoi disappeared like the wind.

A horrible feeling was tickling Samuel's guts; a feeling of powerlessness he had only experienced during his adventure on Metverold. A tiny voice was warning him to get ready for the worst, telling him that terrifying events were about to unfold. The vampires were not satisfied with merely trying to break into the house. They were also mocking him. The monsters were trying to shake him, and were waiting for Samuel to make a mistake. Their plan was probably to torment him until he could endure no more, until the point where he would abandon all reason and try to flee from the house. If he were to make such a mistake, if he got out of the house screaming at the top of his lungs, then they would descend on him before he could even reach the street.

Samuel took a deep breath and silenced the voice in his head. He would not make such a mistake. He would not get out of the house, and he certainly would not invite them inside either. All he had to do was to wait patiently for ...

For what, exactly? He had no idea. Sooner or later, his parents, his sister and Patrick would all come back from the fireworks, and then the vampires could use them to draw him outside. Samuel did not dare imagine what kind of torment they could inflict on his family to force him to show himself. He had to get rid of them before the fireworks were over. He quickly glanced at the time on the stove. It showed ten forty-two.

The fireworks would not start for another twenty minutes. If it was like the year before, the show would last about half an hour. Then his parents would probably make their way to the house, unless they decided to chat with the neighbors before leaving the park.

Samuel estimated he had about an hour, maybe a little more.

The shadow of a strigoi quickly passed through the window above the kitchen sink. A moment later, the same shadow flew by the window next to the front door, and then that of the living room. At the same time, another vampire frenetically pounded on a window upstairs, while the third monster howled through the chimney. Its horrible scream filled the house, and Samuel had to drop his knife to cover his ears with both hands. The scream lasted for several minutes, along with the hammering upstairs, while the shadow of the first strigoi flew across the windows a second, then a third time, always going faster.

Then silence abruptly fell once more.

Samuel remained still for a moment in the vestibule, his eyes closed and his hands on his ears. Cautiously, he opened his eyes and exhaled. Everything was calm now, but he doubted the vampires had decided to abandon their prey. They were most likely getting ready for another attack.

Samuel picked up the dagger he had dropped and sat down on a step. He put his elbows on his knees, clenched the hilt of the dagger in his right hand, and looked straight at the front door before him. If the vampires wanted to force him to run, a little bit of noise would not make him flinch. He would remain seated on the stairs, and he would find a solution to send the monsters away before his parents returned.

With each squeaking of the house frame and each drop falling in the kitchen sink, Samuel's heart tightened. The seconds soon turned into minutes, which stretched endlessly in turn, without anything else happening. Silence reigned outside the house.

Samuel thought the strigois had to be preparing something particularly scary; something that would terrify anyone—but they forgot Samuel was not an ordinary young man. He was the Lorekeeper. He had faced creatures that would send the bravest men fleeing for the hills. He had seen things that would terrify the most courageous boys his age. He certainly would not let himself be scared by the stupid tactics of bloodsucking monsters.

Someone knocked at the front door again.

"You've already tried this one on me!" shouted Samuel defiantly.

"Samuel? Are you there?"

Samuel bounded to his feet and lunged for the door. When he saw Clara's silhouette in the door frame, his heart skipped a beat. Clara opened her eyes in shock when she saw Samuel, but he did not give her time to say a single word. He grabbed her wrist and swiftly pulled her inside. He then glanced at the surroundings. There was no sign of the vampires. He shut the door in a hurry, locked it and set his back against it.

"Are you all right?" he asked Clara, panting.

She looked at him from head to toe.

"Me? Of course I'm all right," she replied. "I should be the one asking you."

Samuel looked down at himself and noticed he still had the dagger in his right hand, and his black t-shirt was soaked in cold sweat.

"I … I mean that … it's not important," he said. "Are you sure everything's okay? You're not hurt?"

Clara put her hands on her waist and frowned at him. She was wearing a black cotton tank top and jean shorts that showed off her athletic legs. Her red hair fell over her shoulders, and her crystal-green eyes were staring at him with a questioning look.

"Samuel Osmond, what the hell is going on? What are you doing with this knife in your hands?"

Samuel looked at the dagger he was holding, then looked up at the young woman again. Clara raised an eyebrow, and Samuel understood she was not going to give up without an answer.

"It's nothing," he said. "I was only training myself with this dagger for the next larping event. That's all."

A movement to his right suddenly attracted Samuel's eyes and he quickly turned his head toward the kitchen, certain he had seen the silhouette of a vampire in the window, over the sink. It turned out to be the shadow of a tree outside. Clara followed his gaze, then turned back to him, waiting for further explanations.

"And what are you doing here to begin with?" asked Samuel, trying to change the subject.

"Your text message," answered Clara. "You wrote that you couldn't come see the fireworks. I wanted to see how you were doing."

"You could have replied to my message."

"Oh, you know, technology and me have never really gotten along. I'm more of an old-world kind of gal, if you know what I mean."

44

Samuel was using all his willpower to remain calm in front of Clara and not spill the truth in a way that would make him look like a complete lunatic. The last thing he wanted was to scare her with stories about vampires. She would never believe him, but it did not change the fact that vampires were still lurking in the area. He had to find a way to protect Clara from them.

"I thought you'd be happy to see me," said Clara. "If not, I can always go away."

She took a step toward the door, looking defiantly at Samuel.

"No! I mean, yes," replied Samuel. "Of course I'm happy to see you, but you can't stay here."

"You want me to go?"

Of course not, thought Samuel. Clara's presence was a blessing that almost made him forget his troubles. It was as if the young woman could confine both of them in an invisible bubble that protected them from sadness and worries. At her side, Samuel felt limitless, as if he could conquer any mountaintop if he set his mind to it. Nonetheless, even with such bliss numbing his mind, he could not bear the idea of putting Clara in danger, and he could not send her outside without any protection. Even if the strigois had remained silent since Clara's arrival, Samuel was convinced they were still out there, spying on the house and its occupants.

"If it were only up to me, you could stay here as long as you wanted to," replied Samuel. "But I'm grounded. If my parents find you here when they come back, things will get even worse for me."

"You're grounded? At your age? What did you do?"

"It's a long story. I—"

"Samuel, did you get caught going on adult websites?"

Blood rushed to his cheeks.

"What? No! It's … Forget it, okay?"

Samuel was thinking as fast as he could. Any second now, the vampires would resume their little game to scare him, and then he would have to explain to Clara what was going on. If he did, either she would run away from him forever, or she would mock him. He had to get rid of Clara before anything happened to her.

An idea crossed Samuel's mind. It was a little farfetched, but it was better than doing nothing.

"Did you see anything strange on your way here?" he asked.

"What do you mean by strange?"

"I don't know. Strange or weird people."

"You mean, besides you?" answered Clara with a grin.

"Okay, I get it! No, I mean people lurking around. For some time now, the neighbors have been complaining about vandalism in their yards or on their cars."

"No, I didn't see anyone."

Samuel thought about the previous night, when Shantel and Patrick had come home. Just before the car stopped in the street and its passengers got out, the vampire had retreated to the shadows. And tonight Clara had seen nothing unusual, despite the three strigois trying to get inside the house.

Maybe the creatures of Metverold—if the vampires did, in fact, come from there—were afraid of humans for reasons unknown to Samuel. Maybe some strange rule forbade them from interacting with men and women in our world, with the exception of the Lorekeepers. It could also be a defense mechanism, to avoid a witch hunt.

In the end, maybe it was not up to Samuel to protect Clara, but rather her presence that would keep the vampires at a distance. Samuel was far from being convinced his theory held water, but he had little choice. He could not send Clara into the street, and he had to drag the vampires away from the house before his family returned home.

"You want to go get some air and look at the fireworks?" he asked.

"I thought you were grounded."

"At my age?" he replied with a wink. "Wait here, I'll be right back. Don't move a hair!"

Samuel climbed the stairs two at a time and ran to his room. However, even in his hurry, he paused for a second at his bedroom door and scanned the room. Once he was sure there was no monster hiding in the room, he stepped in, threw the dagger on the bed and removed his sweat-soaked t-shirt. After applying a new coat of deodorant as fast as he could, he slipped the first clean t-shirt he saw over his head.

Then he cautiously went to the window, pulled the curtains slightly apart and checked the front of the house. There was no sign of the vampires. The neighborhood was perfectly quiet. Maybe the monsters had decided to postpone their attack because of Clara's presence. Maybe his theory was not as farfetched as he had thought.

Maybe he would see the morning sun after all.

Before he went back downstairs to join Clara, he picked up the ivory dice from his desk and put them in a pocket. He then opened one of his desk drawers, took out a pack of mints and flipped one into his mouth. Better to be ready for anything.

He grabbed the dagger from his bed and considered carrying it with him, but when he thought of the explanations he would have to give Clara, he decided to forget about it. He stored it in the desk drawer instead, and then rushed down the stairs as fast as he had climbed them. Once on the ground floor, he suddenly stopped.

The young woman had disappeared.

"Clara?" Samuel called out.

There was no answer. Samuel's heart started racing, while his mind whispered terrifying scenarios.

"Clara!" repeated Samuel, louder.

Still nothing.

Panic suddenly swept over him. He took a step into the kitchen and called her name again, then did the same in the living room, always without getting an answer.

Clara had vanished.

With each second that passed, a knot tightened in Samuel's stomach. He had left Clara alone for less than five minutes and that had been enough for the vampires to grab her. At this very moment, they were probably having fun inflicting the worst torments on her, before feasting on her blood.

With a furious scream growing in his throat, Samuel rushed to the door and leapt outside, ready to fly to Clara's aid.

"Are you coming, Samuel? The fireworks are about to start."

Samuel stopped dead on the front door's threshold, short of breath, his fists clenched by his side. Clara was standing in front of him, her arms crossed on her chest and her face brightened by the moonlight. She was so beautiful that Samuel forgot all his worries. In the darkness, the young woman's green eyes shone like an aurora borealis, and her pink lips were like a flower picked from the most exquisite gardens of Eden. Her flaming hair cascaded down her shoulders.

"Samuel?" she asked. "Is everything all right?"

For barely a breath, Samuel forgot about Metverold, his role as a Lorekeeper, the Yfel and the vampires tracking him. In that moment, all that mattered to him was Clara and the thought of taking her in his arms, embracing her and tasting her sweet kiss.

"Yes, everything is all right," he answered, moving closer to Clara. "Let's get out of here. We'll have a better view of the fireworks from up the street."

Clara answered with a smile that melted Samuel's heart. They turned west and walked for a while, then climbed up the street toward a small hill at the end. Samuel spent most of the time glancing nervously all around them. Even if his theory was true, and the vampires would not dare to come closer because of Clara, he thought the monsters were certainly following them at this very moment, watching from the shadows of the houses and the trees around them.

"Are you sure everything is okay?" asked Clara.

"Yes," answered Samuel, barely hiding the worry in his voice.

"You know, whatever you did to get grounded, I'm sure your parents will have calmed down by the time they return. You can relax. You have nothing to worry about anymore."

Samuel would have preferred it if the only thing on his mind was his parents' attitude toward him. Unfortunately, he could not tell Clara the real reason for his anxiety, and that secret that ate him up from the inside was sometimes even more unbearable than the fear of being attacked by the vampires.

After about ten minutes they arrived at the top of the hill. Here the town had installed a few aluminum benches, scattered around a tree that was supposed to be even older than the town, something Samuel had always doubted. Since the entire neighborhood had preferred to go directly to the park to see the fireworks from up close, this one was deserted at the moment.

Once Clara and Samuel sat down on a bench, Samuel quickly scanned their surroundings. There was still no sign of the vampires. Samuel was tempted to believe the monsters had abandoned their hunt. For now, anyway.

"You know Samuel," Clara said suddenly, "you truly are enigmatic."

"I know, you already told me."

"No. I said you were strange. Being enigmatic—that's different."

"Really?"

Clara threw her head back and lifted her eyes to the stars. "You're mysterious, a riddle to those around you. Being enigmatic arouses people's curiosity, while being strange usually makes them run away. I've met many strange people in my life, but very few who were enigmatic. I have to admit it gives you a certain charisma, even though you usually do everything you can to hide it and put out the image of a perfectly normal boy."

"And it's wrong to want to be ordinary?" asked Samuel.

"Only if you are extraordinary," replied Clara. As she spoke, the first of the fireworks exploded in the sky.

"You really think I'm someone out of the ordinary?" asked Samuel.

Clara slowly turned her eyes to Samuel and looked straight into his. "Let's just say that I still haven't found anything mundane about you, Samuel."

The sky lit up with a rain of green, red and blue lights. The explosions grew more powerful, culminating in a crescendo of multicolored stars, before the show slowed its rhythm to let the spectators catch their breath for a second. On the bench, Samuel slid closer to Clara, his mind lifted by the magic of the stars. He did not think of vampires anymore, or Metverold, or even his parents. All that mattered now was the angelic face of Clara, the perfume of her hair, her big, bright eyes and her delicate lips. He had an irresistible desire to put his arm around Clara's shoulders and bring his lips to hers. He had been dreaming of it for many months now, fantasizing of telling the young woman how his true feelings for her had been tormenting him ever since they met. More than once, he had wanted to speak the words echoing in his heart, but every time his courage had failed him. Maybe tonight things would be different.

"Samuel," said Clara, lowering her eyes.

"Yes?" He slid a little bit closer to her.

"Samuel, please."

Samuel felt his heart shatter.

"I have to go," said Clara without turning to him. "I'm really sorry, I—"

Without finishing her sentence, she quickly got up and walked away. A few moments later, she turned into the street and disappeared, leaving Samuel alone on the bench, his heart in a thousand pieces and his mind in shambles.

For many long minutes, he stayed still, numbed by sadness, unable to order his thoughts. What had he been thinking, exactly? Why had he ruined such a perfect moment by allowing his feelings to take over; feelings that were clearly not shared by Clara?

What an idiot he was!

Above Samuel, the fireworks continued their assault on the darkness, the explosions following each other without letup. He heard the joyous cries of children from the park, as well as the cheers of the adults. Everyone was having fun and enjoying their time with their loved ones, while he was alone and pitiful.

For a moment, he had thought that Clara was also feeling something toward him. After all, she had come to see him at home earlier that evening, instead of simply answering his text message. And Lucien was right: Clara had a habit of always showing up wherever Samuel was. Contrary to what his friend thought, Samuel had entertained the hope that the young woman acted this way because she had a crush on him.

Had he been that wrong in interpreting Clara's attitude toward him?

After another ten minutes, the fireworks reached their pinnacle. Then the last sparks burned out and left the stage for the applauding crowd below. A few seconds later, the shouts and cheers also vanished, and the silence once again claimed dominion over the night.

However, a noise persisted. It was a sound Samuel had not heard until now, since it had been covered by the detonations, but he recognized it immediately. Now that the fireworks were over, the sound was impossible to miss. It was a rasping whistling, coming from somewhere behind him.

Samuel jumped to his feet and turned around. About thirty feet away, the three strigois were watching him, their sharp teeth exposed by their horrible grins. Samuel immediately reached for the knife at his waist, but remembered he had hidden the weapon in his bedroom. He cursed himself, keeping his eyes locked on the vampires. The monsters took a step in his direction, savoring every sign of fear that appeared on his face.

Samuel was defenseless, without any weapons or powers. The only remaining option was to run. Without thinking, he took a step to his right. Maybe if he moved fast enough, he could get around the vampires and run down the street, until he met the crowd coming back from the park. Unfortunately, as soon as he put his foot on the ground, one of the vampires planted himself in his way with phenomenal speed. A moment later, a second monster moved to his left, cutting any hopes of fleeing in that direction.

Samuel was trapped. He would die here, drained of all his blood by three creatures from another world, without anyone ever knowing what had truly happened to him. His hands were shaking and sweat rolled into his eyes. All of this could not be real. Surely he was having a nightmare. After everything he had gone through on Metverold, after all the dangers he had survived, he could not die like this.

At that moment, he felt something warm against his thigh. Samuel plunged his hand into the pocket of his shorts. He pulled it out and opened his fingers. The ivory dice glimmered in his palm with a red glow. Already the light was spilling around his feet.

As soon as they saw the dice, the vampires screamed in unison. The two strigois flanking Samuel turned to the tallest of them, who was still facing the young man. The monster looked at each of its companions in turn, then fixed its gaze on Samuel and growled wildly in his direction.

It understands, thought Samuel.

Without wasting a minute, Samuel threw the dice to the ground, and prayed to every god of Metverold he could think of that it was not too late. If he could not outrun the vampires in this world, maybe he could flee to Metverold and buy some time. He had no idea what he would do when he returned, but it was better than staying here and waiting for his demise.

The dice bounced on the ground and a powerful detonation echoed in the night each time they hit against each other. The vampires screamed and launched themselves toward Samuel, their hands straight out before them. However, one of them had the misfortune of stepping on the red light spilling on the ground, and immediately vanished in a green flame. The two remaining monsters stopped and looked anxiously at each other. Samuel immediately stepped forward, until both his feet were inside the red light.

If the vampires wanted to get to him, they would suffer the same fate as their companion.

As the landscape started to swirl, Samuel's gaze met that of the tallest vampire, probably their leader. The monster growled in anger at Samuel, its face twisted by rage. Its prey was so close, yet impossible to reach.

At least for the moment.

Samuel held the monster's gaze for a few moments, until he heard musical instruments, and the perfume of countless flowers entered his nostrils. A few seconds later, the colors of the night merged with each other, and the Lorekeeper got ready to return to Metverold. Right before he lost consciousness, Samuel saw the vampire smile at him, before sitting on the bench to patiently wait for its prey's return.

Then everything went black.

5

"Samuel! Samuel! Wake up!"

"You think he's dead?"

"Of course he's not dead! Well ... I don't *think* so."

The words floated sluggishly toward Samuel, who was fighting to rid his mind of the dark clouds shrouding it.

"I think we're wasting our time," said a nasal voice. "If you want my opinion, he's dead."

"Stop talking nonsense," replied the other voice. "Samuel, can you hear me?"

This voice was much more pleasant than the first. It was soft and honeyed, as comforting as the smell of warm bread by a baker's window. It covered Samuel's spirit with a peaceful balm, and allowed him to grab hold of his senses again. It was a voice that awakened in him a feeling of familiarity, like an old friend welcoming him with open arms. Slowly his muscles answered to him, and his senses sharpened again. A few moments later he moved the tip of a finger, and finally regained consciousness.

Then he opened his eyes, and his heart nearly jumped out of his throat.

Just a few inches from his nose a horrible face looked at him with red goggling eyes.

Samuel screamed at the top of his lungs.

"Calm down, my boy," said the face, with a creaky voice. "That's your Lorekeeper? Is he always so easy to scare? Because if that's the case, we're already doomed."

"Of course not, don't be silly," replied the other voice. "He has more courage than all of us, but anyone would be scared to death to wake up to a stranger's face a few inches from his own. Step back and let him breathe, by the gods."

Samuel heard a little buzzing close by, and a few seconds later the familiar silhouette of Angeline appeared before him. As soon as he laid eyes on her, he relaxed a little and his heart slowed down a notch.

"Are you all right, Samuel?" she asked.

Samuel wanted to get up before answering, but a sharp burst of pain crossed his skull and made him clench his teeth. Searching the back of his head with the tips of his fingers, he found a little bump already growing on his scalp.

"I'm really sorry," said the hoarse voice. "If I had known you would appear in my humble home, I would have made sure your landing was softer."

"How many fingers am I holding up?" asked Angeline, waving her tiny hands in his face.

"Three," answered Samuel.

"Perfect!" said Angeline. "He's okay."

Samuel painfully raised himself on his elbows and slowly lifted his head. He saw that he was in a room sculpted directly from rock, probably in the heart of a mountain. Like the cold and damp floor on which he lay, the smooth walls and dark ceiling showed no seams or cracks. A few torches hanging on the walls pushed back the darkness in the room, but the flames made eerie shadows dance on the stone surface, and gave the room a gloomy feel.

"Here, drink this," said the dry voice.

An old woman hunched over Samuel and offered him a copper goblet. Before he could ask what was inside, she forced him to take a swallow. As soon as the warm liquid flowed over his tongue and down his throat, a burning sensation spread in his chest and he quickly spit back the beverage, before choking violently. With eyes blurred by tears and his breath short, he turned toward Angeline.

"What did you give him?" she asked the old woman.

"It's tea made with olive leaves," she answered. "I also added a few wild berries, and some vine bark and jasmine root. It will help him get his senses back."

Samuel coughed one last time, and then raised his head again. Soon after, the burning sensation in his chest vanished, and he had to admit that only a few seconds later he had regained full control of his body and mind.

"Where am I?" he asked Angeline.

"We are in Cumae, in southern Italy," she answered.

Samuel stood up a bit straighter and she set herself on the ground next to him.

"And *when* are we?" he asked.

"I don't know the exact date, but it's around 1170 BC."

"So I'm even farther back in time than the last time?"

"Yes. About a hundred years earlier, in fact."

Samuel thought he would never get used to traveling in time like this. He felt lost and powerless and had to use all his willpower to refrain from panicking, since there was only one way for him to get back home: protect the legend.

Brushing off the complaints of his muscles, Samuel got to his feet, but was seized by vertigo and almost lost consciousness again. The old woman quickly made him sit on a wooden bench in front of an ancient table.

"Thanks," said Samuel.

"Be careful," answered the old woman.

Angeline quickly flew toward her.

"Samuel, I'd like to introduce you to our hostess, Deiphobe. She is the Cumaean Sibyl. Deiphobe, this is Samuel, the very latest Lorekeeper."

"Nice to meet you," said Samuel.

Deiphobe looked at him inquisitively, as if she was trying to decide whether or not the young man deserved her trust. She had a hard face, furrowed by a few wrinkles around her eyes and at the corners of her lips, and her skin was a colorless white, which made it impossible to guess her age. Her graying hair was bunched up in a chignon at the back of her head, but a few locks had escaped captivity and hung loosely behind her ears. Her look was sharp and full of wisdom garnered over the years, but her lips were young and vibrant. She was wearing a red toga that bordered on pink, and made Samuel think she was not a small woman. On her shoulder rested a blue shawl made of a light material.

"Let's hope the Parcae made a wise choice," said Deiphobe after a little while. "If you ask me, Angeline, I believe we should rethink our strategy, just in case—"

"That won't be necessary," cut in Angeline. "Samuel is an excellent Lorekeeper and he will succeed. Don't worry about him."

"I pray to Apollo that you are right, little fata," said Deiphobe, "because many men have sought to prove their valor with a journey like the one we will undertake, but very few came back to tell the world about it."

Samuel straightened on the bench and looked at Angeline, suddenly worried about where this conversation was going.

"Angeline, what … what journey is she talking about?" he asked.

Before the fata could answer, footsteps and clashes of metal echoed from a tunnel in front of Samuel.

"By the gods, they're already here!" said Deiphobe. "Stay in this room and be quiet."

The old woman raised her shawl over her head and disappeared into the dark tunnel without offering more information. Samuel jumped to his feet and turned to Angeline, but she signaled for him to stay quiet. They remained still and in complete silence for a few moments, but then curiosity took over and Angeline flew to the corridor, closely followed by Samuel.

The tunnel was in total darkness, and it was only by chance that Samuel avoided hitting his nose on the stone wall when the corridor made a sharp turn to the left. He saw a flicker of light at the end of the dark tunnel, as well as the outline of Deiphobe, who entered another room. In front of her stood a man clad in bronze armor. A scabbard hung from his waist, and a shield was attached to his back. From this distance, it was impossible to see what he looked like.

"Who is it?" asked Samuel in a barely audible voice.

"Achates," answered Angeline, without offering more details.

The newcomer greeted Deiphobe. "Are you the Cumaean Sibyl?" he asked.

"What do you think, Achates?" replied Deiphobe. "Who else would live in solitude under Apollo's temple?"

"You know who I am?"

"Of course. I am the Sibyl, after all."

"So you know the name of the one I travel with, and who just set foot on the Euboean shores?"

"I know who leads you, yes."

Samuel had no idea what was going on. "Who are they talking about?" he asked Angeline.

Achates suddenly moved Deiphobe aside and placed a hand on the hilt of his sword. He raised the torch he was carrying and gazed into the dark tunnel. Fortunately, the darkness was such that he could not make out Samuel and Angeline.

"Priestess of Apollo," he said, "you should stay behind me. We are not alone within these sacred walls."

"Don't be silly," replied Deiphobe as she glanced furiously in Samuel and Angeline's direction. "These halls are old and full of cracks, suitable to make any draft sing. If I were to frighten myself at the slightest whistle, I would go crazy. Come, there is no time to lose. Bring me to your master. He still has a lot of work to do before he reaches his goal, and I'm sure he won't appreciate any delay."

Achates allowed his gaze to linger on the dark tunnel for a few moments, but then he lowered his torch and turned to Deiphobe again.

"You are right, priestess. Follow me. I will lead you to him."

A moment later Achates disappeared. Deiphobe followed him, but before she stepped into the shadows she fired a reproachful glance at Samuel and Angeline. Then she too was gone.

A few minutes later, when they were sure Achates and Deiphobe had left the area for good, Samuel and Angeline walked back into the Sibyl's home. That was when Samuel noticed the fragrance of herbs in the small kitchen. It was mixed with the smell of wild berries simmering in a small cauldron.

The room's furniture was rather simple, limited to a table before which Samuel sat, the wooden bench, a few cabinets and dozens of stone shelves on the walls. Several vases and amphorae of all sizes were scattered on the shelves, and many more plants were swinging from ropes hanging from the stone ceiling. On one of the shelves was a wicker basket containing hundreds of olive leaves.

"Those are for inscribing prophecies," said Angeline when she saw Samuel looking at the leaves.

"Deiphobe is a soothsayer?" asked Samuel.

"A Sibyl. She is a priestess of Apollo, who is the god of prophecies, among other things. Sometimes he speaks through Deiphobe, and sometimes he whispers words she must write on the olive leaves. The problem is that most of the time, no one knows in what order one must read the leaves to learn the true prophecy."

Samuel turned to Angeline. She was still wearing her white toga, as well as the black leather skirt that made her look like a miniature valkyrie. He gave her a quick smile, which she took as a sign to throw herself on his neck and wrap her arms around it.

"I'm really glad to see you're back among us, Samuel," she said.

"I'm also pleased to be here, Angeline."

The two friends embraced for a moment, and then Angeline flew a little way back and landed on the table again.

"Tell me—how much time has passed since our last adventure on Albion?" asked Samuel.

"No more than a couple of weeks."

"Once again time didn't flow the same way here as it did on my world. For me, it has been over two months since I came back home. I must admit, I was starting to miss Metverold."

"Let's hope it won't always be this long between our adventures," replied Angeline. "One thing is for sure: it's always a pleasure to find myself by your side, Samuel."

"And it's always a pleasure for me to fight the Yfel next to the Unshakable Angeline!" He paused for a moment, then added: "Can you tell me who Achates was talking about earlier, or is it a secret I must find by myself again?"

"Of course I can tell you! He was talking about Aeneas."

"Aeneas?"

"A hero of the Trojan war, son of the goddess Venus, and the ancestor of the Roman people. You've never heard of him?"

Samuel shook his head.

"And I guess I'm here to protect this man?" he asked.

"Of course! Why else would the dice have sent you to Metverold? To share a cup of olive tea with an old priestess of Apollo?"

Angeline and Samuel chatted together for a moment, recalling their first adventures together. Angeline shared with the young

60

man the nightmares she'd had about Mumby, following their stay in Albion, and Samuel told her how he had convinced his parents that the souvenirs he had brought back from Metverold were nothing more than replicas. When Samuel touched the subject of Cathasach, however, the little fata's face turned red and she quickly changed the subject.

She indicated a large cabinet in the corner of the kitchen, where Deiphobe stored the many offerings and gifts made to her over the years. Among the dozens of objects of all kinds piled up inside, Samuel found bronze armor that more or less fit him, leather sandals, a military skirt similar to the one he had worn on Albion, and a bronze sword in excellent condition.

Once he had put his armor on and stored his clothes in the cabinet, Angeline guided him to the room where Deiphobe had welcomed Achates a few moments earlier. She called the room the Chamber of a Hundred Doors. The round room, carved directly into the stone, was probably over a hundred yards wide, and the ceiling, supported by four pillars over six feet thick, was just as high from the floor. However, the most breathtaking feature was the number of wooden doors, which gave the room its name. A stairway went along the wall and circled the room a few times, going up to the ceiling like a coil. The wooden doors, all identical to one another, followed the stairs at regular intervals. Here and there, torches hung on the stone walls.

"This is where the god Apollo whispers his prophecies to Deiphobe," said Angeline.

She was hovering in the middle of the room, next to a stone throne sculpted at the same time the room had been dug. Once again, there were no seams or cracks to indicate it had been carried here. It was one with the floor beneath Samuel's feet.

"Why all the doors?" he asked.

"That would be something you should ask Deiphobe. Maybe they lead to other worlds or unknown dimensions, only accessible to the gods and chosen heroes."

Samuel walked over to the closest door, but it did not have any knob to open it. He put his ear flat on the wood. He felt a vibration coming from the other side, and he quickly changed his mind and took a step back.

"It's probably best not to get too close," said Angeline. "Come, let's go get some fresh air, while we still can."

They walked out of the Chamber of a Hundred Doors, through another straight tunnel that was at least a hundred yards long. Unlike the previous one, this corridor was marked by openings to let the light through, and allowed Samuel to see that it was nighttime. Once they were outside, he saw that the entrance of the Sibyl's lair was at the top of a cliff, and at the foot of a gigantic mountain. A small trail to his right wound against the mountainside until it reached a forest below.

Samuel moved closer to the edge of the cliff and closed his eyes. The warm wind picked up his hair and the fresh air of the night invaded his lungs. There was something different about the air here, something magical that belonged to Metverold. Samuel knew his adventure would be full of dangers and obstacles, but for the moment he was happy to be back.

Angeline flew to him and settled on his right shoulder. "Look, we can see Aeneas's boat below," she said.

Samuel opened his eyes and took in the landscape before him. The forest spread for almost a mile, and then the ocean glittered under the starlight. On the shore, Samuel saw the fires of Aeneas's companions, as well as the shadows of the boats that had carried them here.

"So these guys are Trojans, like the people who traveled with Brutus?" asked Samuel.

"Not quite," answered Angeline. "The people traveling with Brutus were descendants of the Trojans, while these people lived inside the walls of the famous city. They witnessed the horrors of Troy's desecration. They are the last survivors of this great nation, and they are now seeking a new place to settle down. If everything goes well, they will soon come to a place called Latium. Some of their descendants will become the Romans, while others will travel with Brutus to Albion. In fact, Brutus is Aeneas's great-grandson."

Samuel watched the fires dance among the branches of the forest below. He heard the chants and the cheers of the men, addressing prayers to different gods for their protection. These men and women would give birth to not one, but two nations: the Romans and the Britons. And once again their survival depended on Samuel.

"Do you think the sorcerer is already here, on Metverold?" he asked Angeline.

"I don't know, but I would bet he is."

"Let's hope that this time we will spoil his plan before it's too late."

Angeline passed her tiny hand through Samuel's hair.

"Don't be so hard on yourself," she said. "We saved Brutus and the legend the last time."

"Yes, but the sorcerer got what he wanted from Aristaeus. He learned where to find the one who knows how to kill a god."

"And that's probably why the Yfel chose this particular legend. This time we know what he is looking for. It's more than we had to work with the last time."

Angeline made her wings buzzed again and flew in front of Samuel.

"We'll succeed, Samuel. We will not let the sorcerer get away with it this time."

Samuel smiled at her, but the thought of his enemies brought back images of the vampires waiting for him on Earth.

"Angeline, can I ask you something?"

"Of course!"

"I thought only the sorcerer and I could travel between worlds. Are there other creatures who can do it as well?"

Angeline's face immediately darkened.

"Why are you asking me this?"

Samuel told her in detail the events of the previous nights, as well as the vampire attack earlier that evening. He then described how the dice had allowed him to flee to Metverold, and reminded her that for the vampires, no more than a second or two would pass before he returned to his own world. When he was done, the little fata's face was as pale as the moon, and her lips trembled.

"Are you sure they were strigois?" she asked.

"Yes."

"This is all very unsettling. Usually it's impossible for the inhabitants of Metverold to cross over to your world, but there are a few ways to do it. These methods aren't at the disposal of anyone, and they require exhausting rituals, but the Yfel doesn't shy away from using them when necessary; when they feel threatened, for example."

"So I should take the presence of vampires as a compliment?" asked Samuel.

"That's not what I meant, but we can guess that the Yfel isn't entirely sure of its plan yet. If it was, it would not waste time with you on Earth."

"Right, but that still doesn't tell me what I need to do to get rid of the strigois."

"That's what worries me the most," said Angeline. "The strigois should never have been able to get this close to you."

"I'm not sure I understand."

Angeline raised her large purple eyes to Samuel.

"The Yfel are not the only ones who send people to your world. Virtus also has agents on Earth, for different purposes. Some of them are there to protect the Lorekeepers. If the vampires were able to get this close to you, it means someone hasn't done their job."

"Okay, but it doesn't help me to know someone hasn't done their job," answered Samuel. "When I return, there will still be two vampires ready to suck my blood."

Angeline shook her head and slammed a fist into the palm of her hand.

"We will not allow it," she said. "I promise we will find a way before you get back home. I can't lose my Lorekeeper while he's in his own world. In any case, we still have time, and more urgent problems to solve. Come, we should go inside before Aeneas and Deiphobe get back."

She floated to the Sibyl's lair, followed by Samuel. When they got to the entrance, Samuel noticed the imposing doors guarding the access to the lair. Forged in massive gold and over ten feet tall, both doors were covered with bas-reliefs portraying scenes as intriguing as they were violent.

"Aren't they magnificent?" asked Angeline. "These doors were sculpted by the famous architect Daedalus. He was an incredibly smart man who did many great things. According to the legend, he took refuge here after fleeing from Minos's kingdom. It's also said that it was he who built the temple to Apollo inside which Deiphobe lives. He made these doors to guard the entrance."

Samuel looked again at the carvings on the doors. The precision and attention to detail were truly stunning. The more he looked at the characters sculpted in gold, the easier it was to imagine they were real and alive.

"What story did he want to tell with this piece?" he asked.

Angeline's wings fluttered, and she moved toward the first door, to the left.

"It's a strange story," she said. "It happened many years ago." She pointed at the body of a young man, riddled with arrows and surrounded by naked men. "Here is Androgeos, son of King Minos. He was killed by the Athenians while he was participating in the Panathenaic Games—sacred games held every four years."

"Why did they kill him?" asked Samuel.

"They were jealous. It is said he was winning all the honors, in every discipline. Unable to beat him without cheating, his competitors decided to murder him instead."

"Talk about good sportsmanship," whispered Samuel.

"When King Minos learned of the death of his son," continued Angeline, "he immediately declared war on the Athenians, as you can see here."

She showed him a bas-relief depicting an army marching toward Athens. A little below, the architect Daedalus had sculpted a funeral urn surrounded by men and women in tears.

"But King Minos soon realized he would not be unable to conquer the city," said Angeline, "since it was under the protection of the goddess Athena. So Minos asked Zeus to intervene, which he did, and the city was struck by a harsh famine. When the Athenians asked the Oracle to tell them how to end this terrible curse, she replied that they must give King Minos whatever he wanted."

"And what did Minos want?"

"He wanted to avenge his son's death, of course. So he stipulated that every nine years, the Athenians would send him seven young men and seven young women, preferably virgins. To select who would be sent, the rulers of Athens put the names of every eligible teen into this urn you see here, and drew the names of those who would be delivered to Minos."

"It's kind of like the Hunger Games of Antiquity," said Samuel with a smile.

"I don't have the slightest idea of what you are talking about, but there was nothing funny about this story. The night of the draw, the whole town of Athens would shed tears for the sons and daughters they had to send to Minos."

Samuel studied the carving of the urn and the scene. It was so realistic that he could feel all the sadness of the parents whose children were chosen to pay their city's debt toward Minos.

"And what did Minos do with these people?" he asked.

"He locked them in the Labyrinth, where the poor souls were devoured by the Minotaur," answered Angeline, pointing to the image of a muscular man with the head of a bull. "In a way, Daedalus was a part of this sadistic ritual, without knowing it, of course."

"Why is that?"

Angeline flew over to the right door, where Samuel saw the image of a city above the ocean, as well as a woman copulating with a bull.

"Daedalus was a brilliant architect," she said, "who once held a desirable position in the court of King Minos. One day the queen asked Daedalus to build a wooden cow, so she could get inside and satisfy certain ... urges. You'll excuse me if I don't go into the details, but the result was she gave birth to a creature that was half man and half bull: the Minotaur. When Minos learned what the queen had done, he asked Daedalus to built the Labyrinth, and locked the Minotaur inside. The beast remained there until Theseus, an Athenian who sought to free his city from the terrible tribute they had to pay, finally killed the Minotaur and freed himself from the Labyrinth, with the help of Daedalus. Furious, the king locked Daedalus and his son Icarus in the Labyrinth."

"But Daedalus managed to flee as well, right?" Samuel asked.

"Of course. I told you he was a genius! He made wings out of wax and feathers for his son and himself, so they could fly toward freedom. Unfortunately, Icarus flew too close to the sun, which made the wax melt, and he plunged to his death. There would be a place for him on this magnificent work of art if his father had had the strength to carve the scene, but he could not."

Samuel studied the bas-relief. At first glance, Daedalus's work looked absolutely breathtaking, but now that he knew the story it told, he could also appreciate the tragedy it expressed.

"Is that what's waiting for me?" he asked Angeline. "Will this legend will bring us to the Labyrinth?"

Angeline turned to Samuel with a smile that did nothing to comfort him.

"Unfortunately, no. The Labyrinth isn't our destination. To be honest, the Labyrinth would have been fun and games compared to where we have to go."

"And you can't tell me where that is?"

"Everything in its own time, Samuel. I can tell you one thing, though: this legend will test your courage like no other, and for that reason, I will be with you every minute of this adventure. It's out of the question that I leave you for even a second."

The idea of having Angeline by his side gave Samuel courage. Usually he had to manage by himself, and he had gotten into hot water once or twice. This time, with the fata's help, maybe he could stay out of danger until it was time to face the Yfel's sorcerer.

A shadow suddenly jumped out of the darkness and grabbed Samuel by the shoulders.

"What are you doing here?" asked Deiphobe. "Aeneas is on his way and he cannot see you."

Without waiting for an answer, the Sibyl walked into her lair, gesturing for them to follow her.

"We should probably do as she says," whispered Angeline. "You won't want to miss what's coming next."

"Why is that?"

"Aeneas may have lived many adventures, but I guarantee he's never seen anything like what's waiting for him inside."

6

From time to time, Deiphobe seemed to have the qualities of a caring mother. She would speak with a soft and understanding voice; she would attend to her guests, and address them with all the kindness in the world. Then, the next minute, her face would darken and she would raise her voice at those who invaded her home. In those moments she would scream unintelligible sentences and push Samuel around, without him knowing the source of her sudden outburst.

Angeline claimed that the life of a Sibyl was not an easy one, and that Deiphobe's mental instability was perfectly understandable. Sibyls did not choose to become priestesses of Apollo. They were instead selected by him, and even though they knew the destiny of men and women who sought them out, they had no power over their own fate. Unlike prophets, who only interpreted and repeated the words of a god, Sibyls were literally possessed by Apollo, and he spoke directly to whoever consulted him, using the poor woman's body to do so. It was no surprise that Deiphobe was anxious, knowing the god was about to invade her mind to answer Aeneas's questions.

Nevertheless, when she yelled at Samuel and then shoved him inside the Chamber of a Hundred Doors, the young man found it hard to take pity on her. After all, it was not his fault fate had selected her to be a god's spokesperson. Without offering any explanations, Deiphobe led Samuel and Angeline to the spiraling stairs and forced him to climb, pointing to a spot behind one of the pillars.

"Hide there, and by the gods, do not touch any of the doors!" she ordered in a voice that made Samuel's blood run cold and left Angeline speechless.

The Sibyl then climbed onto her throne of stone in the center of the room, and prepared to welcome Aeneas.

"Don't worry," whispered Angeline. "Deiphobe may seem strange, but she knows what she's doing. You can trust her."

Samuel decided to use the downtime to learn a little more about the legend he was supposed to protect. He knew Angeline could not reveal all the details, but maybe he could gather some information if he approached the subject from another angle.

"So, I'll have the pleasure of your company for the entire legend?" he asked.

Angeline rolled her eyes at him and put her hands on her waist.

"Samuel, don't try to soften me with flatteries so you can winkle information out of me," she said. "I won't say another word about what's waiting for us."

"All right, I get it. Can you at least tell me more about this Aeneas and why he needs a Lorekeeper, as well as a fata, to protect him?"

Angeline glanced at the entrance to the Chamber of a Hundred Rooms to make sure no one was coming, then turned to Samuel again.

"I gather you never read Virgil's *Aeneid*, right?"

Samuel shook his head.

"I thought so. You see, Aeneas is the son of the goddess Venus, as well as the last prince of Troy still alive. The famous war that set the inhabitants of the city against the Greeks ended a few years ago with the latter's victory, led by the hero Achilles."

"Aeneas fought in the Trojan War?"

"Yes. He was actually Hector's main lieutenant. Hector was the son of King Priam, Troy's ruler. In the conflict, Aeneas defeated many Greek heroes, and he even survived a fight against Achilles, who was said to be impossible to beat. It is said that Aeneas killed close to thirty Greek officers by himself in the course of this war."

"And he managed to escape the city after it fell?" asked Samuel.

"Yes. During that fateful night, when the Greeks entered the city using the famous wooden horse ruse, Aeneas received a message from the gods telling him to flee the city, which was now doomed to fall. The ghost of Hector appeared to him in a dream and ordered him to gather Troy's Penates, and leave the region before it was too late, so Aeneas could accomplish his destiny."

"He had to gather what?" asked Samuel.

"Penates. Idols protecting the homes and families of Troy. In these times, the Penates are almost as important as the gods. Anyway, Aeneas managed to flee Troy carrying the idols, but they were not the only things he brought with him. Despite the fire consuming Troy during that cursed night, he saved his son Ascagne, as well as his father Anchise, whom he carried on his back until they were safe in the mountains."

"Were they alone, all three of them?"

"No. Many of Aeneas's companions were able to escape with him, including Achates, who you saw earlier."

Samuel peeked around the side of the pillar, at the room's entrance. No one was coming, so he continued to question Angeline, hoping to discover what was waiting for him on Metverold.

"What did they do afterward, the survivors with Aeneas?" he asked.

"The successfully reached their boats, and set sail for the sea. However, the goddess Juno, Jupiter's wife, who had favored the Greeks during the war, kept persecuting the Trojans even as they fled. After throwing violent storms at them and causing the death of many of Aeneas's companions, she forced the hero to make his way to the doors of Carthage."

"Why was Juno so mad?"

Angeline shrugged. "Probably just because they were Trojans. Or maybe because one of Troy's princes, Paris, had chosen Aeneas's mother, Venus, as the most beautiful of all the goddesses. The gods rarely have good reasons to do anything, you know."

"And she led the Trojans to Carthage for a specific reason?"

"You could say that," Angeline said. "Carthage was, uniquely, a city led by a woman, Queen Dido. Juno wanted Aeneas to marry her and permanently settle within the city walls. That way, he would abandon his destiny, which was to find a place for the descendants of Troy."

"You mean Brutus and Corineus?"

"Not necessarily. It's true they are two descendants of the Trojans, but the people most often associated with Aeneas are the Romans. They will see the Trojan hero as their one true ancestor, and they will worship him according to his glorious past."

Samuel remembered the documentaries he had seen about Julius Caesar, and some snippets of information surfaced in his memory.

"I thought the Romans descended from Rebus and Ramonus?"

Angeline burst out laughing, but immediately slapped her hands over her mouth to suppress the sound.

"You mean Remus and Romulus. It's true the Romans also worship those two, but what they see in Romulus is the founder of their city, rather than the roots of their nation. In fact, the stories and legends telling of the founding of Rome aren't all that flattering. It's probably for that reason the Romans will consider themselves descendants of the Trojans, and why they will pattern their way of life after them in many ways."

Samuel listened carefully to what Angeline was saying. The more she spoke of the Trojan hero and his importance, the more he felt the weight of his responsibilities on his shoulders. Not only was Aeneas the ancestor of the Romans, a nation that would leave an unprecedented mark on the history of the world, but he was also Brutus's ancestor, a man who would also father a great nation, the Britons. If the Yfel wanted to do maximum damage to the world's history, Aeneas was the perfect target. With his death, the Yfel would erase two very important nations.

And of course, Samuel was the only one who could prevent them from doing so.

"You said Aeneas and his companions stopped in Carthage during their journey," said Samuel to Angeline. "Did they stay there a while?"

"No, not for long, but enough to do irreparable harm to the city."

With a questioning look, Samuel invited Angeline to continue.

"You see, the goddess Juno made Queen Dido fall madly in love with Aeneas," she said. "The queen saw in him a king worthy of her city. The Trojan fell for the queen's charms, and a wedding was organized. However, before the ceremony took place, Aeneas's mother, Venus, appeared before him to remind him of his destiny. A few nights later, Aeneas fled under the cover of darkness, along with all his boats, his companions and their weapons."

"I bet the queen did not appreciate that."

"You can say that again! She stabbed herself with the sword she had offered Aeneas, then threw herself on a flaming pyre."

Samuel looked at Angeline in stupefaction. The fata had a knack for telling frightening stories without thinking twice about the effect they had on Samuel. The tales of war, treacheries and murders she often told him never failed to remind Samuel he was no longer in his own comfortable world.

Metverold was a violent and barbaric place, where death took many forms and could surprise him at any moment.

He wanted to question Angeline some more about the Trojan hero, but they were interrupted by footsteps coming from the tunnel below. A few moments later, a man appeared in the Chamber of a Hundred Rooms.

"Welcome to my home, Prince of Troy," said Deiphobe. "Come closer, so that the god Apollo can see who dares address him."

Cautiously, Samuel looked at the Trojan from his spot higher up the stairs, making sure he was still hidden by the stone pillar. As soon as he saw Aeneas, he was struck by admiration. The Trojan not only looked like a prince; he also had the charisma of a king and the physique of a god. Samuel was almost six feet tall, but Aeneas was taller, and had a body that would have made every Renaissance sculptor drool. His hair, the color of autumn leaves, floated softly over his shoulders, and his sturdy face reflected the vigorous youth coursing through his veins, as well as the wisdom he had acquired during the many battles he had fought. His eyes were a striking blue, and his gaze reminded Samuel of Brutus's.

Aeneas wore magnificent gilded armor, perfectly molded to his chest, and a red cape attached to his shoulder. A leather skirt, decorated with gold and gemstones, encircled his waist, while his leather sandals were laced up to his knees. On his left arm he bore a round shield, similar to those Samuel had seen on Brutus's ship, and at his waist hung a sheath in which he stored his sword, of which only the hilt set with silver was visible.

Aeneas was a spectacular sight, and Samuel wondered why such a man needed him for his protection.

"It is time to inquire about your fate," the Sibyl screamed suddenly, making Samuel jump. "Here he comes! The god is here!"

As she said the words, a bone-freezing gust of wind barged into the room and made the flames flicker over the torches hanging from the walls. Samuel hunched over, trying to avoid the strange gust, while protecting Angeline at the same time. The wind whistled for several seconds, then vanished as quickly as it had come.

Samuel lifted his head and glanced at Deiphobe. The old woman was still seating on her throne of stone, but when he saw her face, a chill ran along his spine. The feminine features of the woman had vanished, and in their place were those of a twisted and delirious being. Her eyes were turned up inside her head, her skin seemed to have lost what little color it had and her mouth was contorted into a frightening grin. Even her chaotic hair had turned white and seemed to have grown down to her waist.

Deiphobe laboriously lifted herself from her seat, then moved closer to the Trojan hero, dragging her feet. Now that she was standing, Samuel could have sworn the old woman was taller than before, even taller than the man in front of her. She panted rapidly, and her heartbeats echoed across the room, while her cavernous breathing seemed to be coming from the bowels of the mountain.

Only when she started talking again did the obscene character of the possession fully strike Samuel. The woman's nasal voice had been replaced by a voice that had nothing human about it. It was a sepulchral voice, which sounded like a legion of demons all possessing the body of the poor Sibyl at the same time.

"You linger to vow and pray, Aeneas of Troy."

The words pierced even the soul of Samuel and almost made him lose all his willpower. He was completely petrified, unable to look away from the scene before him.

"You linger!" repeated the god with Deiphobe's tongue, his voice thundering inside the stone chamber. "You linger, but know that the vast portals of the spellbound house will remain closed until you observe the rites I am owed, Trojan."

The scene taking place below Samuel was unreal. As an impatient god addressed him from the foaming mouth of a poor woman, Aeneas remained still, his face calm and his gaze unshakable. Angeline was right. The Trojan hero had probably never seen something like this, but his courage was unwavering, and Samuel felt admiration for him, and maybe even a little fascination.

"Mighty and Divine Apollo," Aeneas said finally, talking directly to the god with a calm voice, "you who have ever pitied the sore travail of Troy, you who have guided the Dardanian shaft from Paris's hand to the son of Aeacus, it is in your leading that I have sailed without rest all these seas skirting mighty lands. I have traveled to the withdrawn Massylian nations, and to the fields fringed by the Styres, so that we may reach the shores of Italy that seemed always to elude us.

"Today, at last, after we battled countless dangers and overcame unspeakable hardships, my companions and I set foot on the Eubean lands. May the misfortune of Troy stop here, and not follow us any longer. The Fates allow you to it. Mighty sun god, and any gods and goddesses whom Ilius and the great glory of Dardania overshadowed, please spare our nation, the nation of Pergama. I do not ask for any kingdom that was not already promised to me. Show me, as well as my companions, that the time has come, that we can claim a resting place in Latium. Tell us that we can lay down our wandering gods and our Penates, rattled for so long by the storms that our enemies have cast against our ships.

"If you allow this to come to pass, Apollo, god of prophecies, I will ordain a marble temple in your name. I will order a festive day in the name of Pheobus, and I will preserve a mighty sanctuary in our realm, where I will place your oracles and the secrets of destiny uttered to my people. I will name the priests and consecrate the chosen ones myself, O gracious one. Only do not commit your verses to leaves that can fly distorted as soon as you leave this room of stupor, I beg of you. Sing them to me, so that your message is not lost in ambiguities."

Aeneas paused and looked at the woman before him. The Sibyl's face was now as twisted as ever, and her mouth foamed. The god Apollo tried to articulate an answer, but the borrowed body was suddenly seized with spasms, as the Sibyl fought to expel this being from her. Unfortunately for Deiphobe, the battle was already lost, and the god quickly regained the upper hand, disfiguring the woman's silhouette even more.

Suddenly, the hundred doors around Samuel opened all at once and a hundred voices filled the room, accompanied by such forceful gales that Angeline had to hang on to Samuel to avoid getting blown away. The voices spoke with words incomprehensible to Samuel, sometimes uttered in a joyous and almost childish way, and sometimes with such anger that it shook the stones around him.

The voices swirled around the chamber for a few seconds and then vanished, and the god Apollo spoke once more.

"O you who are finally free of the sea's great perils," he said to Aeneas, "heavier clouds still await you on land. Chase away the worries from your heart, for you and your companions will enter Latium, but I must warn you that the Dardanian descendants following you will soon regret setting foot on these lands. I see new wars waiting for you, as well as all the horrors of battle, and the Tiber waters are afoam with blood. Another Achilles is already found in Latium, also goddess-born, and he will stand in your way.

"And you will again find a scornful Juno still after the Trojans. To which Italian nations will you turn in your sorrow? What city will you beg to come to your aid? Once more, a foreign woman will be the cause of great woe for the Trojans. Once more, your heart will be the source of suffering for your people. But do not yield to distress. Look them in the eye with more confidence than Fortune allows you, because the path of salvation, as startling as it may seem, will come from a Greek city."

Once again, Deiphobe's body convulsed wildly and her breathing became so fast, and her face so twisted by pain, that even Aeneas took a step back and briefly looked away. A new icy wind engulfed the room, which Samuel thought was coming straight out of Deiphobe's mouth. The breeze swirled for a moment above their heads, and then escaped through the tunnel that led outside. Soon afterward, the hundred doors slammed shut in unison, a deafening thump that froze Samuel's blood in his veins.

At the center of the room, Deiphobe was slowly catching her breath. The poor woman seemed entirely drained of her energy. With difficulty, she dragged herself up to her stone throne, where she sat down to recover. Aeneas walked up to her and spoke again.

"O virgin, I thank you for allowing me this conversation with the god you serve."

The Sibyl raised her glassy eyes to the hero.

"You speak as if the choice was mine to make, Trojan," she said, "but I assure you that my will has nothing to do with any of this. Now go. Go back to your people and leave an old woman to recover her strength."

But Aeneas walked up to Deiphobe and gently took her hand. "Poor priestess, my heart sheds tears as I must ask you one last request, for I know it will only add to the burden already too heavy for these delicate shoulders to carry. But no trial stands before me with an unknown face. Apollo's words have already been said to me. I foresaw it all. I have already lived through it in my mind. I know what destiny awaits me, and I have but one request to ask of you."

"Such a fool," replied Deiphobe. "What is it, this wish that would so afflict a priestess to the god of prophecies?"

"Since it is here, they say, that one can find the way to the Acheron marsh, grant me the privilege of seeing my father's face, since he is the one who visited me in a dream and who instructed me to come see you."

A doubt crept into Samuel's mind, just as a shiver tickled the back of his neck. The hero's father had visited him in a dream?

"Is Aeneas's father still alive?" he asked Angeline in a strangled voice.

Before she could reply, Deiphobe answered Aeneas:

"Poor Aeneas, was the fall of Troy not enough of a misfortune? Are the exile of your people and the trials that await you not a heavy enough burden, that you wish to go where it is forbidden to go?"

Aeneas remained silent, and she continued:

"Prince of Troy, son of Anchises, born from the blood of gods, know that it is easy to descend into Avernus. Night and day, the gates of dark Pluto stand open. Retracing your steps and climbing back into the light of the day—that is the true task."

Once again, Samuel turned to Angeline. The doubt in his mind was quickly turning into a worry that twisted his guts.

"Avernus? The dark Pluto? What is she talking about?" he whispered.

Angeline only looked at him, biting her lip.

"Gracious woman," said Aeneas, "have pity on the father and the son. It is not in vain that Hecate gave you power over the sacred groves of Avernus. If Orpheus brought back the Manes of his wife, and if Pollux redeemed his brother by exchange of death, I beg of you, show me the way."

This time, Samuel understood exactly what the Trojan was talking about. Their journey's destination was without a doubt now. Samuel turned one last time to Angeline, unable to say a word. The fata stared at him with a look of compassion and fright. She understood Samuel's fear, since she was just as terrified by the place they were all going.

"Priestess of Apollo," Aeneas said, "I beseech you, open for me the door that leads into Hell."

7

The words of Aeneas echoed in Samuel's mind, as if a voice was mocking him from the depths of the abyss.

The Underworld.

Hell.

That was what waited for him in this legend.

Nightmarish images surged through Samuel's mind. Memories of Hollywood horror movies and scary stories he had read. He could already see the rivers of fire flowing around him, the flames licking his soft skin. He pictured demons of all shapes residing in this cursed place, each more horrible than the last. He could even feel the heat of Hell's fires on his face, and sweat beading on his back.

Samuel still had his eyes fixed on Angeline. He was unable to even twitch a muscle, as if the mere fact of moving would start the wheel of time again, and would begin a countdown until he found himself standing at the gates of Hell. Angeline had not looked away either, staring at Samuel with her wide purple eyes. She seemed just as mortified as he was, maybe even more. Samuel only had the imagination of those from his own world as a point of reference, but Angeline had probably already set foot in the Underworld, and she knew exactly what kind of horrors were waiting for them.

After a moment, Samuel found the strength to turn around and stretch his neck. Below, in the middle of the Chamber of a Hundred Doors, Aeneas was still talking with Deiphobe.

"If you possess the desire to cross the Stygian waters twice, and to twice see the dark walls of Tartarus," said the Sibyl, "—if your intention to set out on this senseless task is as inflexible as the pillars of this room, then listen to what you must do before anything else, you fool. There is a bough, with a soft stem and golden leaves, hidden among the leafage of a shady tree, consecrated to the queen of the Underworld. It is protected by the depths of a woodland, and by the dimness of a dusky vale. However, it is impossible to penetrate the depths of the earth without having first taken the bough from the tree with golden leaves. It is the offering Persephone has established for her beauty, and without it, the road to Elysium is hidden. Once you have found this bough, pluck it according to the rite. If the Fates allow you to enter Pluto's kingdom, then the bough will come away easily, but if the access to the dominion of death is denied, there is no strength in this world that will tear it free."

Aeneas remained still a few moments, but when he opened his mouth to speak, Deiphobe abruptly cut him off.

"Listen! Listen to me!" she screamed. "You do not know, alas, but the remains of one of your companions lie cold on the shores. While you question me, his body defiles your entire fleet with death. Before you do anything else, lay him in a suitable resting place, hide him in a tomb, and lead black sheep to the altar of sacrifice. May those be your first expiations. Only then will you see the Stygian groves and the realm that has no roads for the living."

As soon as her instructions were given, the Sibyl closed her eyes and fell silent, and her inert body dropped softly to the throne of stone. Aeneas watched the woman with piercing eyes, his gaze reflecting all the courage of his ancestors and his determination to see his father Anchises, even if he had to fight all the demons of Hell to do it. He stayed still for a moment, and then, without ceremony, turned and walked out of the Chamber of a Hundred Doors. Once Samuel and Angeline were certain the Trojan would not come back, they came out of their hiding spot and climbed down the stairs. Cautiously they walked to the throne of stone and the motionless body of Deiphobe. The poor woman's face was no longer twisted by the god who had possessed her, but the signs of the battle she had led against Apollo were clearly visible in her suddenly aged features.

"Is she all right?"

"I think so," said Angeline. "I had heard of this legend, but it's the first time I have participated in it myself. I have to admit, I wasn't ready to see this poor woman be tortured like that by a god."

"She looks like she's aged ten years."

"That's no surprise," said Angeline. "The effects of such a possession on the human body must be horrible. I believe Deiphobe hasn't even reached her thirties yet."

Samuel looked at the face of the poor woman with pity and a certain sense of companionship. Though she had not requested it, some celestial being decided her life would be spent in solitude. Like Samuel, she had been chosen to fill a specific role. However, his did not affect his body in any way. At least, he didn't think it did.

"Why do the gods need her to speak with people?" he asked.

"Deiphobe would be better suited to answer that, but I believe it's because of the true form of the gods, which is unbearable to the human eye. In order to speak with you, they must first adopt a form acceptable to your mind. Sometimes it's the shape of animals, but other times, it's through chosen people, like Deiphobe, who must carry this burden."

"We should let her rest," said Samuel.

"You're right. In any case, I believe we have much to discuss, you and I."

A few minutes later, Samuel and Angeline were back in the kitchen of the Sibyl's lair. A fire still crackled under the chimney, and a small pot hung over the flames. Samuel glanced inside and saw a bubbling stew. It looked almost like oatmeal: grains of wheat were mixed with herbs he did not know. Despite its repulsive appearance, the concoction gave off a pleasant fragrance, and Samuel grabbed a wooden spoon and dipped it into the pot.

"If I were you, I wouldn't bring that spoon near my lips," said Angeline.

"Why not?" asked Samuel.

"Because one sip of that stew will send you to the land of dreams for a few days."

Samuel carefully put the spoon back on the shelf.

"If you're hungry, eat some bread," Angeline said, pointing to a basket on the table. "Our journey will be harsh, and you will need all your strength. Food isn't easy to find where we going."

Samuel noticed that Angeline was careful not to mention the name of the place waiting for them, as if the mere fact of pronouncing it made their adventure horribly real. It was absurd, but Samuel understood Angeline's sentiment. Like her, he had no desire to utter the syllables that designated this infernal place.

However, the fact remained that Angeline was right. He did not know how much time he would spend in the Underworld, and he would be advised to take every opportunity he had to eat something. Samuel sat at the wooden table, took the basket and grabbed the piece of bread inside. It was so dry that he could probably have used it as a weapon against the vampires.

"You must have many questions," said Angeline.

She gently floated to the table and landed in front of Samuel.

He nodded, and dug his teeth into the piece of bread. With the help of every muscle in his neck, he triumphantly tore off a piece, which he chewed for a while.

"Are we really going to Hell?" he asked.

Angeline nodded.

"And can you tell me what's waiting for us there?"

She shook her head. "I can't tell you anything that pertains to the legend," she said, "but I can tell you about this place we're going."

"Who's Pluto." he asked. "I doubt the Sibyl was referring to the planet, right?"

"Pluto is the Roman equivalent of the Greek god Hades," Angeline told him. "He is the ruler of the Underworld. Unlike his counterpart, the kingdom of Pluto does not share his name, but Pluto and Hades are identical in most other ways, and their domains are one and the same."

"I don't really understand what you mean," said Samuel. "They are both masters of the same place?"

"It's more complicated than that. Technically, Pluto and Hades belong to two separate mythologies, but the Greek and Roman mythologies are very close to one another. You see, after the conquest of the Mediterranean region, the Romans took over the Greek culture, as well as their religious beliefs. Then, in the years that followed, they changed the names of the gods, probably in an attempt to give the illusion that those beliefs were their own. That is why Zeus became Jupiter, and Hera is now Juno, and Hades was renamed Pluto. They are the same gods, but they belong to different mythologies. The Romans even went so far as to co-opt some of the Greek legends so they would tell how their people came to be instead."

"In that case, why did the Sibyl speak of Pluto, even though Aeneas is a Trojan? Shouldn't she have called him by his Greek name, Hades?"

"I see you are paying attention to the small details," said Angeline. "It's one of the many things that make you an excellent Lorekeeper. Indeed, it would be perfectly logical for the Greek names to be used in this legend, but if you remember, Metverold only exists through the narration of the legends. In other words, for a legend to play out here, someone in your world must be telling it or reading about it at this very moment. Without people to read the legends, we wouldn't exist. So, even though this story takes place in a time where the Greeks still dominated the Mediterranean Sea, and a Trojan is the main character, the fact remains that it is a Roman story. It was written by Virgil, under direct order from Augustus, first emperor of the Romans. The story is told in their language, with the name of their gods. That's why we are going to the kingdom of Pluto, and not Hades."

"But it's the same place," said Samuel.

"Yes, identical in every way."

"So, if I get this right, Aeneas wants to descend to Hell to meet his father."

Angeline nodded. "Aeneas is destined to become the ancestor of the Romans," she said, "but there are still doubts lingering in his mind. Even if his mother is a goddess, the road traced for him isn't always easy to follow. He needs to be guided. It's for this reason his father visited him in a dream. He asked the hero to come visit him in Hell, because that's where Aeneas will remove any uncertainty about his fate and become the true father of the Roman nation."

"Once again, the fate of a whole nation is in jeopardy, right?"

"Why else would you be here?" answered Angeline, a smile on her lips.

Samuel smiled in return. Angeline was right. The Yfel would not waste their time with insignificant myths. They had chosen this legend with a specific goal in mind, and once again Samuel had to discover what it was.

"So I have to protect Aeneas from the Yfel sorcerer," he said.

"*We* must protect Aeneas," corrected Angeline. "Don't forget that this time I'll be with you for the entire mission. I will not let you out of my sight while we are strolling around in the land of the dead. Who knows what demon you'd fall upon if I wasn't there to look after you!"

"Is that why we must hide from Aeneas? So he doesn't see you, or figure out there is an invisible presence with us when we're in Hell?"

"Not exactly," answered Angeline. "We must remain unseen by Aeneas because he cannot know of your presence. You see, unlike the legends we saved before this one, there is no army among which you can hide. There aren't thousands of minor characters you can mingle with to stay out of sight. This legend only has three characters: Aeneas, Deiphobe and Anchises, the hero's father. If you were to simply join them, you would immediately change the story. We can't take that risk."

"But I teamed up with Brutus on Albion, and Uther Pendragon in Britain. Why would it be more harmful to the legend if I were to join Aeneas this time?"

"Because, in the previous stories, your actions were easy to attribute to someone else. If enough time passes, history can forget some characters and credit their actions to their companions, but when a legend only has two or three characters, it's much harder to do. Do you understand?"

"I guess, but how am I supposed to protect Aeneas if I can't walk next to him? Are we going to have to follow him from a distance, hoping he doesn't spot us?"

"We'll have to follow or precede him," said Angeline. "Don't forget the Yfel sorcerer knows the story and will most likely lay some traps. We will have to find them before Aeneas falls in their midst."

Samuel swallowed hard and took another bite of the bread.

"And that's not all," added Angeline. "The kingdom of Pluto is a different place from those we visited until now. Many of Hell's dwellers know of the Yfel's and Virtus's existence, as well as the battle raging between them. Most of them stay outside of the conflict, but some have decided to associate with one side or the other. This peculiarity, specific to the Underworld, makes things much more dangerous for us, since some demons will try to kill us just to gain the Yfel's favor."

"Okay, but then how can I protect Aeneas without drawing his attention, or the awareness of a demon looking to fall under the Yfel's good graces, or even the attention of the sorcerer? You'll have to excuse me, but I doubt that my presence will go unnoticed in a place like this."

"I believe I can be of help with that particular matter," called out a powerful voice.

As soon as he heard the voice, Samuel's stomach twisted in a knot. It was a familiar voice, but also the voice of a stranger. It seemed to be the sum of a hundred different voices, while remaining unique.

In front of him, Angeline had her mouth open and her skin was covered with goose bumps. She stared over Samuel's shoulder toward the tunnel leading to the Chamber of a Hundred Doors. The bright eyes of the fata were wide open in surprise, but also filled by fear.

Carefully, Samuel put the piece of dry bread on the table, lifted his right leg over the bench, and turned toward the tunnel. What he saw left him speechless as well. Deiphobe was floating a few inches above the ground, like a specter from beyond the grave. Her eyes were turned in her skull, and her mouth was covered in white foam. Her hair floated wildly behind her head, and her arms were straight up before her, as if an invisible puppeteer controlled her every move. She opened her lips once again, and the god who had taken possession of her spoke to Samuel:

"You are Virtus's emissary, the messenger of the Parcae. You have been chosen to protect our world as well as yours, Samuel Osmond, guardian of the gods, but you have yet to face dangers like those awaiting you at this hour."

Drops of sweat slid down Samuel's neck. His hands were clammy and his legs trembled. A god was speaking directly to him. Should he reply? Should he throw himself to his knees?

Many questions rushed through his mind, but none crossed his lips. The last thing he wanted to do was to offend anyone and earn himself a horrible punishment in retaliation.

"Apollo, is that you?" asked Angeline behind him.

The Sibyl's head nodded.

"And you, Unshakable Angeline," said Apollo, "your story is known by all of us. We know the trials you had to endure, and the woes that afflicted your existence, but we also know of your heroic deeds and the victories you have won. Still, know that nothing you have experienced until this day can prepare you for the dangers lurking in my uncle's kingdom."

Samuel turned to Angeline. What was the god talking about?

The fata's face turned scarlet, and she quickly spoke again.

"O mighty and powerful Apollo, we thank you for your warnings, but if you don't mind, I doubt your presence within these walls is only ascribable to your desire to give us a few words of caution."

"As usual, you are right, Angeline. Before you stands an unparalleled enemy, forces that make even the mighty gods of Olympus tremble. The Yfel is getting ready for a strike that will shake the foundations of our world, and risks changing Samuel's own in a way that is impossible to predict, even for the gods. Only you can prevent it, and that is why I offer my help. Samuel, your journey to the realm of Pluto will be most arduous, and among the many challenges you will face, to stay in the shadows, unseen by Aeneas or by those who could wish you harm, will be the hardest. I can help you succeed. There is an object unlike anything else in this world, which will be of great help to you for your adventure in Hell: the Helm of Darkness."

As soon as the god pronounced those words, Angeline gasped and clung to Samuel's armor.

"The Helm of Darkness is a crown of onyx belonging to my uncle, the mighty Pluto," Apollo went on. "This object renders invisible whoever wears it. It will allow you to keep your presence hidden from Aeneas and the denizens of Hell, but be warned, for the powers of the Helm of Darkness are not without a price."

Angeline's hand tensed even more around the leather straps of Samuel's armor. "A ... a price?" she asked.

As if in answer, the possessed Sibyl turned and disappeared into the tunnel leading to the Chamber of a Hundred Doors. Samuel turned to Angeline, who glanced at him with terrified eyes.

After a moment, Samuel found the strength to get up, doing his best to control the spasms in his thighs. Making sure he still had his sword at his waist, he took a few steps toward the tunnel, and then went in after Apollo. When he got to the Chamber of a Hundred Doors, the god was sitting on the stone throne, his hands raised to the ceiling.

"The Helm of Darkness is powerful," he said suddenly in a voice that echoed through the chamber, "but it is not unlimited. It will not work on every creature of the Underworld. Some of them are immune to its power. You will have to be careful not to think yourself invisible to everyone, Samuel."

"Okay," answered Samuel, not knowing what else to say.

"And that is not all!" thundered the god.

Angeline yelped and took cover behind Samuel. The young man took a step back and almost crushed her against the wall.

"The powers of the Helm of Darkness come at a price," repeated the god, "and for many mortals, this price is too high to pay."

A door suddenly swung open on Samuel's right. Past the threshold was a tunnel shrouded in total darkness.

Samuel did not like the turn of the events one bit.

"The Helm of Darkness feeds on the fears of the one wearing it," said Apollo. "Should you be foolish enough to put it on your head without first having mastered your fears, it will take hold of your mind and make you live the most terrifying nightmares you can imagine. It would rob you of your sanity, and submit you to an eternity of indescribable torments. Therefore, before you can use the helm, you will have to face your most intimate fears and learn to control them. Only then will you have the strength to place the Helm of Darkness on your head to help you in the task awaiting you."

Samuel turned his eyes to the door.

"And ... and what do I need to do to master my fears?" he asked.

Deiphobe's pointed to the open door with a bony finger. "Behind that door you will find the answer to your question. To earn the Helm of Darkness, you will have to venture alone into this tunnel that leads between two worlds. There you will face the three deepest fears that torment your soul. Should you survive this trial, you will find the Helm of Darkness and take possession of it."

The god turned his white eyes to Samuel and the young man saw that Deiphobe's face was different now. Pain and struggle no longer twisted it. Instead, it displayed sadness, and even a hint of fear.

"Samuel, I beg of you, find the courage to succeed," said Apollo, with a single voice this time. "Only you can save our two worlds. Only you can foil the Yfel's plan. Only you can save my sister, Lorekeeper Samuel."

With these words, the Sibyl's face turned white, her eyes closed, and her arms fell heavily on either side of the throne.

About ten minutes later, Deiphobe regained consciousness and opened her eyes. Although Apollo had released his grasp on the poor woman's body, she still bore the signs of her struggle with the god. Her eyes were streaked with red, her hair was disheveled, and her lips were covered with dried foam. The glow of the torches around the room reflected on her sweaty face, and her skin seemed to have aged several years.

When Deiphobe tried to straightened herself, she groaned in pain, her muscles still aching. She tried to speak, but the words remained stuck in her dry throat. Angeline gestured to Samuel, and he ran to the kitchen. He came back a few seconds later with a copper goblet filled to the brim with cool water. In his short absence, Angeline had flown closer to Deiphobe and was stroking her hair, urging her to remain calm. When Samuel presented the goblet, the Sibyl thanked him and brought it to her lips. Even if the majority of the water ended on her robe, what little she managed to drink seemed to help, and she finally spoke.

"We do not have much time," she said.

"Don't think about that for now," said Angeline. "Drink some more water."

"No, you don't understand," replied Deiphobe. "Aeneas is searching for the golden bough to offer Persephone, but his quest will be quick. He is a resourceful man who will not take long to find what he is looking for. As soon as he comes back, we will have to leave for Pluto's kingdom."

Samuel was still holding the goblet under the Sibyl's chin, not knowing if he should pull it back or insist she drink more water.

"We?" he asked. "Surely you're not coming with Angeline and me?"

The Sibyl turned to him. "My boy, let me give you a bit of advice that could save your life one of these days. If you want to survive in a world like Metverold, you need to learn never to trust appearances. As they say in Latium, *be wary of silent rivers, for they are usually the deepest.* Know that I am not as weak as I look. I have experienced things in my life that will make this journey look like a walk in the forest. When you have fought back a god of Olympus trying to get control of your body, then you can tell me what I can or cannot do. However, to answer your question: no, I am not coming with Angeline and you. It is with Aeneas that I will cross the Acheron, and who I will walk with in Elysium."

"She speaks the truth," Angeline said. "Without her, Aeneas has no idea of the road to follow, and he would get lost in the Underworld. If that were the case, he would never find his way back to the surface. Deiphobe will be his guide, and I will be with you for the same reasons. Virtus cannot afford to lose its Lorekeeper in the depths of Hell!"

"I certainly won't argue with that," answered Samuel.

Deiphobe interrupted the conversation and painfully climbed down from the throne of stone. As soon as she set foot on the ground, she turned to Samuel and, taking the goblet from his hand, pushed him toward the open door.

"Come, my boy. We have lost enough time as it is, and you must find the Helm of Darkness. Aeneas will be back soon, and you must return before he and I descend into Hell, or else we risk getting too far ahead of you."

Samuel did not dare resist the tired woman, but he had no desire to enter the dark and eerie tunnel in front of him.

"Wait!" he said. "Are you sure we absolutely need this Helm of Darkness? Maybe we could manage without it."

"Don't be absurd," said Deiphobe. "Apollo himself ordered you to find it. Do you dare defy the command of the sun god?"

He shook his head. "All right, I'm going," he said. "No need to push me like that. Angeline, are you coming?"

Angeline floated next to Deiphobe, looking just as terrified as Samuel.

"She cannot go with you," cut in the Sibyl. "You heard the sun god. You must face your fears and master them on your own."

This time, Samuel straightened his legs and resisted the old woman's efforts to push him forward. "I have to go by myself?" he asked.

Angeline flew over to him and gently stroked his cheek with her hand. "Deiphobe is right," she said. "If you want to master what scares you the most, you have to go alone. But don't worry, Deiphobe and I are absolutely confident you will return victorious from this journey."

"Don't be so sure, little fata," said the Sibyl. "Do you know a single legend that tells the story of a hero crossing the threshold of one of these doors?"

Angeline looked daggers at the old woman, but Deiphobe ignored her.

"You don't, because none of them ever came back. If there are no heroes to return, then there cannot be a story to tell. They were all quickly forgotten."

Samuel took a deep breath and placed a hand on his sword, and then took a nervous step toward the open door. When he found himself standing at the threshold, he slowly slid the blade out of its sheath and turned to the Sibyl and the fata.

"Angeline, do you mind?" he asked, raising his weapon before him.

The fata flew closer, placed both her hands on the blade, closed her eyes, and whispered a spell in a language unknown to Samuel. A few moments later, the blade glowed with a purple light.

Samuel thanked her with a nod, and turned toward the dark passage again. Despite the glow of his weapon, he could not see more than a few feet in front of him. The oppressive darkness seemed to fight back the light, as if it were a living thing that refused to concede a shred of its territory.

Samuel hesitated a few more seconds, but just as he was about to turn and wave to his friends one last time, Deiphobe rushed to him and violently pushed him inside. Samuel staggered across the opening, and then the door slammed shut behind him with a deafening thud.

8

As soon as the door closed behind him, Samuel turned and dropped his sword. With an energy sustained by fear and despair, he banged with all his might on the stone wall. His heart was racing and he screamed as loudly as his lungs allowed, begging Angeline and Deiphobe to let him out. In just a few seconds his courage had vanished, leaving behind an irrepressible terror.

He desperately searched the rock, hoping to find a handle or another way to open the door and go back the way he came. Unsurprisingly, he only found a cold, hard wall. All he managed to do was give himself aching hands and scratched fingers.

Without completely accepting his fate, Samuel picked up his sword, turned toward the darkness behind him and raised the blade over his head. Although the light Angeline had given him was magical, it was barely able to push back the darkness. Samuel looked at the passage in front of him, but he would not have been able to see any less had his eyes been shut. He was unable to distinguish the floor or the ceiling, or even the walls by his side. It was as if he had stepped between two universes, lost in a space that did not truly exist.

Samuel could hardly control the twitching of his muscles, but he still managed to place one foot in front of him, then the other. Which way was he going? He could not have said. All he could see was a darkness so thick it was dizzying. With each step Samuel took, he had to fight two battles that were quickly stealing all his energy. First, he had to control his muscles and impose his will on them, so they did as he commanded and kept him moving forward. Then he had to rein in his mind, which, suddenly deprived of all its markers, threatened to go crazy at any moment.

He shuffled on for a few minutes, or maybe several hours—it was hard to tell. As soon as he dared to think about the passing of time, his mind whispered he would never get out of this place; that he would forever be a prisoner of this world where only darkness existed.

Samuel was still trying to convince himself that was not the case when he suddenly heard a familiar noise in front of him. Immediately, his stomach dropped to his heels, and the hair stood up on his nape. The noise was weak and far away, but it was impossible to mistake. He had heard it every night for a week now, through his bedroom window.

Samuel stood still and pricked up his ears. A laborious whistling came from somewhere in front of him, a sound he thought he had left behind when he had crossed into Metverold.

It was the whistling of a strigoi.

"It's only an illusion," whispered Samuel to himself.

But was it? Was the noise only there to summon one of Samuel's fears that he had to master? Should he simply ignore the chilling sound and keep going forward?

He was still thinking things over when a green light appeared about twenty yards from where he was, barely bright enough for him to see three shadows that made him shiver in terror. Samuel immediately recognized the bald skulls, misshapen ears and black coats worn by the vampires who had attacked him in his own world.

They were really here, right in front of him. Somehow the gods had brought the three strigois here and put them in his way.

Samuel glanced over his shoulder, but saw nothing except total darkness. It was futile to think about going back the way he had come, since he was sure the stone door was still sealed shut. He only had one option left: fight the monsters tracking him, once and for all.

Not surprisingly, it was much easier said than done. His legs obstinately refused to take a single step forward, and the tremor in his arm seemed to increase the weight of the sword tenfold, so he could barely keep it in front of himself. If he wanted to have even a small chance of surviving, Samuel had to calm down and regain control over himself.

A little farther ahead, the strigois were still not moving. They were probably waiting for him to cast caution to the wind and rush blindly toward them, so they could finish him off in one bite.

The green light that had unveiled the vampire's presence grew brighter, revealing to Samuel exactly where he was. What he saw then sent his mind spiraling.

What he had mistaken for stone under his feet was, in fact, the pavement of a street. Farther ahead, the street changed to a green lawn, enclosed by a white picket fence. At the end of this lawn stood a familiar building: his parents' house.

He was back on his own world.

The gods had not brought the vampires to Metverold. They had instead sent Samuel back to his world, in front of his home. He had momentarily left the world of legend to stand in the middle of the street he had walked every day for most of his life.

A warm breeze gently stroked Samuel's face, carrying with it the perfumes of summer and the fragrance of meadows. Above him, the dark sky was peppered with stars, among which shone a dazzling full moon. On each side, the street was totally deserted, without even a single light coming from the neighbors' windows. There was no horrified scream at the sight of the vampires, no hasty slamming of a door. All Samuel could hear was the rustling of the leaves, the swirling of the dust around him, and the whistling of the vampires.

Samuel had still not moved a muscle when he noticed the vampires were not at all interested in his presence. In fact, they had their backs turned to him. They were watching the white house of his parents, about twenty feet in front of them. A light suddenly went on in the second floor, and Shantel's silhouette appeared in front of a window. She seemed to be in a conversation with someone in her room, and when she disappeared, Samuel's mother took her place at the window. Shortly after, a dim light outlined a third shadow on the ground floor, which Samuel guessed was his dad, probably searching the refrigerator for something to nibble.

A terrifying thought crossed Samuel's mind, and when the vampires took a step toward the house's front door, this thought became horribly real.

"No," whispered Samuel.

He had understood what the strigois planned on doing. They did not intend to attack him. The monsters did not seem to even be aware of his presence. Their plan was much more frightening. They had decided to attack Samuel in a different way, delivering a strike he could not parry or evade. They had decided to attack his family. Samuel tightened his fingers around the hilt of his sword, until he could feel each of the leather straps marking his skin. A new energy was flowing in his veins, chasing away all the anxiety that had gripped his will until now. The air around him started bursting with electricity, and the hair on his arms stood up. His jaw clenched.

It was one thing to attack him, but it was another to hurt his family. They had nothing to do with his role as the Lorekeeper, and Samuel would not let anyone harm them because of him.

As the strigois got closer to the house, Samuel discarded the last remnants of fear lingering in his mind and loosed his anger. He let out a scream so powerful the vampires jumped as they turned to him, and then he leapt toward them without even taking a moment to establish an attack plan.

Caught by surprise, the strigois barely had time to see him running at them. They pulled their lips back to reveal sharp fangs, but before they could do anything, Samuel was on top of them. Blinded by rage and worry for his family, he struck out in every direction with his sword. He was content to slay his foes in any way imaginable. With his eyes shut, Samuel struck from left to right, and then upward and downward, without ever stopping to evaluate the efficiency of his moves.

After a while, Samuel realized that each time his blade met the body of a vampire, it did nothing more than slice through the air. It was as if he were fighting three ghosts or three illusions.

Nevertheless, the vampires screamed in terror. They yelled for almost a minute under Samuel's onslaught, and then the three monsters' silhouettes vanished, as if they had been a mirage in a desert. A moment later, Samuel's home also disappeared, and the darkness reclaimed its dominion over this place of mystery. Samuel found himself alone in the dark again, covered in sweat and out of breath.

What did it all mean? Had he passed some kind of test? It did not feel like it. He actually thought he had been quite reckless when he let his emotions get the better of him and ran to his enemies like he did. But when he had seen his family in danger …

Suddenly, Samuel understood the aim of this little exercise. All this time, he had thought he was scared for himself; that he feared the vampires because of his life. But his concerns had always been for the security of his family. If the vampires, or any other monster from Metverold, were to attack him, in his own world or in this one, Samuel could defeat them. He had the necessary tools to defend himself, but his family was vulnerable. His parents, his sister and his friends did not possess the knowledge he did, or the necessary abilities to fight back. It was up to him to protect them.

He was the Lorekeeper, a soldier of Virtus, but he was also a protector of his own world, of his family and the people around him.

A rumble rose from the depths of the cave, and the ground started quaking with such force that Samuel had a hard time maintaining his balance. At the same time, a large boulder rolled on his right, revealing an opening through which a blue light escaped.

Samuel had passed his first trial. He had found the true source of one of his fears. He now had to continue his journey and face the next challenge.

Still cautious, he made his way to the opening and walked into the light.

Once on the other side, the first thing Samuel noticed was the familiar smell, where the stench of sweat mingled with the scent of cleaning products and microwaved pizzas. He heard laughter and shouts, as well as an electronic voice talking unintelligibly somewhere above him. When the scene around him came into focus, he realized he was in a long corridor. The floor was monotonous white tile, and the walls were covered with yellow paint that seemed over twenty years old. Along the walls were dozens of metal lockers, with several boys and girls around his age walking between them. Some carried books in their arms, and others had heavy backpacks.

After a moment, Samuel understood where he was. The gods had transported him to his school, probably sometime between two classes.

A horrified cry behind him made Samuel jump, and he turned swiftly, his sword still in his hand. A young student he had seen a few times looked at him with a terrified look. She clung to her books and held them to her chest as if she were trying to shield herself. Right next to her, another young girl stared at Samuel, then dropped her backpack and ran away.

Whispers spread around Samuel, and alarming screams shot out from every direction.

Samuel lowered his eyes and understood why he was generating such agitation in the corridor. He was standing in the middle of the students wearing Trojan armor and carrying a sharp gladius in his hand.

"Uh," he mumbled. "No, wait, I—"

What could he say to the people around him? What explanation could he provide to explain his presence, his outfit and, most important, the weapon in his hand. Moreover, he was covered in sweat and dust, and certainly did not smell like roses.

"Would you look at this dumbass!" yelled a voice behind him. "You think you're in one of your stupid games?"

Samuel turned and saw Danny standing before him, arms crossed over his chest. Behind him, his two acolytes cackled like frenzied hyenas.

"What's going on?" said Danny. "You had nothing to wear other than your stupid toys, is that it?"

"No," answered Samuel. "You don't understand. I ... I am—"

"A dumbass," said Danny. "We already knew that."

Samuel wanted to say that he could explain everything, but before he could utter a word, the students around him all burst out laughing at the same time. Heartened by Danny's insults, they no longer looked afraid by Samuel's appearance.

A little farther ahead of Samuel, Clara squeezed her way through the students. She pushed two of them aside and stood in front of the young man.

"Samuel?" she asked, looking at him with worried eyes. "What are you doing?"

"Clara, I can explain everything," replied Samuel.

His answer only seemed to boost the students' laughter around him. *Really?* they were saying. *He can explain why he was dressed like this?*

"There's something you don't know about me," said Samuel, trying to make himself heard over the laughter. "I … to tell you the truth, you see, I'm—"

"Shut up, you bunch of dumbasses!" Danny commanded the other students. "Let's see how he's going to explain his ridiculous costume."

Samuel never looked away from Clara, and she kept looking straight into his eyes. She was waiting for an explanation from Samuel, and by the look she gave him, she prayed for this explanation to be convincing so they would all leave him alone.

Samuel sheathed his sword. He took a deep breath, and decided to tell her the truth.

"I am the Lorekeeper," he said.

As soon as the words passed his lips, he felt as if a gigantic weight had been lifted off his shoulders. A moment later, the laughter around Samuel increased twofold. Amid them, the voice of Danny rose above all the others, shouting more insults.

However, Samuel easily ignored the name-calling. He had his eyes locked on the only person whose opinion truly mattered: Clara. She had not moved, and she was still looking into his eyes. After a few seconds, she crossed her arms over her chest and took a step toward him.

"Can you repeat that?" she said.

"I am the Lorekeeper," answered Samuel.

Clara slowly nodded her head and a particularly unpleasant feeling coiled around Samuel's guts. The look of the young woman had just changed. It had gone from worried to something else. It was the kind of look usually reserved for the foolish and the witless.

"And why are you the Lorekeeper?" she asked, trying to hide a chuckle.

"Because the dice chose me."

This time she could not help herself and let a tiny laugh slip through.

"Dice? Some dice told you to dress like Brad Pitt in Troy, to arm yourself with a sword, and protect the legends, is that it?"

"Yes. No! It's much more complicated than that. There is this parallel universe called Metverold, and—"

Now Clara was laughing without holding back and joined her voice to those of the other students in the hall.

"A parallel universe?" she repeated, laughing. "And it's inhabited by leprechauns and faeries, right?"

Samuel's heart shattered into a thousand pieces. He had finally told Clara who he was, and she had thrown it back in his face, laughing. She was mocking him, and had joined the others to ridicule him.

"Yes, there are faeries," whispered Samuel, lowering his eyes. "And pechs, fatas, and evil sorcerers."

He could hardly believe it. He had thought Clara was different from the other girls his age. He had hoped she would understand, that she would at least agree to hear his story before deciding if he was telling the truth. But she had opted to mock him instead. In the end, she was no better than Danny and the others.

Samuel raised his eyes again and saw Lucian, who was also laughing enthusiastically with the other students, pointing at Samuel and joking with the boys next to him.

"Lucien? How can you mock me like this?" asked Samuel. "You saw the dice for yourself. You saw with your own eyes the engravings on their sides. I said we had imagined it all because I could not tell you the truth, but deep in your heart, you have to know it was not our minds playing tricks on us."

Lucien looked at Samuel and his laughter slowly faded. The rest of the students turned their heads to the red-haired boy. A light of hope appeared in Samuel's mind. His best friend would not let him be turned into a fool like this. Lucien had seen what the dice could do. Now, with the eyes of every student fixed on him, he would seize the occasion to confirm Samuel was telling the truth. Maybe all was not lost. Maybe Clara would even regret having laughed at him, once she heard what Lucien had to say.

Lucien looked over the crowd of students around him, and then he said, "I have no idea what you're talking about, Samuel."

No armor could have protected Samuel from Lucien's words. They pierced his heart.

"You've always had a prolific imagination," added his friend. "Maybe it's time you grew up and put these stupid ideas aside."

The crowd around Samuel exploded into laughter at once, their enthusiasm multiplied by the treason he had just been the victim of. Even Clara had now moved closer to Danny to share jokes with him, her eyes blurred by tears. Lucien joined them, whispering something that made them fall on the ground and roll around in laughter.

It was too much for Samuel. Something inside him snapped and he burst out: "That's enough!" His voice thundered in the corridor. The students fell silent and turned to him, holding to one another.

"I couldn't care less what you think of me," added Samuel. "I am the Lorekeeper, whether you believe me or not. I didn't choose this role. I didn't ask the gods to name me their protector. It is they who have chosen me, okay? I didn't ask for anything. To be frank, I didn't want this responsibility at first. I thought they had made a mistake, that I would not be good enough, but I was mistaken. I am the Lorekeeper and I will not relinquish this duty. Someone has to protect our world from those who seek to change it, to remodel it for their own purposes. If I don't do it, who will? One of you, maybe? How about you, Danny? Who among you wants to take my place, to fight dragons, giants, vampires and other infernal monsters?" When Samuel stopped talking, silence reigned in the hall. No one dared to answer him, not even Danny.

"That's what I thought," Samuel said. "You're all so quick to mock me, but deep inside you're all cowards. You would rather laugh than confront the nightmarish creatures trying to destroy our world. Well, I'm not afraid anymore. I accept this role. I am the Lorekeeper and it is a part of me. If you have a problem with that, I don't really care."

Danny was the first to vanish, quickly followed by his two acolytes. The rest of the students disappeared in a cloud of smoke, one by one, until only Clara and Lucien were left. Lucien looked at Samuel and gave him a smile filled with admiration, and then he vanished as well, leaving Samuel alone with Clara.

"You're right, Samuel," said Clara. "Never forget that you are the Lorekeeper, and that you were chosen because only you can protect us. No one else can beat the Yfel's sorcerer. You don't protect these people to gain their sympathy or their approval. You do it because they depend on you, and their world needs your protection. They will never know what you have done for them, but believe me, Samuel, *I* am grateful!"

Before Samuel could answer, Clara blew a kiss in his direction. Then she faded away as well. A few moments later, the school faded into the dark. Soon, all that was left was himself and a dim purple halo coming out of the sheath at his waist.

Sliding his sword out again, Samuel remembered all of this had not been real, that it was only another trial. He had just confronted the second of his three biggest fears, and it was one he had underestimated. It was not a fear that was easy to picture, like the vampires and the safety of his family. It was a much more subtle fear, one that touched him in the deepest part of his being.

It was the fear of being mocked for what he was: the Lorekeeper. It was the fear of being ridiculed for something that was an integral part of who he was, something that was impossible to discard. And this trial had taught him this fear was futile. He had no reason to be ashamed of his role, to be fearful of being discovered. Being the Lorekeeper was a part of him. It was in his blood, in his veins. He had to embrace this role without holding back, and then the opinion of others would not matter. He would even feel some pride in being the one chosen for this responsibility.

To be honest, he had to admit it was an honor to be chosen, and if the occasion ever presented itself to do it all over again, he would not change a thing.

A new door opened on his left, and this time it was a red light coming from the other side.

Samuel had overcome the second trial, which was to ignore the opinions of others and fully accept his role as the Lorekeeper. There was only one test left now before he could find the Helm of Darkness. His face set with determination, he walked through the door and into the red light.

As soon as he crossed the threshold, the door slammed shut behind him, and the red light vanished. Samuel found himself in the dark again, the only light the purple glow from his weapon.

He took a few cautious steps forward. He tried to pierce the darkness with his eyes, but could not distinguish the slightest detail.

"If you could only see yourself," a voice echoed in the darkness. "Always alone and pathetic, completely lost in the dark. As usual, you have no idea of what is going on and Virtus is doing nothing to help you out."

He recognized the voice as soon as he heard the first words. It was the voice of his sworn enemy: the Yfel's sorcerer. Was this the last trial that awaited him? Did he have to confront his fear of the sorcerer?

His answer arrived with a green light in front of him. Within this light he saw his enemy, still wearing his long, dark robe, his head hidden by the hood. He had both hands inside the sleeves, but Samuel knew that one of them was closed around the hilt of a sword. He had seen the sorcerer draw his weapon at lightning speed, and there was no doubt his enemy would not be taken by surprise.

"You're not real," said Samuel. "You're just an image of my true enemy. You're nothing more than an illusion designed to scare me."

The sorcerer burst into a laugh that echoed around Samuel.

"Don't be an idiot," said the sorcerer. "You really think I will let you pass all three trials to get the Helm of Darkness? You see, as I understand it, without the Helm, you can't stroll around Hell without being spotted by the friends of Yfel dwelling there. And if you can't safely walk around, then how do you expect to protect Aeneas?"

Once again, the sorcerer erupted in cavernous laughter, but this time Samuel did not let him finish. Without warning he launched himself at his foe, his weapon held high before him. However, instead of taking out his own sword, the sorcerer turned and fled to Samuel's right. The green light mysteriously followed him, until he came to a halt after about thirty yards.

"You think you're clever?" said Samuel. "You think I'll just wait for you to get the drop on me when I least expect it?"

Once again, Samuel ran to the sorcerer. Once again, his enemy refused to face him and fled to his left, floating a few inches above the ground. He flew for a couple of seconds, then made a sharp right turn, always pursued by Samuel. After a moment, Samuel stopped, and the sorcerer did as well.

"What kind of game are you playing?" asked Samuel. "Are you going to make me run like this all night, or are you going to find the courage to face me?"

This time, instead of fleeing, the sorcerer moved closer to Samuel, catching him by surprise. A sinister laugh whistled through his teeth. He stayed still before the young man for a few seconds, and then abruptly lifted his head toward him. Just as he was about to pull back the dark hood and reveal his identity, the green light disappeared, and the area fell into total darkness once again.

"My dear Samuel, you'll never learn. You still throw yourself into the traps I lay for you without thinking twice."

The sorcerer's voice seemed to be coming from everywhere at once. Samuel turned around, trying to find the direction from which the sorcerer would attack.

"You still think I'm just an image; that I am part of your stupid trials. You're so convinced you are right that you have followed me without asking yourself if it was a wise decision. Do you even know where you are?"

Samuel did not understand what the sorcerer was getting at. The trial was rather simple: Samuel had to fight his enemy and defeat him in order to face his fears. However, the sorcerer seemed to have no intention of facing him. He looked happy to simply play hide and seek with him instead.

"You see," added the sorcerer, "I knew you would think my presence here was part of your ultimate test. I was convinced you would think you only had to kill the big bad sorcerer to get to the Helm of Darkness. All I had to do was show myself, and you followed me in haste, like a good little doggy. However, this is not your final trial. In fact, you never reached the place where your test is taking place. You didn't listen to the voice of reason, and now you are completely lost, alone between two worlds, without any possibility of finding your way back."

"You're lying," said Samuel, but his voice trembled.

"It doesn't matter whether you believe me. You lost, Samuel. You failed even before the legend started. What a Lorekeeper you are! Now, you'll have to excuse me, because I have a hero to kill, and a nation to eradicate before it even sees the light of day. Unlike Virtus, the Yfel doesn't leave me alone in this violent world. They told me how to get out of here, and in a few minutes I will feel the warm Italian sun on my face again. It's unfortunate that you won't share the same fate. Still, I do wish you all the best, Keeper of nothing at all."

As soon as he heard the sorcerer's last words, Samuel instinctively knew his enemy was telling the truth, and that he had just vanished. The words echoed in Samuel's mind and absolute terror spread into the deepest part of his being. The sorcerer had told the truth. Samuel was not in the last trial he had to overcome. His enemy had led him far from it, through a world that did not make any sense, where only darkness existed.

Now he was utterly alone, and completely lost in eternal blackness.

He screamed in horror, but the words vanished into the abyss.

9

The fright taking root in Samuel's guts grew at an alarming rate. Like a tidal wave surging on a barren plain, the terror spread to the most remote corners of his mind. Around him, the darkness seemed to thicken, and Samuel worried that at any moment the ground would disappear from under his feet, or the ceiling would come crashing down on his head.

Should he let go of his mind's reins and flee blindly? His legs were begging him to do so, but Samuel knew that losing control of his willpower would only worsen the situation. Without any markers to guide him, and without any idea of where he was, isolated in utter blackness, he would only get farther away from the exit.

Samuel cursed the sorcerer out loud. His enemy had made a fool of him. He had used his convictions and his newfound courage, fueled by his previous successes, to set the perfect trap, and Samuel had thrown himself into it like a complete idiot.

Samuel turned slowly. He could not stay still here, waiting for death to come. He had to try and find his way out, but which direction should he go? No matter how hard he peered, he could not see a single detail. Everything was black, black, black.

After a little while, he took a step forward, in the direction that seemed the most like the one he had come from earlier. Of course, it was only an intuition. To tell the truth, he had not the slightest idea if it was, in fact, the direction he had arrived from.

Samuel walked for about ten minutes. He would not have been able to say if he was really walking in a straight line or if he was going in circles. Keeping his sword close to his body, he cautiously set his foot down with every step, praying to the gods of Metverold that he would see a boulder or a stone wall, but neither ever came.

After a moment, terror yielded to despair. How could he hope to get out of this place alive—a place that existed between two worlds? For all he knew, this place went on forever in every direction.

On the verge of abandoning all hope, Samuel collapsed to the ground and crossed his legs. He thought of Angeline and Deiphobe. Had they already guessed Samuel would never come back from this cursed place? Were they still waiting for him, entertaining the futile hope he would appear at one of the hundred doors? And if that was the case, what would they think when they understood Samuel was lost forever? Deiphobe had mentioned that none of the heroes who had come here before him had returned from this wretched place. Would the fata and the old woman assume the same fate had befallen him? Samuel could not see how they would think otherwise. Angeline would certainly be inconsolable for a while, but she would eventually accept it and would wait to get a new Lorekeeper assigned to her. And all the time, Samuel would be condemned to wander in this place that did not exist, until he died of exhaustion or hunger, alone and forgotten by all.

Completely drained by hopelessness, Samuel put his sword on his knees. His head fell until his chin bumped his chest. He sighed.

He would die here. The sooner he accepted it, the easier it would be for him.

For several long minutes, he stayed still and in silence. He listened to his breathing. He had his eyes fixed on the blade of his weapon, his gaze locked on the purple glow. Angeline had many powers, but she was unable to help him now.

He was alone, abandoned by all.

Samuel raised his head again.

How could he say something like that? Angeline would never abandon him. She would not let him rot in this dark place and wait for a new Lorekeeper to be placed under her care. Angeline was a warrior, a faerie without equal who never let anyone push her around. She would not leave him here. She was not only his fata; she was his friend and his guardian angel. She had always been there for him, since the very first time he had set foot on Metverold. She had even broken the rules a few times, without fearing the consequences, so Samuel could live and complete his mission.

Once Angeline realized Samuel needed her help to get out of this place, she would move mountains to find him before it was too late.

Samuel also thought of Cathasach, the pech with prodigious strength. He thought of Merlin, Brutus and Corineus. He saw the face of Malloy again, and Uther Pendragon, as well as his brother Ambrosius and all the people he had met in his previous adventure—all the friendships he had built on Metverold. If these people could be of any help in rescuing him from this dreadful place, Angeline would not hesitate to recruit them, consequences be damned, and they would answer her call without thinking twice.

Samuel jumped to his feet.

He was not alone. Angeline and his friends were with him. They would never let him die here, alone in total darkness. If they could, they would fly to his rescue, and would not hesitate to put their lives in danger to get him out of here.

For the third time, a boulder rolled in front of Samuel, revealing a door hidden until now. This time, a white light was coming through the opening.

Samuel stayed still for a second or two, surprised to see this exit suddenly revealed to him. What did it mean, exactly? Had he successfully passed his last test? The sorcerer had led him away from this last trial, so how was this possible?

Suddenly, everything became clear, and he smiled. The sorcerer had never actually been here with him. It had only been an image of his enemy. All this time, Samuel had been in the center of this last trial, and now he understood what it was. The ultimate fear he had to face, the fear that always paralyzed his muscles and blurred his judgment, was not the fear of fighting the sorcerer and dying by his hand. After all, he would give his life to save the legends and in doing so, his own world.

No, the *true* fear was the fear of being abandoned on Metverold. It was the dread of finding himself completely alone, without any possibility of going back home. What scared him most was to be forgotten at the bottom of a dark cavern, to be left to himself, without any hope of seeing his family and friends again. Without any hope of seeing Clara again.

But now he understood that this fear was ridiculous, that it had no foundation. Angeline and his friends would never desert him like this. They were there for him, and would always come to his aid. Now that he understood the true nature of this fear, and that he had chased those thoughts away, the last door opened for him—the one leading to the Helm of Darkness.

With a smile still on his lips, Samuel walked to the door and into the white light.

Unlike the previous two doors he had entered, as soon as this one closed behind him, Samuel did not find himself in complete darkness. He was instead at the top of a gigantic staircase, carved directly into the stone of the mountain. Before him was a cavern of titanic dimensions, so vast he could not see the end of it. Above his head, he saw an enormous vault, several thousand feet high, supported by massive stone pillars. Phosphorescent stalactites hung from the ceiling and washed the cavern in blue light. On each side of the cave, cascades dumped glittering water into rivers below, which all converged in the center of the cavern. The rivers then divided again to go around a small rocky hill, at the top of which was a black altar.

Samuel immediately guessed what rested on it: the Helm of Darkness.

He slowly made his way down the stairs, his eyes wide open so he missed nothing of this magnificent place. Although the purple glow of his sword was no longer needed, Samuel still held the blade before him. He had overcome three terrifying trials to get here, and there might be more surprises waiting for him on the way to the hill at the center of the cave.

Once at the bottom of the stairs, Samuel carefully stepped forward on an old stone road, where it was easy to twist an ankle. After about twenty yards, he reached a bridge straddling the place where two rivers joined. The racket from the waterfalls on each side of him was deafening and he could barely hear his own thoughts. Out of curiosity, he stopped for a moment and peeked over the bridge's handrail. What he saw then was worthy of the most stunning fairytales. Rather than simply reflecting the glow from the stalactites, the river produced its own light. Millions of luminous dots of all colors danced before his eyes.

Samuel had to use all his will to break the spell and turn away. A few minutes longer and he would surely have abandoned himself completely, forgetting even his mission. As he kept walking, he wondered if that was the reason the river shone like it did. Maybe the hypnotic lights were one last trial, just to measure the willpower of those brave enough to venture here.

A few minutes later, Samuel climbed the hill at the center of the cave. On the onyx altar lay the Helm of Darkness. When he saw the object, Samuel was slightly surprised, and even a little disappointed. He had thought the Helm of Darkness would be a magnificent metallic helm, forged in the darkest pit of Hell and made of a metal unknown to man. He had thought it would be rather big and heavy, adorned with countless gems and made for the head of a god. But on the altar before Samuel was a simple crown. It had been forged in black metal with glints of silver, but it did not have any jewels set in it other than a small red pearl at the front. It was so small that Samuel thought for a moment it wouldn't fit his head.

This was why he had faced his worst nightmares and his most terrifying fears?

Samuel let his sword slide back into his sheath and grabbed the black crown. He moved it closer to his face, turned it before his eyes and studied the object more closely. He noticed several strange symbols engraved on the inner surface. The finesse of the work was remarkable, and Samuel thought he might have criticized the crown a little too quickly. Evidently it held immense power, and did not need superfluous decoration to prove it. After all, Apollo had told Samuel he needed to vanquish his fears before putting the Helm of Darkness on. The god would not have put him through all those trials for a common crown.

He hesitated for a moment, then raised his arms and placed the crown on his head.

As soon as the Helm of Darkness was in place, a strange sensation spread through his body. It was as if a fog enveloped him, slowly freezing his muscles. First he lost the sensation in the tips of his fingers, then his toes. A few seconds later, a tickling spread in his hands and feet, before climbing along his arms and legs.

Then Samuel understood why he had to master his fears before putting the helm on his head.

Without any warning, all his senses were attacked by invisible forces seeking to scare him. Out of the corner of his eye, he saw the outline of the strigois. They vanished as soon as he turned his head in their direction, only to appear again on the other side. With them came a bitter wind that blew along his spine and up the back of his neck. He then heard the mocking laughter of a dozen people around him, their voices muffled as if he were in a dream. He heard the insults and bad jokes he had always feared. Even worse, a feeling of isolation was growing in his mind that pushed him toward complete despair. His courage faded, replaced by a desire to lie down on the ground and wait for death.

The first reflex Samuel had was to remove the Helm of Darkness from his head, but he stopped himself at the last moment. He guessed this was exactly what the dark crown wanted. The helm was feeding on his fears and was urging Samuel to put the magical object back on the altar, where it would stay for eternity. It was a mechanism designed to ensure only the deserving ones could use the helm.

Samuel closed his eyes and took a deep breath. This is why Apollo had sent him to face his fears. He wanted to give Samuel the force to master the Helm of Darkness, so he could wear it without fear.

Samuel focused on his successes and how he had overcome those fears. He thought of his family and how he would do anything to protect them. He thought about his role as the Lorekeeper—a role he now fully assumed and appreciated, honored to have been chosen by the gods. Finally, he thought of his friends, Angeline and Cathasach, who would never leave him alone on Metverold, and who would never abandon him.

Slowly the feelings of despair and vulnerability receded. The artifact was doing all it could to resist him, but he was determined to impose his will on it.

Finally, after several long minutes of battle, the helm conceded and ceased its attack on Samuel's mind. The tingling under his skin was still there and limbs were still numb, but he now had full control of the situation. He had dominated his fears.

Samuel lowered his head, closed his eyes and took off the Helm of Darkness. When he opened his eyes again, he was no longer in the cave.

"Samuel!"

He turned just in time to see Angeline throw herself at his neck. Behind her, Deiphobe was looking at him with bewildering eyes, her face frozen by surprise.

"You … you came back!" said the Sibyl, hardly believing what she was saying.

"Of course he came back!" shouted Angeline. "I *told* you never to doubt my Lorekeeper."

Samuel glanced around him. Without knowing how, he was back in the Chamber of a Hundred Doors. Was this real? One minute he had been standing in the heart of an endless cavern, and an eye-blink later he was back in the Sibyl's home.

"How did I get here?" he asked.

Angeline let go of Samuel's neck and flew back a few inches.

"I don't know," she said. "Deiphobe and I were just talking about Aeneas's legend, and when I turned around there you were, standing with your eyes closed."

She lowered her eyes to the black crown Samuel was holding in his right hand.

"Is that the Helm of Darkness?" she asked with a trembling voice.

Samuel held the object up. "Yes."

"I thought it would be bigger," said Angeline.

Deiphobe stepped forward slowly, a shaking hand raised before her. With a bony index finger, she pointed at the Helm of Darkness.

"I don't believe it," she said. "After all these years, someone has finally managed to bring this treasure back to our world. How did you do it?"

"It wasn't easy," said Samuel, his eyes fixed on the crown. "I thought I would have to fight dreadful monsters or giant insects, but in the end the trials were designed to make me identify what my real fears were. I had to discover what frightened me the most before I could master it."

"And you pulled it off like a true hero!" said Angeline. "Can we have a little demonstration?"

116

Samuel hesitated a moment, then placed the Helm of Darkness on his head. Right away, the numbing sensation spread to his legs and arms, but this time the Helm did not try to dominate him by using his own fears.

"That's it?" asked Angeline. "I don't see anything special."

"That's because you exist outside of the mythologies," said Deiphobe. "The Helm of Darkness has no effect on you, but for most of the beings inhabiting our world, Pluto's crown will render Samuel invisible. However, the helm isn't foolproof. Some creatures living in the Underworld are also immune to its power, and they will be able to see you, Samuel. You will have to be very cautious, and you as well, Angeline. You may be invisible to most of the inhabitants of this world, but you will be subject to the same rules as Samuel in the Underworld."

"You mean I won't be invisible?"

"Not to everyone. You won't draw attention like the Helm of Darkness will, but don't go thinking you will be completely ignored."

Deiphobe then turned to Samuel.

"You should attach the helm securely to your waist. If you wear it on your head all the time, it will eventually dominate you. If you let down your guard for even a moment, it will take control of your mind. Use it only when necessary."

Carefully, Samuel lifted the onyx crown from his head and tied it to the rope around his waist.

"And now what do we do?" he asked.

"Now we wait for Aeneas to finish the rites and bring us the golden bough," replied the Sibyl. And with that she turned and disappeared into the tunnel leading to the kitchen.

"I like her, but she's strange," said Angeline, before following the woman.

Samuel smiled and went after them as well.

10

The flames rose mercilessly against the night. They stretched gracefully to the stars as if trying to touch the celestial vault and draw the attention of the gods. Carried by the ocean's warm and misty breeze, they danced carelessly under the moon, their hypnotic light like the waves of the sea.

As Aeneas watched the flames consume the funeral pyre where the body of his companion lay—poor Misenus!—he found himself thinking of Troy. Images of that terrible night when the Fates had allowed the Greeks inside the city walls would remain etched in his memory until he died. He could still hear the horrified screams of his fellow Trojans, as rivers of fire ravaged their homes and reduced their lives to ashes. He would never forget escaping the doomed metropolis, carrying his father Anchises on his back and pulling his son Ascagne behind him. He saw once more the last images of his wife Creusa, before she got lost in the bloodied alleys of Troy. Even after all this time, he still shed tears for the poor woman.

One of the logs at the base of the pyre suddenly crumbled, and the hero's companions took a few steps back, but Aeneas remained still. He managed to momentarily cast away the memories of this infernal night that had sent him into exile with these men, but they had been replaced by other baleful thoughts.

The funeral pyre for Misenus was the latest in a long series of funerals he had attended since the fall of Troy. Many of his companions had met their doom following him in this journey, among them his own father, Anchises, who had not survived the dangers of the sea.

However, the Trojans were not the only victims of Juno's wrath. The queen of Carthage, Dido, had also met her tragic end in the funeral flames. She who had welcomed Aeneas and his companions in her city, and whose only crime had been to allow her love for the hero to grow inside her. She had known a most appalling fate, preferring to throw herself on the sword she had offered to Aeneas and abandon her body to the pyre rather than see the Trojan hero sail away from her.

Aeneas closed his eyes and clenched his fists. Too many men and women had been sent to Pluto's kingdom because of him. It was time for his people to end their journey. It was time for them to find a place to settle down, and to build a new city where they could find peace and prosperity.

"Poor Misenus," whispered Achates, next to Aeneas. "Never again will we hear the marvelous sound of his horn. Why did Poseidon wish the death of such a talented young man? Why did the god of the sea throw his body against the black reefs?"

"For the same reasons Juno persecutes us," answered Aeneas. "For the same reasons the gods do anything at all: envy and vanity."

"My friend, I know that your heart is crying for the loss of many of our companions, but I beg of you, beware of the words you say. Blasphemies are a particularly bad omen for the journey you are about to take."

Aeneas turned to Achates, smiled and put a hand on his shoulder.

"As usual, you are right," he said. "I know that you are also saddened by the loss of Misenus. I apologize."

"There's nothing to apologize for," replied Achates. "But if you must, you should address those words to Jupiter instead of me."

Aeneas's companion raised his eyes to the stars.

"Tomorrow, when the flames have carried our friend to the Underworld," he said, "we will look for the golden bough the Sibyl told you about."

Aeneas tightened his grip on his friend's shoulder and his smile grew a little wider.

"Why wait for tomorrow?" he asked. "Have the men dig a sepulcher for Misenus and place the ashes inside as soon as you can."

"Aeneas, is it wise to undertake a journey to the Kingdom of the Dead at such an hour, while the sun still hides over the horizon?"

"Do you truly believe the Avernus will be more welcoming if I go in the midst of the day?" asked Aeneas.

Achates shook his head.

"Then why delay my encounter with my father any longer?" Aeneas said. "Don't worry about me, my friend. If the gods had wished for my doom, I would already by wrestling Hector on the Fields of Elysium. In my absence, I put the protection of our companions in your hands."

Aeneas offered his hand to his companion, who shook it without lowering his gaze.

"Be careful," said Achates. "Who knows what horrible beasts linger in the depths of Hell."

"I will be prudent," replied Aeneas. He turned and walked resolutely into the night, toward the place the Sibyl had indicated. Aeneas walked until he could no longer hear the prayers of his companions and silence was again the master of his surroundings. After a while he came to the top of a small vale, at the bottom of which was a forest ten times as wide as Troy had been. Somewhere in these woods was the golden bough.

"If only the golden tree would reveal itself to me," whispered Aeneas, searching the forest with his eyes. "What the Sibyl said about Misenus was only too real, but how can she think I will find the object of this quest in such a large forest?"

He had barely pronounced these words when two doves came down from the sky and landed in the grass in front of him. Aeneas immediately recognized his mother's birds and quickly said a prayer for them.

"Birds of Venus, be my guides," he said, "and if there is really a path to the offering I must bring with me, may your flight lead my steps to the grove and show me where the bough casts its shadow on this fertile soil. And you, my divine mother, don't leave me to my doubts. Guide my footsteps toward my destiny, so that my people can finally have the peace they deserve."

As soon as Aeneas said these words, the doves took off and soared into the night toward the forest. The hero quickly ran after them, rushing down the hillside. Without wasting a second, he disappeared among the oak and olive trees, his eyes locked on the birds. He ignored the branches whipping his face as he ran.

After some time, Aeneas came to a small clearing washed by the moon's pale light. A gigantic olive tree stood in the middle of the clearing, solitary and splendid.

The two doves floated to the majestic tree and settled on one of its large branches. They started cooing melodiously. Aeneas walked over to the tree. The trunk was as large a small house, and the branches were so heavy with olives they hung toward the ground. The rustling of thousands of leaves reminded the hero of the ocean's song, and the scent of the olives brought back memories of his youth, spent running in the fields around Troy.

Aeneas raised his eyes to the doves. A golden glow filtered through the foliage above them. He immediately guessed the glow came from the bough he needed, and he set about climbing the tree. Being careful not to damage the bark and the sacred fruits, he slowly pulled himself to the spot were Venus's birds waited, then seated himself on a branch as wide as a full-grown man.

Carefully, he parted the leaves where the golden light shone, and laid his eyes on the divine bough. Its splendor left Aeneas speechless. The golden branch was no more than a foot long, but its light almost rivaled the sun. It was straight and garnished with perfectly rounded leaves, as well as tiny emerald olives.

Never had Aeneas seen an object like this, and he understood why the queen of Avernus desired such a treasure.

Aeneas extended his hand to take the bough, but hesitated at the last moment. The Sibyl had mentioned that if the gods granted him access to the kingdom of Pluto, then the bough would easily yield. However, if the gods decided he was not worthy of walking in the fields of Elysium without first meeting Death, then the branch would be impossible to pick. Aeneas closed his eyes, whispered a prayer to Jupiter and Venus, and closed his fingers around the bough. He took a deep breath and tugged on the tiny branch.

It detached as easily as if he had picked a ripe apple.

Aeneas sighed in relief and opened his eyes. As soon as he had picked the golden bough, another one appeared in its place, identical to the one he held between his fingers. The hero admired the bough for a few seconds, then put it in a small leather satchel at his waist and quickly climbed down the tree. Once on the ground, he thanked the two doves for showing him the way, then he ran toward the mountain and the Sibyl's home.

"And you think this boy is the Yfel's sorcerer?" asked Angeline.

"I don't know," replied Samuel, "but Patrick claimed that he gave him the black dice."

Samuel was sitting in front of the oak table, in Deiphobe's lair, while Angeline paced up and down before him. As usual, she considered this piece of information from every angle, stroking her chin. Samuel had taken advantage of the little time they had to tell her about his discussion with Patrick—omitting the part where he had threatened the young man with a sword, of course. Angeline would certainly have scolded him for his carelessness. Instead, he had only said Patrick had mentioned the black dice when he had seen Samuel's own white dice.

"Do you know anything about this Simon?" asked Angeline.

"Not really," answered Samuel. "My friend Lucien is closer to him than I am. I only know he goes to the same school I do. He's a shy boy who hardly mixes with anybody."

Angeline flew in circles over Samuel's head. "That would make him an easy target for the Yfel," she said. "They tend to favor those who stay outside of society. It's probably easier to convince them that a new world would be a better place for them."

"Agreed, but I'm having some difficulty picturing Simon as the sorcerer," said Samuel. "He's shy, but he doesn't look particularly troublesome."

Angeline put her feet down in front of Samuel again and stared into his eyes.

"Once again, you underestimate the Yfel, Samuel," she said. "Their influence on the sorcerers they choose is without equal. They can change the most unassuming boy into a bloodthirsty murderer with a simple snap of their fingers."

Samuel swallowed hard at the thought that Simon could have become a being of unprecedented cruelty. It was so hard to believe. As he was about to reply, Deiphobe burst into the room and pounced on him.

"Get up quick!" she said as she pushed on his shoulders. "The moment has arrived. Aeneas is coming and we must be ready."

Samuel got up with a strange feeling in his guts. The discussion with Angeline had almost made him forget their destination, but now it was time for them to descend into the Underworld.

Deiphobe pushed him aside and walked over to a wooden cabinet at the back of the kitchen. She grabbed a goatskin bottle hanging next to the cabinet, and then turned to the black pot where the mixture of wheat and honey still brewed. With the help of a copper ladle, she delicately filled the goatskin with the warm mixture. She pinched the leather bag shut and swung it over her shoulder.

"Follow me, both of you," she said, and left the room to walk back to the Chamber of a Hundred Doors.

In the chamber, Deiphobe told them to climb the stairs again and go back to their hiding spot, behind a pillar. Then she sat on her throne of stone, pulled her shawl over her head, and waited for the arrival of the Trojan hero.

A few moments later, Aeneas entered the room, proudly exhibiting the golden bough.

"I have accomplished all the rituals you ordered me to do, Sibyl," he announced. "And I have with me the offering you required. Now show me the way to Pluto's kingdom."

Deiphobe looked at the hero and the bough he held. She slowly got up and climbed down from her seat.

"Fool," she said. "Are you certain you fully comprehend the magnitude of your quest? You, who have already sustained so much misfortune, are you sure you want to face this new trial? Is it really your desire to descend into Hell and risk never coming back out?"

Aeneas put the bough back in the leather pouch at his waist. He stood straight before Deiphobe and nodded once.

"All right, then. Follow me," Deiphobe said. She passed in front of Aeneas and disappeared into the tunnel leading outside. The Trojan hero glanced one last time at the hundred doors around him, then turned and left the room as well.

Angeline and Samuel waited a few minutes, just to be sure the hero would not come back, and then they too climbed down from their hiding spot and left the Sibyl's lair. Outside, the fresh night breeze gently brushed Samuel's face, and the full moon's blue rays washed over the landscape.

"This way," said Angeline. "We must not let Aeneas and Deiphobe gain too much of a lead on us."

Without waiting for Samuel's answer, the fata soared toward a path that wound down the mountainside before disappearing in the forest below. Samuel ran after her, already cursing the pebbles in his sandals.

"Angeline, wait for me!" he shouted in a strangled voice. He rushed down the slope and reached the forest in only a few seconds. He followed the path until he reached a fork, where Angeline waited for him. As soon as she saw him, she darted to the right, taking the road that led deeper in the forest, and Samuel quickly turned after her. He guessed the path to the left must lead to the beach where Aeneas's companions had anchored their ships.

The forest was immersed in darkness, and if Samuel had not already been on his way to the scariest place that could exist, he would surely have felt a few shivers as he slipped among the pine branches and oak trees. He even ignored the howling of the distant wolves and the rustling of bat wings over his head. After the trials he had just faced, it would take more than a few little critters to scare him.

Once or twice, Angeline glanced over her shoulder to make sure Samuel was still following her, and he noted the tiny smile on her lips. She had probably sensed the new confidence flowing through his veins.

They followed the path for about thirty minutes, until the forest ended in a small beach of black volcanic sand and a lake of baffling calmness. The stench of sulfur was heavy in the air, and Samuel noticed the bats and birds of the night avoided flying over the surface of the water. The moon illuminated the area with its spectral light and Samuel was able to observe the sadness of his surroundings. All around the lake, the forest stopped abruptly, and no branch or root ventured onto the beach. It was as if Death itself lived here. Samuel could not hold back a shiver.

They had arrived at the entrance of Hell, there was no doubt about it.

"Look over there," whispered Angeline.

Samuel followed her gaze. A few hundred yards to his right, Aeneas's torch illuminated the Trojan and Deiphobe. As they watched, the forest parted to allow access to the mountainside.

"What are they doing?" asked Samuel.

"They have to observe other rites and offer more sacrifices," answered Angeline. "Once the blood has been spilled, the door to Hell will open for them."

"Where do they find all these animals?" asked Samuel. "Everyone seems eager to sacrifice around here."

Angeline burst into laughter that she quickly muffled with her hand.

"You're right, but that's just the way things are," she said. "People from this era are very superstitious. And who wouldn't be? These poor souls just survived a war triggered by the pride of their gods, and they are persecuted because of a goddess's jealousy. They feel powerless and they seek help in any way they can think of."

"I guess, but is it going to take a while?"

"Why? Are you in such a hurry to descend into Hell?"

"Of course not," answered Samuel, "but if we wait here all night, I fear I may fall asleep. Let's just say I didn't get much sleep in the last twenty-four hours."

Angeline led Samuel to the fringes of the woods and perched herself on a branch.

"You can get some rest if you want," she said. "It will take a couple of hours for them to complete the sacrifices, unless

Aeneas quickly finds a pair of wild bulls. I'll keep my eyes open and let you know when they are done."

Samuel lowered his eyes to the ground. It was covered with dry leaves, pebbles and roots. It was not the Hilton, but he had slept in similar conditions before. He did his best to gather the dead leaves into a pile and lay down. He squirmed for a few minutes to get comfortable, but was soon fast asleep.

Samuel was abruptly pulled out of his dreams by the howling of dozens of wolves and the trembling of the earth beneath him. Before he could comprehend what was going on, he jumped to his feet and unsheathed his sword, scanning for signs of danger with his tired eyes. As the racket was becoming unbearable, and the animals of the forest added their voices to those of the wolves, Samuel heard Angeline trying to get his attention.

"Samuel!" yelled the fata. "Come here, quick!" Angeline was hovering over the black beach and gesturing.

"What's going on?" he asked, scrambling to his feet.

When he reached her on the beach, the fata pointed to where he had seen Aeneas and Deiphobe, a few hours earlier. A fissure about a hundred feet high now fractured the mountainside. At the foot of this crack was a gaping hole, surrounded by a grotesque face sculpted directly into the rock. Its eyes were filled by rage, and it had a mouth as dark as a starless night and razor-sharp teeth. It could only mean one thing.

"Deiphobe has opened the door to Pluto's kingdom," said Angeline in a quavering voice.

Samuel let the tip of his sword fall into the black sand.

The moment had come. He was going to Hell.

11

The Yfel sorcerer peeked over his shoulder and raised his eyes to the cave's ceiling. The mountain shook for a few more seconds, and then the tremor slowly receded and silence fell once more. With a smile on his lips, the sorcerer looked at the passage on the other side of the cave. The shaking mountain only meant one thing: The Cumaean Sibyl had opened the door to Hell, and Aeneas's journey had begun.

Samuel is probably with him, thought the sorcerer.

Just thinking about taking his revenge on the Lorekeeper made the sorcerer smile more broadly. During their last encounter, Samuel had managed to get out of his grip, with the help of Aristaeus, but things would be different this time around. The Yfel was the master of the Underworld, and the sorcerer would not lack the weapons to eliminate his enemy once and for all.

However, he had to put aside his desire for vengeance and focus on his work. He had a task to complete and time was of the essence. He only had thirty minutes or so before the Trojan would reach the cave—barely enough time to set his trap.

The sorcerer recited an incantation in a language dating from a time when humans were still learning to stand up straight. Each of the words required an excruciating physical effort to pronounce, and the price to pay for each syllable was a little bit of his humanity, but it was nothing new for him. Being the

Yfel's sorcerer was an honor and, if need be, he would offer even his soul to unlock all the secrets of his own power.

Unfortunately, the Yfel still kept him on a leash. If it were up to him, he would fight Samuel at the very start of the legend, right here in this cave. He would eliminate him without much ceremony, and then he would be free to complete his mission, but the Yfel seemed determined to avoid another duel between the two enemies. The instructions given to the sorcerer were clear: set the traps and focus on his mission.

Bunch of cowards, thought the sorcerer. *I will play their little game, but if the occasion presents itself, Samuel will taste my blade, no matter what they may think.*

During his first two battles with the Lorekeeper, his enemy had been lucky to come out alive. The sorcerer had been forced to leave Metverold before killing Samuel, but at least he had completed his missions with his head still attached to his neck, which was more than he could say for Mumby.

A mocking grin appeared on the sorcerer's face when he thought about the horrible boggart. He remembered how the creature had strutted under his nose, and how it had mocked him and pretended to be immortal.

What an idiot! thought the sorcerer.

For his last mission, the Yfel had imposed the silly little leprechaun as a chaperon for him, but this time they had sent the sorcerer on his own. He had deduced that they fully trusted him again, given the way he had obtained the name of the one who knew the secret of the gods' immortality. The high-ranking officers of the Yfel were probably kicking themselves for having doubted him. It could also be that no one wanted to follow him into Hell, given the way the previous adventure had ended for Mumby. He couldn't care less. As long as he was left alone, he could focus on his mission and show them all he was not the kind of person to take lightly.

The sorcerer finished his incantation. Using the tip of his sword, he etched strange symbols into the stone wall. He did not know where this knowledge of ancient languages came from, but he could clearly see the hieroglyphs in his mind, and only had to copy them on the stone. His role as the sorcerer offered him a privileged link to the universe, and to the forces that had waged battle against each other a long time ago. As soon as he finished tracing the last symbols, an ageless energy grew inside the cave. It was the Yfel energy, begging to be released and projected onto a chosen target.

The sorcerer took a few steps into the cave and looked at his surroundings for a moment. He wanted to take a few minutes to carefully study each possibility and make the best possible choice. Which of them would pose the greatest challenge to Samuel and Aeneas? They all seemed like valid choice, and there was no doubt each of the creatures before him had the potential to kill the Trojan hero and his bodyguard. After a few seconds of hesitation, he made his choice.

"I'd like to see you get out of this, Samuel," whispered the sorcerer.

He recited one last spell and raised his hands before him. The Yfel energy that had gathered in the cave flowed toward him, and formed a bright sphere before entering his chest. The energy surged along his arms to the tips of his fingers, and was propelled like lightning at the target designated by its master.

Once he was done, the sorcerer quickly walked back to the large opening behind him. He needed to get out of here quickly, before he fell victim to his own trap. As he was leaving the cave, he heard the acute screams of the creatures in the cavern. With a smile on his face, he left the area quickly and resumed his journey.

12

Angeline and Samuel entered the fissure in the mountainside and they walked through a tunnel so narrow that Samuel had to move sideways. Above him, the rough stone walls rose to a vertiginous height, the ceiling lost in the darkness. The passage was so tight that he could not shake the thought that the mountain might close in on them at any moment and crush them like mosquitoes.

Just as that thought rose, thunder exploded in the passage and it shook wildly. Angeline let out a scream and grabbed Samuel's hair. Behind them, the mountainside sealed itself, and they were in complete darkness. From now on it would be impossible to retrace their steps and leave the same way they had come in. They had no choice other than to keep moving forward. A second later, Samuel heard Angeline whisper a few words in the language of fairies, and the fata's blade lit up with a purple glow. Samuel took out his own sword and did a few contortions to raise it before him in this narrow tunnel, and Angeline repeated her spell on the young man's blade.

"Are we in the Underworld now?" asked Samuel.

"Not yet," answered Angeline, "but we will soon be there. At the end of this corridor, there is a chasm we must cross. We'll walk through an antechamber and there will be a final cave from which a tunnel leads to Hell."

"So what's the plan?" asked Samuel after they had walked on for a few minutes.

"For now, all we have to do is follow Aeneas from a distance, without him noticing us," Angeline said. "Our role is to prevent the sorcerer from attacking him, and nothing more. We have to make sure Aeneas does what he came here to do."

"You mean having a chat with his dad."

"Yes, among other things. It's the ultimate goal of his journey, but on his way to Elysium, there will be other important moments Aeneas hasn't foreseen. These moments are significant for the rest of the hero's story. It will be up to us to make sure each of these steps unfold as they should."

"And you think we can do it by staying out of sight like this? I can barely see in front of us. The sorcerer could be attacking them at this very moment and we would have no idea what was going on."

As he said these words, Samuel almost toppled over when the ground suddenly dropped away to a sharp slope.

"See?" he said. "I can't even see where I'm going."

Angeline chuckled. "Don't worry about it," she said. "For now, Aeneas is perfectly safe. Deiphobe is a most surprising woman. You shouldn't doubt her because of her strange appearance. As long as we are in the world of the living, she can communicate with the gods and ask for their help. If the sorcerer were to attack Aeneas, she would know how to defend him until we got there."

"But her power will disappear once we're in the Underworld, right?" asked Samuel.

"To tell you the truth, they aren't real powers. Let's just say that she has a privileged connection with the gods. And to answer your question: yes, this link will be severed once we are in Pluto's kingdom. It will be up to us to protect the Trojan, but if it reassures you, in a few minutes we will reach the Chasm of Orcus. We will easily spot them there, and can make sure they are safe."

As she had predicted, about fifteen minutes later they reached a gigantic cave, split in two at the center by a narrow ravine. Samuel jumped out of the tunnel as fast as he could, and stopped dead in his tracks. The landscape before them was breathtaking. They were in an enormous vale hidden in the heart of the mountain, only accessible by the secret passage they had just come through. Above them, millions of phosphorescent stones sprinkled the vault and brightened the cave like stars.

"It's incredible," said Samuel.

"I have to admit I was not expecting such wonderful scenery," replied Angeline. "I had heard of the Chasm of Orcus, but I would have never thought the vale in this place to be this magnificent."

Before them, the stone path descended steadily toward the bottom of the vale, where it entered a thick forest of birch, pines and oaks. Like the cave, the forest was divided down the center by the ravine. In the middle of the trees, a bridge of stones linked the two sides of the ravine, and Samuel saw two silhouettes crossing to the other side.

"Aeneas and Deiphobe," he said, pointing.

"They already have quite a lead on us," Angeline said. "We should hurry and go down toward them before they reach the passage to Hell."

Samuel nodded, slid his sword into his sheath and walked down the stone path, followed closely by Angeline. After a few moments, they reached the fringe of the forest, where the sinuous path continued its course. As soon as Samuel set foot between the first trees, thousands of bats flew up in a deafening racket, blocking the light from the vault for a moment. When the last of the bats had disappeared into the recesses of the cave, Samuel glanced over his shoulder. Angeline signaled for him to keep going, and he resumed his walk toward the ravine.

He had taken just a few steps into the forest when dozens of eyes appeared among the foliage above his head, as well as between the branches of the trees around him. Immediately, Samuel placed a hand on the hilt of his sword, but Angeline grabbed his arm before he could draw his weapon.

"Samuel, wait!" she said. "I wouldn't do that if I were you. These creatures are the protectors of the vale. If we keep going without touching anything and without damaging any of the trees they will leave us alone, but at the slightest sign of aggression they will be on us faster than you can pull that sword out of its sheath. You may be gifted with a sword, but trust me, they are much too ferocious for us and there are too many of them to deal with."

Samuel would never doubt Angeline's words, but when one of the creatures came closer, he could not help clenching his fingers tighter around the hilt of his weapon. The little being did not look like anything he had seen before. A little over a foot tall, it had an egg-shaped head, with wide, almond-shaped yellow eyes and a mouth filled with sharp teeth. Its skin was gray and covered in scales, and on its head, four jagged horns pointed to the sky. The creature was armed with a spear and on its chest dozens of tiny knifes hung from a cracked leather vest.

"Pygmies," said Angeline. "They are generally harmless, but let's not linger any longer than we have to."

As more creatures like the first one gathered around them, Samuel let go of the hilt of his sword and took a step forward, then another. The creatures hiding in the foliage followed his every move with their yellow eyes, but did not come any closer. Samuel hastened his pace, and a few minutes later, they reached the bridge crossing the ravine. They quickly stepped onto it, and Samuel turned around to look behind them. In the forest, thousands of eyes watched them.

Samuel walked over to the stone balustrade guarding each side of the bridge, just so he could shake the uncomfortable feeling of being watched in distrust. Since it was about knee-high, he set one foot on top of it, and pushed slightly on the stone to gauge its solidity. He bent his head slightly forward. At the base of the ravine, at least a thousand feet below, a river coursed between the stone walls and disappeared in the distance. Before vertigo sent his mind swirling, he straightened again and took a few steps back, until he was in the center of the bridge again.

"Come, Samuel, we must hurry," said Angeline, already on the other side of the bridge. "Aeneas and Deiphobe will soon enter the Underworld."

Samuel quickly reached her and they crossed the forest on the other side in a hurry. Once again, their movements were monitored by hundreds of pygmies, and Samuel only briefly dared imagine what would happen to anyone foolish enough to snap a twig and build a fire here. A few moments later, they climbed the path to the other side of the cave, where the road once again disappeared into a dark tunnel. Before setting foot in it, Samuel glanced one last time at the vale. Would he see this landscape again? Would he cross the stone bridge a second time on his way back? He had no idea, but he wanted to keep in mind the beauty of this place, for he doubted he would see such a sight where they were going.

The new tunnel looked exactly like the one that had led them to the vale. It was just as narrow, and the ceiling was so high that Samuel could not see it. A sense of claustrophobia similar to the one he had felt earlier threatened to grab hold of his will again, and he quickly unsheathed his sword, which was still glowing purple.

Finally, after ten minutes of squeezing between two rough stone walls, Samuel saw a light at the end of the tunnel. A moment later, he also heard muffled voices and Angeline pulled slightly on his armor to signal him to stop. With a wave of her hand, she put out the purple glow of their weapons, and they quietly moved forward until they reached the opening before them.

The tunnel led to a small circular room carved directly into the rock. A fire burned at its center, and on the other side of the flames Aeneas and Deiphobe were talking with each other.

"Here is Grief," said the old woman to Aeneas.

At that moment, Samuel noticed several statues, each about seven feet tall, scattered around the little room. Even in the uncertain light of the flames, the realism of the work was such that Samuel feared for a moment the statues would come to life and attack them. Fortunately, instead of fending off stone enemies, Aeneas walked over to the statue Deiphobe indicated, the one she had called "Grief." It was of a woman dressed in a long garment that covered her head. She was looking at the ground before her, a hand on her forehead and the other on the wall of the cave, as though she were trying to keep her balance. Clearly the sculptor had wanted to represent all the sadness the poor woman felt following the loss of someone dear to her.

A few yards away from her stood a muscled man clad in imposing armor, with a helm on his head. He had a spear in his right hand. In his left, he held a gigantic square shield, which barely concealed a sword sheathed at his waist.

"What about him?" asked Aeneas, indicating the man of stone.

"He represents War."

"You mean this is the god Mars?"

"No," replied Deiphobe. "Mars is the god who controls war, like a master controlling his dog. A master can sic his dog wherever he pleases. Likewise, Mars holds War on a leash, and can direct it wherever he desires."

Aeneas studied the figure representing war for a moment, then moved on to the next statue. This was a man covered with a shroud and hiding his face in his elbow. Deiphobe indicated it was Sickness, which not only attacks the body of men, but also their pride.

"We have to continue our journey now," said Deiphobe. "We still have a long way to go, Prince of Troy, and we do not have time to admire these mysterious works of art."

Aeneas nodded and followed the woman to an opening on the other side of the room. Once they had disappeared into the tunnel, Samuel and Angeline stepped into the room as well, careful not to make a sound. Samuel looked over the statues that encircled the fire.

Angeline told him about the others. The first represented Old Age. It was a woman with a wrinkled face, leaning on a knotty walking stick. Then came the statue of Fear, which was a man with his hands on his heart, his mouth and eyes open so wide his face was horribly twisted. Then came a naked man hunched over himself, with nothing other than his skin on his bones, representing Hunger. Poverty was depicted by a mother and child holding hands, with tattered clothes on their backs. Samuel noticed their faces did not look afflicted by dread or sadness, like the rest of the statues, but rather expressed the love they had for each other.

On the other side of the room, the statue of a woman with snakes on her head, her face distorted by anger, represented Discord. Next to her, the statue of an empty cloak, with a large hood pulled over an invisible head, represented Death. Beside it stood its sibling Slumber: a half-naked woman asleep, her face devoid of expression.

The last statue, next to the sleeping woman, was the most complex and shocking of them all. It displayed a naked man, half crouching, his hands covering his ears. He had his mouth wide open, as if screaming at the top of his lungs, and madness filled his eyes. Behind him, three women with horrible faces were shrieking at him.

"What does this statue represent?" asked Samuel.

"Remorse," answered Angeline. "This poor soul is assailed by the three Furies, who will persecute him until his death. Remorse is one of the feelings men tend to underestimate, but it can easily lead the strongest of them to madness. Even if he can ignore their screams for a while, in the end the Furies' victim always succumbs to their accursed song. Then the poor soul takes his own life, hoping to find peace in Death."

Samuel lingered for a moment before the statue. The poor man seemed terrified, ready to do anything to escape the shrieks of the Furies behind him. The Fury in the middle held a six-lashed whip in her right hand, each strap ending in razor-sharp claws. Her hair consisted of vipers attacking each other, and her eyes were masked by a soiled blindfold.

"This is Tisiphone," whispered Angeline who had come closer to Samuel. "Next to her are her sisters Alecto and Megaera."

Alecto's face was distorted by rage. Her mouth was foaming and her eyes were mad with anger. She held a dagger with a curved blade in one hand and tried to scratch the poor man with the other. The third Fury, Megaera, looked just as terrible as her sisters. She was getting ready to strike the man with a flaming torch in her left hand, and her face expressed a limitless anger for the women's victim.

"And who is he, exactly?" asked Samuel, pointing at the poor man.

"I don't know," answered Angeline. "Probably someone who has committed a murder or some other terrible crime. The Furies seems to be especially hard on him, and I believe that—"

She was interrupted by a frightful scream, coming from the tunnel through which Aeneas and Deiphobe had left the room a few minutes earlier. Samuel immediately drew his sword and ran into the narrow tunnel, without giving Angeline time to cast the purple glow on his blade.

"Samuel!" she yelled. "Wait for me!"

She quickly followed after Samuel, but he was moving as fast as he could through the passage. He had let himself be distracted by the statues, and now Aeneas was in danger. There was not a moment to spare.

Aeneas held his shield and sword before him, while his scream bounced from one stone wall to the other. The massive cavern he stood in sent the scream back at him a few more times, as if mocking him, and then silence fell.

"Stay behind me, Sibyl," he ordered, and took a cautious step forward, his eyes still locked on the monsters around him. At the center of the cave, a hundred foot elm stood at the top of a small hill. Moon rays leaked through several openings in the ceiling, washing the area in a gloomy and unearthly light.

"Trojan, lower your weapon," said Deiphobe.

Aeneas ignored her and swung at the air a couple of times. *The gods may have chosen her,* he thought, *but she knows nothing of the dangers of the real world.* The monsters lingering in this cave were among the most dangerous the Earth had ever known, and although they did not seem to have spotted them yet, they would soon feel their presence in their lair.

A giant as tall as three men walked over to them with a slow and steady pace. He had three heads and six arms, and Aeneas immediately identified him as Geryon. It was said that only Hercules had successfully defeated the immortal warrior, using an arrow dipped in poison from the hydra.

The Lernaean Hydra itself was pacing at the back of the cave, easily recognizable by its six dragon heads. The beast was gigantic, and each of its steps made the ground shake. However, the tremors were nothing like those resulting from each step taken by Briareus, a Hekatoncheires. As tall as the elm in the center of the cave, the giant was believed to possess a strength unlike anything else in the world, probably because of the hundred arms arranged in five columns around his torso.

"Please, pious Aeneas, lower your sword and put your shield down," repeated Deiphobe, placing a hand on the Trojan's shoulder. "There is nothing here that can do us any harm."

"What are you talking about?" said Aeneas. "We are surrounded by the worst creatures to ever walk the Earth, and you want me to sheath my weapon?"

Deiphobe stepped in front of Aeneas and walked confidently toward Geryon. Aeneas quickly followed her, and when he tried to pull her behind him, he saw the giant make a right turn and walk away from them, as if he had not seen them.

"These creatures aren't real," said Deiphobe. "They are only images, placed here to scare those foolish enough to try finding the road leading to the Underworld. They are mere illusions, nothing more."

Aeneas slowly lowered his shield and let the tip of his sword drop to the ground. Was the Sibyl speaking the truth? A dozen centaurs galloped by him, with their horse bodies and human torsos. Each was armed with a spear and shield, and all looked so real that a chill ran down the Trojan's spine.

"Are you sure they are only illusions?" he asked.

Deiphobe walked over to him and placed a comforting hand on his arm, making him lower his sword even more.

"I am absolutely sure," she said. "Pluto placed them here to protect the entrance of his kingdom, but since he could not use the true creatures, he decided to use images of them. That is why he chose the most horrible creatures, so they would frighten any intruder with their appearance alone. Come, I want to show you something."

Aeneas hesitated a moment, his eyes fixed on a chimera flying circles over them. The creature was among the most terrifying, with its lion head, the body of a goat, a snake tail, and the wings of a bat. The monster glided for a few seconds longer, then landed heavily a few yards from the hero. That was when the Trojan noticed the three Gorgons, farther into the cavern, and quickly averted his eyes. It was said that these women were so hideous that one look was enough to petrify whoever laid eyes on them.

At Deiphobe's insistence, Aeneas sheathed his weapon and risked a glance at Medusa and her two sisters. He did not know if the Gorgons' images were true to the real monsters, with their snake hair, their empty eye sockets, and their scarred faces, but the mere sight of these illusions was enough to cause nausea. Quickly, Aeneas turned away and followed Deiphobe. The woman walked to the tree at the center of the cave. They reached a pair of pools, one on each side of the path, and two horrible creatures emerged from the water. Deiphobe soothed Aeneas once again with a composed voice.

"These are images of Scylla and Charybdis," she said.

The monster on the left, Scylla, was probably thirty feet tall. It had the face and body of a young woman, but her mouth contained three or four sets of razor-sharp teeth, not to mention the dozens of tentacles under her arms, each ending in the head of a snake. Charybdis looked just as frightening. She resembled a giant squid, with a mouth wide open and spitting out large waves of black water.

Aeneas resisted the temptation to grab his sword again as he passed between the pools, and once again the creatures completely ignored the two intruders. After a few seconds, they retreated to the depths of their respective pools, leaving only a few bubbles at the surface as a sign of their presence.

When Deiphobe and Aeneas reached the top of the small hill, the Sibyl lifted her eyes to the branches of the giant elm.

"This is the Elm of Dreams," she said. "It is said that each leaf carries a dream for the world's sleepers—a message from an ancestor, or a prophecy from a god."

She had barely pronounced these words when one of the leaves detached itself from a branch and flew up to the ceiling, lifted by an invisible breeze. The leaf fluttered for a few seconds, rising higher and higher until it disappeared under the vault.

"It's truly amazing," said Aeneas.

"Yes, but one must stay vigilant," said Deiphobe. "Some of the dreams here are nothing more than empty promises; dreams with no purpose. Sometimes it is not easy to discern the true messages of our ancestors from the lies of the gods."

Aeneas turned to Deiphobe and looked straight into her eyes.

"My father came to see me in a dream," he said firmly. "Just as Hector warned me of the fall of Troy in my sleep, my father Anchises visited me and asked that I come speak with him in the Underworld."

"I don't doubt it, Trojan. Just be careful who speaks to you in those dreams. Your enemies are as powerful as they are cunning."

With these words, Deiphobe walked down the opposite side of the hill, toward the back of the cave, where there was another opening. Aeneas raised his eyes to the leaves one last time. Then he shouldered his shield and followed the Sibyl.

Samuel watched at the Trojan hero walk away from the Elm of Dreams, and then swept the cave with his eyes. The monsters might not be real, but they were still frightening.

"You are *sure* these monsters are not real?" he asked for the tenth time.

"Absolutely certain!" answered Angeline in an exasperated tone. "They are only illusions, and what's more, they aren't all that good. A quick glance is all that's needed to see they are not even aware of our presence."

Samuel looked toward the elm at the center at the cave. Another leaf fell from a branch and took flight toward the vault of the cavern. He followed it with his eyes for a few seconds, but his gaze was quickly drawn by something he had not noticed before. About three hundred feet above the ground, two creatures were perched on a stone ledge. The creatures looked like nude women, but instead of arms they had long bird wings, and their faces were almost completely hidden by large beaks. Their hair was prickly on their skulls and they had bird feet, with a sharp claw at the end of each toe.

"What are those?" he asked, pointing.

"They are the harpies Aello and Ocypete," answered Angeline. "Harpies are remarkably cunning and vicious. You have no idea how much of a pain they can be to deal with. It's a good thing they're only illusions, or else we would be in serious trouble, believe me."

"Okay, but if they are only illusions," Samuel said, "why are they following Aeneas and Deiphobe with their eyes?"

Angeline studied the two creatures perched on the ledge more closely. After a few seconds, she covered her mouth with her hand and muffled a tiny yelp.

"By the gods!" she said. "The harpies are real!"

13

"We have to do something," said Angeline, pointing at the creature diving toward the Trojan. "The harpies aren't just illusions. They are real, and Ocypete is diving straight for Aeneas."

Without thinking twice, Samuel jumped out of the tunnel and ran toward the Elm of Dreams. On the other side of the tree, Aeneas and Deiphobe were leisurely climbing the stone steps to another tunnel, unaware that a harpy was swooping down on them like an eagle on its prey.

"Wait for me!" yelled Angeline, darting after Samuel. "What are we going to do?"

"I don't know yet," answered Samuel. "I'm improvising."

Unfortunately, he was not lying. He had no idea how to stop Ocypete's attack against Aeneas. Samuel was still much too far away to physically do anything, and he would never reach the harpy before it grabbed the Trojan in its razor-sharp talons. What's more, Samuel could not attract the attention of the creature with a scream, since Aeneas would also hear it and discover the young man's presence. The legend would then be changed, while they were still only in the first act of the story.

The harpy descended rapidly toward Aeneas. As soon as she reached him, the hero would turn around to defend himself—if he had a chance to do so—and he would see Samuel. The result would be the same: the legend would be changed.

Samuel hastened his pace, his sword heavy in his hand and the Helm of Darkness banging against his thigh with each of step.

The Helm!

Everything had happened so fast that Samuel had completely forgotten he had the Helm of Darkness with him. He halted next to the hydra's image, and quickly untied the belt around his waist. Angeline passed by him in a hurry and stopped, turning back.

"What are you doing?" she asked.

"The Helm of Darkness will make me invisible," replied Samuel. "With any luck, I'll be able to attract the harpy without Aeneas seeing me."

"But he will hear you, won't he? You think the Helm of Darkness will completely hide your presence?"

Samuel's fingers moved so fast they seemed to tie themselves in a knot rather than untie the linen thread holding the crown to his belt.

"I don't know," he replied, "but it's worth a try. Unless you have a better idea."

Angeline remained quiet.

When Samuel had finally untied the knot, he quickly raised his eyes to evaluate the situation. Ocypete was now less than fifty feet away from Aeneas. The harpy wheeled a few times over her prey, positioning herself for the final assault. It would only be a few seconds before she was on the Trojan. Samuel did not have a moment to spare. He got the Helm of Darkness free and placed it on his head. As soon as he felt the weight on his skull, he opened his mouth:

"Hey! Ocypete!" he screamed, praying to the gods that the Helm of Darkness also hid his voice from Aeneas. "Over here! Leave Aeneas alone or else you'll have to deal with—"

Samuel fell silent. He did not need to scream to draw Ocypete's attention. As soon as he placed the Helm of Darkness on his head, the harpy had swiveled in midair. Behind the monster, next to Aeneas, Deiphobe had also turned around and was now looking at Samuel, her eyes suddenly filled with horror. She quickly pulled Aeneas up the stone steps. As soon as the Sibyl and the hero disappeared into the opening on the other side of the cave, Samuel looked at the harpy again. She was flapping her powerful wings and floated motionless over the ground, her eyes locked on Samuel. The young man remembered Apollo had told him some creatures were immune to the power of the Helm of Darkness, and could even be drawn to it. Clearly, the harpies belonged to this category.

Ocypete flapped her large wings a few more times, soaring higher in the cave, her eyes never leaving Samuel. She hovered for a few more seconds, then shrieked and dove toward the young man. Samuel rapidly checked to see if Aeneas was coming back into the cave after hearing the scream, and was relieved to see he was not. Deiphobe had probably found an excuse to convince the Trojan to keep going on the road to Hell.

"Samuel," whispered Angeline. "I hope you have a plan to get rid of the harpy, because she does not seem to appreciate the interference one bit."

Samuel dug his heels into the ground and raised his sword. His plan was not particularly well thought out, but it would have to do. At least the hardest part was behind him. He had managed to get the attention of Ocypete and draw her away from Aeneas, without the hero realizing he was followed. As for what came next, it could hardly be more simple. He now had to defend himself against the creature diving in his direction. Fortunately, Samuel was confident he could defeat the creature without much difficulty.

Next to him, Angeline followed his lead and quickly took out her tiny sword. Her purple eyes narrowed, and she pressed her lips firmly together. Samuel saw in her eyes that, just like him, she believed they could vanquish this monster and be on their way without much delay.

Farther ahead, the harpy passed over the Elm of Dreams. She was now about a hundred feet away from them. Any moment now, she would dive straight for her prey.

But this prey won't go down so easy, thought Samuel. *Come here, I'll—*

Something hit him violently on the back of the head, and he tumbled to the ground, raising a cloud of dust. Before he could understand what was going on, flashes of pain stabbed at his skull and blurred his vision.

"Samuel!" Angeline called out.

The young man painfully raised his head, brushing the dust away from his eyes with the back of his hand. He looked up to the Elm of Dreams and realized what had happened. How could he have been so foolish? He had been so determined to draw Ocypete's attention that he had completely forgotten about the second harpy on the rocky ledge. The creature had taken advantage of his carelessness to fly around the cave and attack him from behind. Now she was gliding toward the Elm of Dreams with a series of sharp screams that resembled a mocking laugh.

As Samuel was about to get up he noticed something that made his heart sink. He clutched the top of his head. His eyes had not deceived him—the second harpy, Aello, was holding the Helm of Darkness in her talons.

Samuel jumped to his feet, but as soon as he stood up straight, he had to duck again to avoid Ocypete's assault. He barely had time to dive forward and avoid the creature's sharp claws as she passed at lightning speed above his head.

"Angeline!" yelled Samuel, getting up a second time. "The harpies have the Helm of Darkness."

The fata turned toward the young man and shot him a panic-stricken look. Behind her, Ocypete was flying in a large circle along the cave wall, getting ready to make another pass. Samuel had to get the Helm of Darkness back, but he would never be able to do so if he had to defend himself against Ocypete's attack at the same time.

"Angeline, you have to help me," he said. "I need you to take care of Ocypete. I can't fight her and recover the Helm of Darkness at the same time."

The fata turned toward Ocypete. The harpy was coming toward them at full speed, her shriek even more piercing than the first time. Angeline clenched her fingers around the hilt of her sword and nodded.

"You can count on me," she said. "You take care of Aello, and I'll take care of this one."

As soon as she had spoken, Angeline made her wings buzz and darted like an arrow toward Ocypete. The fata screamed, and did a few spirals and loops to fool the harpy and avoid her claws. She then went straight for the monster's face and stabbed her cheek with her tiny sword. The harpy yelled in pain and masked her face with one of her wings.

Meanwhile, Aello was still flying toward the ledge, about three hundred feet from the ground. Samuel had to prevent the harpy from reaching her lair, or else he would lose all hope of ever getting the Helm of Darkness back.

He slid his sword into its sheath, picked up a couple of rocks and ran after the harpy. Without taking the time to estimate the distance between himself and Aello, he hurled the first stone at her. The projectile missed its target by a good twenty feet, but the noise it made as it ricocheted off a boulder attracted her attention. This hesitation was enough to slow down the creature and Samuel hurriedly threw a second stone, smaller than the first. This time the projectile missed Aello by less than a foot. The harpy made another mistake when she turned toward Samuel. Without hesitation, he threw a third rock.

This time the stone hit Aello square in the face, and the horrible creature crashed violently into the grass, midway between the Elm of Dreams and the harpies' lair.

Samuel quickly grabbed the hilt of his weapon again and swung the blade out of its scabbard. He redoubled his efforts, reaching into every corner of his body for the last ounces of energy still available. In front of him, Aello was twisting on the ground, and dozens of feathers flew around her contorted body. The harpy had fallen on her back, and in this position her wings were more of a nuisance than anything else.

As he dashed toward her, Samuel heard Ocypete's chilling screams and Angeline's insolent replies. At least the fata was keeping the first harpy busy.

Samuel passed by the Elm of Dreams and kept going without missing a step. His heart was racing in his chest and his mouth was as dry as a desert, but he could not slow down. Farther ahead, Aello had calmed down and was turning onto her belly. She got up on one knee, and Samuel knew she was about to take off again.

"Give me back the crown!" he shouted, hoping to gain a few precious seconds.

Aello slowly got up to her feet and turned to Samuel with a mocking grin. He was now less than thirty feet from the creature. Samuel raised his sword and jumped forward, swinging his weapon in a circle before him.

Unfortunately, Aello took off at the last moment, and the blade found nothing but air. Samuel lost his footing and fell face-first on the ground. Above him, he heard Aello's mocking laughter as she flew away, lifted by her powerful wings.

Samuel rolled over and jumped back to his feet, his sword still in his hand. He looked up just in time to see the harpy reach the ledge and disappear into a hole.

He had failed. Aello had successfully stolen the Helm of Darkness. Could he protect Aeneas and the legend without Pluto's onyx crown? He doubted it. Apollo would not have submitted him to impossible trials if Samuel did not need the Helm of Darkness. Samuel inspected the rock wall below the ledge. It offered no foothold that would allow him to climb to the harpies' lair. Even if he managed to ascend halfway, the risk of falling and breaking his neck was much too great. If he wanted to get the Helm of Darkness back, he would have to find another way to get up there.

He turned to Angeline and Ocypete. They were still locked in an acrobatic dogfight, fifty feet above the ground. The harpy's face was lacerated by tiny cuts and even with all her efforts she could not get her hand on Angeline, who kept swirling around with surprising agility. For the first time, Samuel noticed that Ocypete's face looked exactly like Aello's, and he wondered if the harpies were sisters. The idea that these creatures could be linked together gave root to a new plan in Samuel's mind, and he quickly ran toward Angeline and the harpy.

"Angeline!" he yelled. "Don't let Ocypete get away! Those little pests have stolen the Helm of Darkness, and she's going to pay for it."

Samuel had said the words in such an aggressive tone that Angeline turned to him for a second, her face filled with surprise and worry. He had declared his intentions with enough force for Aello to hear them, which was crucial for his plan.

"Stop playing around with her and get it over with," added Samuel, as he winked at Angeline.

The fata hesitated for a second, then shrugged and turned to face the harpy once more. When Samuel reached the Elm of Dreams, he slid his sword back into its sheath and began climbing the gigantic tree. He had reached the first couple of branches when he heard a shriek that turned his blood to ice. Looking at Ocypete and Angeline, he saw the harpy lying on the ground, thrashing about in pain, with purple smoke floating above her. A little higher, Angeline looked back at Samuel.

"What?" she asked. "It's what you wanted, isn't it?"

Before answering, Samuel turned and looked at the ledge. There he saw Aello, drawn out by the scream of her companion. When she saw the convulsing body of Ocypete,

Aello shrieked in turn and threw herself over the ridge, opening her large wings.

"Yes, that's perfect," Samuel yelled to Angeline.

He resumed climbing the tree immediately. Fortunately, his muscles remembered the games he had played with Lucien when they were younger, and he hopped from branch to branch with the agility of a squirrel. Each time he jumped, leaves carrying dreams flew toward the cave vault, but he did not worry about them. In a few seconds he reached the top of the elm.

Once his head was out of the foliage, Samuel quickly glanced around. On his left, he saw Angeline circling over Ocypete. Her body still smoking, the harpy was looking at Angeline with worried eyes and did not dare to get back up. Samuel turned his eyes to his right and saw Aello speeding toward Angeline. As he had hoped, the harpy was not paying him any attention and only wanted to help her companion.

She was flying in his direction at full speed, her eyes locked on the fata. When she was no more than ten feet from the tree, Samuel flexed his knees and jumped with all his might, throwing his hands in the air. His left hand caught nothing but air, but the fingers of his right hand grabbed one of Aello's talons.

Caught by surprise, the harpy let out a scream, but she frenetically flapped her wings and flew higher, above the tree, pulling Samuel with her.

As soon as his feet left the branches and he found himself hanging in the air, Samuel regretted going through with his plan. What was he thinking? What could he do now? This would surely end with him plummeting to certain death.

He quickly chased these gloomy thoughts from his mind and grabbed Aello's other talons with his free hand. Questioning himself would not do any good now—it was much too late to turn back. Aello tried to get rid of him with a few acrobatic maneuvers, but Samuel held on firmly. Below, he heard

Angeline yell all kinds of reprimands, but he ignored them. He waited for the harpy to stop her aerial ballet, and then proceeded to climb the creature.

A few moments later, he was sitting on the harpy's back. Immediately he placed both his hands over her eyes. Aello shrieked acutely and instinctively lifted her head, which made her fly even higher in the cave. Samuel clenched his legs around the creature's body. He pulled Aello's head again to his right and she immediately turned in that direction, flying at full speed toward the cave wall, still blinded by Samuel. Just before they smashed headfirst into the wall, Samuel pulled on the harpy's head. The monster glided so close to the wall that her left wing brushed against the stone with each flap.

Samuel kept his hands over Aello's eyes, but he had his own eyes locked on a point below them. Still trying to direct the harpy, he judged the distance between him and the ledge. When he thought the time was right, he let go of the creature, swung his right leg over her back and jumped down.

The force of the impact was greater than he had anticipated, and when he crashed on the stone ridge, his body rolled uncontrollably until he toppled over the edge. At the very last moment, he threw his right hand over his head and grabbed hold of the stone.

He hung for a few seconds, his feet dangling, trying to catch his breath. Somewhere in the cave, Angeline was screaming his name and launching herself like an arrow toward him, and Samuel thought she had every reason to fear the worst.

His plan was utterly stupid. Even if he could climb onto the ledge—which would be a miracle from the position he found himself in—how was he going to get back down?

Samuel shook his head and raised his left hand to the stone ridge. After a few seconds of trying to find something to hold on to with the tips of his fingers, he finally had a firm grip on the stone and tried to pull himself up. Unfortunately, it was much more difficult to do than the stuntmen in the movies made it look like, and he only managed to lift himself a few inches.

Panic was quickly growing in Samuel's guts. To make things worse, when he glanced over his shoulder, he saw the harpy Aello loop around behind him and dive at full speed in his direction. The look she gave him left little doubt of her intentions.

Samuel tried to gain a foothold on the stone wall to his right. His arms were getting tired, and his fingers were sliding toward to edge of the ledge. Each gesture on his part brought him a little closer to falling down.

Using all his strength, Samuel swung his right foot toward the cave wall and miraculously found a foothold. Right away, he pushed himself up with his leg, trying to reach the edge of the ridge with his knee. A quick peek behind him revealed the harpy was now barely twenty feet from him.

It was too late.

Samuel closed his eyes and clenched his muscles, bracing for the impact. Maybe with some luck he would keep his grip on the ledge.

A detonation thundered in the cave and small fragments of rocks hit Samuel in the neck and on the backs of his arms. Without trying to understand what had happened, he pulled with all his might and finally managed to drag himself onto the stone ridge. He rolled and took out his sword, but rather than finding himself facing a furious harpy, Samuel's eyes crossed Angeline's gaze. The fata's eyes shone with a purple light so bright that he was forced to lower his head. He then saw the body of Aello tumbling down the cave wall, before crashing to the ground below.

"Grab the Helm of Darkness and let's get the heck out of here," Angeline said.

Without waiting for an answer, she dove toward the harpy.

Samuel had never seen Angeline like this, and he suddenly regretted all the times he had been harsh with her. Obviously she had much more power than she let on.

Samuel pushed aside the questions surging through his head and entered the small cave on the ledge. He had only taken a few steps into the shadows before he saw the Helm of Darkness resting on a regular stone. With a sigh of relief, he took the onyx crown and quickly tied it at his waist. The cave stretched deeper into the mountain, but Samuel had no intention of exploring it any more than he needed. He walked back out of the cave and took a few cautious steps toward the edge of the ridge.

Below, Angeline was flying circles around Aello, striking her with her sword each time she passed in front of her face. On the other side of the cavern Ocypete had recovered enough to stumble to her feet and wander around, though she was still unable to take flight.

How am I going to get down from here? Samuel wondered.

That was when he heard a sound behind him, like an acute and cavernous breathing.

"Oh come on!" he whispered.

He turned and found himself facing a third harpy, who had remained hidden in the lair until now. Unlike her two sisters, she was covered with black and gray feathers, and seemed to be twice the size of Aello and Ocypete.

"Thhiefff!" whistled the harpy.

"It's you who have stolen it from me," answered Samuel. "The Helm of Darkness is mine."

"Llliarrr!"

The harpy said the word with disdain and a rasping voice like a blade against a whetting stone. She remained still for a moment and looked Samuel from head to toe. Then she jerked forward, and Samuel instinctively took a step back, forgetting where he was for a second. When the heel of his foot found nothing but air, his stomach turned to stone, and cold sweat beaded on his neck.

"Angeline!" yelled Samuel. "I think we have a new problem."

"What is—" the fata dove forward to avoid one of Aello's wings. "What is it now?" she asked.

"There's a third harpy."

The silence that followed did nothing to reassure Samuel. The creature before him studied the young man for another second, then took a step toward him. She opened her wings and raised one of her taloned feet at Samuel. He put a hand on the hilt of his sword, but hesitated before pulling it out.

"Does she have black feathers?" asked Angeline from below.

"Yes."

"By the gods, I had completely forgotten about her," said Angeline. "Celaeno the Sinister."

Upon hearing her name, Celaeno smiled, letting Samuel see teeth as sharp as the tip of arrows.

"You'd better leave us alone," said Samuel, sliding his sword a few inches out of its sheath.

He did his best to speak with a commanding tone, but his trembling voice did not help at all. The harpy tilted her head to the side, blinked and then, without warning, lurched at Samuel with a deafening scream.

Samuel let go of his sword and dove to his right. He barely avoided Celaeno's attack, and seized the occasion to grab one of the harpy's wings. In one swift move, he pivoted and jumped onto the back of the creature, pushing with all his might on her neck. The harpy swung over the edge of the ridge and dove at full speed toward the ground. She was stronger than her two companions, and pulled herself back up despite Samuel's efforts. As much as Samuel tried to put all his weight on his hands, he could not control the harpy's flight like he had done with Aello.

Celaeno flapped her powerful wings a few times and rose even higher, toward the center of the cave and the Elm of

Dreams. When she passed the top of the tree, Samuel decided it was now or never and jumped from her back. He tumbled through the branches of the giant elm, and crashed to the ground between two roots. He would certainly have a few bruises, but nothing seemed to be broken.

However, his relief was short-lived. Above him, Celaeno circled around the cave's ceiling, her eyes fixed on him. At any moment now, she would dive toward the young man. Samuel flattened himself against the trunk of the Elm of Dreams, trying to shield himself from the attack, but as soon as the bark scratched his shoulders, Ocypete grabbed his wrists with her talons. She had been lurking behind the tree, waiting to strike.

Samuel pulled with all his strength, but the creature was too powerful. From the corner of his eye he saw Celaeno do one last circle, and then she plunged down to him, while Ocypete kept his body pinned to the Elm of Dreams' trunk, his arms behind him and defenseless.

Suddenly, a tremor shook the cave. Celaeno halted abruptly, and Ocypete let go of Samuel. The young man quickly ran away from the tree. After sprinting fifty feet or so he turned around, drawing his sword. What he saw left him speechless.

Next to the Elm of Dreams, Angeline floated about twenty feet above the ground. She was completely still and surrounded by dozens of miniature purple lightning flashes, which jumped in all directions, forming an energy bubble around her. Her skin seemed to glow like the moon, and her eyes gleamed with such an intense light that Samuel had a hard time looking at her.

"I've had just about enough of you three!" shouted Angeline.

Samuel barely recognized his friend. Her voice was loud and stern, and seemed to be coming from the very depths of the mountain.

Angeline rose a few feet higher, and suddenly opened her arms and threw her head back. A powerful shockwave spread across the cavern, shaking the Elm of Dreams and throwing Samuel on his back. The harpies were not spared, and all three flew a short distance before crashing face-first into the solid ground.

"You will leave us alone now!" screamed Angeline, still in that cavernous voice that made Samuel shiver. "You will go back to your lair and let us be on our way. I order it by the will of the Parcae."

A second shockwave spread across the cave, and Samuel had just enough time to flatten himself on the ground to avoid getting pushed farther back. The harpies did not move as fast and flew back once again, before hitting the ground a second time.

The largest of the three, Celaeno, was the first on her feet. She immediately turned toward Angeline and let out a shriek that would have sent the hardest men running, but the fata remained still. A little farther on, Aello and Ocypete also got back on their feet, but rather than imitating their sister, they quickly took off toward the ledge, and then disappeared into their dark lair. Celaeno studied Angeline and Samuel, screamed one last time and then took off as well and joined her two companions.

Samuel looked at Angeline again. The fata had regained her normal appearance and was quickly flying toward him, her little wings buzzing.

"Are you all right?" she asked when she reached him. "Did you recover the Helm of Darkness?"

Samuel slowly nodded.

"Very well," added Angeline. "Let's not waste any more time and get out of here."

"Angeline, how did you—"

"I don't want to talk about it."

Samuel slowly straightened. He sheathed his sword and followed the fata toward the exit where Deiphobe and Aeneas had left the cave earlier. As they walked, he raised his eyes to the ledge, but saw no sign of the harpies.

"What did you do to them, exactly?" he asked.

"I said I didn't want to talk about it!" answered Angeline, before she disappeared into the dark tunnel.

Obviously, Angeline had not revealed everything about herself, but he decided to wait until she was in a better mood to press the issue. He glanced one last time at the cave behind him and was relieved to see the harpies had not found the courage to follow them. As he was about to turn around again and step into the tunnel after Angeline, he noticed several strange symbols etched in the stone wall. Tiny green sparks ran along the symbols, and he concluded it must be some spell left there by the Yfel's sorcerer. It was probably how he had given life to the harpies.

"Angeline!" Samuel called out. "Do you mind coming here for a second?"

The fata flew back and looked at the symbol inscribed in stone.

"I think the sorcerer did this," Samuel said. "It's probably how he—"

Before he could finish, Angeline raised a hand over the symbols and said a word in a language he did not understand. The inscription on the wall started to vibrate, and then vanished.

"I don't want to talk about that either," whispered Angeline, before disappearing again into the tunnel.

14

"Are we there yet?" asked Samuel, dragging his feet on the rocky ground.

"I don't know," snapped Angeline. "It's not like I come here every year for the holidays, you know. You didn't expect the Underworld to be easily accessible by just about anyone accidentally stumbling around here, did you?"

Of course not, Samuel wanted to reply, but kept his thoughts to himself.

The road leading to this realm had to be littered with insurmountable obstacles, and a tiny voice at the back of his mind whispered for him to be careful. Even though he had triumphed every time he faced adversity so far in this adventure, this voice told him he might soon regret his wish of moving on to the next act. It was whispering that the previous trials would seem like a walk in the park compared to what was waiting for him in Pluto's kingdom.

Samuel shook his head to quiet the voice and looked at Angeline, a little ahead of him. She had covered their weapons with the purple glow, and the light gave her a ghostly look. After the way she had gotten rid of the harpies, Samuel was dying to bombard her with questions about her power, but he managed to hold his tongue. They walked forward in silence, the road barely lit by the purple glow of his sword and Angeline's weapon. Looking at the purple bronze, Samuel thought he should have found a shield to bring on this adventure. It would have provided additional protection for himself, but also, the surface of a shield would have emitted much more purple light than the blade of his sword.

Lost in thought, he did not immediately notice a low murmur.

"Listen," said Angeline. "Do you hear that?"

Samuel was happy to note that the fata's tone was friendlier. Beneath his feet, the passage suddenly sloped sharply downward.

"What is it?" he asked.

"That is the sound of the dead," answered Angeline. "We are now officially in Hell."

Hearing those words made Samuel's blood turn cold.

For another ten minutes, the slope kept going down toward the Earth's womb. Then the tunnel twisted in a series of curves, each tighter than the last. With each step, the constant murmur grew louder. What had been only a faint whisper at first was now a vibrant and muffled clamor. The deeper he penetrated the tunnel, the more he noticed the nuances in the strange noise. At last, turning a corner, Samuel saw a light at the end of the corridor, and then he understood the nature of the noise he heard: they were thousands of supplicating voices and countless screams of agony. A few moments later, Angeline and Samuel emerged from the tunnel, and what he saw then seemed straight out of the mind of a mad artist.

Before them was a colossal valley, divided by a river as dark as a starless night. To Samuel's left, the blurry shape of a distant mountain was outlined against the horizon, its summit besieged by dark clouds and vivid lightning. To his right was a cliff a few miles high, like an impenetrable wall, at the foot of which the dark river disappeared. Raising his eyes, Samuel saw a titanic vault stretching from the top of the cliff until it disappeared over the horizon. Gigantic stalactites threatened to plummet to the world below, and roots of unseen trees hung between them.

In the distance, beyond the black river, was a murky forest, followed by a field that blended with the horizon. To the left of the field, a river of flames flowed furiously, and then merged with the main river. On the other side of the plain, a third river cut through the valley, parallel to the blazing stream, until it also merged with the black river. Other than the flames of the river and the lightning gashing the sky, thousands of blazes burned across the valley and provided a sinister and eerie light.

Even more troubling than the landscape in front of Samuel and the stench of sulfur floating in the air was the spectacle unfolding on the shores of the black river, at the end of the road Samuel and Angeline had to descend. Tens of thousands of men, women and children pressed against one another, hands above their heads, faces twisted by despair. Pleas and lamentations rose above the crowd—supplications that would tear apart the heart of the coldest man.

"Are these ... ?" Samuel began, but couldn't summon the courage to finish his question.

"Yes," answered Angeline. "These are the souls of the dead."

"Why are they moaning?"

"For different reasons. Some simply don't understand what has happened to them. Others do not accept their fate and try to plead their case, so they can go back to their loved ones. And then there are the lost souls, doomed to wander the shores of the River Acheron, without ever being ferried across to the other side."

Angeline pointed to a large ferry, moored to a wharf as old as the world, on which was piled a crowd of mourning people. The vessel had a ghastly look, with a single sail in tatters, several holes punched in the hull and a wobbly railing, but what sent a chill down Samuel's spine was not the ramshackle ship swaying over the dark waves. It was the sight of its helmsman, standing at the bow of the ship.

"That's Charon," whispered Angeline. "The first guardian of Hell. He is tasked with ferrying the souls of the dead across the waters of the Acheron, and dropping them on the opposite shore so they can continue their journey into the infernal kingdom."

Samuel could not turn his eyes away from Charon. He had already heard the legends surrounding this famous character, and had seen the illustrations made by the artists of another time, but none did justice to the spine-chilling appearance of the old man.

Charon's silhouette overshadowed the crowd before him. Samuel guessed the ferryman was almost ten feet tall. He wore a dirty rag, which was tied over his right shoulder and fell to the blackened boards of his vessel. A hood kept his face in eternal shadow, except for a white beard falling over his chest, like a waterfall coming out of the side of a mountain. One of his frail-looking arms rested on a knotty walking stick. With the other, he signaled some of the souls to come aboard, and pushed away those who were not welcome on his ferry.

Suddenly, one of the souls on the wharf—a young man of about thirty years of age—started getting anxious and darted toward the vessel, without being invited to climb aboard first. The soul pushed aside the other shadows on his way, even shoving some into the black waters of the Acheron, where they disappeared with agonizing cries. Quickly, the crowd on the deck stirred, with the commotion twice as wild near the ferry.

Charon raised his twisted stick and pointed it at the shadow pushing his way toward the helmsman. His cavernous voice echoed in the valley, as powerful as the scream of a thousand dragons. On the wharf, the young man's soul fell to the ground and screamed in pain, while the people around quickly lost their nerve and fled from him, some even climbing on their neighbors to do so. Samuel then saw a shadow quickly approaching from the horizon. Large wings moved with force behind the creature, and it came closer with extraordinary speed. When it passed over the Acheron, Samuel saw that the creature had blazing eyes, a body covered with scales and sharp claws at the end of its fingers and toes.

The demon circled the crowd a few times, then dove for the wharf, where it landed with such violence that some of the wooden boards exploded. A few seconds later, the monster took off again, carrying the soul of the young man between its powerful hands. The poor shadow screamed in horror, but the demon ignored it and rapidly carried him toward the place it had come from. When it disappeared over the horizon, Samuel did not dare imagine the fate awaiting the poor soul.

"Let's go," said Angeline after a moment of silence. "We can't allow ourselves to be scared by such events. Don't forget we have a mission to complete."

She glanced at the crowd for a moment, and then indicated a small group below, and a little farther ahead. "There, I see Aeneas and Deiphobe. Let's move closer before they disappear in the crowd."

Samuel was still stunned by the scene that had just unfolded before their eyes, but his body mindlessly followed Angeline's instruction, and they slowly walked down the ramp to the river.

When they were within fifty feet of the first souls, an upsetting thought formed in Samuel's mind. Would the souls of the dead ignore him or would they be upset, thinking he was mocking them by his presence—he who was still alive? Would they stand against him or would they let him pass without any trouble? And if the souls of the dead became agitated because of him, would that draw the attention of Hell's ferryman, the ominous Charon?

Samuel saw again the image of the young man being carried away by the winged demon.

"Look, Aeneas is right there," whispered Angeline as she pointed to the Trojan. "Let's get a little closer to him."

Samuel looked at the hero and Deiphobe amid the crowd. With a sigh of relief, he noted the souls around them completely ignored their presence: they were too busy wending their way to Charon's vessel. What's more, save for a few that showed signs of a violent demise, most of the souls had a human appearance, similar to Aeneas, Deiphobe and Samuel.

Angeline, who was invisible to those around them, dead or alive, zigzagged through the souls, closely followed by Samuel. Since it was the ideal occasion for them to get near the hero without alarming him, they only stopped when they were less than twenty feet from Aeneas. Because Aeneas had never seen Samuel before, and he had no reason to suspect he was being followed, he would believe the young man was simply another soul among the thousands standing on the shores of the Acheron. Samuel took the opportunity to scan the crowd around him. When he had first seen all these souls, he had thought about how easy it would be for the sorcerer to lay another trap for them in this place. The sorcerer himself could be hiding among the souls and closing in on the hero without Samuel noticing him, if he were not vigilant.

"Angeline, would you mind doing me a favor?" he asked. "I'd like you to fly above the crowd and have a look around. Make sure the sorcerer isn't hiding in the shadows around us."

"You got it."

The fata quickly took off and circled above the crowd a few times, studying the faces of those pressing around Samuel. The young man stretched out his neck as much as possible and also looked at the faces walking around him. At first he did not notice anything unusual, but after a moment Samuel became aware of a particular man acting oddly. Unlike the other souls around them, this man was not trying to make his way toward Charon's ferry. He was, rather, walking against the crowd and getting closer to Aeneas, his eyes locked on the hero.

Samuel placed a hand on his sword and pushed his way toward Aeneas. As he was sneaking between the men and women around him, he positioned himself to intercept the incoming man before he could reach the Trojan hero. When the man was less than twenty feet from him, Samuel quietly slid his sword a few inches out of its sheath and stood ready to intervene. The man was rather well-built, with a square jaw and striking eyes. His clothes and hair were dripping with water, and his skin was blue and covered with goose bumps.

When the man was less than six feet from him, Samuel took a step toward him, slid out his sword some more and moved to block the man's way. Just as he was about to face the man, he heard Aeneas's voice behind him.

"Palinurus!"

The incoming man's face lit up with a smile, and he jumped into Aeneas's arms. Aeneas welcomed him with a few friendly pats on the back.

"Aeneas!" said Palinurus, bursting into tears. "It's really you!"

Samuel let his sword slide back into its sheath. Evidently the man was a friend of Aeneas, and not an assassin sent by the sorcerer. A few seconds later, Angeline flew back next to Samuel and perched on his shoulder.

"Who is the man talking with Aeneas?" asked Samuel.

"His name is Palinurus. He was the helmsman of Aeneas's vessel until recently. One night, as he was manning the ship's helm, Palinurus disappeared without anyone knowing what became of him."

Samuel looked at the two Trojans, who could not stop embracing each other and exchanging salutations.

"Palinurus," said Aeneas, "tell me which god has taken you from us and cast you down into the sea's icy water. Apollo, who is yet to deceive me, had told me you had nothing to fear, and that you would reach the Ausonian coast with us. Is this how the sun god keeps his promises?"

Samuel crept a little closer to the two men and the Sybil. The woman spotted him and shot him a scolding look. Samuel stopped immediately.

"Apollo did not delude you, Aeneas," answered Palinurus. "It wasn't by the hand of a god that I found Death. The helm you appointed to my care, and to which I was clinging dearly, was violently pulled into the dark waters, dragging me after it."

Angeline turned to Samuel.

"In truth, it's the goddess Juno who yanked the helm," she whispered in his ear.

"Juno?"

"The wife of Jupiter, who is the Roman version of Zeus."

Angeline had answered as if what she revealed was obvious, but Samuel's head was spinning as he tried to keep track of all the links between the gods and goddesses playing a part in this legend: Pluto was the Roman version of Hades, who was the uncle of Apollo, who apparently kept the same name in both mythologies—while Juno was the wife of Jupiter, making her Pluto's sister-in-law and Apollo's aunt ...

"Pious Aeneas, even when the waves sought to swallow me, I did not tremble for myself as much as I did for your ship, suddenly deprived of its rudder and steersman," Palinurus said. "I feared it would be overwhelmed by the sea's gathering waves."

"Brave Palinurus," replied Aeneas. "What became of you then? Why do you find yourself here, asking to be brought to the forbidden shore of the Acheron?"

"For three stormy nights, the south wind rolled me in the icy water of the endless sea. The fourth dawn was barely upon me when a wave lifted me up, and I finally caught a glimpse of Italy's blessed coastline. Drawing from every drop of courage still within me, I swam to shore, where I safely landed, as the god Apollo had promised. However, I had barely closed my eyes to get my strength back when barbarous people attacked me without mercy, ignorantly deeming me a worthy prize. Now the waves hold me, and the winds toss me on the shore. So, I beseech you, pious Aeneas, son of Anchises, by heaven's pleasant light, by the air you breathe, by your father and by the hope of Iulus who grows by you, O invincible hero, rescue me from these distresses. Cast earth over my remains, I beg of you.

You only need to seek the port of Velia, and you will find me easily." With these words, Palinurus fell to his knees before Aeneas and lowered his head between the Trojan's feet, clinging to the hero's garments.

"Or, if there is another way," added Palinurus in a voice strangled by tears, "if your divine mother shows you how, lend a pitying hand to your cursed companion and take me with you across the Acheron, so that I may find a quiet resting place in death."

The poor man had barely pronounced these words when Deiphobe addressed him with a voice verging on hysteria: "Where does this foolish longing come from, Palinurus?" she yelled as she waved her arms wildly. "You who are without a burial, you would behold the Stygian water and the Fields of Judgment? Without an order from the gods, you would reach the opposing shore and try to make your way to Elysium? Cease hoping your prayers can bend the immutable decrees of the gods."

"According to Roman beliefs," whispered Angeline to Samuel, "a dead person must be put in the ground to be allowed across the Acheron and granted access to Pluto's kingdom. Those who do not receive the funeral rites must wander for a hundred years on this shore, waiting for permission to travel to the opposing shore."

"I thought they only had to pay the ferryman with the two silver coins, which the families usually placed on the eyes of the dead," Samuel said.

"That's only one of the many rituals. The Greeks and the Romans were not known for the simplicity of their ceremonies."

Samuel studied poor Palinurus, who was trying to kiss Aeneas's feet, still begging the Trojan not to abandon him on this shore for the next century. The hero pleaded to the Sibyl with his eyes, inviting her to take pity on his companion, but Deiphobe looked to the stars and threw her hands in the air.

"Poor Palinurus," she said, placing a gentle hand on his shoulder. "Remember these words that will bring solace in your woeful case: celestial portents will force the bordering cities to purify your bones, raise a tomb for your remains and pay the tomb all the honors you deserve. And know that this place will eternally bear your name, Palinurus. Once these deeds are accomplished, you will be invited onto Charon's ferry to find the rest you deserve."

The hapless soul got back to his feet with Aeneas's help. With eyes reddened by the tears, he looked incredulously at the hero.

"You can trust her," said Aeneas, placing a hand on his friend's shoulder. "She is a priestess of Apollo, a Sibyl, who knows the designs of the gods. They will not forget you, my dear Palinurus, and your name will remain etched in the memories of generations to come."

Once again, the poor man's eyes filled with tears, but this time his face brightened with a radiant smile. Palinurus took Aeneas in his arms and refused to let him go. The Sybil had to pull with both hands to separate the two men.

"We have to continue our journey," she ordered Aeneas, glancing toward Samuel and Angeline. "We must be seated in Charon's boat before it leaves this shore, as Hell's ferryman will not wait for us."

Before Aeneas could protest, Deiphobe pushed him farther into the crowd, leaving Palinurus behind them. Samuel and Angeline followed through the souls of the deceased, and when they passed by Aeneas's steersman, Samuel heard him murmur prayers for Apollo, grateful to the god for sending the Trojan hero. Now that Palinurus knew that the gods would not abandon him to his fate, he would wait for his turn to cross the Acheron with a lighter heart.

Samuel made a mental note to check if the helmsman was still remembered, and if there was indeed a place named after him somewhere in Italy.

Leaving Palinurus behind, Samuel sneaked through the crowd after Aeneas. He made sure he kept a safe distance between himself and the hero, so he would not raise any suspicions on the Trojan's part.

"Angeline, can you keep an eye on Aeneas from the air?" asked Samuel. "I fear we may lose him among all these souls."

She took off right away with a buzzing of wings that only Samuel could hear, while he kept moving forward through the crowd. The closer he got to the wharf and the water, the more the people around him were pressed against each other, to the point where Samuel had to use his shoulders and elbows to squeeze through. Farther ahead, he saw the soiled rags of the sail floating over Charon's ferry, as well as the silhouette of the helmsman.

With each step he took toward the wharf and the creaking ferry, Samuel's stomach tightened a little more. He clenched his fingers around the hilt of his weapon, and put the other hand on the Helm of Darkness attached to his waist. Feeling the crown against him, and sensing its power that begged to be released, Samuel regained some of his courage. He had faced his worst fears to get the onyx crown, and he now knew what truly scared him. Charon, though he was a chilling character, was not part of his fears.

Samuel raised his eyes to the vault. Angeline hovered above the crowd and snapped her head in every direction, like a bird looking for danger. When she saw Samuel looking at her, she pointed to Charon's vessel and signaled that everything was going smoothly.

Samuel scanned the crowd for Aeneas, and found him and the Sibyl next to the ferry. Samuel moved closer and carefully climbed up the dock's stairs after them.

Without warning, Charon raised his knotted staff and struck the wharf with prodigious strength. A hundred bombs exploding in unison would not have produced a more powerful detonation. Samuel immediately covered his ears with both hands, while the crowd of mournful souls quickly stepped away, leaving only Aeneas and the Sibyl in front of the ferryman. Charon slowly leaned over them, like a centennial oak bending under a stormy wind, and then he pointed at them with a twisted finger.

"Whoever you are, you who marches toward our river, stop immediately," said Charon in a rasping voice. "Tell me what brings you to this place, for this is the land of Shadows, of Sleep and slumberous Night, and I am forbidden to carry any living being in my hull."

Aeneas parted his lips to reply, but Charon did not allow it. He struck his boat once more with his staff, and then spoke again in a powerful voice filled with a timeless rage.

"It is forbidden to take living souls across the Acheron's water," he repeated. "Besides, woe was me to have accepted on my ferry, when they came here, Alcides, Theseus and Pirithous, born of gods and unconquered. One of them put the chains around the guardian of Tartarus, and dragged him cowering from the throne of my lord Pluto. As for the others, they all tried to ravish the queen of Hell from the chamber of this valley's king."

The Sibyl stepped in front of Aeneas, while at the same time Angeline came down next to Samuel.

"Samuel, we have a problem," whispered Angeline.

But before Samuel could inquire what it was, Deiphobe spoke to Charon with a defiant look in her eyes, even though the ferryman was at least three times her size.

"We have no such perfidious intentions in mind, Charon, so you can stop worrying," she said. "My companion's arms do not bring war here, and we will leave the huge guard dog undisturbed, free to frighten the bloodless ghost forever with his eternal barks. And the chaste Persephone can sleep peacefully in her uncle's place. The Trojan Aeneas, renowned in goodness and in arms, goes down into the deep shades of Erebus to meet his father, nothing more."

She then dug inside her garments and produced the golden bough she had tasked Aeneas to find.

"If such piety does not move you, then at least recognize this golden bough, which will be offered to the queen of this realm to buy our passage."

As soon as he saw the offering, Charon straightened on his staff, and his anger vanished. He remained still for a moment, looking the bough as if he was witnessing a forbidden love for the first time in millennia. Then, with a wave if his bony hand, he tossed aside the souls piled on the wharf in order to clear the way for Aeneas and Deiphobe. He also pushed with his dry fingers the souls already seated on the ferry, and ordered them off his ship. When some refused to obey, he simply tossed them overboard.

"Samuel, you have to listen to me for a second," said Angeline, pulling on a lock of the young man's hair.

Samuel barely heard the fata's words. As he watched Aeneas and Deiphobe climb aboard the ferry, a worrying thought occupied his mind.

"I know," he said finally. "We do have a serious problem." He turned to Angeline. "How are we going to cross the Acheron?" he asked. "We are not dead yet, and we have nothing to offer Charon to pay for our trip. He will never agree to carry us."

Angeline looked at Samuel with her large purple eyes, her face pale with anxiety. "And that is not our only worry," she replied. "Look at the other side of the river."

Samuel followed her gaze, and his heart skipped a beat.

On the other side of the Acheron, on the shore toward which Aeneas and Deiphobe were now sailing, the sorcerer watched him, his hands hidden in his dark robe.

15

Charon's ferry was gliding in silence on the dark waters of the Acheron, slowly sailing away from the lamenting crowd. The incessant creaking of the blackened planks and the hull's sinister wailing had replaced the moaning of the dead. Despite the sail's pitiful condition, the rags of soiled fabric swelled under the yard, lifted by a mysterious wind pushing the vessel across the river to the Underworld.

Hell's ferryman, the sorrowful Charon, stood at the ship's stern, motionless over the wooden helm. With one hand he leaned on his walking staff, and with the other he maneuvered the wheel and guided his gloomy vessel. On the shore behind him, Deiphobe saw the decaying wharf and the crowd of souls on the rotten planks. Somewhere among these poor souls were Angeline and Samuel.

Had they anticipated the first real obstacle in their journey? Had they thought of a strategy to cross the Acheron after she and Aeneas had? When the Sibyl sent Aeneas to get the golden bough that would grant him access to Pluto's kingdom, did Samuel guess he would need to find something else to enter this place as well?

Deiphobe doubted it.

The Lorekeeper had been chosen by the Parcae, and she did not dare to question their decision, but Samuel did not look to her as if he knew how legends really operated or what he needed to do to survive on Metverold. He seemed completely lost.

May the gods help us, thought Deiphobe.

She turned to Aeneas. The hero was standing at the ship's bow, his eyes locked on the incoming shore. This was what a *real* Lorekeeper should look like, she thought. Unlike Samuel, Aeneas inspired courage and confidence. The Trojan had the makings of a true hero. He was a man able to round up his companions and lead them to victory.

This was a man who was ready to face the demons of Hell just so he could learn his true destiny.

Deiphobe sighed and lowered her eyes. Maybe she was being too harsh on Samuel. After all, Angeline had mentioned it was only the Lorekeeper's third adventure on Metverold. He still had a lot to learn, while Aeneas had been born in a time marked by conflict, and had survived the famous Trojan War. He had spent practically his whole life fighting enemies, each more ferocious than the last. And it was important to remember that Aeneas was the son of a goddess—a considerable advantage in times like these.

Deiphobe stood and walked over to Aeneas at the ship's bow. Angeline trusted Samuel, and the Sibyl decided that was enough for her. The Lorekeeper might not be the mightiest warrior she had ever met, but he was certainly resourceful. He had even survived Apollo's trials to get the Helm of Darkness. Angeline and the young man would find a way to cross the Acheron and catch up with them. She just had to be patient.

"Tell me, priestess of Apollo, what is waiting for us on the forbidden shores of Pluto's kingdom." said Aeneas.

"A perilous journey," Deiphobe answered. "Why did you embark on such a foolish adventure, Prince of Troy?"

"Because it is the will of the gods," answered Aeneas.

The Sibyl remained quiet, her eyes still on the Trojan's face. After a moment, Aeneas spoke again:

"I know this journey appears to be reckless in the eyes of my companions," he said. "My men believe I'm risking my life unnecessarily, and I don't need the revelations of my father to continue my quest. Each of them blindly follows me through thick and thin, trusting I will lead them to the promised land, where we will finally know peace." He turned to Deiphobe, and she saw his eyes were glimmering with tears. "This blind trust has cost the life of more than one of them, like poor Palinurus. Because of me, their children will grow up without a father to look after them, and their wives will have to live without a husband to protect their house. I need to know these sacrifices were not in vain. I need to know I'm not leading these men to their demise. I need to know that Troy's Penates will not be carted across countless lands, each more violent than the last. That is why I'm taking this dangerous journey."

"In that case, let us hope the answers you find will put your heart at peace, Trojan," replied Deiphobe.

Out of the corner of her eye, she noticed movement on the incoming shore, a little to the right, and turned just in time to see a shadow disappear in the darkness. At that moment, the ferry softly dug itself into black sand. For a moment, Deiphobe studied the place where she thought she had seen a shadow, fearing she already knew who was hiding in the darkness. If the Yfel wanted to attack Aeneas, this was the ideal moment to do it, since the Lorekeeper was stuck on the opposing shore, among the souls of the deceased.

A shiver slid down the Sibyl's neck. Then she raised her eyes and her heart froze as soon as she glanced at the landscape before them. It was not the first time she had witnessed the horrors of Pluto's kingdom, but it was the first time she had set foot in it. It was one thing to see the blazing hills in frightening visions, but it was another to smell the pungent stench of sulfur and to feel the eternal heat on her cheeks.

Without the slightest hesitation, Aeneas jumped out of Charon's boat. Turning, he offered his help to Deiphobe. The

Sibyl placed a hand on his strong shoulder, and the Trojan took her by the waist. With little more effort than he would need to push a chair, he lifted the Sibyl and gently set her down on the shore. When the black water of the Acheron came closer to them, they quickly took a few steps back to avoid dipping even the tips of their toes.

Once they were out of reach of the cursed water, Deiphobe slowly turned and let her eyes wander over their surroundings. The black sand stretched for a little over a hundred yards before her, and then it was replaced by long strands of red grass, the like of which she had never seen on Earth. When she saw a fuming stone hill a little ahead of them, her hands became clammy and sweat beaded on her forehead. The life of a Sibyl was not for the weak of heart, and few things could scare a woman whose body and voice were stolen by envious and spiteful gods, but when she thought of what was hiding behind the hill, Deiphobe found herself paralyzed by fear. It was not the last hurdle they would have to conquer on this journey, but it was one of the most frightening.

Fortunately, the Sibyl had come prepared, but all the precautions in the world would not calm her worries.

She turned to thank Charon for carrying them here—after all, she would eventually require his services again one of these days—but he had vanished, together with his cursed ship.

"I think we can safely assume we will not be leaving the same way we came," said Aeneas.

Deiphobe opened her mouth, but before she could answer the ground jerked beneath their feet. A few seconds later, a blood-freezing roar echoed behind them.

"Is ... is that what I think it is?" asked Aeneas, his face suddenly pale.

"Yes, and we must hurry," answered Deiphobe. "You may be strong, Aeneas, but believe me, you have no desire to face a monster like this."

Deiphobe darted toward the fuming hill without waiting for the Trojan's reply. She had to act quickly, and she had no time to explain the details of her plan.

When she reached the first blades of red grass, Deiphobe grabbed the leather wineskin she had prepared in her lair a few hours earlier. The liquid it contained had been suggested to her in a vision a few months earlier, and she had no reason to doubt its effectiveness, but her heart constricted a little when she dared imagine what would happen if the potion failed to produce the desired effect.

May the gods look upon us, she thought.

Behind her, Aeneas followed in a hurry. Fortunately, he had guessed they needed to act with haste, and refrained from bombarding her with questions.

Another growl echoed on the shores of the Acheron, accompanied once more by a tremor that shook the ground, more powerful than the previous one. The shock took Deiphobe by surprise, and the wineskin suddenly slipped from her fingers. Her heart raced when she saw the bag fall to the ground, but Aeneas quickly caught it before the precious liquid spilled.

"I don't know what's in this skin, but I imagine we will need it," he said, handing over the wineskin to Deiphobe.

"It will allow us to pass before the guardian of Hell without leaving any limbs behind," replied the Sibyl.

"In that case, I suggest we do not waste a single drop."

When they reached the hill of fuming stones, Deiphobe signaled to Aeneas to slow down and stay close to her. They quietly moved forward until they reached a boulder at least ten feet high. Deiphobe peeked around it. Relieved, she saw that the monster was still in its lair. If it were to spot them before it saw the wineskin, the creature would certainly jump on the two intruders and ignore the potion.

"Throw this skin as far as you can," said Deiphobe, giving the leather bag to Aeneas.

The Trojan stepped in front of the old woman and spun the wineskin at the end of the leather strap with a deftness that came from years of training with a sling. Once he had gained enough momentum, he let go of the leather strap, and the skin flew more than fifty yards. Deiphobe quickly pulled the Trojan behind her.

A third tremor shook the ground, then a fourth, and a terrible growl echoed around them. A few seconds later, a huge black paw appeared on the other side of the hill, and the guardian of Pluto's kingdom came out of his lair.

With a clenching heart, holding her breath, Deiphobe watched the beast move closer to the skin, drawn by the smells of meat and honey she had mixed with the herbs when concocting the sleeping potion. The beast sniffed the air a few times, and then it licked the ground where the liquid was pooling. With tremendous relief, the Sibyl saw the beast ferociously jump on the wineskin and devour it whole. Satisfied, Deiphobe leaned back on the boulder and signaled to Aeneas that everything was fine.

After waiting for ten minutes, Deiphobe and Aeneas slowly moved out of hiding and walked over to the inert body of the beast. Its cavernous breathing lifted its scaly chest, but the monster remained motionless, deeply asleep under the effect of the potion.

"This is truly prodigious," whispered Aeneas.

"Let's not linger," Deiphobe said. "I doubt Cerberus will be in a good mood when he wakes up, and I don't know how long the effects of the potion will last."

Let's just hope Samuel and Angeline do not wait too long before passing here, the Sibyl added to herself.

16

How had everything spun out of control so quickly? One moment Samuel was standing next to Aeneas with the situation well in hand; the next he was watching Deiphobe and the Trojan sail without him toward the Yfel's sorcerer. On the other side of the river, the sorcerer had disappeared, but Samuel knew he was still there, hiding in the shadows and waiting for his chance to pounce on Aeneas.

"What are you going to do?" asked Angeline.

"I don't know," replied Samuel.

Even though he tried to look at the problem from every possible angle, he had no bright ideas. Samuel was stuck on the rickety wharf, watching Charon's ferry reach the other side.

"We have to find a way to get aboard that boat," he told Angeline.

"And how do you plan on doing that?" she asked. "We have no golden bough to offer, and you heard what Charon said: only the dead can get on his ferry. He will never agree to carry us while we are still breathing."

Samuel watched as the vessel approached the opposing shore and saw Aeneas and Deiphobe disembark on the beach. With several hundred yards now between him and them, he wondered if the sorcerer would attack right away, or if he planned to ambush them farther ahead.

Suddenly Charon's ferry disappeared in a fog, which dissipated as quickly as it had come.

"What the ...?" whispered Samuel, and then his attention was drawn by a movement downstream. He turned and saw Charon's vessel, with the gigantic helmsman at its bow, gliding toward them. In a racket of creaking and cracking, the ship came alongside the old dock and the ferryman slowly moored his vessel with cables of hemp. Then Charon resumed his eternal sorting of the souls, accepting some aboard and pushing others back with his hand.

Samuel was a little over twenty pace from the ferry. All around him, souls pressed against each other, trying to make their way to the front and embark on the ultimate voyage toward eternal rest. Some shot him odd glances, but for the most part they completely ignored him.

"What if I flew over to the other shore to see what's going on?" suggested Angeline.

"I don't think it's a good idea," replied Samuel. "The Acheron is pretty wide, and the sorcerer would see you coming a mile off. You remember what Mumby did when he saw you coming on Albion? The sorcerer could easily cast a spell in your direction and send you plummeting into the dark waters." A shiver shook her tiny body. "What do you suggest we do, then?" she asked.

Samuel tightened his fingers around the Helm of Darkness. An idea had taken root in his mind a few moments earlier, but it was rather risky.

"Maybe I could get on board without being seen," he said.

"And how are you going to do that?"

He looked down at the Helm of Darkness to show Angeline his intentions.

"The Helm of Darkness makes me invisible to the inhabitants of the Underworld," he said.

"Yes, but it also makes you a target for some of them. Did you already forget about the harpies?"

"Of course not, but the harpies were not technically creatures of the Underworld. They were spawned by the Yfel's sorcerer. Besides, I think it's worth the risk. If the Helm can make me invisible to Charon, I'll be able to sneak through the shadows and get aboard the ferry."

Angeline placed her fists on her hips and looked at Samuel with doubtful eyes.

"Is that your genius plan?"

"If you have a better idea, by all means tell me."

Angeline seemed lost in thought for a moment. Then she let her shoulders fall and gave up.

"All right," she said, "But how will *I* slip under Charon's nose?"

"You're already invisible to most of the characters we meet, Angeline. I'm almost certain you're also invisible to him."

Angeline raised her eyebrows, but Samuel quickly put the Helm of Darkness on his head before she raised new objections. She was probably wondering what would happen if his plan failed and Charon saw him. It was better not to think about that for now.

As soon as the onyx crown rested on his head, a numbing feeling spread across his body, right up to the tips of his fingers and toes. Samuel immediately became aware of the artifact's tremendous power—a force trying to grab hold of his will and sending him frightening images. But Samuel had already mastered each of the fears the Helm of Darkness was trying to use against him, and he did not let himself be dominated this easily. After a quick battle with the crown, the pressure on his mind receded and he regained full control of his thoughts.

Around him, the closest souls had astonished looks on their faces, as they searched for the young man who had been standing there a few seconds ago.

At least I'm invisible to the dead, thought Samuel.

He took a deep breath, seized his courage with both hands, and sneaked through the souls gathered on the wharf. With each step he took toward the ferry, his heartbeat quickened and his feet seemed to become heavier. Around him, startled souls were pushed out of the way by his shoulders, and were questioning this mysterious presence slipping among them. Angeline clung to his armor, her face buried just below his shoulder.

"Keep going," she whispered. "Everything is going well for now."

Before them, Charon was sorting the souls. Those who were refused permission to climb aboard burst into tears, while those we were authorized to get on rejoiced at the thought of meeting their loved ones again.

Samuel was now less than a dozen steps from the end of the pier. Just a little bit more and he would be on the ferry. He forced himself to keep calm, turning his eyes to Charon's emaciated silhouette. The ferryman was still leaning on his walking staff, directing the souls with his free hand.

Samuel took two more steps.

It was now impossible to sneak any farther between the souls. Samuel could only let himself be carried by the crowd, which was slowly bringing him closer to the vessel. At this point, even if he had wanted to turn around it would have been impossible to walk away. He could hear the ship's creaking, and every moan coming from the hull rolling over the dark waves of the Acheron. He heard the water splash against the ferry's rotten wood, and the wind flapping the rags of the decrepit sail.

Samuel took another step.

He now heard Charon's powerful breathing, as if it came from the bowels of the Underworld itself. Samuel smelled his foul breath and the stench of scum on his gray garments. Hell's ferryman was so close that Samuel could have extended his arm to touch him.

Behind him, Angeline stiffened her grip on Samuel's armor and buried her face deeper between his shoulders.

Charon was standing to their right, still watching the crowd and sorting the souls in front of him.

Samuel could hardly believe it. His plan was working. Charon had not seen him, and he was about to climb aboard the ship.

After a sign from Charon, the soul in front of Samuel happily jumped aboard the boat. It was a woman about fifty years of age, with long hazel hair and large hips. She gave Samuel the impression she had labored rigorously all her life, and had probably left many kids in tears with her death. He thought he would surely sit next to her on the ferry.

He took one last step forward, and a deafening thunder exploded over the Acheron, quickly chasing away the courage and confidence Samuel had up to this moment. He saw Charon's staff come down hard before him, blocking his path. Trembling from head to toe, Samuel slowly turned his head toward the ferryman.

Charon was leaning over Samuel, his dark hood on the verge of swallowing the young man.

"Who goes there?"

Charon's voice shook Samuel's soul.

"Who tries to slip aboard my ship under my nose? I know you are there, fool. Show yourself! Reveal the identity of the one trying to mock Hell's ferryman."

Samuel was frozen by fear, unable to move a single muscle. Behind him, Angeline pulled harder on the leather straps as she tried to bury her face even deeper in Samuel's back.

Charon leaned forward some more.

"Show yourself!" he screamed.

Samuel was trapped. In front of him, the souls already on board were looking in his direction, trying to make out who Charon was talking to. He imagined a similar confusion was on the faces of the souls in line behind him.

Samuel briefly thought about staying perfectly still and waiting for Charon to doubt there was actually someone there and resume his work, but this idea quickly vanished when Hell's ferryman struck the wharf with his knotty staff again. Charon was no fool. He had been carrying out his task since the beginning of time. If he believed an invisible being was trying to sneak aboard his ferry, he would never doubt his instincts.

There was only one thing left to do. Slowly Samuel raised his trembling hands to his head and lifted the Helm of Darkness.

"What are you doing?" yelled Angeline, now panic-stricken. "He's going to see you!"

Samuel did not answer. He was too paralyzed by fear to emit the slightest sound.

As soon as the onyx crown left his head and he appeared to all, screams of stupefaction and fright were heard among the souls around him. A murmur spread across the crowd behind Samuel, as the most distant souls asked their neighbors what was happening on the dock.

Charon tilted his head to the side and moved closer to Samuel. The cold, fetid breath of the ferryman nearly made Samuel gag.

"Who are you?" asked Charon.

"My—my name is Samuel."

"What are you doing here, Samuel? Why do you seek to deceive Hell's ferryman?"

Samuel's throat stiffened, and the words remained stuck in his gullet. Would Charon believe him if he told the truth? Hell's ferryman had refused passage to Aeneas before the Trojan showed him the golden bough, even though the hero had nothing but good intentions. Nothing indicated his judgment would be different with Samuel.

"I was not trying to deceive you," replied Samuel in a faltering voice.

"Liar!" spit Charon.

Angeline squealed behind Samuel.

"Please," said Samuel, "you have to believe me. I'm not here to make a fuss or anything."

"Liar!" screamed Charon again. "You are here to free the soul of a close friend and defile the decrees of the gods, is that it?"

"No, not at all! I'm here to protect the Trojan Aeneas, who you just ferried to the other side."

"If you are traveling with Aeneas, why did you not cross the Acheron with him?"

"Well, to tell you the truth, it's rather complicated. You see, I'm the Lorekeeper and—"

Charon struck the railing once again with his staff. The detonation made every soul around Samuel jump back.

"The Lorekeeper!" yelled Charon. "Virtus's lapdog! This explains everything!"

"You know who I am?" asked Samuel, a glimmer of hope in his voice. "So you know about the battle raging between Virtus and Yfel?"

Charon straightened, and his bony silhouette loomed over Samuel.

"Oh yes, I know the story of Virtus and Yfel. I also know they are willing to violate the divine laws to reach their goals."

The last words were spoken with so much spite that the hope building in Samuel quickly vanished. Obviously Charon did not have any sympathy toward the two factions fighting each other on Metverold.

"I don't want to violate any divine law," said Samuel cautiously. "I only want to protect the Trojan Aeneas. And since you have ferried our enemy—the Yfel's sorcerer—across the Acheron, why do you deny me access to your ship?"

"Impossible!" answered Charon. "No one crosses the Acheron without my knowledge."

Samuel wanted to reply that the sorcerer had fooled Hell's ferryman, but he thought that offending Charon was probably the best way to make sure he never crossed the Acheron.

"You're right," said Samuel. "It was stupid to believe I could fool you with the Helm of Darkness, and I hope you will accept my apologies."

Charon burst into a laugh that sent the ferry pitching violently.

"Accept your apologies? You are mocking me again, Samuel."

"No! I'm not making fun of you, I—"

"Silence!" yelled Charon. "I've had enough of my sisters' trickeries. If it amuses them to think they guide the world, let them do it somewhere other than on my river. I am the sole master here, and no one will tell me whom I can ferry across."

"Your sisters?" asked Samuel.

Angeline raised her head for the first time, as surprised as he was by Charon's declaration.

"Who are you talking about?" Samuel said.

"The three Parcae, of course!" replied Charon. "They are not the only ones free of the gods' will. The old decrees give me the freedom to manage the Acheron's crossing as I wish, and if the Parcae think they can send their puppet and that I will bend to his demands, I will show them how wrong they are."

A worrying feeling was growing inside Samuel. Charon's words had been said with profound disdain, and he did not like the turn the discussion was suddenly taking.

"Please," said Samuel, raising his hands, "there is no need to get angry. I'm only following orders. I'm sure the Parcae had no intention of—"

"Quiet!" growled Charon in a voice that shook the Acheron's shore.

Two flaming lights appeared in the impenetrable darkness of the hood. The lights intensified until they became two blazing globes, and for the first time in over a millennia, the crowd gathered on the old wharf saw the burning eyes of Hell's ferryman.

"Not only do you seek to fool me," thundered Charon, moving closer to Samuel, "but you also suggest I am ignorant of my sisters' and their pawns' scheming?"

"No, you don't understand," said Samuel, taking a step backward.

"It's you who do not understand the gravity of your action," replied the ferryman. He muttered a few words in an unknown language, and then he slowly lowered his staff and pointed toward Samuel.

"Oh no," whispered Angeline. "By the gods, not this."

"You want to cross the Acheron, you fool?" asked Charon. "Very well, I will grant your wish."

A horrible shriek echoed over the Vale of the Dead, like a horde of furious dragons. The souls of the deceased around Samuel hastily stepped away from the young man, and a few unfortunate souls were pushed into the dark waters of the Acheron during the panic that followed.

Now standing alone at the end of the wharf, Samuel turned his head toward the horizon. In the distance, over the kingdom of Pluto, the silhouette of a winged demon appeared in the sky and came toward him. Terrified, Samuel turned to Angeline, who had her hands over her mouth, her face as pale as her white tunic.

"Angeline," said Samuel. "What do I do?"

The fata shook her head, her eyes locked on the incoming demon. If she had a solution for Samuel, she did not find the strength to say the words, and remained paralyzed by fear.

When Samuel turned to the demon again, he saw that it was now close to the river. In a few seconds it would dive toward the prey Charon had designated, and would carry it to a forgotten corner of Hell.

"Now you will know the price of defying the divine laws," said Charon with a grating laugh.

What followed happened so fast that Samuel found himself pinned to the ground before he could realize what was going on. Powerful hands seized his shoulders, and razor-sharp claws pierced his flesh. Before he had a chance to defend himself, he was lifted into the air by the demon. When his feet left the rotten planks of Charon's dock, Samuel could still hear the ferryman's rasping laughter, as well as Angeline's screams, calling out his name in a voice broken by tears.

And above all, Samuel heard his own voice, crying out in horror.

In a second, Samuel was almost a hundred feet in the air, his feet dangling over the murky waters of the Acheron. He tried to free himself from the demon's grip by twisting his body, but it was no use. The monster was holding him firmly, and even if he managed to get free of his clutches, Samuel would fall right into the forbidden river. As frightening as his current situation was, he had no desire to find out what kind of monsters lurked beneath the surface of the Acheron.

"Samuel, can you hear me?"

Fear was like a fog so dense over Samuel's mind that he barely heard Angeline's voice. The only things he was fully aware of were the sharp pain in his shoulder and the black waters of the Acheron below his feet.

"Samuel!" repeated Angeline with more persistence. "Help me!"

This time, the fata's words made it to his mind, and Samuel saw she was flying next to him. With her needle sword she was striking the wrists of the demon.

"Help me set you free," she yelled.

"It won't do any good," Samuel called back. "The fall would kill me."

"Don't be stupid! You really want to find out where this demon is taking you?"

Samuel looked at her. Maybe it was better to take his chances in the waters of the Acheron after all. For the first time since the demon had taken him, he lowered his eyes to his hands. His left hand still held the Helm of Darkness, which he promptly attached to his waist. With his right hand, Samuel tried to draw his sword, but the demon guessed his intentions and grabbed his wrist with one of its agile feet. Samuel tried to get free, but the demon's claws were firmly planted on his wrist.

"Angeline, my hand ... I can't get to my sword."

The fata quickly charged toward the demon's foot and with all her strength thrust her tiny sword into its ankle. The demon howled in pain and let go of Samuel's wrist. The young man immediately grabbed his sword with his right hand. Blindly, he struck over his head, but the demon dodged the first two blows. Only with his third strike did Samuel hit the monster's ear, and the demon shrieked in pain again. He let go of Samuel's left shoulder. Before the demon could seize him again, Samuel grabbed the demon's free wrist and struck the claws that still held his right shoulder. With another cry of pain, the monster let go. Now, the only thing preventing the young man from falling was his own grip on the demon's wrist.

"Climb onto his back," yelled Angeline.

Easy for you to say, thought Samuel, but since he did not have a better idea, he pulled himself up the demon's arm, parrying the monster's attacks with his sword.

"You must find a way to force it down," Angeline told him.

Ignoring the pain in his shoulders, Samuel encircled the demon's waist with his legs, and pressed against its body. Now Samuel's face was right under the demon's chin, and the monster immediately tried to bite his head.

"Be careful!" yelled Angeline.

Letting go of the demon's wrist, Samuel punched the demon's face a few times. Then, with his free hand, he grabbed one of its wing's membranes. Ignoring the burning in his shoulder and the pain in his wrist, Samuel pulled himself onto the monster's back. Before the demon could get rid of its passenger, Samuel lunged forward, passed his left arm around the demon's neck and struck his skull with the hilt of his sword. The demon swung its arms around and fought back, but it still dove toward the ground, unable to maintain its trajectory. Samuel tightened his grip on the monster's neck and struck it some more, each blow pushing the demon farther down.

"Hold on!" shouted Angeline.

Samuel barely had time to let go of the demon's head and grab hold of its wings before the monster violently crashed into the shore. The force of the impact sent Samuel flying forward and rolling in the black sand, but he quickly jumped back to his feet, before the demon could recover his senses.

"Nice landing."

The voice froze Samuel's blood.

He immediately turned his eyes to the right and saw the Yfel sorcerer standing there. Slowly, Samuel's sworn enemy walked toward him. Then he leaned forward and picked up a dark object: the Helm of Darkness. It must have come loose during Samuel's fall.

"What have we here?" said the sorcerer.

On Acheron's shore, the demon pulled itself up. It looked at the two men in front of him for a moment, then let out a shriek so frightening that Angeline quickly hid behind Samuel. The monster took a step toward Samuel, firmly set on recovering his prisoner.

"I think I'm going to have a little bit of competition for your head," said the Yfel's sorcerer.

1 7

A misty wind blew over the waters of the Acheron, carrying the moans of the dead souls toward the depths of the Valley of the Dead. The wind followed each curve of the River Styx, on which the gods swore the most sacred oaths, and ran upstream to the Forest of Suicides. Facing the Styx, the blazing waters of the Phlegethon violently coursed toward the Acheron. The heat from the eternal flames made the horizon wobble and licked without pity those foolish enough to get too close. Between the flames lurked the silhouette of a distant mountain, with permanent clouds covering the summit.

Samuel did not have the luxury to admire the landscape. He did not have time to marvel before the titanic vault over his head, or observe the gigantic pillars supporting the world of the living above him. A furious demon sought to carry him to a place forgotten by the gods, and a faceless sorcerer blocked his way. Even worse, the sorcerer now held the Helm of Darkness that Samuel had dropped.

Samuel could not afford the slightest moment of inattention, or everything would be lost.

The demon opened his mouth and produced another shriek that echoed in Samuel's soul. The demon was only a head or so taller than Samuel, but its body was covered with massive muscles, and its powerful arms seemed as wide as tree trunks. Its face looked human, but its eyes were as black as the abyss, and its mouth was filled with razor-sharp teeth. On its skull, horns were ranged in a line from forehead to nape, and its large wings were like those of a bat.

Samuel quickly glanced over his shoulder and saw that the sorcerer had not moved. Maybe he was hoping the demon would get rid of the Lorekeeper without him having to lift a finger.

Samuel decided to ignore the sorcerer for now, and focus on the demon.

"Angeline, would you keep an eye on our Yfel friend?" he asked.

"All right, but I beg you, don't leave me alone with him," answered the fata.

"I'll do my best."

Samuel took a step toward the demon. The move seemed to surprise the monster, who was probably used to seeing people running as fast as their legs could carry them. It stopped for a moment, and then a grin appeared on the demon's face, and it came toward its prey. When Samuel was a few steps from the demon, he attacked without warning. The demon growled in rage. It swirled to its left and avoided Samuel's strike with surprising speed. The demon struck him with its elbow between the shoulder blades, and sent him to the ground.

The demon pounced on Samuel and tried to grab him by the shoulders again, just like it had done on Charon's wharf, but this time Samuel was ready for the attack and rolled over on the ground, throwing a handful of black sand in the demon's eyes as he did so. The monster screamed with rage once more. Samuel jumped to his feet.

With a powerful flap of its wings, the demon rose several feet in the air, before charging directly at Samuel. The young man had just enough time to dive forward and avoid the sharp claws, and the monster cried out in frustration before rising higher above the Acheron.

The demon launched another attack. Once again, Samuel ducked at the last moment and barely dodged the demon's claws. He tried to strike the monster with his sword, but the demon flew by so fast that Samuel only split air.

"Focus!" cried Angeline.

He wanted to reply she was not helping with such remarks, but the fear was so obvious in the little fata's voice that he remained quiet. Samuel got back to his feet and followed the demon with his eyes.

As the monster circled and got ready to attack once more, Samuel thought it might be best to listen to Angeline. He took a deep breath, closed his hands around the hilt of his sword and shut his eyes. After all, he was the Lorekeeper, and he had several powers at his disposal, including an unbelievable ability with a sword.

Samuel remained still for only a few seconds, but it was enough. As soon as he closed his eyes and focused his attention on the leather hilt of his weapon, a familiar sensation spread in his arms and his guts. It was not an aggressive sensation, like the one he felt whenever he placed the Helm of Darkness on his head. It was more like a light warming his spirit; an energy spreading across his body. It was a power shrouding and protected him, and a strength that comforted his soul. It was a feeling that nothing was impossible; that no creature, no matter how frightening, could beat him.

The sensation lasted for only a brief moment. Then it receded, and Samuel opened his eyes.

He was ready.

The demon charged at him with blazing speed. Its claws were razor-sharp, its fangs like daggers, and this time it seemed determined to come down on its prey with all of Hell's fury.

Samuel dug his heels into the black sand and turned slightly to the side. He lifted his weapon close to his face and held the blade parallel to the ground. As the demon swept toward him with bloodcurdling screams, Samuel saw in his mind the scene that would follow. Everything was so clear now, so precise—all that was left was for him to execute the movements.

Samuel counted down in his head: *Three ... two ... one!*

He suddenly pivoted to his right and the demon dove into the black sand. Without waiting for the monster to regain its senses, Samuel completed the turn, and planted a foot on the demon's lower back. Raising his sword above his head, he brought it down with all his might, aiming between the monster's shoulders.

But just before the tip of his sword pierced the demon's flesh, lightning struck Samuel and sent him flying through the air.

"Not so fast," said the sorcerer.

"Samuel!" called Angeline as she flew toward the young man.

All of Samuel's muscles clenched in agony, and every inch of his body hurt excruciatingly. As Angeline touched his cheek, a burning sensation made him think his entrails were on fire.

"What did you do to him?" screamed Angeline at the sorcerer.

The fear was gone from her voice, replaced by a deep rage.

"I only prevented him from making a big mistake," replied the sorcerer. "He was going to kill this demon, even though it's strictly forbidden by Virtus. You must not change the legends, remember?"

"You filthy bastard," spat Angeline between her tears.

The sorcerer turned toward the shore. "But now," he said, "I believe your new friend is really pissed off. If I were you, I would not stay between him and the Lorekeeper."

Samuel was twisting in pain on the black sand, unable to tell if the distant voices he heard were part of his imagination or not. Then a series of little slaps struck his cheek.

"Samuel, please wake up!"

Samuel recognized Angeline's voice and the last moments came back to his memory. He moaned and opened his eyes, but his head fell forward and his chin bumped his chest.

"That … I … what?" he mumbled.

Behind Angeline, the sorcerer burst into diabolical laughter.

"Samuel," said the fata, "you have to get a hold of yourself."

A lengthy grumble whistled between Samuel's lips, and he swung his head from left to right. His entire body was numb, and his mind was swimming.

Running out of patience, Angeline struck him as hard as she could.

"Samuel!" she yelled.

He startled, opened his eyes wide and jumped to his feet.

"What?" he said. "What's happening?"

Just then he spotted the demon coming toward him, face disfigured by rage, and reality rushed into Samuel's mind. He was in Hell, on the shores of the Acheron, fighting a ferocious demon, while the sorcerer watched the scene. Samuel should have been terrified, but he'd had enough of being a victim. It was no longer fear that coursed in his veins, but anger and rage. He'd had enough of always being the prey.

Samuel clutched the hilt of his sword and darted toward the demon. He screamed in anger and raised his sword over his head. The distance between the demon and himself shrank quickly, and a few seconds later he jumped on his target without holding back.

At the same moment, a terrifying roar echoed in the valley. The savage howl hid the sorcerer's laugh and the rustling of the Acheron, and its echo spread to the darkest pits of the dead kingdom. Samuel's muscles all clenched at once, but the fear he saw on the demon's face frightened him even more than the roar.

"It's about time," said the sorcerer when the growl receded. "It seems we're going to have some company."

Samuel's gaze jumped between the sorcerer, Angeline and the demon. The latter seemed to have lost all desire to attack Samuel, and was instead backpedaling toward the Acheron, its mouth open wide and its head lowered between its shoulders.

After a few more steps, the demon turned, opened its broad wings and rapidly flew over the dark river. It rose higher and higher, until it finally vanished over the horizon.

Samuel turned toward the valley of the dead as the ground shook beneath his feet. Next to Samuel, Angeline looked at him with eyes widened by fear, her skin whiter than snow. The sorcerer was no longer laughing. He turned to Samuel.

"As always, it has been a pleasure to see you, Samuel," said the sorcerer, the hissing and rasping voice barely hiding the irony of his words. "Unfortunately, I have to leave you. I have quite a busy schedule, and I need to respect it if I want to change this legend. I'm sure you understand. After all, we both have our orders to follow, right?"

"My orders are very simple," replied Samuel. "I only need to prevent you from succeeding."

The sorcerer gave a grating laugh. "Has no one ever told you that vanity is a capital sin?" he asked. "You speak as if you've already won, but in reality you're still just as lost as before."

"We know you're trying to kill a god," said Samuel defiantly.

"Congratulations," replied the sorcerer. "You must really be a genius to have come to that conclusion. Tell me, how do you think I will do it, exactly?"

"It doesn't matter," Angeline cut in. "We will not let you do it, whatever it is you plan on doing."

"Would you look at that," said the sorcerer. "Looks like she found a bit of courage. Be careful, you might think you're more powerful than you really are, little fata."

Samuel took a step toward the sorcerer, raising his sword.

"Don't you dare touch a hair on her head, or you'll regret it," he said, moving in front of Angeline.

The sorcerer threw back his head, and his laugh echoed on the shores of the Acheron. Samuel examined the Helm of Darkness his enemy still held in his left hand.

"We have to get back what is ours," he murmured to Angeline.

A new tremor shook the Underworld, along with another infernal growl that seemed to be coming from the bowels of Earth itself.

"How?" asked Angeline with a strangled voice.

Samuel had no idea.

"You're pathetic, Samuel," said the sorcerer. "As usual, you are swimming in the dark. You're lost in a fog of stupid rules and useless obligations. How do you hope to prevent me from fulfilling my mission, when you don't even know where Aeneas is at this very moment?"

The sorcerer raised the Helm of Darkness for all to see.

"And you've managed to lose the only advantage you had in our very first encounter!"

Samuel took a step toward the sorcerer, closely followed by Angeline.

"What use is this stupid crown to you anyway?" asked the sorcerer. "What did you intend to do exactly? Proclaim yourself king of Hades and recruit the help of its inhabitants?"

Samuel took another step, while the sorcerer had his eyes on the Helm of Darkness. With the hood constantly shrouding his face in darkness, it was impossible for Samuel to know if his enemy was looking at him or not. He risked his luck again and took another step forward. Behind him, Angeline brandished her tiny sword, ready to follow him when he launched his attack.

"Why don't you give it a try?" asked Samuel. "You'll see for yourself what the crown is capable of."

The sorcerer turned the Helm of Darkness before his face. Even with the knowledge given to him by the Yfel, he did not look like he knew what the helm was. Since the Yfel had no reason to think Apollo would help Samuel and provide him with the mythical artifact, the sorcerer's superiors had not thought it necessary to mention the Helm of Darkness.

"You think I'm stupid?" asked the sorcerer finally. "If you insist I put this thing on my head, it's probably because there's a catch. It doesn't take—"

His words were lost in another growl. This time, the scream came from just over the smoking hill in front of Samuel. Whatever it was that produced such howls was quickly approaching Samuel and the sorcerer. The latter had probably come to the same conclusion, since he quickly glanced over his shoulder. Samuel seized the opportunity and moved a little closer. He was now less than twenty feet from the sorcerer. A few more steps and he would be able to jump on him.

"Don't tell me you're scared?" said Samuel. "And here I was, thinking you were so dreadful and without any fear. Maybe deep down, you're just a coward who hides in the darkness of his hood to avoid being ridiculed."

"Don't speak nonsense," answered the sorcerer. "We both know I'm not scared of you, or anything for that matter."

"Then give me my crown and let's see which one of us comes out victorious," said Samuel.

The sorcerer raised the crown before his eyes again.

"You think yourself stronger than anyone," added Samuel, "but you're exactly like the rest of us. As soon as you find yourself facing the unknown, you're scared. You're terrified of facing what you don't understand."

Another tremor made Samuel's legs wobble. The sorcerer ignored it and observed the Helm of Darkness for a few more seconds. Then he turned to Samuel.

"You think I'm scared of you or this rubbish?" he said. "I'll show you what an Yfel sorcerer is capable of."

As the sorcerer raised the Helm of Darkness over his head, Samuel slid a foot forward and stepped closer to him. Behind him, Angeline was holding her breath.

As soon as the sorcerer placed the helm on the hood covering his face, his body was seized by overpowering tremors, and his limbs twitched uncontrollably. Samuel knew the onyx crown was attempting to take control of the sorcerer's mind using the fear of his enemy. Since he had not been through the same trials Samuel had to get the Helm of Darkness, he was not prepared to defend himself against the attacks.

The sorcerer cried out in horror, and his screams were echoed by a growl so powerful that the smoking hill shook behind him. Samuel almost lost his footing when the ground suddenly jerked beneath him, but he quickly regained his balance and leapt toward his enemy. As he grabbed a fold of the sorcerer's robe, the sorcerer threw the crown away and tripped over a rock. He immediately fell on his back, dropping his weapon.

Samuel seized the opportunity and jumped on him. Out of the corner of his eye, he saw Angeline rush to pick up the Helm of Darkness.

The sorcerer was struggling like a devil in holy water. For months now, Samuel had been trying to find out the identity of the sorcerer, and now his enemy was at his mercy. All he had to do was to extend a hand and pull back the hood. He would discover the face of the one hiding in darkness. He would learn the identity of the one trying to kill him.

Samuel hesitated for a moment. What if it was someone he knew? What if the sorcerer was someone he trusted? What would happen then? Would he have to kill him? Could he convince Angeline and Virtus the sorcerer did not deserve to die?

The cold laugh of the sorcerer pierced Samuel's ears.

"Poor Samuel," said the sorcerer. "Here I was, at your mercy, but you're too stupid to take the opportunity presented to you. Now your hesitation will cost you dearly, because you're going to have to let me go and run as fast as you can."

"What are you talking about?"

"Um … Samuel?" said Angeline in a quavering voice. "I … I think we should listen to him and not stick around too long."

Samuel turned to Angeline, being careful to keep his sword under the sorcerer's chin. The fata still held the Helm of Darkness in her little hands, but her eyes were wide with fear. As she took a step back, moving toward the furious waters of the Acheron, Samuel followed her gaze to the smoking hill. What he saw made him jump to his feet.

Ahead of Samuel, a gigantic dog was coming around the hill. The ground shook with each of its steps. The beast was as high as a house, and its immense body was covered in scales as dark as the night. Its powerful legs ended in claws that were each as large as a man, and its thirty-foot tail slashed at the air like the whip of a demon.

However, what was particularly horrible about the beast were the three heads trying to bite each other. Their mouths were open to reveal rotten, slimy fangs, between which he saw the decaying remains of their victims. Their blazing eyes scanned the area, searching for new prey.

Samuel took several steps back, and was immediately joined by Angeline. The sorcerer took advantage of the diversion and jumped to his feet, picking up his sword at the same time.

"Samuel, allow me to introduce you to Hell's watchdog, Cerberus."

He pronounced the name of the beast loudly enough to draw the monster's attention. As soon as it heard its name, the infernal dog turned all three heads toward Samuel and produced such a powerful growl it would have made the harshest demons run for cover.

"I'm sure you will be an excellent playmate," whispered the sorcerer, before he disappeared in a cloud of green smoke.

At that moment, Samuel understood he had never had the upper hand over his enemy. All this time, the sorcerer had been mocking him. He had merely been playing with the Lorekeeper, patiently waiting for the trap to close, and now, while Aeneas was traveling even farther away from him, Samuel had to face a monster straight out of the deepest abyss of Hell.

18

Every time to ground shook beneath her feet, Deiphobe's heart sank and her blood curdled. Every time a ferocious roar echoed from the shores of the Acheron, she was momentarily paralyzed by a gut-wrenching feeling.

Standing on the path leading farther into the Underworld, Deiphobe looked back at the landscape she and Aeneas had left behind. Despite the distance, she could see the tumultuous waters of the Acheron, as well as the black beach running alongside the river. She also saw the cursed, smoking hills on the left, one of which housed the lair of Hell's guardian, Cerberus—a beast so horrible even the gods did not dare come near it. Instead, they had sent a mortal to fight it, convinced that Hercules would fail in his task.

Why had she not warned the Lorekeeper of the danger lurking on the other side of the forbidden river? Why had she not prepared him to face such a frightening monster? But if she had done, would Samuel have agreed to follow them on this perilous journey?

Deiphobe chased away these questions, which she knew were useless anyway. The many years she had spent serving Apollo had taught her it was no use questioning the past. The Fates, who imposed their will on men and gods, had no obligations toward anyone. The sisters—Nona, Decima and Morta—tirelessly wove the life threads of mortals and immortals alike, measuring the desired length and cutting the cloth in the selected spot. Those who suffered from their work had no right to say a word about it. Therefore, it was useless to torture oneself with alternatives and "what if" scenarios.

If the Parcae had wanted Deiphobe to warn Samuel of Cerberus's presence, they would have whispered the words in her ear. For the same reason, if the Fates had not wished Samuel to fight the beast, Deiphobe's sleeping potion would have lasted long enough for the Lorekeeper and Angeline to pass by its lair without waking up the monster.

Unless, of course, Samuel had fallen victim to outside influences. After all, the Yfel had sent a sorcerer into Pluto's kingdom.

"Sibyl? Is everything all right?"

Aeneas's voice came from so far away that she thought for a moment the Trojan was now part of this place, just like the souls of the deceased passing by on either side of Deiphobe.

"Yes," she answered without turning her eyes from the hills.

Another growl from Cerberus shook the vale, sounding even more aggressive this time. The scream was filled with unbound hostility. There was no doubt anymore in Deiphobe's mind that Cerberus had noticed the Lorekeeper, and was probably charging at this very moment. All that was left for her to do was to hope Virtus had chosen the right champion, and that he would get out of this mess without too many injuries.

Unable to endure any more of this, she turned around and walked over to Aeneas, who waited a little farther down the road.

"Is something bothering you, priestess of Apollo?" asked the Trojan.

"Nothing that concerns us," she replied. "Let's keep going. We still have a long road ahead of us."

Fearing Aeneas would ask another question, Deiphobe stepped in front of him and hurried away. They could do nothing more for Samuel now. The Lorekeeper had to get rid of

Cerberus by himself and find a way to catch up to them on his own. After all, he was not the only one with a mission.

The path beneath their feet was covered in blue dust. To their right stood a dark forest, with trees that seemed to be made of ashes. From time to time, a tearful wail rose above the treetops, but Deiphobe ignored the cries of the tortured souls and kept walking along the path without so much as a glance in their direction. Across the road, fields of grass as high as a man stretched as far as the eye could see. On this side, not a sound could be heard. There were no moans or cries. Deiphobe hated this place, which reeked of death and sadness. She had heard horrible stories about the creatures lurking in the grass of these plains, and she thought it best not to stay longer than necessary in the area.

After a little while, the path veered to the right and climbed up a small hill. Once at the top, Deiphobe finally saw the first building of the Underworld, several hundred yards in front of them. It was not as sumptuous as Pluto's palace, but neither was it as scary as Tartarus's. Entirely made of black onyx, the building was about a hundred yards wide and over a hundred feet high. The facade was adorned with dozens of columns as dark as the night, aligned at the top of a series of stairs as wide as the building.

Above the structure, hundreds of winged creatures circled the area, keeping an eye on the crowd of souls passing between the onyx pillars and making their way inside.

"Tell me, priestess of Apollo. What is this dark place?" asked Aeneas.

"It's the court of King Minos," answered Deiphobe. "This is where the souls of the deceased are judged and sentenced according to the life they lived, the crimes they committed or the death they chose."

"They are judged based on the death imposed on them? Isn't that unfair?"

Deiphobe pointed to a group of souls on the right side of Minos's court. There, the ill-fated were expelled from the tribunal and cast directly into the raging waters of the River Styx, their screams muffled by the violent waves.

"You misunderstood me, Prince of Troy," said Deiphobe. "I said they were judged according to the death these souls have chosen while they still lived. This is what happens to those whose own innocent hands dealt them death, who flung away their souls in hatred of the light of day. See now how they would give anything to go back to the upper air and endure their poverty and sore travail, but the fate opposes it, and the waves of the River Styx lock them in the unlovely pools."

The Sibyl then pointed to the left of the courtroom. There, the souls of the deceased were pushed out of the king's tribunal against their will and led through the tall grass running along the path. Even from this distance, they could hear their screams and heartbreaking moans.

"And yet those who preferred the torments of the River Styx to the light of the sun can consider themselves lucky not to suffer the fate of the souls trudging down this path," said Deiphobe.

"Where does the path lead?" asked Aeneas.

"To Tartarus."

Deiphobe resumed her walk and went down the other side of the hill, toward King Minos's court. Behind her, Aeneas remained still for a moment, observing the poor souls condemned to spend eternity inside a prison from which none could escape, be it a god or a mere mortal.

"Come on!" shouted Deiphobe. "We've lost enough time as it is already."

The words were said in a tone that left no room for argumentation and Aeneas ran after her. Less than half an hour later, they were climbing the stairs to King Minos's court.

At the top of the onyx steps, Deiphobe pushed Aeneas between two pillars and into the tribunal. Glancing behind her, she saw a silhouette appear at the top of the hill. It was a man dressed in a long black robe, with a hood hiding his face, and Deiphobe immediately understood he was not the Lorekeeper.

Deiphobe looked at the sorcerer for a moment, cursed under her breath and hurried inside to join Aeneas.

Their enemy was on their heels, and there was not a second to lose.

19

Samuel dove into the black sand, barely avoiding Cerberus's sharp fangs. Behind him, the beast's jaws slammed against one another, like thunder rolling on the shores of the Acheron. One of its three heads produced a growl fit to wake the dead, while another stretched its neck toward Samuel. Boiling foam dripped between its fangs, and each time a droplet of the gooey slobber fell to the ground, a wisp of smoke floated over the beach.

Cerberus was deceptively fast for a beast its size, and with its three heads relentlessly attacking, Samuel was under the impression he was fighting a pack of angry wolves. He had hardly jumped to his feet when he needed to roll backward again in order to avoid one of the monster's paws. Samuel finished his tumble just before falling into the Acheron's dark water, and quickly moved to his right to get away as fast from the cursed river as he could.

"Angeline, if you have any bright ideas, now would be a great time to share them!" yelled Samuel.

The fata was circling Cerberus's three heads, trying to get its attention to provide a bit of a breather for Samuel. Unfortunately, each time one of the heads showed any interest, the other two remained locked on Samuel.

"You wouldn't have some honey cakes with you, by any chance?" asked Angeline.

"Honey cakes?" replied Samuel, as he lurched under the monster to avoid getting bit again. "What the hell are you talking about?"

"Forget it," said Angeline. "I think we should—"

"Careful!" yelled Samuel.

Angeline turned her head at the last moment, and just managed to avoid Cerberus's snake tail, which snapped violently next to her.

"What if we run away?" asked Angeline, catching her breath. "We'll never kill Cerberus."

"I doubt we could put any distance between us and this beast," answered Samuel.

"Okay then … why don't you put the Helm of Darkness on your head?" said Angeline. "Once you're invisible, you'll be able to flee without this horrible thing being able to follow you."

Samuel lowered his eyes to the onyx crown hanging from his waist. When Cerberus had appeared from behind the smoking hill, he had immediately tried to disappear by placing the crown on his head. Unfortunately, his action had had the reverse effect. Cerberus had immediately turned all three heads toward the young man, and had charged him without hesitation.

"The helm doesn't work on it," said Samuel.

"It must be because of the relationship between Cerberus and his master, Pluto, to whom the crown belongs. Watch out!"

Samuel raised his eyes just in time to jump to his right and avoid the monster's fangs again. He stepped behind Cerberus and quickly backpedaled toward the hills, farther from the boiling water of the Acheron. Hell's guardian quickly turned toward its prey, then let out a shriek that it seemed to freeze time for a moment. It pounced on Samuel again. Once more, the young man ducked to the ground to avoid the attack. Finding himself directly under Cerberus, he tried to hit the monster with his sword, but the skin was covered in scales as hard as steel. "How did the heroes of Antiquity beat Cerberus when they passed by this place?" asked Samuel as he hurriedly got back to his feet.

"Most of the time they put it to sleep with an offering of honey, or with music," answered Angeline, flying as fast as she could around the beast. "But since we do not have any cakes or a harp, I don't know how we can put it to sleep, or even distract it for a moment."

"So, you're saying no one has ever vanquished this monster?"

"Only one survived a direct fight against Cerberus: the demigod Hercules."

"If only Virtus had given me his prodigious strength," said Samuel. "My ability with a sword is completely useless against Cerberus."

Angeline dashed between the slimy fangs of Hell's guardian and soared like an arrow toward the vault, drawing the attention of two of the three heads.

"Did I hear you right?" she yelled to Samuel. "You're complaining about your powers?"

"No, that's not what I meant," replied Samuel, jumping back to avoid one of Cerberus's paws again. "I only said I would have liked the dice, or the Parcae, to give me powers that were more appropriate for—"

Samuel did not finish his sentence. Instead, he stayed still, his mouth partly open, and his look somewhere else. An idea had come to mind. He understood how to get rid of Cerberus.

"Angeline, I need you to get all of its attention for a few seconds," he said suddenly.

"Are you out of your mind?" yelled the fata.

"Please, do as I say."

Angeline sighed in protestation, and then she rolled her eyes to the sky and dove right for one of Cerberus's heads. Without stopping, her lips pressed firmly against each other, she lightly bent her wings and quickly straightened, passing just over the muzzle. As she did, Angeline kicked the monster right on the snout. Cerberus instantly roared in rage and tried to bite the fata with one of the two remaining heads. Angeline circled before the monster, diving for the ground, and then came back up along the beast's right flank. When she was close to the third head, which was still looking at Samuel, Angeline raised her sword and plunged the blade directly into one of Cerberus's large nostrils. Once again, the monster produced a howl to freeze the blood, and this time all of the beast's three heads followed Angeline's flight over the Acheron.

As soon as Cerberus turned to pursue Angeline, Samuel sheathed his sword, closed his eyes and quickly sat down on the black sand. Each second mattered, and it would be the only chance he would get to execute his plan. He could not afford the smallest hesitation. He had to trust Angeline and believe she would hold the monster's attention while Samuel was vulnerable.

He took a deep breath, focused on the air entering his lungs and emptied his mind. He forgot the smell of sulfur, the growls of Cerberus and the fear tangled in his stomach. He chased from his mind the images of Aeneas and Deiphobe fighting off the sorcerer on their own, or Angeline stuck in Cerberus's jaws. He slowly pushed the air from his chest, visualizing all his worries exiting his body as he did.

After a few seconds of relaxation, a pleasant sensation began to grow deep inside Samuel. It was a lovely warmth filling his chest, as if a stranger had built a campfire in front of him. This warmth quickly spread across his entire being and wrapped around him like a comfortable sheet, soothing his heart and soul.

After a little while, Samuel's body began to vibrate, as a new energy was flourishing in each molecule of his being. This energy converged from his limbs to his heart, and then rose to the top of his skull, ready to be directed.

Samuel then focused on the target he had chosen. With all fear gone, he summoned the image of Cerberus to his mind. He saw the infernal dog's three heads, its snake-like tail and the scales covering its powerful body. He even heard the roar of the monster.

When he had a precise image of the monster in his head, Samuel focused on the message he wanted to send Cerberus. He could not kill the monster, but maybe he could convince it they did not mean any harm. After all, he had connected with a dragon during his first adventure on Metverold. Getting in touch with a ferocious beast like Cerberus could not be that much more difficult. Still, he had to make sure he had the right message in his mind. Even the slightest mistake could mean Cerberus would misinterpret the message. The monster would immediately turn his attention on the one trying to invade his thoughts, and would charge him with a ferocity rarely seen in Hell.

Samuel could not have said how long he remained still, but after a while he held in his mind an image that seemed appropriate. It showed Angeline and himself, calm and smiling, without weapons, with their arms open. With this image, Samuel believed he would convey a message of peace and friendship with Cerberus. He hoped the monster would no longer see these two strangers as a threat, but rather as allies it needed to let through.

Once he was satisfied with the exact image he wanted to send, Samuel focused on Cerberus's picture. He fixed his attention on the middle head of the beast. In all likelihood, this was the one commanding the other two, as well as the entire beast. With his eyes still closed, Samuel created a link between the gigantic head and his own. The energy gathered at the top of his skull stretched toward the beast, until it became a conducting thread he could use to send his message.

As soon as the energy connected with Cerberus's mind, Samuel was violently assaulted by unbounded rage and a murderous madness. The dark spiral that boiled in Cerberus's mind almost propelled Samuel out of his trance state, but he managed to keep calm and control his fear. A few seconds later, he was able to cast aside the violent feelings of the monster, and he seized the image he had chosen a few moments earlier. Samuel sent this image along the conductive thread, right into Hell's guardian spirit.

Roars of rage echoed in Samuel's mind. Still, the young man remained immobile, with his eyes shut. The growls continued for a few more seconds, and then they diminished, and were replaced by grim moans and new cries of anger. Samuel understood the screams could only be heard by him. He was inside the heads of Cerberus. He had established a link with the beast, but had failed to deliver his message. Rather than calm the monster, Samuel's incursion into its mind had only enraged him more. Now Cerberus roared to push the intruder out of its heads.

Even worse, the ground suddenly jerked beneath Samuel, and he guessed the monster was no longer paying attention to Angeline.

Samuel dismissed the fear still trying to control his mind. He had successfully created a link with the monster, and although his message had not been interpreted the way he had hoped, he had to maintain the link.

He had to try again.

Samuel heard Angeline shout at him, but he could not decipher what she was saying. The ground shook more violently beneath him, but he did his best to ignore it.

He focused on his mission instead. He brought forth in his mind an image of Aeneas and Deiphobe, walking along a path in the Underworld. He tried to show all the importance these two characters had for Metverold and his own world. He concentrated on the Trojan and his descendants, joining images of the Romans and the Britons. He added the image of the Yfel sorcerer, closing in on the Trojan hero and the Sibyl, his silhouette hidden by the shadows. He gave his enemy a most menacing appearance, and went so far as to add an image of the sorcerer sneaking under Cerberus's snouts.

As a finishing touch, Samuel added his own image between the sorcerer and Aeneas. He was trying to make Cerberus understand he was not here to steal anything; that he was here only to protect the hero. He included Angeline next to him, as well as the god Apollo, who had given him the Helm of Darkness. He was trying to show the guardian of Hell he was not here to fool him in any way, and that he absolutely had to continue his adventure, since it was the will of the gods.

When he was satisfied with the result, Samuel sent the images along the link of energy he had created between Cerberus and himself, ignoring the growls and the tremor beneath him.

A few seconds later, the enraged screams vanished and the ground stopped jerking. Complete silence fell on the shores of the Acheron.

Carefully, Samuel opened his eyes, and his heart nearly jumped out of his chest.

Just a few inches from his face, Cerberus's middle head was watching him with flaming eyes. The monster's mouth was wide open, and long strings of slobber stretched between its teeth, a few inches from Samuel. Behind the head, the beast's sides were pumping furiously.

A little farther on, Samuel saw Angeline, her hands over her face and her skin pale.

Cerberus watched Samuel for a few moments that stretched to an eternity. The monster seemed to be wrestling with opposing feelings, not knowing anymore if it should do its duty and devour this intruder, or if it should let him go on his way so he could protect the one sent by the gods.

Finally, Cerberus took a step back, then another. It turned one of its heads toward the smoking hill housing its lair, and slowly walked in that direction. On the way, the other two heads tried to bite each other, displaying the conflict still raging in the beast's minds.

It was only when Cerberus disappeared from view that Samuel realized he had been holding his breath since he had opened his eyes. On the verge of passing out, he took a deep breath and welcomed the oxygen with full lungs. A second later, Angeline hurried to him and threw herself at his neck.

"I thought it was going to eat you alive," she said, her eyes glittering.

"I must admit that, for a moment, I thought the same thing," answered Samuel.

"How did you … I mean, what did you do exactly?"

"I only told the monster we did not want to harm it, and that we had no intention of bringing back a soul with us. I showed it we were only here to protect Aeneas."

"You told it that?"

"Yes, with my power of communion. Remember? You're the one who told me about the power, during our first adventure."

Angeline slapped her forehead. "Of course!" she said. "Why didn't *I* think of that?"

"I remembered the power was for communicating with animals, and since it had worked with the red dragon I thought it might work with Cerberus. It may be the most terrifying dog in the universe, but it's still a dog."

Angeline smiled at him with admiration.

"I'm so proud of you, Samuel. Well done!"

Samuel smiled back at her, then got to his feet and tied the Helm of Darkness at his waist.

"I can't take all the credit," he said. "If you hadn't kept his attention with your aerial gymnastics, I would never have had the opportunity to establish a link with it. You can be proud of yourself as well, Unshakable Angeline!"

The fata's cheeks turned bright red as she slid her sword back in its sheath.

"Come, we've lost enough time as it is," Samuel said. "The sorcerer already has a large lead on us and we must find Aeneas before he does."

Angeline nodded in approval and followed Samuel on the path leading farther into the vale.

After he had walked a few yards, Samuel stopped for a moment and glanced behind him at the Acheron and Cerberus's lair. He knew more horrible dangers awaited them in the Underworld, but no matter what they would face, he only wished for one thing at this very moment: that there was a way other than this one to get back to the world of the living.

20

After leaving the shores of the Acheron, Angeline and Samuel followed a road between, on one side, fields of grass as high as a man, and on the other a dark forest, until they reached the top of a small hill. There, Samuel saw a majestic building of titanic dimensions, built entirely of black onyx.

"This is King Minos's court," said Angeline. "This is where the souls of the deceased are judged according to the acts they committed while they were alive. The king weighs the value of their soul, and then he pronounces his verdict. Some are condemned to an eternity of suffering, but for the most part they are invited to follow the road to Elysium."

"What is Elysium?" asked Samuel.

"A peaceful place, where the worthy souls go to relax as they wait to be called to the surface again and start a new existence."

"The Romans believed in reincarnation?"

"Yes," answered Angeline. "They believed in the immortality of the soul. According to them, after a certain amount of time spent in Pluto's kingdom, the worthy souls and the souls of the sinners who had served their time could return to the surface. They would choose a body and destiny, drink the water of the River Lethe to forget their stay in Hell, and climb back to Earth."

"I thought Hell was reserved for criminals and sinners," said Samuel. "I thought the good souls were lifted to Heaven or some sort of nirvana, where angels and cherubs would agree to all their wishes."

"That's true for some religions," answered Angeline, "but in the Greek beliefs, as well as the Romans', each and every soul ended here, in the Underworld. For them, Hell is divided into several regions, where the souls are sent depending on the life they lived, to suffer the sentences dictated by Minos. As for the sky, it is reserved for the gods."

A few minutes later, Samuel and Angeline climbed the black steps leading to the court of King Minos, and then slipped between two pillars to access the tribunal's antechamber. Once inside, Samuel was astounded by the scene before him. Standing in the middle of a crowd of souls, he swept the gigantic room with his eyes, and tried to take in the immensity of the place. The building was impressive when seen from outside, but once inside the walls, Samuel had the feeling the enormity of the room was trying to impose its will on him. It was as if the anteroom had been designed to underscore how insignificant the mortals were compared to the gods. Men and women were only grains of sand slowly pouring inside a celestial hourglass, with no control over the moment they would fall to the other side.

Next, Samuel observed the souls pressing against him. Just like the crowd he had seen on Charon's wharf, this one consisted of men and women of all ages. Most of them had lived full lives, but others had been plucked from the light of the sun before they had even had a chance to leave the family nest. The hardest to look at were the young mothers, who had entered death with their children, condemned to carry the tiny bodies of their babies for all eternity. Samuel could not help but take pity on them, and wondered if it was not punishment enough for the poor women, no matter the actions they had committed while they lived.

Over the noisy crowd, a balcony encircled the vast room, and several bridges of onyx linked the two longest sides.

Hundreds of sentinels stood on the balcony, motionless and impassive, observing the crowd of deceased souls below. Samuel guessed they were the courthouse guards, since they were at least three times the size of an average man, were clad in golden armor and wielded spears and shields. When a small group of souls tried to force its way to the entrance of the tribunal, creating a moment of panic among the crowd, two of the guards pounced on them, and carried the rebellious souls through a door on the other side of the room.

"We will never find Deiphobe and Aeneas," whispered Angeline to Samuel.

Samuel had to admit she might be right. With the snail's pace at which the crowd was moving toward Minos's tribunal, they might very well never leave this room. Around them, thousands of deceased were trying to reach the front of the antechamber, where two large steel doors stood open. Samuel tried to see what was on the other side of the doors, but he was still too far away. He hoped the courthouse only had one antechamber, but he could be wrong. Maybe there were other rooms like this one, where lost souls piled on each other, like a crowd in a train station at rush hour, waiting for the human wave to carry them before the ultimate judge: King Minos.

Samuel glanced once more at the guards posted around the room. Had they spotted him? Did they know a living soul was walking among the dead? Or maybe, since he was still breathing, he was invisible to them. Samuel lowered his eyes to the Helm of Darkness at his waist. If he put Pluto's crown on his head, would he be invisible to the sentinels, and could he sneak through the front of the crowd?

He was dying to put the helm on his head, but he remembered the effect it had had on the harpies and on Cerberus. Rather than make him invisible, the Helm of Darkness had enraged those Samuel was trying to hide from. Considering the number of guards posted on the balcony and the impatient crowd around him, Samuel preferred not to risk it. He felt like he was standing in a barrel of gunpowder, and feared the Helm of Darkness would become the spark if he put it on his head.

"What do you suggest we do?" he asked Angeline.

"You should try to sneak to the front and cross the steel doors," replied the fata. "I'm sure the tribunal is just on the other side."

"Okay, but the sentinels will spot me. They might come get me if I make a fuss, like they did with the small group earlier. I broke free of a demon trying to carry me away once, but let's not push our luck."

"If you say so, but don't forget Deiphobe and Aeneas are counting on us. We have to find them before the sorcerer catches up to them. In fact, we will be lucky if he hasn't already got his hands on them. Our enemy has a good head start on us."

Angeline was right. Samuel could not stay still like this, shuffling forward with the crowd. The way things were going, he would spend the next year in the antechamber of King Minos's court. What's more, he was positive the sorcerer had not quietly waited for his turn to pass in front of Minos. His enemy had certainly forced his way across the crowd, and Deiphobe and Aeneas had probably done the same. After all, the storyline of this legend did not stretch for months.

Samuel decided it was worth trying his luck. If the other living souls had managed to move to the front without the guards grabbing them, he could do it as well. However, he did not dare to use the Helm of Darkness. After all, Aeneas and the sorcerer had not needed it. The trick was to move carefully, with calculated gestures. The sentinels were probably watching for any movement of panic amid the crowd. All he had to do was avoid creating a fuss that would generate a chain reaction.

Samuel took a step forward and pressed on the man before him. The man weighed at least three hundred pounds and obstinately refused to yield even an inch.

"Excuse me," said Samuel in a barely audible voice. "Sorry."

The potbellied man tilted his head and turned slightly toward Samuel, but refused to move. Fortunately, a woman who was standing to the man's right turned around as well, and Samuel quickly slipped his shoulder between her and the man. The latter sighed heavily in protestation, but quickly turned his attention back to the steel doors ahead.

Samuel smiled timidly at the women and slid in front of her, looking for another opening for his next step.

"Faster," whispered Angeline.

"I'm going as fast as I can," answered Samuel.

A young man in front of him moved aside to glance over his shoulder. As he looked at the Lorekeeper with questioning eyes, Samuel seized the opportunity to sneak in front of him.

For what seemed like an eternity, Samuel squeezed through the crowd and repeated the same ritual: he excused himself to those in front of him, slipped his shoulder between two souls, and dragged his foot on the black onyx floor. As he moved, he kept an eye out for the sentinels above. Once or twice, he thought one of them turned its head in his direction, but every time he was relieved to see it was only his mind playing tricks on him.

He had his eyes raised to one of the bridges crossing over the crowd when he suddenly hit a brawny man, who was at least two heads taller than Samuel. The colossus turned to him.

"Where do you think you're going like this?" he asked in a rasping voice.

"I'm really sorry," answered Samuel. "I didn't see you."

The giant leaned over Samuel. The young man briefly peeked around him and saw the steel doors less than twenty feet from where he stood.

"That's strange," replied the colossus. "Seems to me like you still have your eyes. Maybe they aren't working properly. Because if they are, I'm having a hard time believing you did not see me."

"I assure you I didn't see you. Please accept my apologies."

Samuel turned away from the man, fearing he would draw the attention of the guards. Unfortunately, the colossus did not intend to let him off the hook that easily, and caught him by the shoulder.

"Don't you dare turn your back on me, you little shit," said the man. "I think you were trying to sneak—"

Samuel did not let the man finish his sentence and elbowed him as hard as he could in the stomach. He'd had enough of these bullies trying to scare him, and he did not have time to waste. Although he had just set foot in the Underworld, Samuel had already fought three harpies, a demon, a sorcerer sent by the Yfel, and a giant three-headed hellhound. He would certainly not be stopped by an idiot who was used to scaring everyone with a twitch of his muscles.

However, Samuel had to be careful not to stick around too long. Already, the sentinels closest to him had turned their heads in his direction. Now they seemed to be evaluating if the situation required their attention.

"You're going to pay for this!" screamed the colossus, who had not seen the guards taking an interest in him.

He shoved aside a woman, who yelled sharply, and then pushed another man out of his way. Immediately, the other souls around them got their feet tangled and tumbled against one another, with screams of protestation echoing from the crowd.

Samuel hunched his back to hide among the souls and took advantage of the confusion to make his way to the steel doors. Out of the corner of his eye, he saw the sentinels swoop down on the colossus and the souls around him, but he hoped that once on the other side of the steel doors, he would be out of danger.

"Hurry up!" yelled Angeline behind him.

He only had a few feet to go now. Ignoring caution and subtlety, Samuel straightened up, shoved the surrounding souls out of his way, toppled a man with a gaping wound on his left side and jumped through the opening in front of him. As soon as he passed the steel doors, he turned to watch the scene unfolding behind him.

With relief, he saw the sentinels had only grabbed the colossus, and none of them was coming toward the steel doors. The colossus shrieked in horror and tried to free himself, but his efforts were in vain. A few moments later, he disappeared through a door on the other side of the room, which immediately closed behind him.

Samuel turned and hurried away from the steel doors. The sentinels seemed to have completely ignored him, but he preferred not to pull the devil's tail by staying too close to the antechamber.

Fortunately, this new room was less crowded than the first. Once he was past the initial bottleneck, Samuel was able to walk more freely and look around.

The room was almost as large as the previous one, with a ceiling of black stone almost a hundred feet high, and a gigantic chandelier hanging in the middle. A balcony ran along the perimeter of the room, and more guards were posted there, but they did not pay Samuel any attention. Under the balcony and along the center of the room, endless rows of wooden benches were arranged on each side of a red carpet, which was wide enough for five men to walk abreast. Unlike those in the antechamber, the souls here were not pressed against one another. Some of the deceased carelessly walked between the benches, but most of them sat on the wooden seats, quiet and motionless.

"Patrimus!"

The solemn voice seemed to be coming from everywhere at once, including the most secluded corners of Samuel's soul.

About thirty feet from Samuel, a man slowly stood and left the bench he was seating on. With sluggish steps, he dragged himself down the red carpet and walked toward the front of the room. A few souls turned around to watch him, but most were content to stay still.

Unable to quell his curiosity, Samuel stepped forward and moved a few feet down the central aisle. When Patrimus reached the end of the carpet, Samuel saw he was indeed in a tribunal, where souls were judged on their actions. Before Patrimus, in the middle of the praetorium, stood a desk at least twenty feet tall. Behind this desk, a giant with a long black beard leaned forward to study the puny man standing before him.

"It's King Minos," whispered Angeline to Samuel. "You saw images of his story on the golden doors at the entrance to the Sibyl's lair. He is the one who ordered the construction of the Labyrinth so he could lock the Minotaur inside."

Samuel had his eyes locked on Minos. The king listened to the man before him with a steady look. He was dressed in a black toga, over which cascaded his long dark hair and wavy beard. In his right hand, he held a gavel big enough to smash a house, and with the other he took a piece parchment from the top of a pile higher than the desk behind which he sat.

A few moments later, after he had heard Patrimus's arguments and studied what was written on the parchment, Minos robustly struck a piece of stone with the gavel and declared his verdict.

"Elysium," he announced.

Instantly the man before him burst in tears and thanked the judge profusely. A moment later, two golden sentinels appeared on each side of Patrimus and led him behind Minos, to tall, white double doors that opened in complete silence. As soon as the opening was large enough, Patrimus hurried between the two doors, which closed behind him. The two guards vanished in turn, and King Minos took another parchment from the pile.

"Ligeai!" he thundered.

This time it was a young woman who walked down the central aisle. Unlike Patrimus, she was shaking like an autumn leaf and took forever to walk up to the king. Samuel watched her for a while, and then swept the room with his eyes, studying the souls who waited for their name to be called.

"I don't see Aeneas and Deiphobe," he said to Angeline.

"And yet they had to come through this place," answered the fata.

"Could they have snuck under Minos's nose?"

"No, that's impossible. No one can get out of here without Minos seeing them. The doors won't open otherwise. Plus, the king did let them through, because he knows Aeneas is pure-hearted and the destiny awaiting him is crucial. As for Deiphobe, she is a poor woman who suffered all her life because of the gods. When she passes away, she will have a golden carpet leading her all the way to Elysium."

Samuel continued to observe the souls in the tribunal. At the end of the aisle, the young woman named Ligeai erupted in tears, throwing herself on her knees and shouting cries of supplication Samuel could not make out clearly.

"And what about the sorcerer? Do you think he also came through here?" asked Samuel.

"I don't know, but if he wanted to follow Aeneas, he had to come to King Minos's court. There's simply no way around it."

"I doubt his past actions would allow him through the white door leading to Elysium," murmured Samuel.

Suddenly the room darkened, and the silence became absolute. The chandelier's flames diminished until they were barely brighter than the embers of a dying fire, and the air turned as cold as a glacier.

"Tartarus!" thundered Minos abruptly, his voice echoing across the entire tribunal.

Upon hearing the verdict, the young woman before him screamed in horror and fell to the ground. Two horrible creatures appeared on either side of her, their bodies covered with blisters and their faces deformed by dozens of scars. They grabbed her by the arms and dragged her to a charred door on the left side of the courtroom. It opened with a screech, and the young woman was carried away through the door. When it closed behind her, an explosion made Samuel jump. Then the chandelier lit up again, and the tribunal returned to its normal state.

"I don't know what that poor girl has done to deserve being sent to Tartarus," said Angeline with a shiver, "but I thank the gods this legend doesn't force us to go there."

As Minos called forth another soul to appear before him, Samuel was still stunned by the scene he had just witnessed. The look of terror he saw in the eyes of the woman as she was being dragged to the door would haunt him for many nights to come.

A cold hand grabbed Samuel by the arm, startling him. He quickly turned and came face to face with Deiphobe's pale visage. The Sibyl's angry eyes were looking right through him.

"Where the heck were you, by the gods?" asked the woman. "I've been waiting here for over an hour!"

Before Samuel could answer, Angeline hurried between him and Deiphobe.

"And you—you could have warned us Cerberus would be awake when we got there!" she yelled, pointing an accusing finger at the Sibyl. "Or better yet, that Charon would not agree to carry Samuel across the river!"

"And what else? Do I have to do your job as well as protect Aeneas?" replied Deiphobe. "You are the ones in charge of protecting the hero, not me. It's up to you to make sure nothing happens to him."

Before Angeline could add fuel to the fire, Samuel broke in.

"Where is Aeneas?" he asked.

"Not far away," answered the Sibyl. "He is on his way to Elysium, but he stopped to chat with an old acquaintance. Under normal circumstances, I would have pressed him to keep going, but given the incompetence you're displaying, I had to improvise! I pretended I needed to make sure we were still on the right track, and stayed behind to wait for you."

"You left Aeneas by himself?" yelled Angeline. "You left him alone in the Underworld, with the sorcerer on your heels?"

Deiphobe rolled her eyes and planted both her hands on her waist.

"I am not the one responsible for his protection, fata. You are! I am merely his guide here. I'm already taking enough risks as it is by coming here and talking to you." Deiphobe paused for a second, pinched her nose, and looked at the souls around them. "Besides, the sorcerer isn't following us anymore," she added after a moment.

"What do you mean, he's not following you?" asked Samuel. "Are you sure?"

"It seems our enemy had other schemes in mind," answered the Sybil. "He entered King Minos's courtroom a few minutes after Aeneas and I did, but he did not exit through the white door like the Trojan."

Angeline's lips started to tremble.

"Which ... which door did he use then?" she asked, choking on the words.

Deiphobe turned to the left, and pointed at the blackened door through which dreadful creatures had carried Ligeai. "That one," she answered. "It seems to me that if you want to find out what your enemy is planning, you're going to have to enter Tartarus."

Samuel had just enough time to put both his hands under Angeline to catch her before she fell to the ground unconscious.

21

As soon as Angeline regained her senses, Deiphobe left Samuel and the fata to find Aeneas. Without waiting for the king to call her name, the Sibyl stood before Minos, so he would judge her and let the woman go on her way. Just like he did every time Deiphobe lived the legend, King Minos carefully studied her with his piercing eyes, then took a parchment from the pile to his left. Deiphobe had no clue what was written on the parchment, but as usual the judge indicated that she should exit through the white door and follow the road to Elysium.

When Deiphobe returned to Aeneas, she found him on the side of the road, in the midst of a conversation with the soul of a woman she identified as Eriphyle. The poor woman still bore the wounds inflicted by her perfidious son Alcmaeon, and Deiphobe could not help but smile in satisfaction as she thought about how the young man had paid for his crime and had been persecuted by the terrible Furies for his matricide. The three avenging sisters had pursued him relentlessly until madness seized his spirit.

To the west of the road leading to Elysium were the Wailing Fields, stretching to the blazing waters of the Phlegethon. To the east was a forest of thorny myrtles and weeping willows. This region of Pluto's kingdom was devoted to the souls whose hearts had been wounded by love, and its poison had led them to their demise. These poor shadows were sentenced to wander the gray grass and dark forest, with their aching hearts their only companions. Her journey in this region was a rare occasion when Deiphobe thanked the gods for having chosen her to be their voice on Earth. Her role as a Sibyl forbade her from knowing love, and every time she witnessed the tears eternally rolling down the cheeks of the souls around her, she thought herself lucky.

She reached Aeneas's side at the same Eriphyle was saying goodbye to the Trojan.

"What cruelty inhabits the gods, that they would punish this woman in this manner?" asked the hero. "Why don't they allow her eternal rest in the fields of Elysium rather than leave this poor soul to wander this way, with nothing but the memories of a doused love to keep her company?"

"It is not our place to question the wishes of the gods," answered Deiphobe. "Let's continue our journey, Prince of Troy. The road to Elysium is long."

Aeneas nodded and resumed his walk along the Wailing Fields, but he had not taken five steps when he stopped again. He had his eyes fixed on a soul at the fringes of the forest, and Deiphobe felt her heart constrict, since she knew what was coming for the hero. She would have given anything to prevent what had to happen, but it was not her right to do so. Aeneas had to face his destiny, and he had to witness the wounds left by his actions. These lessons would turn him into the man he was supposed to become: nothing less than the father of a glorious nation.

Aeneas seemed to hesitate for a moment, and Deiphobe hoped that maybe this time he would not recognize the woman who had given her life for his love. Maybe, for once, the gods would be merciful and would spare him the sadness that would be etched in his heart forever, but Deiphobe knew this hope was in vain.

Without warning, Aeneas darted toward the edge of the forest, where stood the soul of Carthage's dead queen, the beautiful Dido. The Trojan did not know Deiphobe already knew every detail of their journey in Hell, and that she had witnessed the lovers' reunion many times before. He did not know the mechanisms of the universe, nor the forces that battled each other on Metverold. In his mind, the only conflict that had had any influence on his world had been a war between the Greeks and the Trojans.

When the hero came to the soul of the woman whose beauty could give sight back to the blind, he grabbed her by the arm and made her turn to him.

"Poor Dido," he said. "I was not duped by the news. With the sword in your hand, you went to the end of your despair."

When the queen of Carthage laid her eyes on the one who was the cause of her misfortunes, her face remained emotionless, and she did not say a word or show any sign of surprise. Deiphobe's heart cried out in pain as she thought of the sufferings the poor woman must have endured. She had welcomed Aeneas into her home while the hero was going through his darkest hour. She had given asylum to him and his men, and had offered her body and heart to the Trojan hero. And he had taken them without holding back, until the gods intervened and reminded him of his mission.

"Am I really the cause of your death, then?" Aeneas asked Dido. "I swear by the stars, by the heavenly powers and by all that is sacred beneath the Earth, that I was unwillingly forced to leave your shores. It was the gods, who now force me to pass through this shadowy place, this land of moldering overgrowth and deep night, whose orders drove me forth."

Aeneas tried to meet Queen Dido's eyes, but the beautiful woman looked past him, her gaze fixed somewhere behind him, her face resolute and unchanging.

"I beg you to believe me, my queen," Aeneas said. "I could not foresee you would feel such pain at my departure."

This time, Dido shook her arm free of the hero's grip. Once again, Deiphobe's heart broke when she saw the gaping wound the queen still bore in her belly, where she had plunged the sword she had first offered Aeneas.

As soon as the hero let go of the queen's arm, she turned toward the forest, and then walked away between the trees, without glancing back even once.

"Stop!" the Trojan called. "Do not withdraw from my gaze. Is it me that you flee? I beg of you, do not leave like this, for it is the last time the Fates will allow me to speak with you."

But the queen kept walking. Aeneas's words did not move her any more than they would disturb marble from Paros. Just before she vanished into the forest's shadows, Dido returned to the soul of a man who Deiphobe knew was her first husband: the faithful Sychaeus, who had never stopped loving her.

"Come now, Trojan," said Deiphobe as she laid a hand on Aeneas's shoulder. "There is nothing you can say that will comfort her heart. We must continue our journey now."

Aeneas raised tearful eyes to the Sibyl, and then nodded. They quickly returned to the path crossing the Wailing Fields and resumed their travel toward Elysium.

As they walked, Aeneas turned his eyes to the west, and saw a mountain on the horizon, its summit hidden in ominous clouds. A tumultuous river encircled the mountain, and on the other side of the white waves stood a large, dark building. A colossal door guarded the entrance of the spine-chilling building, and from its roof sprang an iron tower that almost rivaled the mountain's height. At the top of this tower sat a most frightening woman. Her eyes were blindfolded, her head rested in her hand and she wore a bloodied gown. In her right hand she led a six-lashed whip.

Deiphobe stopped and turned her eyes to the cursed mountain as well. They could hear the cries of the damned locked inside the dreadful building, as well as the clash of their chains and the shrill sound of grinding metal.

"Tell me, priestess of Apollo, what crimes are punished in this place?" asked Aeneas. "Tell me the torments used to torture those sent there. What are the causes of the terrible wails coming to my ears?"

Deiphobe sighed deeply, and then she answered: "Illustrious leader of Troy, the divine laws forbid the pure man to pass this wretched threshold, but when Hecate entrusted me to watch over the sacred groves of Avernus, she also taught me how the gods punish those sent in this place. She told me that Rhadamanthus, brother of King Minos, holds ruthless power in this place. He sends to the torture chambers those who committed secret crimes, and he forces them to confess evil deeds they boasted to have hidden while they lived, and pushed back their atonement until it was too late. At his command, the avenging Tisiphone, armed with her whip, tramples on the shivering sinners and flogs them, summoning at the same time her merciless sisters. Only then do the cursed doors you see shriek and roll on their hinges with a horrible rattling. Inside, the monstrous Hydra stands guard, with six black, gaping mouths. It watches over the old sons of Earth, the Titans, vanquished by thunderbolt and hurled into the deepest abyss. Likewise, the Hekatoncheires, whose hundred arms have no equal in their strength, roam the cursed tunnels of the mountain, watching over prisoners like Aloeus's two sons, poor Salmoneus, and Phlegyas." Deiphobe paused for a moment, chasing the images of torture and torments she had seen more than once in her visions. "This place you see is Tartarus," she went on, "and even if I had a hundred mouths, a hundred tongues and an iron voice, I could not describe to you all the crimes that are punished within these walls; nor could I enumerate the many torments administered in its dark cells."

As she said these words, Deiphobe looked upon the road leading to this terrible place from King Minos's court. Somewhere along this cursed path, Samuel and Angeline were walking toward the most terrifying place in existence.

Deiphobe was never inclined to call upon the gods. She had enough of them whenever they took possession of her body.

However, in this moment, she prayed to those who were tasked with watching over the mortals.

She did not pray for herself, but rather for Samuel and Angeline, so they could find the courage to overcome this terrible trial that awaited them.

22

Samuel looked over his shoulder and saw the onyx walls of King Minos's courthouse. Since he and Angeline had left the tribunal, the charred wooden door had not opened again, and he wondered if it would open for them if they decided to turn back now. Angeline said a few times that no one had ever come back from Tartarus, but it was not every day someone willingly made the journey to this place. Maybe the king would make an exception and welcome them back if they turned around. Maybe he would even be relieved to see Samuel had regained his senses.

He saw again the surprise in King Minos's eyes when Samuel and Angeline had asked him to open the cursed door for them. The king revealed that a similar request had been made a few moments earlier. He had questioned Samuel on the reasons pushing him to follow the sorcerer to this place from which no one ever came back. Samuel had explained it was his duty, as the Lorekeeper, to find his enemy, protect the legend, and discover the Yfel's ultimate plan. Minos listened carefully to Samuel's words, and agreed to let them through. Fortunately, the king had not requested the help of the hideous creatures who had dragged the young woman through the same door.

Samuel looked at the mountain standing against the horizon. He did not like stepping out of the legend like this, but he, Deiphobe and Angeline had all agreed it was the best thing to do. If the sorcerer sought to enter Tartarus, it must be because he had a good reason to do so, and Samuel had to find out what it was, with Angeline's help. Until they returned, Deiphobe would keep an eye out for danger.

That is, if they ever did return.

"Do you think this detour is part of the sorcerer's plan to change the legend?" asked Samuel.

Angeline was sitting on his right shoulder, her eyes on the dusty path before them. Her little body jerked when she heard Samuel's question, and then she turned to him.

"I don't know," she said. "I must admit it's not a very rational thing to do on his part. It's almost as if he was trying to eliminate us, rather than attack Aeneas."

"That's what I think as well. He is trying to get rid of us, or at least slow us down. The sorcerer is leading us toward Tartarus to shake us off, and then kill Aeneas more easily. Unless he really does intend to enter Tartarus."

Angeline shuddered upon hearing the name of the dreaded place before them. Evidently this was the last place in the world she wanted to set foot in.

"If that's the case, it's a pretty lame plan. Even for a sorcerer of Yfel, Tartarus is a particularly dangerous place. He would be taking an enormous risk by entering simply to put some distance between Aeneas and us."

Samuel had his eyes locked on the enormous mountain before them, at the foot of which stood Tartarus. The clouds veiling its summit seemed to roll more ferociously with each step he took.

"What makes Tartarus so terrifying?" asked Samuel.

"Many things," replied Angeline. "To begin with, it's a place no one has ever escaped from. Once you're inside, you're a prisoner for eternity."

"If it's impossible to get out of Tartarus, what would the sorcerer gain by going in?"

"I don't know. Unless he plans to get outside help. For instance, the giants and the Hekatoncheires were among the first to be locked in the pits of Tartarus by the Titans, but they were freed by Zeus and the gods of Olympus, to help them in the Titanomachy."

"The Hekatoncheires?" asked Samuel. "Like the one we saw in the cavern of the Elm of Dreams?"

"Yes. They are giants much taller than those you faced on Albion, endowed with a hundred arms and unimaginable strength. In fact, because of their unmatched physical power, they are now the wardens of Tartarus. They roam the halls of the prison and oversee the punishment of the prisoners in this horrible place."

"Who are they, the prisoners of Tartarus?"

Angeline flew a little ahead and turned around without looking Samuel directly in the eye.

"They are the cruelest and darkest beings humanity has ever known," she answered. "Only those who committed the most atrocious crimes are sent to Tartarus, as well as those whose actions have put the entire world in danger."

Samuel stopped and looked at Angeline. "In other words, Tartarus is full of people who could provide precious help to the Yfel," he said.

Angeline paused in turn and put a hand over her mouth, her eyes suddenly wide.

"You're right!" she said. "Why didn't I think of that before? If the Yfel needs an assassin to kill a god, Tartarus is the ideal place to find one. Even if it were only to find new recruits for its fight against Virtus, the cells of Tartarus abound with monsters to fill their ranks. Now that I think of it, maybe the sorcerer really plans on entering the prison. Maybe he is the external help a soul needs to break free of this place."

Samuel resumed walking, though his steps dragged.

"So the sorcerer's real goal is to facilitate the escape of one of Tartarus's prisoners," he said.

"It would be an excellent reason for choosing this legend," Angeline said. "Along with eliminating Aeneas and the Romans from history—and probably the Britons at the same time—the Yfel could also count on a new assassin picked from among the most horrible beings that ever existed."

"What we need to do now is find out who the sorcerer intends on breaking free."

Angeline circled Samuel a few times, stroking her chin.

"We know the Yfel is trying to kill a god," she said. "The giant Aristaeus told you as much on our last mission. We also know the Yfel target may be one of Apollo's sisters, as he told you himself. That would mean she is one of Zeus's daughters—or one of Jupiter's, for the Romans—which makes her a powerful goddess. It would take someone at least as powerful to completely erase her from Metverold and from mythology."

"The Titans have already waged war on the gods, right? Maybe the sorcerer wants to free one of them."

"It's true that they already fought against the gods of Olympus, but the Titans lost the battle," answered Angeline. "The Yfel will probably want to recruit someone who hasn't known defeat already."

"Okay, but isn't that the case for most of Tartarus's prisoners?" asked Samuel. "No matter what each of them planned to do, if their schemes had succeeded, they would not be rotting away in a cell at the bottom of a prison where no one wants to go."

"You're right," said Angeline. "In that case, we cannot eliminate the Titans from the equation yet." She shuddered once more as a chill passed through her tiny body. "I must admit that I hope with all my heart we are wrong," she added. "If the Titans were to get free of their chains, it would be terrible for Virtus, but also for the Yfel. Those monsters are simply impossible to control. Their leader, Kronos, who was already half mad before spending several millennia at the bottom of the abyss, would be a true calamity for whoever tried to use him."

"Be that as it may, I still think we should not exclude them at this moment. Are there any other prisoners the Yfel could try to break free?"

Angeline made one last circle around Samuel, then took her usual place on his shoulder again. "The list of prisoners in Tartarus is long," she said with a sigh. "There is King Sisyphus, who was sentenced to push a boulder up to the top of a steep hill."

"That doesn't seem like such a terrible fate," said Samuel.

"Oh, but his torment doesn't end there. Each time he is about to reach the top of the slope, the boulder breaks free and rolls back down, and the king has to start all over again. Sisyphus's punishment is eternal frustration, since he will never manage to push the boulder all the way to the top."

"Still, I thought this place was more frightening than that. It doesn't seem *that* terrible."

"Oh yeah? All right, then. How about the torment Zeus imposed on the giant Tityos after the monster tried to rape Leto, Apollo's mother? The giant is stretched out in a cell in Tartarus, and two vultures constantly feed on his liver, which eternally regenerates. What do you say to that?"

"I'd say those birds are probably pretty obese by now," answered Samuel.

Angeline shot him a look. "It's not funny, Samuel! Tartarus is not a joke."

"All right, I'm sorry. I only wanted to lighten the mood."

Angeline looked at him for a moment, and then she smiled. "I'm sorry," she said. "I didn't want to use that tone with you. It's just that ... it's just that this place scares me like nothing else."

"I know," said Samuel. "I'm afraid too, but I remind myself we will be in there together, you and I. You'll be able to count on me, and I know you will do your best to protect me. It's much better than being alone in this cursed prison."

"You're right!"

"And I don't know who could protect me better than the Unshakable Angeline!"

"Nonetheless," said Angeline after a moment, "we will have to be on our guard. We must not forget that the sorcerer will certainly place a few traps for us along the way. If he plans to free a soul from Tartarus, he must know we will not let him succeed."

"We will be careful," said Samuel, grabbing hold of the Helm of Darkness at his waist. "And we still have Pluto's crown to help us, if need be."

Angeline nodded, and Samuel was relieved to see he had appeased the fata's worries, however slightly. Of course, she was probably still as scared as he was to set foot in Tartarus, but at least they might be able to do so without being overcome by fear.

They walked along the gloomy road for another half hour or so, until they reached a river of flames. Angeline told Samuel it was the Phlegethon, the river on the other side of the Wailing Fields that flowed parallel to the River Styx. According to a legend, the goddess Styx was in love with the god Phlegethon, but this love was forbidden by Hades—or Pluto, according to the Romans—and that was why both rivers ran their course without ever touching.

Fortunately, a stone bridge spanned the flaming river, and Samuel was able to cross safely to the other side. He did so hurriedly, however, fearing the soles of his sandals would melt on the burning rock.

After the blazing river, the road led down a vertiginous cliff, weaving between the rocky ledges and sharp walls. For more than an hour, Samuel and Angeline climbed down the steep slope toward the bottom of the valley, careful not to trip on loose stones. As well as avoiding the constant threat of falling,

Samuel also had to keep looking up, since more than one stone avalanche almost crushed them in their descent.

When they reached the foot of the cliff, Samuel and Angeline resumed their journey to Tartarus and went along a sinuous road that twisted and curved between boiling marshes and scrubby trees. Now, closer to the mountain, Samuel noted how gigantic it was. It occupied almost all of the horizon, and the summit was so high it was impossible for him to see the storm raging at the top. No vegetation had taken root on the barren sides of the mountain, and its stark appearance was only matched by the desolation at its base.

At the foot of the mountain, Tartarus stood in all its horror. From this distance, Samuel thought the Titans' jail was probably ten times the size of King Minos's court. Thousands of gargoyles with blood-freezing faces were aligned along the massive structure, and clear water poured from their twisted mouths, down to a foaming river.

"Those are the tears of Tartarus's tormented souls, feeding the River Cocytus," said Angeline.

Two impenetrable doors guarded the entrance, and a tower of iron rose over the prison. At the top of this tower was a woman with frightening features, blindfolded and dressed in a bloodied gown. She was sitting motionless, and Samuel did not dare imagine what would happen if she suddenly woke up.

"Who is she?" he asked in a strangled voice.

"Tisiphone," answered Angeline, her voice trembling. "She is one of the three Furies, the avenging sisters who persecute those who committed horrible crimes. The Furies plague their victims until they take their own lives, and then they torture them in the Underworld."

This time it was Samuel who shuddered. Tisiphone was particularly eerie and terrifying. Her hair was made of vipers and a six-lashed whip in her right hand still dripped with the blood of her last victim.

"I have this feeling that I've already seen her somewhere," whispered Samuel, fearing to draw the attention of Tisiphone.

"Yes. The Furies are represented by a statue in Hades' antechamber, which we crossed to get here. It was the room right before the cavern of the Elm of Dreams. The statue showed the three Furies screaming into the ears of a poor man, pushing him to commit suicide."

Samuel remembered the statue she was referring to, and thought the image sculpted by the artist did not give justice to Tisiphone's terrifying appearance. He did not dare imagine what kind of terrors inhabited the poor souls pursued by the Fury and her sisters.

Suddenly, Tisiphone raised her head and let out a shriek that forced Samuel and Angeline to cover their ears with their hands. Still screaming, the eldest of the Furies jumped from her metal seat and down in front of the two rusty doors of Tartarus. Only then did Samuel see the sorcerer's silhouette in front of the black building.

Before his enemy could move, Tisiphone pounced on him like a lioness on her prey and pinned him to the ground. With one hand she held him down, and with the other she struck him with her whip, its crack echoing across the barren land. A few moments later, Samuel heard a chilling screech that petrified him, as the gigantic doors of Tartarus rolled open on their hinges. As soon as the space between the two doors was sufficiently wide, two women lurched outside, stepping on one another. Their appearance was just as repulsive as Tisiphone's, and Samuel realized they were the two remaining Furies.

Without wasting a second, with quick and precise movements, Tisiphone's sisters grabbed the sorcerer and rapidly dragged him inside. Curiously, the sorcerer did not scream in terror and allowed himself to be dragged without much resistance. Samuel thought his capture was probably part of his plan, and his stomach turned to knots thinking he would also need to suffer the same fate to follow him inside Tartarus.

When the doors closed with a deafening clap of thunder, Tisiphone stopped her shrill screaming and flew back to her metal throne. There she sat again, leaned her head in her left hand and promptly fell asleep once more, waiting for her next victim.

Samuel swallowed hard, thinking that would be him.

He could not have said how long he remained still, petrified by the scene that had just unfolded before his eyes. On each side of the road, bubbles of mud burst across the marsh, while unknown insects threatened them with their incessant chirping. After a few more minutes, Angeline finally broke the silence.

"Samuel, are you still willing to follow the sorcerer?" she asked.

"Unless you have another idea to prevent him from breaking someone out of Tartarus, I don't think we really have a choice."

"We could wait for him to get out," suggested the fata. "Maybe with a bit of luck, the wardens of Tartarus will do their job and keep him locked in there forever."

Samuel turned his head slowly and looked into Angeline's eyes.

"Do you really believe it's possible?"

"No, not really," she said, lowering her eyes. "The Yfel would not have sent him here if they were not sure he would succeed."

"That's what I think too. We don't have any other choice but to go in."

Angeline lifted her head and looked at the somber building. She took a deep breath. "Well then, let's go," she said. "But I beg of you, do not leave me alone inside this place."

"You don't have to worry. As long as we're together, I know we can do this."

With renewed confidence, and a courage bolstered by Angeline's presence by his side as well as the Helm of Darkness tied to his waist, Samuel moved toward Tartarus with his head held high, ready to face the dangers inside the prison.

Standing in front of the doors to Tartarus, which were at least a hundred feet tall, Samuel realized that the only way he was going to get inside was to wake the Fury and get dragged in by her sisters.

Angeline looked at Samuel with worried eyes, and he knew she had come to the same conclusion. At least she would not have to suffer the wrath of the Furies. Angeline would be able to slip inside as soon as the doors opened even slightly. Samuel, on the other hand …

He preferred not to think of the lashes he would have to endure, and focused on his mission instead. He had to stop the sorcerer before it was too late. His heart was racing and his hands were clammy. He nodded to Angeline, then raised his eyes to Tisiphone. The Fury was still asleep, waiting for her next victim.

Samuel took a deep breath and opened his mouth to call out.

"I wouldn't do that if I were you."

Samuel's heart nearly slipped through his lips when he heard the voice behind him. Fortunately, his scream remained stuck in his throat. Slowly, he turned around.

A man was standing close to him, staring into his eyes with a piercing look. He had long gray hair dangling below his knees and a braided beard that fell over his chest. He was wearing a purple toga and held a golden scepter in his right hand. With the other, he was stroking his beard, studying the young man before him.

"Unless, of course, you want to be on the receiving end of Tisiphone's lashes," the man said. "Some people are into that sort of thing, after all."

"Who are you?" asked Samuel.

The man opened his arms. "Where are my manners? Let me introduce myself. I am Rhadamanthus, son of Zeus and king of Crete. If you are here, it means you have already met my brother, King Minos." Rhadamanthus bowed lightly. "Well, I *used* to be the king of Crete," he added. "Nowadays, I'm only a judge in Pluto's kingdom."

Angeline flew in front of Samuel and addressed the man in a quavering voice.

"I thought Minos was the judge of the souls," she said.

"My brother is the first judge, but he is not the only one. He sends the souls of the deceased to all corners of Avernus, but he is not flawless. Sometimes he sends to these parts souls that do not belong between the walls of Tartarus." Rhadamanthus studied Samuel from head to toe. "Like you, for instance," he said. "Not only are you not dead, but you also don't belong in there, Samuel."

"How do you know my name?"

"I know many things about you, now that you stand before me."

"Your brother did not make a mistake with Samuel," Angeline cut in. "He let us through because we have a mission to accomplish."

Rhadamanthus did not break his stare on Samuel, which made the young man uneasy.

"You seek to follow the Yfel's sorcerer inside Tartarus," said Rhadamanthus. "Why is that?"

"Because I need to prevent him from finding what he wants," answered Samuel.

"And what do you think he wants?"

"We believe he wants to break out one of Tartarus's prisoners," answered Samuel.

Rhadamanthus raised an eyebrow and a smile appeared on his lips.

"Impossible," he said. "No one gets out of Tartarus without my consent, and even a decree from the gods cannot force my hand. Your enemy is seeking something else."

"What is he looking for, then?" asked Samuel.

"That I do not know," replied Rhadamanthus. "All I know is that he came here and asked me to open the doors for him.

After reading his soul, I concluded his place was among the prisoners and agreed to his request. This man's soul is darker than most of those inside Tartarus. However, you don't belong here, Samuel. You don't deserve to be locked away in Tartarus and suffer the torments dispensed between these walls. Turn and walk away without looking back."

Rhadamanthus's suggestion was certainly tempting, but Samuel could not turn back. He had to follow the sorcerer, even if it meant going to the bottom of the abyss.

"Believe me, nothing would please me more than going home," he said after moment. "But it's impossible. I must prevent my enemy from succeeding, or both our worlds could be changed forever. If the sorcerer finds what he is looking for, everything will be lost."

Rhadamanthus burst out laughing. Immediately, Samuel raised his eyes to Tisiphone. The Fury was still sleeping on her metal throne.

"Samuel, you may be Virtus's chosen one, but you still have so much to learn," said Rhadamanthus. "No one can get out of Tartarus, period! It's impossible. The doors only open when Tisiphone orders it, and the prison walls are impenetrable." Rhadamanthus raised his scepter toward the stone building overshadowing Samuel. "What you see here is only Tartarus's entrance," he added. "The real prison is located beneath the mountain, buried under millions of tons of rock. The first level alone is several hundred feet beneath the surface, and I'm not even talking about the wardens roaming the tunnels. What's more, even if a soul managed to escape their vigilance, it would have no chance of finding its way out of this place. It's a labyrinth that would make the ingenious Daedalus turn green with envy. You can trust me, Samuel—the Yfel sorcerer is never getting out of this place. Our two worlds have nothing to fear anymore."

Samuel wanted to believe Rhadamanthus. He wanted nothing more than to trust that the walls of Tartarus would hold the sorcerer for all eternity and would prevent him from killing a god, but he could not. A voice deep in his soul was saying the sorcerer would not make such a mistake. He would not willingly throw himself into a hole he could never get out of. The sorcerer had to have a plan to recover his freedom, and Samuel could not run the risk of letting his enemy win.

"Your Majesty," he said, "I have no reason to doubt your words, or your prison's efficiency, but I still ask that you let me enter Tartarus. I've fought my enemy several times already, and if there is one thing I am absolutely sure of, it's that he always has a plan. If he offered himself to you this way, it's because he is confident he can find his freedom again, and if he gets what he wants and escapes, then the life of a god will be in danger. I must get into Tartarus."

Samuel could hardly believe he had said the words. Rhadamanthus watched him for a moment, still stroking his long, braided beard. He seemed to weigh Samuel's words. Since the dawn of time, no one had escaped the prison by himself. For Rhadamanthus, the idea that one could even think it was possible was pure madness. But on the flip side, he had to know Virtus would not have sent Samuel after the sorcerer if it was not crucial to the survival of this world.

Finally, Rhadamanthus made a decision.

"All right," he said. "If that is your wish, I will let you enter, but I must warn you, the same rules apply to all the prisoners of Tartarus, including you two. Once inside, I will have no means of helping you. No one will be able to come to your aid. You will be prisoners of Tartarus, just like every other soul already locked inside. You will spend all eternity between the walls of the most terrifying prison that ever existed. Are you absolutely sure you want to enter, knowing all this?"

Samuel nodded. Angeline flew closer, placed her tiny hand on his shoulder and nodded as well.

"Then it is decided," said Rhadamanthus.

He opened his arms and the screeching of the doors made Samuel's heart jump. The young man quickly raised his eyes to Tisiphone, sure that she was pouncing on him at this very moment, but to his surprise the Fury was still sleeping.

"Congratulations, Samuel," said Rhadamanthus. "You will be the first to pass through these doors on your two feet. What a shame you won't be able to get out the same way."

Samuel looked at Angeline. She nervously nodded once more and took out her sword. They were ready. Samuel took a step toward the doors. When he stood on the threshold, he paused for a moment, and looked behind him one last time. He could not help himself, but smiled a little bit as he thought he would give anything to stay in Hell rather than continuing his journey.

"One last thing," said Rhadamanthus. "Once inside, know that you will be at the mercy of my other brother, Sarpedon. He is in charge of overseeing the prisoners' punishments, but no one has seen him for centuries. It's impossible to foresee how he may react upon seeing you, but if I were in your place, I would do my best to avoid him."

"Thanks for the warning," Samuel said.

Without ceremony, he stepped over the threshold and into Tartarus. As the hinge moaned and the doors closed behind him, Samuel glanced one last time at Rhadamanthus.

"Good luck, Samuel," said the king.

Then the doors banged shut, sealing Samuel's fate.

23

After a little while, the screams of Alecto and Megaera became almost bearable, and the sting of their long, crooked nails in the sorcerer's flesh was reduced to an insignificant distraction. He could even tolerate the cold stone hammering against his feet and knees. However, what he was unable to accept, what made him suffer down to the deepest part of his soul, was the humiliation of being dragged like a common thief.

He had been sent here to help them, and these two hags, as horrible as they were stupid, had lugged him across the corridors of Tartarus as if he was a vulgar criminal.

If they only knew the truth, they would treat me with respect and admiration, thought the sorcerer.

But the two Furies did not know who he was, and he could not tell them anything. It was one of the rare rules the Yfel had imposed on him. He was free to do as he pleased to change the legend, but it was absolutely forbidden to reveal anything to the three infernal sisters.

In order to forget the embarrassment he had to endure at the moment, the sorcerer focused on the Yfel's ultimate goal. He wondered what would happen to the world after the universe had been put back on the right track. What the Yfel planned to do was so significant it was impossible to predict the consequences of their actions, but one thing was for sure: he would have a prominent place in this new world, where the sinners would be punished with justice, and where debauchery would be eradicated.

But for now, the sorcerer had to bite his tongue and suffer the humiliation.

For over an hour, Alecto and Megaera dragged him across the dusty floor, carrying him deeper into Tartarus. They climbed down hundreds of steps, crossed dozens of corridors and passed by thousands of doors, until finally they arrived at an empty cell. With surprising force, the two horrible women shoved the sorcerer to the back of the cell, and then rushed inside after him. With a vicious grin on their faces, the Furies stepped toward the sorcerer to inflict the first of many sufferings he was entitled to—just a little taste of what eternity had in store for him.

But before Alecto and Megaera's bony fingers could grab him again, the sorcerer dug into his robe and produced a dagger with a wavy blade. He immediately placed the weapon between himself and the Furies, and showed the two women the hilt of the dagger, sculpted in the image of three ancient gods, long forgotten by men. A green glow appeared along the blade, and then it spread across the floor and walls of the cell, revealing filthy chains and a pool of fresh blood on the stone.

As soon as they saw the light, the two Furies shrieked in horror and cowered in the corner, trying to protect themselves from the light with their feeble hands.

The sorcerer smiled in the shadow of his hood, satisfied with the effect produced by the antediluvian weapon. The Furies were revolting creatures of ancient mythology, and they were among the most terrifying beings the world had ever known. Once, they had been renowned for their unbounded ferocity and total lack of compassion. Now, two of them writhed in pain at his feet. Of course, the dreadful women were not at the peak of their power, and the strongest of the three, Tisiphone, was absent, but the sorcerer still drew satisfaction from seeing these women who had disrespected him suffer.

"That will teach you to toss me around like a vulgar thief," he spat at the Furies. He took a step toward them, and the two horrible women clutched each other, their faces twisted by fear. "Now, you will listen to me carefully," said the sorcerer. "You will do exactly as I say, or I will not hesitate to use this dagger."

He was bluffing, of course. He could not harm them—not with dagger, nor with anything else for that matter, but the Furies did not know this. They had forgotten who they truly were.

This is all going to change soon, thought the sorcerer.

"For starters, you will get me out of this rat-hole," he said. "Then you will lead me to one of your prisoners. You will bring me to the one who knows the secret to the gods' immortality."

24

Samuel thought he had set foot in another world, or had entered an unknown dimension, completely different from the one he was coming from. It was as if his steps had taken him outside the universe, and he was now stuck between two worlds, in a space that time and light did not dare to approach.

Even before he had moved a muscle, Samuel regretted his decision to follow the sorcerer into this sepulchral place. Claustrophobia pushed against his mind and whispered that, in this place, the laws regulating the exterior world did not apply. He was now in a unique universe, reduced to the space between these walls, where anything could happen and nothing was certain.

A purple glow pierced the darkness to Samuel's right. When the shadows fled before the light, he thought he heard frightened cries. Inside Tartarus, darkness ruled, and it did not appreciate that its reign was contested.

Without saying a word, Angeline raised her tiny blade toward Samuel. When he looked into the fata's face, he thought for a second someone had kidnapped his friend without his knowledge, and replaced her with a more sinister version. Her cheeks were hollow, and she had shadows beneath her eyes. Her nose seemed to be longer, and her lips were so pale they looked ice cold.

When he saw the look Angeline gave him, Samuel realized he must not look any better.

He took out his sword as well and raised the blade toward the fata. Angeline placed a hand on the cold metal, and a moment later a purple glow spread across Samuel's weapon, illuminating the room they stood in. Samuel took a few cautious steps forward.

The purple light revealed that they were at the entrance of a titanic hall, encircled by a wall that disappeared in the darkness overhead. A dozen archways in the wall provided access to dark passages. The arches were so high that the tallest giant could have walked under them, and Samuel shivered thinking of the creatures roaming the halls of this cursed place.

In the center of the hall stood the statue of a man. He had a beard cascading down to his knees, a head as smooth as marble, and a stone hammer in his hands. His body was covered with a long toga, and his face admitted the new prisoners of Tartarus with a look of eternal rage. His gaze plunged into Samuel's eyes, and though it was only a statue, each hair on the young man's body stood on end.

Angeline flew a little bit ahead and attentively examined the area. Floating six or seven feet above the ground, she turned her head in all directions, looking for a familiar detail, or a sign to bring her some comfort.

But there was no comfort to be found in Tartarus. The place breathed anger, suffering and damnation.

"What do we do now?" asked Samuel.

"We have to find the sorcerer," said Angeline, looking up to the hidden vault and peering into the archways.

"The question is: which of these tunnels did he use?" she said.

Samuel walked to the center of the room, but was careful to remain at a distance from the statue in the middle of the hall. He had the feeling the stone eyes were following his every move. "We know that two Furies brought him here," said

Samuel. "There has to be a main corridor they use to carry their prisoners farther in, before throwing them into a cell."

Angeline flew a little higher, and the light from her sword brightened the wall around them a little more. When she passed close to the statue's face, Samuel's heart clenched, thinking the man would suddenly come alive and catch the fata in his stone hand.

Fortunately, the statue remained perfectly still.

Samuel walked away from it and toward one of the arches. Once he was close, he studied the work on the stones around the opening. Hundreds of symbols were carved there, and when he saw dried blood on some of the ancient runes a shiver tickled the back of his neck.

"Do you understand anything these symbols say?" he asked Angeline.

She did not answer, and seemed to be hypnotized by a face sculpted over another archway, about ten yards from Samuel.

"Angeline!" he repeated, a little louder. "Can you read these runes?"

As soon as he said the words, Samuel felt a pinch in his gut. He had tried to keep his voice in check, but his words echoed down the black tunnel before him, until they vanished in the darkness.

Samuel held his breath, not daring to move a muscle, his eyes locked on the passage.

Just as he was going to let the air out of his lungs, a distant growl came to his ears, like an answer to his shout. Then a second shriek echoed, similar to the first. It was immediately followed by a third, and then a fourth, each as frightening as the first.

Something had heard his call, and their presence was no longer a secret.

Another roar came from within the tunnel, and Samuel was certain the creatures making the shrieks were quickly approaching.

"Angeline?" he whispered in a trembling voice. "Angeline, could ... could you come here for a second?"

The fata flew up to Samuel.

"What's going on?" she asked.

Her voice was barely louder than a whisper, but Samuel felt as if every soul in Tartarus had heard it.

"I ... I think we have a problem," he muttered.

Angeline opened her lips to ask what he was talking about, but she was interrupted by two simultaneous growls that blocked the words in her throat. Her face turned pale, and the light from her sword started shaking.

"What ... is ... that?" she asked.

"I was hoping you could tell me," replied Samuel.

New shrieks tore through the tunnel's darkness, louder this time. The creatures, whatever they were, would soon be here.

A tremor shook the rocky ground.

"We can't stay here," whispered Angeline.

"I agree," answered Samuel, before turning and sweeping the hall with his eyes, "but which tunnel are we supposed to use?"

Angeline darted like an arrow, just as another batch of growls echoed behind Samuel. She quickly passed before each tunnel, stopping briefly to study the darkness in the last one, but rapidly abandoned the idea. It was impossible to see where the tunnels led. When the ground jerked again beneath his feet, Samuel ran away from the arch as well and to a tunnel on the other side of the room.

"This way," he said, without any reason to explain his choice other than the fact it was the tunnel farthest from the horrible growls.

Angeline dove straight for him and stopped just over his head.

The ground shook again, with more force this time.

"I don't know," said Angeline. "I can't see anything."

She flew from one arch to the other, and Samuel saw in her panicked movements that fear was taking control of her will.

"I don't know where to go!" she yelled, her voice strangled by tears.

Half a dozen shrieks answered her. The creatures were now very close. A few more seconds and they would appear in the hall. The ground shook with more violence, and the tremors were coming at a faster pace. There was not a moment to lose. Samuel and Angeline had to make up their minds.

But before they could move, a snake head as big as a man appeared under the stone arch, and it was only by a miracle that Angeline avoided the fangs snapping next to her.

"Angeline!" cried Samuel.

Another snake head passed through the arch, identical to the first, followed by a third one, which turned toward Samuel, and then the foot of a dragon shook the ground, its claws sending bits of stone flying. When the rest of the beast's body appeared under the arch, Samuel saw he had made a mistake thinking more than one creature were coming at them. In reality, there was a single creature with many heads, and he immediately recognized the Lernaean Hydra he had seen in the cave of the Elm of Dreams.

Only this time, it was not an illusion. The hydra trying to devour Angeline was real.

As three more heads appeared under the arch, followed by the scale-covered body of the monster, Samuel turned to the first tunnel he saw, without take time to notice which one it was. He and Angeline did not have the luxury of choosing anymore. They had to flee.

"Angeline!" he shouted again. "Let's get out of here!"

The fata did a few spins and rolls to avoid the hydra's attack, and then she flew ahead of Samuel and into the dark tunnel. Samuel glanced one last time over his shoulder, barely avoided one of the hydra's mouths, and hurried after Angeline.

Samuel ran as fast as his legs allowed, without daring to look behind him. His heart was beating furiously and sweat stung his eyes. Behind him the hydra roared, and the ground shook with every step it took. Farther ahead, Angeline's silhouette was speeding a few feet above the ground, visible only because of the purple glow of her sword. Samuel kept his eyes locked on her, since he did not want to imagine what would happen if he lost her and found himself alone in this dark place. Like him, Angeline never turned her head to see how far behind the hydra was.

For what seemed like an eternity, they went deeper inside Tartarus, always getting farther from the sealed door at the prison's entrance. Every time Angeline chose to make a sharp turn into a new tunnel, rather than follow the one they were in at the moment, Samuel knew they were only getting more lost in this labyrinth, and their chances of ever getting out were quickly vanishing.

Along with the dozens of corridors they crossed in their escape, Angeline and Samuel passed hundreds of doors, most of them closed and probably locked. More than once, Samuel heard screams of terror and supplications, but they were always muffled by the hydra's shrieks.

"Don't slow down!" yelled Angeline, daring to look over her shoulder for the first time. "We're starting to lose the monster."

The fata's words gave some hope back to Samuel, and he ran with everything he had left. A few moments later, they turned into a small, dark passage, and then through a large open door on their left. Without thinking twice, Angeline and Samuel were turning here and there, trying to lose the hydra in Tartarus's maze.

Finally they arrived in another hall, just as big as the one at the prison's entrance. In the center of the room, where the statue of the old man had been in the first hall, a set of stone steps at least thirty feet wide went down to the lower levels. The wall that encircled this room was adorned with dozens of torches producing blue or green flames. A single large archway led to a new passage.

"This way!" yelled Samuel, without taking the time to study the room.

He hurried down the stone staircase. The steps were almost three feet high, chiseled straight into the rock, and their surface was as smooth as marble. Samuel quickly jumped from one step to the other, being careful not to trip. If he were to take a tumble here, he would certainly break his neck in the fall.

The stairs went down in a spiral toward the depths of Tartarus, and when they had made a complete revolution around the central pillar, Samuel stopped for the first time, unable to take one more step. His lungs were burning like hot coals, and the pain in his sides felt as if he had repeatedly been stabbed. He leaned on the cold stone and tried to quiet the drumming of his heart.

A few seconds later, he heard the monster enter the hall and move to the stone staircase. Samuel cautiously peeked toward the top of the stairs. There he saw the horrible beast, its six heads constantly fighting each other, stopping only to sniff the air and search for their prey. For several seemingly endless minutes, the hydra stayed at the top of the staircase and searched for Samuel's silhouette. Once or twice it almost climbed down the first step, but each time it hesitated. After a little while, the hydra erupted in a chorus of spiteful howls and exited the room through the tunnel it had come from.

Only then did Samuel realize he had been holding his breath the entire time. Muffling the noise with his elbow, he quietly exhaled and took in a new breath of foul air. The stench immediately attacked his throat, and he had to suppress a violent cough.

"Did you notice how the hydra hesitated to come down the stairs?" Samuel asked Angeline. "It's almost as if it was scared of following us down here."

Angeline looked toward the bottom of the staircase. "Maybe we shouldn't go down this way then."

Samuel watched her for a moment. The poor fata was terrified. Tears made her purple eyes shine like stars, and her lips trembled. He also feared the monsters roaming the lower levels of Tartarus, but so far he had been able to contain this fear. The trials he had overcome to master the Helm of Darkness had opened his eyes to his true fears, for which he quietly thanked Apollo.

"Don't worry, Angeline," he said, as calmly as he could. "As long as we're together, you have nothing to worry about. I won't let anything happen to you. You have my word."

Angeline turned to him and stared into his eyes for a moment. "You're right," she said, swallowing her tears. "After all, I am the Unshakable Angeline. It's about time I lived up to my title."

"If you ask me, you honor your title in each of our adventures. There is no one else I would rather be with at the moment, Angeline."

That drew a little smile from Angeline, and Samuel smiled back.

"Come, let's keep going," he said. "We still have to find the sorcerer."

"You're right," said Angeline. "But we can't go back up there. The hydra is probably hiding and waiting for us somewhere around the corner."

Samuel turned to the steps descending into the darkness below.

"Then we have to go this way," he said. "As we said before, if the sorcerer is risking his life to find one of Tartarus's prisoners, it's probably because this soul is particularly significant. I bet prisoners that important are locked up in the deepest levels of the prison."

Angeline nodded, and they were soon on their way deeper into the abyss.

The staircase spiraled down into the darkness for several hours, carrying Angeline and Samuel always deeper into Tartarus. At first, Samuel had bounced from one step to the other with little difficulty, but after constantly turning left for a while, vertigo settled in, and he asked Angeline to slow down a little. On their journey, they crossed many gigantic landings and obscure corridors, and each time they looked at each other hesitantly before resuming their descent. The more time passed, the more worried Samuel became. Tartarus was enormous, and finding the sorcerer in this maze of staircases and dark passages would be like finding a grain of rice on a sandy beach. Still, they had to succeed, because it was not only their mission that depended on it, not only the fate of two worlds, but also their salvation. They had to find the sorcerer before he left Tartarus because they needed him in order to escape this horrible place. Samuel was sure the Yfel had not sent the sorcerer into the depths of Tartarus without a plan to get him out, and if Samuel ever wanted to feel the sun on his face again, his freedom was tied to his worst enemy.

At the bottom of the staircase, the air was even fouler and damper than it at been on the upper levels. The stench of rot assaulted Samuel's nostrils. Even Angeline was trying to bury her nose in the crook of her elbow. As soon as they climbed down the last step, she coughed violently, and Samuel quickly pressed her against his chest to muffle the sound.

After a little while, the smell became more bearable and Samuel took a few steps forward, closely followed by Angeline. A bone-chilling wind went through his body, carrying with it distant cries and sorrowful complaints. Surely this was where the worst criminals humanity had ever known were locked up, which meant it was also on this level that the most horrible torments imaginable were administered.

Samuel tightened his grip on his sword, finding some comfort in the leather hilt, and then took a few more steps. The purple light from his blade spread across the floor and the damp walls, revealing a place so dark that Samuel felt its blackness right down to his core.

He shot Angeline a look over his shoulder, and saw she was holding her weapon with both hands in front of her. The fata nodded at him, and Samuel walked away from the black stone stairs. Each of his steps was like inhuman torture, and every rustle of his sandals against the ground sent a chill down his neck. Even the light whistling of his breath between his lips seemed like a racket that could be heard for miles around.

Angeline and Samuel walked along a narrow tunnel for about ten minutes, and passed in front of dozens of massive, blackened doors. Sometimes a small barred opening revealed a bit of a cell's interior, but Samuel averted his eyes from those. From the rattle of the chains, the grinding of metal and the screams he heard, he feared that a single glance into one of these forbidden rooms would be enough to make him lose his mind.

Once a naked arm slipped through one of the openings, and searched for its freedom in vain. Samuel had just enough time to notice the smoke rising from the red skin before the poor soul was pulled back into its cell by an unseen torturer, and the window slammed violently shut.

At the end of the dank corridor, Angeline and Samuel found themselves at a fork. The darkness in the left corridor seemed as solid as a stone wall, but the right passage reeked so horribly it was impossible to think of venturing in without a mask.

"Left?" suggested Angeline, in a flat and barely audible voice.

Samuel nodded, and they stepped into the darkness, the purple glow of their weapons barely pushing at the shadows around them. The corridor slithered for a little while, offering the two intruders nothing more than uneven footing, oppressive walls, and a vault oozing slime. Then the passage widened into some kind of hall, from which more tunnels branched. Samuel slowly walked into the room. The walls of this room were garnished with several balconies, with a steel door at the back of each. One again, he heard dreadful sounds coming from behind the doors and hurried out as fast as he could.

At the back of the hall, Samuel and Angeline reached another staircase, and descended once again into the unfathomable depths of Tartarus. A nod from Angeline indicated to Samuel that she trusted him, and he started down the stairs, holding his weapon before him to pierce the darkness beneath his feet.

The staircase turned to the left, then to the right, before going straight down into Earth's womb. How far were Samuel and Angeline from the surface? He had no idea and, to be honest, he preferred not to think about it. He had the feeling that ever since the start of this legend, he was always moving downward, and he had no desire to imagine the millions of tons of rocks that were over his head at this very moment.

When they finally reached the bottom of the stairs, what they saw verged on madness. After going through a stone arch so high it was almost impossible to see the top, they came to a vast cave. The tiny balcony on which he stood for the moment was so minuscule compared to the enormity of this cavern that he hesitated to step forward. He felt as if they were tiny insects inside a grain silo.

All around the cave, torches as big as trees illuminated the place with bright red flames, revealing a breathtaking scene.

About fifty yards below the balcony on which Samuel stood was a ledge of stone going around the cave. Several stone bridges leapt from the ledge and crossed at the center of the room, forming a strange star with many branches, and the platform in the middle of this star stood over a bottomless abyss. Between the stone bridges were a dozen gigantic chains, dropping out of the darkness above Samuel's head and disappearing into the void below. Each of the links was at least five or six times his height, and Samuel did not dare imagine what sort of creatures needed such chains to hold them.

What was even more frightening, and what made the hair on Samuel's nape stand on end, was the monster at the center of this abyss, standing on the platform in the middle of the star. It was a giant Samuel had seen only once before. He was five times as tall as those he had fought on Albion, and his body was a pile of muscular arms, going down his chest in several rows.

"It's a Hekatoncheire," whispered Angeline. "A giant with a hundred arms."

Samuel remembered seeing the image of one of these giants in the cavern of the Elm of Dreams, but it had probably been reduced because of the size of the cave. The real size of a Hekatoncheire surpassed anything he could have imagined, and just thinking about fighting a creature like this made his mouth go dry and his stomach churn.

From somewhere deep down in the abyss, a long moan rose like a hurricane. The growl went on for several seconds and shook the entire cave, and then it slowly receded. One of the titanic chains twisted, and then jerked violently, provoking a deafening clang that forced Samuel to cover his ears. When everything fell silent again, he looked into Angeline's eyes, and saw she also understood what creatures were hanging somewhere deep in the bottomless pit.

"The Titans," she whispered.

Samuel nodded. "The very first inhabitants of Earth are directly beneath our feet," he said in a shaky voice.

"By the gods," said Angeline, "Kronos and his brothers really are locked in here."

"And if we found them, the sorcerer can also do it."

Angeline made her little wings buzz behind her and flew over the stone railing surrounding the balcony. Samuel stretched his neck, trying to get a better view of the cave.

For now, the Hekatoncheire had his back to them, inspecting the massive chains on the other side. For a second, Samuel wondered if the hundred-armed giant did not also consider himself a prisoner of Tartarus. After all, he was destined to spend eternity in this room, without ever feeling the sun on his face or breathing the fresh air at the surface.

"There!" Angeline murmured suddenly, pulling Samuel out of his thoughts. "The sorcerer! He's over there!"

Samuel followed the fata's gaze and immediately recognized his enemy's shape in the shadows on the other side of the room. The sorcerer was here, and it appeared he was trying to free the Titans. He had a bit of a lead on Samuel and Angeline, but not much. He had not seen them yet, and Samuel still had the element of surprise.

"We have to get down to the stone ledge," Samuel whispered.

"There's a way over here," said Angeline.

Behind Samuel, a little path descended from the balcony to the ledge surrounding the cave. He hesitated for a moment, because once he was on the ledge below, he would be exposed to his enemy, but after pausing for a second he went down. He had no other choice. The sorcerer would soon put his plan in motion, and Samuel had to prevent him from succeeding.

Careful not to make a sound, Samuel walked down toward the stone ledge. He kept his eyes locked on the Hekatoncheire, only shooting quick glances at the sorcerer, who was about a hundred yards ahead of him.

Curiously, the sorcerer had not moved since Samuel first saw him. He wanted to believe it was because his enemy had not noticed his presence yet, but a tiny voice at the back of his mind told him to move with extreme caution.

When Samuel passed in front of a second immense arch, another growl echoed from the darkness below, shaking the walls of the cave. Samuel thought his heart was going to jump out of his chest when the chain next to him suddenly jerked.

At the same time, the sorcerer raised his head and extended an arm toward Samuel. The young man barely had enough time to duck to avoid a green ball of fire, which exploded behind him and sent pebbles flying. Without wasting a second, Samuel jumped to his feet and got ready to dodge a second attack from the sorcerer, but his enemy had disappeared.

"Samuel," said Angeline in a shaking voice. "I think we should get out of here."

Samuel turned to the middle of the cave and immediately knew why she was so scared. On the stone platform, the Hekatoncheire looked at him, his horrible face twisted by rage. As soon as he saw Samuel, the hundred-armed giant lurched toward him with surprising speed.

"This way!" yelled Angeline.

She quickly soared to a balcony above them and out of the cave into an unknown passage. Without hesitation, Samuel turned on his heels and followed her through an arch of vertiginous height, before darting inside a large corridor, so dark he could barely see Angeline's purple light before him.

"Angeline, not so fast!" he yelled. "Wait for me!"

Behind him, Samuel heard the inhuman screams of the Hekatoncheire, as well as the thunder of his steps on the rocky ground. A boulder as big as a horse flew by Samuel, and he ran faster.

In front of him, Angeline was making turns in the different passages, going left, then right, flying as fast as her wings allowed her. Samuel did his best to keep up with her, but the ground was mucky, and he slipped often. The giant was not gaining on him, but he was not falling back either. Samuel had to find a way to shake him loose before his legs weakened, since he was certain the giant would not tire anytime soon.

"Angeline!"

"Hurry up!" answered the fata ahead of him.

"Wait for me!"

He saw Angeline's tiny silhouette disappear into a tunnel to the right and he hurried after her. He ran across a forge, where fires burned with such intensity his vision was momentarily blurred by the heat. On the other side of the forge, he came to a tunnel stretching to the left and right. He paused for a second and rapidly turned his head in both directions.

Only then did he understand he must have taken a wrong turn somewhere. He had lost sight of Angeline. Horrified, Samuel realized he was now alone, separated from his only ally in this terrifying place. Still stunned, he did not hear the Hekatoncheire come after him, and realized too late what was happening.

When the giant's fist struck him, Samuel collapsed into darkness, his will numbed by despair.

25

"We have to keep going, Aeneas," said Deiphobe. "We must finish what you started with the golden bough."

The Trojan nodded, and then resumed his walk along the winding path. Ever since his encounter with the poor Dido, Aeneas kept glancing over his shoulder. Maybe he was hoping the deceased queen would come to him again, or perhaps he was still fighting a battle with his mind to stop him from turning around and going back to her.

They had already been delayed, and could not afford to waste any more time. The meeting between Aeneas and his father Anchises was crucial for the birth of the Roman people, but it was not the only reason pressing the Sibyl to walk faster on the dusty road. If they did not reach the Fields of Elysium in time, their chances of finding Anchises in Pluto's kingdom were slim, and if they could not find Anchises it would be impossible to get out of the Underworld.

Deiphobe quickly chased away the idea of being stuck in this horrible place. Quickening her pace, she hurried up a small hill covered in blue grass.

"Here are the walls built in the Cyclops' forge," announced Deiphobe when they reached to top of the hill. "Behind these walls stands the palace of the goddess Persephone, to whom you will give your offering to be allowed into Elysium."

A river of clear water coursed a little ahead, beside a forest of trees with emerald leaves. On the near shore stood an immaculate wall in the middle of a field of tall, soft grass. Dozens of statues were ranged along the top of the wall, representing magnificent nymphs and young nude gods, offering a striking contrast with the scenery accompanying Aeneas's journey up to this point.

A golden roof was visible over the wall, delicately outlined against the dark horizon. Hundreds of birds flapped their wings over the palace, and their aerial ballet made for a graceful spectacle across the red sky. On each side of the palace, two towers rose to an incredible height, their walls covered with ivy and clematis of all the colors of the rainbow.

"How can a place of such beauty exist in this infernal world?" asked Aeneas.

"Don't be fooled by the look of this place," answered Deiphobe. "This palace, as magnificent as it may be, is still a prison for the one who lives there. This is where the ill-fated Persephone was imprisoned, after her uncle Pluto kidnapped her to make her his wife. Now, during the months she spends in the Realm of the Dead, Persephone stays behind this wall of ivory, protected from the horrors of her husband's domain. There, she patiently waits for spring to come back, when she will be allowed to climb to her mother again staying in the Overworld until the leaves turn red and fall from the trees."

As soon as she said those words, Deiphobe resumed her walk and went down the hill toward Persephone's palace, quickly followed by Aeneas. The road led them to the base of the white wall, and then curved along the immaculate rampart and continued farther into the Underworld. Beyond Persephone's palace, Aeneas and Deiphobe saw a foggy marsh, where the path they followed lost itself.

"Before we can continue on our journey," said Deiphobe, "you must observe the rites that will grant you access to Elysium, where your venerable father is resting. The road that winds through the Marshes of the Damned will lead you to your doom, but if your heart is purified, and if your soul is washed by the waters of the goddess who is mistress of this palace, then the true path leading to the shores of the River Lethe will be revealed to you."

The Sibyl led Aeneas to the center of the white wall, where a large marble altar stood, as well as a fountain from which flowed water so clear that the splashing it made was the only clue to its presence. Following Deiphobe's instructions, Aeneas removed his armor and washed his body in the cold water offered by the goddess Persephone. Once he was done and he had put his armor back on, Aeneas gently deposited the golden bough on the marble altar and took a step back.

A second later, the landscape beyond the palace started quivering slightly, as if intense heat had suddenly filled the area. The following moment, the Trojan hero was stunned to see the foggy marshes slowly fade away. The path, which had been lost among the dead trees and the muddy ponds, roiled and then stretched again in a different direction. Aeneas saw a magnificent field on either side of the road, at the exact spot where the murky swamp had been a moment ago.

"This is incredible," he said, his eyes fixed on the horizon.

"Only the purest souls or the mortals who receive the blessing of the goddess can see the road to Elysium," said Deiphobe.

"Is that why I needed the golden bough?"

"The sacred branch is the key, yes. It's proof that you are worthy to receive Persephone's blessing. Without it, nothing you could do would make this path reveal itself to your eyes. Come, the road will only stay open for a short while. We should hurry before it disappears again."

As she stepped on the new path and both of them walked by the goddess Persephone's palace, Deiphobe turned around and looked behind her for a moment. In the distance, the cloudy top of the mountain housing Tartarus was still visible. The Sibyl had a thought for Samuel and Angeline, and she prayed to the gods that they were safe and could find a way to catch up with them before it was too late.

26

What Samuel saw when he opened his eyes made no sense. He should have been at the bottom of a dark cell, lying on a cold and soggy floor, or chained to a dank wall in front a torturer who would take pleasure in showing the young man what eternity had in store for him. Instead, he lay in a field. Lime-green grass danced under a warm breeze. The scents of spring tickled his nostrils, and the rays of a bright sun warmed his skin.

Samuel raised himself on his elbows and looked around, baffled. He remembered the large cave at the bottom of which hung the Titans, held by gigantic chains. He also recalled the sorcerer, and the ball of green fire he had thrown at Samuel. The young man now understood that the sorcerer had wanted to draw the Hekatoncheire's attention to the Lorekeeper.

Samuel shuddered, thinking of the grotesque body of the giant with a hundred arms. He then remembered his flight through Tartarus's tunnels, following Angeline, who was moving at incredible speed, completely terrified by the monster chasing them.

"Angeline," whispered Samuel.

He recalled losing sight of the fata in Tartarus's maze. In the confusion, he had probably taken a wrong turn and gone in a different direction than Angeline. Then he had hesitated, just long enough for the Hekatoncheire to reach him and knock him out with its massive fist.

Samuel touched the back of his skull. He rotated his shoulders and stretched his neck. Curiously, he did not feel any pain. After getting hit with such violence, he should have been in pretty bad shape, but nothing indicated he had any fractured bones, or that his body was covered with bruises.

Samuel stood and felt at his waist. A second later, his throat clenched like a fist. His sword and the Helm of Darkness were no longer tied to his belt. The only thing still there was the leather pouch containing the dice. Heart racing, he turned and searched the grass, but did not see anything. Someone had taken his weapon and the onyx crown.

What did it all mean?

Where was he?

The green field stretched as far as the eye could see in every direction. There was absolutely nothing to break the horizon. It was simply baffling. Was he alone? How had he gotten here?

Birdsong made Samuel startle, and he quickly turned around. Where there had only been grass a moment ago, he now saw a small grove. The bird circled the treetops for a little while, and then came toward Samuel and looped around his head. A few seconds later, it fled to the grove and vanished between the lush branches of the oaks and birches.

Without any other options, Samuel took a few steps and followed the bird to the grove. When he got to the first trees, he saw a stream coursing between them, and a small waterfall that produced a soothing music. Without taking the time to look carefully around, Samuel walked into the grove and to the crystal-clear water of the stream. When he reached the waterfall, he fell to his knees and plunged his hands into the cool water. He splashed some on his face and swallowed big, refreshing gulps. As soon as the cold water flowed down his throat, his entire body seemed to come to life again, and strength coursed in his veins once more.

Samuel closed his eyes for a moment and took in the woody fragrance. When he opened his eyes, a young woman was on the other side of the stream. She was seated on a magnificent wooden chair, and wore a gown as blue as the sky. On her head was a crown with seven stars, and her long hair the color of autumn gently fell over her shoulders. In one hand, she held a wooden spindle, around which she spun cotton thread with fiber she pulled from a distaff planted in the ground. Despite the speed at which she worked, the quantity of fiber never changed at the end of the wooden staff.

"Greetings, Samuel," said the young woman, without raising her eyes from her work.

Her voice was like a chorus of angels.

"My name is Nona," she said. "You must have many questions."

Samuel was speechless. A moment ago, he was being pursued by a terrifying giant in the dungeons of the most horrible prison that could exist, and now a young woman with breathtaking beauty was engaging him in conversation, in the middle of a forest that had appeared out of nowhere.

"You ... you know who I am?" he asked, getting to his feet.

"Of course I know who you are. You are Virtus's champion, the Lorekeeper. You were chosen by my sisters and me to preserve the balance between good and evil on Metverold."

"You're a Parca?" asked Samuel.

"That is one of the many titles men gave us. I'm the youngest of the three, the one who spins the threads of the life of every man, woman and even gods living on Metverold."

"I'm not really in a beautiful grove in the middle of a green field, am I?" asked Samuel.

"I'm afraid you're not, no," answered Nona.

For the first time, she raised her azure eyes to Samuel, though she never ceased spinning.

"It's only your consciousness that is here, with me," added the Parca. "Your physical body is still locked in Tartarus. I wanted to talk with you for a moment before you continued your mission, so I brought you here."

Samuel lowered his eyes to the stream.

"My mission … it's not going so well."

"Don't be so hard on yourself, Samuel. Your adventure is far from over. You still have many trials to overcome, but also more occasions on which to prove your courage. You can't give up at the first obstacle."

Samuel raised his head. Nona was looking at him with an affectionate smile on her lips, while her hands carried out her work with great agility. With her right hand she held the fiber between the wooden distaff and herself, and with the left she spun the spindle on her thigh, twisting the fiber into a soft and robust thread.

"Why did you want to speak with me now?" asked Samuel.

"Because it is imperative you do not leave Tartarus without first speaking with one of its detainees."

"Leave Tartarus?" said Samuel. "I doubt I'll ever be able to get out of there. I should never have set foot in that place."

"Once again, you're too hard on yourself, Samuel," said Nona. "It's usually in darkness that one hopes to find light again. Your story is far from over, but your mind is still shrouded in doubt. Learn to trust yourself, Lorekeeper."

Samuel lowered his eyes once more. He had kept his dread at bay for most of this adventure, but his journey in Tartarus had turned to disaster. Casting aside his doubts was not easy.

"Who is he, this prisoner I have to talk to?" he asked.

"That is for you to discover," answered Nona. "The sorcerer has already found this man, and retrieved the information he needed."

"I thought the sorcerer was trying to free a Titan, or another prisoner."

"That's what we believed as well," said Nona, "but the Yfel has more than one trick in its bag. The sorcerer only needed to acquire information to move on to the next part of his plan."

Samuel looked up into a bright blue sky. What kind of information did the Yfel want, if they were ready to brave the horrors of Tartarus to obtain it? Then he remembered what Aristaeus had revealed to him, on the island of Albion.

"He wanted to learn how to kill a god," said Samuel.

"You are correct," said Nona. "And now we have every reason to believe he is in possession of this secret. If we are to have a chance to prevent the Yfel from using that information, we have to know what the secret is ourselves."

"I understand, but don't you already know the secret information?" asked Samuel. "After all, you are a Parca, a mistress of Virtus. The threads of the lives of gods pass through your own hands."

Nona smiled at him again, as if he was a child asking obvious questions.

"Our universe does not operate in such a simple manner. Once the length of a life thread is decided, we can no longer intervene. With regard to the gods, this thread can be remarkably long, even endless, but it still falls under the same laws governing mortals. If there were a way to cut this thread prematurely, and if the Yfel got hold of it, it would be catastrophic for all of us, including your own world, Samuel."

"All right. I will try to find this prisoner, but I'm not doing anything before I find Angeline. I need her to succeed, and I will never abandon her in a place like Tartarus."

"You can stop worrying. You will find the fata again, but not right now. For the moment, she is with the sorcerer, and you can do nothing for her."

"I beg your pardon?" said Samuel. "Angeline is in the hands of our enemy, and you want me to leave her there?"

"That is not what I said," replied Nona. "I said there was nothing you could do for her at the moment. Besides, she is already outside of Tartarus, with the Yfel's sorcerer. As long as you are locked between the walls of this prison, there is no way you can help her."

"Then tell me how I can get out of Tartarus and I will find her."

"Everything in its own time, Samuel. To escape Tartarus, you need to find the prisoner who knows the secret of the gods. Only then will you know how to recover your freedom. Your salvation is tied to the secret of this man."

Samuel did not particularly like the way this conversation was going. He suddenly had the urge to quit this place and search for Angeline. She was at the mercy of the Yfel sorcerer, and there was no way he was going to simply abandon her to her fate.

"In a few minutes, you will wake up in one of Tartarus's cells," declared Nona, as if she could read his mind. "But before you leave me, I have a gift for you."

Nona paused her work for a moment and leaned over a basket on her left. Samuel was certain it had not been there a few moments ago. Nona lifted the wicker lid, put her hand inside and pulled out a thread about a yard long. The bird who had led Samuel here flew over to the Parca, took the thread in its beak and carried it to Samuel, who delicately took it.

"When you awake in your cell, hand this thread over to your jailor," said Nona. "Tell him I gave it to you, and it is a present owed to him since his first true heartbeats."

"I … I don't understand," said Samuel.

He looked at the golden thread for a second.

When he raised his eyes, the stream and the trees around him had vanished, as well as Nona. He was alone in the middle of the field of green grass again. Suddenly the wind picked up, and a distant rumble covered the rustling of the grass around him. Samuel turned his head toward the rapidly incoming noise, and saw a gigantic tidal wave rush toward him, destroying everything in its path. Before he could run, the wave crashed over him and everything went black.

The crisp water splashed on Samuel's face and forced its way up his nose and down his throat. As he tried to get his breath back, the water spilled into his lungs and his throat immediately clenched. With his eyes still closed, Samuel was seized by a violent cough that felt like he was getting punched in the chest.

After a short while, he calmed down a little and finally got his senses back. Even before he opened his eyes, he realized he was leaning slightly forward, his wrist held back by rings of cold metal. When Samuel finally opened his eyelids, all the horror he had forgotten during his conversation with Nona soared back from the deepest corners of his mind.

He was in Tartarus, chained to the wall of a putrid cell. The stench clung to his skin and stung his eyes.

Before him, a plump man held a wooden bucket filled with black, viscous water. He was wearing an animal skin around his waist and a black hood over his head. His greasy body was covered with horrendous scars. When he was about to throw the water at Samuel's face again, Samuel quickly let him know he had regained his senses.

"All right! All right! I'm awake," yelled Samuel, tugging on the chains keeping him pinned to the wall.

The man hesitated, then shrugged and doused Samuel's face with the murky water again. The young man pressed his lips firmly to avoid swallowing a single drop.

"That's enough," said a voice at the back of the cell. "This is no way to treat our guest."

A man appeared from the shadows and stepped toward Samuel. He was tall, with a completely hairless head and chin. His jaws and cheeks were finely sculpted, and his eyes were as dark as the deepest pits of Tartarus. He wore a black robe and held Samuel's sword in one hand. In the other, he had Pluto's Helm of Darkness.

Suddenly, a scream froze Samuel's heart. He turned his head to his right and beyond the open door of his cell he saw Tisiphone's two sisters, the Furies who had dragged the sorcerer into Tartarus. From this close, they were much more horrible than he had imagined. The two dreadful women looked at him, their bulging eyes filled with unfathomable rage, while the vipers they had for hair tried to bite each other.

"Shut up, you two!" yelled the man in black.

The Furies cowered in fear, like two critters scared by a predator.

"Please forgive these two crones," the man said. "This day hasn't been the easiest for them." He studied Samuel for a moment, and then looked at the Helm of Darkness.

"Quite an interesting artifact, this crown of onyx," he said, bringing the Helm up to his eyes. "Not everyone can wear this kind of crown. In the wrong hands, it is a very dangerous object."

"Who are you?" asked Samuel, barely hiding the tremor in his voice.

The man shot him a furious look.

"I should be the one asking you that question!" he yelled. "You're the one who dared sneak into my home, even though you are not a shadow yet."

Samuel wanted to look away, but there was something hypnotic in the man's gaze; something that inspired fear and commanded respect at the same time.

"However, you are right," continued the man. "It's not very courteous of me to hold you prisoner without telling you the identity of your jailer. My name is Sarpedon."

Samuel held his breath. Sarpedon! The forgotten brother of Minos and Rhadamanthus. The latter had advised Samuel to avoid his brother at all costs, since he had no idea how he would react upon seeing the young man strolling through the eerie tunnels of Tartarus.

Evidently, Sarpedon had not appreciated it very much.

"Your turn now," said Sarpedon. "Who are you?"

"My name is Samuel."

"And what are you doing here?"

"I am the Lorekeeper. I have been sent by Virtus to find the Yfel sorcerer and prevent him from changing history."

Sarpedon burst out laughing. The torturer and the Furies joined him, creating a grim clamor that made Samuel shiver.

"Virtus? Yfel?" asked Sarpedon in a doubtful tone. "Are you mocking me?"

"Not at all. I assure you that—"

"Silence!"

Sarpedon struck Samuel's head with his elbow and nearly knocked him senseless again. The young man's upper lip split open under the force of the impact and blood filled his mouth.

"Please, you have to believe me," he said, spitting blood on the ground.

"You think I'm stupid?" asked Sarpedon. "Virtus and Yfel don't exist. They are only legends we tell fallen gods to scare them and put them back in their place. Don't think I'm a fool like those imbeciles."

"I assure you it's true. Virtus is real. The Parcae have chosen me to—"

This time Sarpedon hit Samuel fiercely in the ribs with his knee. A sharp bolt of pain flashed through his guts, and Samuel coughed up the air from his lungs, but he immediately shoved the pain aside. He had to stay focused on his mission and convince Sarpedon to let him go. This legend, the future of Metverold and Angeline's life depended on it.

"The Parcae are nothing but dirty liars," said Sarpedon. "Long ago they made me a promise, in exchange for my services in this rat hole. I've been waiting for centuries now, abandoned and forgotten in Hell's shithole. I understood long ago I had been fooled, and that I would never get what is so dear to me."

It suddenly became clear to Samuel why Nona had summoned him before he regained his senses. It was not only to talk to him about the Yfel sorcerer and a prisoner of

275

Tartarus. She had summoned Samuel because he had to bring Sarpedon what he wanted more than anything.

He turned his eyes to his left hand, then slowly opened his fingers. In the palm of his hand was the golden thread given him by the youngest of the Parcae.

"I ... I think I have what you want," whispered Samuel.

Sarpedon turned and shot him a dark look.

"If you believe your fate cannot be worse than it already is, Samuel, you are mistaken," said Sarpedon. "I suggest you don't mock me. It would be a terrible mistake on your part, I can assure you."

"Please, I beg you, you have to believe me. I have no intention of making a fool out of you. Look in my left hand. You'll find what you have been waiting for for so long."

Sarpedon held Samuel's gaze for an interminable second, and then he turned his eyes to the young man's left hand and slowly stepped forward. When he saw the golden thread, his chin fell to his chest and his eyes widened in amazement. He immediately let go of Samuel's sword and the Helm of Darkness.

"Where did you find this?" he asked Samuel in a biting tone.

"It was given to me by one of the Parcae. She asked me to hand it over to you. She said you would know what it was."

Sarpedon cautiously moved his fingers closer to Samuel's hands.

"Could ... could it really be possible?" he asked, delicately taking the golden thread. "After all these years ..."

"Do you believe me now?" asked Samuel.

Sarpedon studied the golden thread as if it were the most precious treasure that existed on Metverold. Without turning his head, he waved the other hand and the torturer stepped closer to Samuel. With a few precise movements, he unlocked the chains holding back the young man and freed him from the irons.

"Thanks," said Samuel. "Can I have my sword and the Helm back?"

Sarpedon finally stopped staring at the golden thread and turned to Samuel. After a moment of hesitation he nodded, and Samuel quickly picked up his weapon from the ground, as well as the onyx crown. He briefly thought about keeping his sword in his hand, and maybe even using it to make his way out of here, but instead he slid it back into his scabbard. He might not have all of Sarpedon's trust yet, but at least he had made him lower his guard. Showing even the slightest hint of hostility would only make things worse.

"Is it true then?" asked Sarpedon. "Virtus, Yfel, the battle between the energies governing our universe—all of that is true?"

"Yes," answered Samuel. "You really don't have any idea what's going on out there, do you?"

"I have been in here for a very long time, Samuel. Many centuries have passed since I had any contact with the outside world. For all I know, my brothers think I'm completely mad, or worse."

Samuel could not help but smile.

"Let's just say your brother Rhadamanthus is worried about you."

Sarpedon placed the golden thread in a small pouch and hid it inside his robe.

"He's always been the one who worried the most about us three," said Sarpedon. "So, if you really are the Lorekeeper, Virtus's hero, it means the one who came here before you was a true sorcerer of Yfel."

"Yes," Samuel said.

Sarpedon immediately turned his eyes to the two Furies, who cowered against one another. When his gaze crossed theirs, they exploded in a chorus of shrieks and sharp cries that made Samuel grind his teeth and press his hands to his ears.

"Silence!" yelled Sarpedon. "I should have known he had power over your feeble mind. Now I understand how he was able to escape your grip."

"Sarpedon, I have to ask you something," Samuel cut in. "The sorcerer came to her with a specific goal in mind. He wanted to speak to one of your prisoners and discover a secret that could change your world and mine forever. I must find out this information if I want to have a chance of stopping him before he puts his plan in motion."

"I will bring you to this prisoner," answered Sarpedon. "You'll have to meet him anyway, if you want to get out of here. Follow me."

Without waiting another second, Sarpedon stepped out of the dark cell and walked by the two Furies. Samuel followed, but hesitated for a moment before crossing the cell's threshold. In the dark corridor, the two horrible women with vipers on their heads watched him with unbounded anger.

"As long as I'm with you, you have nothing to fear from those two hags," said Sarpedon.

Keeping Sarpedon's words in mind, Samuel put a hand on the hilt of his sword and stepped out of the cell as well, passing by the two Furies. As soon as he was in the tunnel, he hastened his pace after Sarpedon. Behind him, the two terrifying women got up on their feet and followed him, staying at a safe distance in his wake.

Sarpedon led Samuel through Tartarus's maze for almost an hour, until they reached a large, thick wooden door. Sarpedon signaled to the hooded torturer, and the potbellied creature produced a silver key, which he used to unlock the door. When he pushed on the damp door, the hinges screeched. Once the opening was wide enough, Sarpedon slipped inside. Samuel quickly peeked over his shoulder, and when he saw the Furies moving toward him, he hurried after their master on the other side of the door.

The cell where Samuel found himself was unlike anything he could have imagined. Instead of a small room with dank stone walls, the cell was a cave about fifty paces wide, and at least twice as deep. The cave's ceiling was only twelve feet over Samuel's head, and the ground was covered in a carpet of green, luscious grass. At the center of this strange grotto stood a magnificent apple tree, its branches weighed down by juicy fruit, and at the foot of the tree was a majestic pond filled with crystal-clear water.

In the middle of this pond, a man stood waist-deep.

One of the branches stretched over the man's head, and the most delicious-looking apple Samuel had ever seen dangled a few inches from his forehead. When the man raised his arms to the apple, the branch bounced out of his reach, and the water level rose to his chest. A second later, the poor soul abandoned the idea of picking up the apple, and decided to drink some of the cool water instead. However, when he leaned forward, his mouth open to suck in the precious liquid, the water receded to his knees, and the branch over his head came down to its original position, dangling the apple in front of his eyes again.

"Samuel, let me introduce you to Tantalus," said Sarpedon.

Tantalus ignored the intruders in his cell and resumed his little routine. He tried to catch the apple, which fled out of reach again, and then he tried in vain quench his thirst with the water of the pond.

"For his crime," said Sarpedon, "Tantalus was sentenced by Zeus to never satiate his hunger or quench his thirst. The object of his desire constantly seems within reach, but he will never get it. It's an eternal torment of temptation."

Samuel could hardly believe what Sarpedon was saying. A man called Tantalus, condemned to be eternally tantalized. He wondered if the word originated from the poor man's name.

"What did he do to deserve such punishment?" he asked Sarpedon.

"We blame Tantalus for many crimes, but his ultimate sin was to serve his own son to the gods, during a feast he had organized to ask for their forgiveness, after he stole ambrosia, which is the food of the gods."

Tantalus leaned forward again to quell his eternal thirst, but once more the water level receded to his knees. The poor man burst out crying, and his tears dripped into the pond.

Sarpedon walked over to the apple tree and picked up a scarlet apple. When he hungrily bit into the fruit, the juice trickled down his chin.

"So, Tantalus," said Sarpedon, "a little bird told me you had some company today. You do know that visits are strictly forbidden, don't you?"

Tantalus ignored Sarpedon. Drying his tears with the back of his hand, he tried once again to catch the apple dangling over his head.

"Tantalus," insisted Sarpedon. "You know what happens when you ignore me like this. Perhaps you'd like me to ask Megaera to stick around for the next ten years? The last time she did, you guys had some fun."

With these words, one of the Furies hurried closer, her eyes suddenly bright with the anticipation of torturing the poor man for the next decade. Right away, Tantalus's face turned white and his hands started shaking.

"Sarpedon, I beg you, don't do this," he said. "It's not my fault! They are the ones who brought the intruder here!"

He pointed to the Furies with a finger wrinkled by centuries spent in the water.

"I know," said Sarpedon. "Nonetheless, this man wanted information you possessed, and I'd like to know what you told him."

Tantalus looked at Sarpedon defiantly. The warden took another bite of the apple, and bits of its flesh spilled on the grass, close to the pond.

"And what do I get out of it?" asked Tantalus, following each bit of fruit that fell with crazy eyes.

"You continue your little game in peace, without the two Furies to cheer you along," answered Sarpedon. "And if the information is as juicy as this fruit, maybe I'll let you have a taste of this apple."

Tantalus's eyes lit up upon hearing these words.

"It was the Yfel's sorcerer," he said excitedly. "He wanted to know how to permanently kill a god, and to make sure he would never come back—that he would be completely erased from history."

"And you, sneaky Tantalus—you know this secret?" asked Sarpedon.

"Yes, I know what needs to be done," answered the man as he stretched his arms toward Sarpedon. "You all think I stole the secret of ambrosia, and that I killed my beloved son so he would be devoured by the gods, but those are lies spread by Zeus. In truth, my crime was to discover the poison that allows one to kill the inhabitant of Olympus."

"We're listening," said Sarpedon, taking another bite of the plump apple.

"The secret lies in the ambrosia," said Tantalus. "It's a poison that can only be swallowed by those who don't have mortal blood in them, and since the gods don't have blood coursing in their veins, they are immune to the effects of ambrosia and can appreciate all its benefits, such as immortality." He paused for a moment and his lips cracked into a grin that made Samuel shudder. "However, if one were to mix human blood with ambrosia and feed it to a god, then the beverage would become a deadly poison, since the god would put blood inside him as he drank. I discovered this secret and, with the help of my son, we dropped a little bit of our blood into the cups reserved for the gods. We'd had enough of being at the mercy of these jealous, perverse and arrogant beings. But Zeus discovered our trickery, and after he sentenced me to this torment, he invented a story about me serving my beloved son for dinner, in order to hide the truth. And now that you know my secret, *give me that apple!*"

Sarpedon watched Tantalus for a moment, chewing. Then he threw the fruit over his shoulder. The apple rolled away on the grass.

"You promised!" screamed Tantalus.

"I did nothing of the sort," answered Sarpedon calmly. "Count yourself lucky I'm leaving you alone to your torment, Tantalus." He then turned to Samuel. "There. Now we know what the Yfel wanted."

Samuel was appalled. His enemy now knew how to erase a god from Greek or Roman mythology, and he only needed a few drops of blood to do it.

27

Angeline's skull buzzed like a swarm of bees.

Flashes of pain shot across her neck, and her mind tried to find its way through a thick fog of confusion.

For several seconds, Angeline fought to regain control of her body and get her senses back. After a short while, she cautiously opened her eyes and painfully got to her feet. A dense darkness prevented the fata from seeing farther than the tip of her nose. She took a few careful steps in a random direction, her hands stretched out before her. She had only moved a few inches when a slender shape appeared before her. As she walked a little closer, Angeline understood it was a rusty bar. She repeated the exercise in several other directions and quickly concluded she was locked in a cage.

Confusion threatened to become panic, but Angeline took a deep breath and managed to keep what little calm had not abandoned her already. Was she still inside the dreadful Tartarus? She did not have the slightest idea. How long had she been unconscious? Another question she could not answer.

Angeline lowered her eyes and saw she still had her weapon with her. She took out her sword, put a hand on the blade, and recited the ancient words that had been transmitted to her by her ancestors. A moment later, a purple glow spread across the blade. The light was not enough to reveal anything other than the cage she stood in, and Angeline repeated the spell on the small crown she always had on her head. As soon as the glow from the crown joined with that of the sword, she finally got a glimpse of where she was. Angeline saw that the cage was suspended at the end of a chain, a little over three feet above the ground. Above the cage, the chain disappeared into the darkness, and it was impossible for Angeline to know how high the vault was.

When she walked over to the bars, she noticed she was in a relatively small cave, without any distinctive detail about it. However, when she raised her eyes and saw the entrance of the cavern, her heart raced and her wings started buzzing behind her. In the distance, she saw the mountain hiding Tartarus, which meant she was no longer in the prison.

However, her joy was short-lived. She might be outside the prison, but she was still a prisoner; not to mention that she had no idea where Samuel was. Maybe he was still stuck inside the impenetrable walls of the Titans' prison.

Once again, fear pressed on her mind, and Angeline decided to recall the last moments she had spent in Tartarus. She remembered the Hekatoncheire seeing Samuel, and they had immediately run away. She recalled flying as fast as she could through the tunnels of Tartarus, darting like an arrow between the cell doors, and turning into the passages without thinking twice. How long had she fled like that, without knowing where she was going? She did not know, but she still remembered the dreadful feeling when she realized Samuel was no longer behind her. Without her knowing exactly when, her protégé had probably taken a wrong turn and fled in a different direction than the one she was going.

Angeline fell to her knees in the rusted metal cage. How had she let fear dominate her so easily? She was here to look after Samuel, and had abandoned him to his fate at the first opportunity. Tears blurred her vision as she saw terrifying images in her mind—images of Samuel wandering the sinister halls of Tartarus, yelling her name in vain.

Angeline dried her tears and jumped to her feet.

Now is not the moment to act like a mama's fairy, she thought.

She had to devise a way to get out of this rusted cage and find Samuel. He needed her, and she had to be strong for him.

Once again, she tried to summon the last moments she could remember. After she had realized Samuel was no longer following her, she stopped for a few seconds to catch her breath. She then tried to retrace her steps to find her protégé, but without success. Instead, she had wandered through the murky passages of Tartarus, doing her best to ignore the wails of the poor souls being tortured behind closed doors. She could not say how she managed to get there, but after a while she had found herself in the cavern where the Titans were imprisoned.

Tartarus terrified her more than anything she could imagine, and the Titans scared her just as much, but Angeline had been unable to quiet her curiosity. Since she had thought she was alone in the cavern, she had flown to a gigantic chain suspending one of the first inhabitants of Earth over the abyss. Unfortunately, though she had tried to pierce the darkness with her eyes, she had not been able to catch a glimpse of a Titan silhouette.

She remembered hearing a sound behind her and glancing quickly over her shoulder. The mere memory of the sorcerer standing so close to her was enough to turn her stomach upside-down. She had been completely paralyzed by his presence, and he had knocked her out with embarrassing ease.

"Some fata I am," whispered Angeline.

She was supposed to protect Samuel from the sorcerer and the dangers of Metverold, but she could not even defend herself.

Once again, Angeline shook her head. She could not afford to let despair settle in. After all, the situation could be worse. To begin with, she was alive. That was a considerable advantage. And she was alone for the moment, without anyone to keep an eye on her. If she wanted to get out of this jam, it was now or never.

Angeline put her weapon on the floor and walked to the bars of her cage. Without really believing she could break them, she pulled with all her might on two of the bars. As predicted, the bars remained perfectly still.

Angeline looked around, searching for the lock. That was when she saw a little padlock hanging on the side of the cage. Without wasting another moment, she took it between both her hands and closed her eyes. Just as she did when she wanted to infuse a metal with Virtus's energy to generate a purple glow, Angeline focused her energy on the padlock in her hands. The strength of Virtus quickly filled her chest and spread along her arms, until it reached the tips of her fingers.

But when she wanted to pass the energy to the padlock to unlock it, an acute flash of pain made her jump back as if lightning had just struck her.

She then understood the sorcerer had enchanted the padlock with his own Yfel energy.

Angeline got back to her feet and leaned her face against one of the bars. Doing her best to keep her spirits up, she swept the dark cave with her eyes.

"I hope you're doing better than me, Samuel," she whispered.

The sorcerer looked at the mountain standing over Tartarus. Most of the people laying eyes on such scenery shivered in horror thinking of the torments imposed between the prison's walls, but the sorcerer could not help but smile. He even let a few rasping laughs slip out of his throat, because he had a genuine desire to rejoice.

The legend was coming to an end, and everything was going exactly as he had planned. Well, almost everything. He would have liked for the harpies to take care of Samuel before he set foot in Pluto's kingdom, but he never really believed they would succeed. The Lorekeeper had already proven he knew how to defend himself, and if the sorcerer was honest, he would have been a little disappointed if his enemy had been killed by such stupid creatures. Still, the harpies had been useful. They had allowed him to gain a little bit of time to cross the Acheron before Aeneas.

Then there was the fight against Cerberus. When he had planned his mission, the sorcerer had decided not to use the three-headed dog against Samuel, since the monster was too unpredictable, but when he had seen the Sybil use a sleeping potion to walk safely by the beast, the opportunity had been too good to pass up. The sorcerer had doubted the potion would last for very long on a monster of Cerberus's size, and when he had seen Samuel cross the Acheron on the back of a demon, he had decided to set a simple trap for him. So he had hindered Samuel, just long enough for Cerberus to wake up.

He had to admit he had been surprised to see Samuel survive his fight against Cerberus. The sorcerer still did not understand how he had done it, but it did not matter now. He had simply put in motion the next phase of his plan, which was to lead Samuel into the deepest abysses of Tartarus. The sorcerer could easily have slipped inside the prison without Samuel knowing where he was, but it would have made the rest of his plan more complicated. Since he was convinced he was the only who knew the secret of escaping the Titans' prison, he had preferred to draw Samuel after him and get rid of the Lorekeeper once and for all. Now he knew the secret to the gods' immortality, and the Lorekeeper was locked in a prison from which he would never get out. Just thinking of the horrors Samuel would suffer at the hands of Tartarus's tormentor made the sorcerer's smile widen. *The Yfel will be proud of my work*, he thought. And why not? Not only had he obtained the secret to the gods' endless life, along with eliminating the Lorekeeper once and for all; he had also captured a fata of Virtus. There was no doubt the Yfel would be able to extract precious information from her, and the sorcerer only hoped he would be allowed to assist in the little pest's interrogation.

The sorcerer walked over a small hill, then followed the path down the opposite side. Someone else might have been shocked by all these successes, but not the Yfel sorcerer. He had planned it all and calculated everything more than once. He had studied this legend, as well as the inhabitants of the Underworld. He knew every danger and every dark corner of this dreadful world, and because of this flawless planning, his enemies were now scattered across Hell and Aeneas was at his mercy.

A few moments later, he came to a great wall of immaculate white ivory, behind which was the palace of Queen Persephone. At the center of this wall was a fountain. The sorcerer approached it and passed a gloved hand into the water. He heard the splashing, but the droplets were so clear they remained invisible to his eyes.

So this is where the souls come to purify themselves, he thought.

Once again, he could not help but grin thinking about the gods and the ridiculous rites they imposed on the men and women of this world. A simple funeral turned into a festival lasting several days, and a common war required so many animal sacrifices that the soldiers died of hunger before the first battle even took place, which led to more funerals, requiring more sacrifices, and this went on and on until a bull became more precious than gold in this world of fools.

And if a poor soul dared to miss a single of these rituals and did not follow the instructions to the letter, the gods would get angry with him, and his entire town would be struck with a hundred-year curse.

"Time to put these impostors back where they belong," whispered the sorcerer.

He slowly walked over to the altar next to the fountain. Beyond the wall, the road stretched across a murky and noxious marsh. Of course, the sorcerer knew this marsh was only an illusion, where the souls trying to reach Elysium without King Minos's consent were lost forever. There was a ritual that existed to open the passage to deserving souls like Aeneas, but the sorcerer knew he would never be admitted to the heavenly fields, no matter how many times he washed his body with the tears of Persephone.

Fortunately, he did not need to enter Elysium to eliminate Aeneas and erase the Romans from history. All he had to do was use the stupid rites against the dumb gods who demanded them.

With a smile still on his lips, the sorcerer stretched out his hands and grabbed the golden bough from the altar. The ritual allowing Aeneas to enter Elysium in the flesh required two things: to purify his body with the water from the fountain, and to offer a golden bough to Persephone. Without the sacred branch, Aeneas was not authorized to walk the Fields of Elysium, and his presence would draw the ire of Hell's queen.

As soon as the sorcerer took a step back, with the golden bough still in his hand, a terrible shriek tore the silence that usually reigned around the ivory palace. It was a howl that bit like a winter wind, a screeching scream like a blade on a grindstone. The moan continued for several lengthy seconds, and then it died, replaced by a thunder that shook the ground.

If the Yfel sorcerer had been a simple mortal, he would certainly have run away without looking back, but he was not a common man. He knew what followed, and he did not want to miss a second of it. The last part of his plan was about to unfold, and it was with a smile on his face that he waited for what came next.

Ominous clouds gathered over Persephone's palace, and blinding lightning flashed through the red sky. Roaring, the storm moved over the white wall. When the clouds passed over the top of the rampart, the shadow of a woman slid along the stone, then across the green grass. As the storm reached the path leading to Elysium, the shadow stood up and took the form of a beautiful nymph with ivory skin, dressed in a gown as black as a starless night. She took a few steps toward the marsh, and then vanished in a fog and disappeared a few seconds later, along with the storm following her.

When the landscape returned to its normal state and the marsh appeared again on either side of the road, beyond Persephone's palace, the sorcerer could not hold his laughter anymore. The Lorekeeper was stuck in Tartarus, the fata tasked with protecting him was his prisoner, he had obtained the secret to the gods' immortality and Aeneas was going to die without him having to take out his weapon.

My job is far too easy, thought the sorcerer as he turned his back to the palace of ivory.

A majestic meadow stretched around Aeneas and Deiphobe. The turquoise grass gently wavered under a pleasant breeze, and sweet perfumes caressed the Sibyl and the hero. In the distance, they saw a forest of beautiful trees, with large branches and leaves a striking jade. Just over the treetops, a magnificent sun spread its soft rays over the landscape.

"Welcome to Elysium," said Deiphobe.

"It's absolutely breathtaking," answered Aeneas, his mouth hanging open.

"This is where the deserving souls come to lounge after death, and live pleasant days until their return to Earth," added the Sybil.

They continued their journey across the fields until they came to the shore of a river so clear Aeneas could distinguish each grain of sand at the bottom. They followed this river for a short while, and arrived at a beach of pure white sand, where several souls were playing and laughing together. A few of the deceased had gathered in a chorus and were singing to the gods, while others were wrestling nearby to measure each other's strength.

On a boulder farther down the beach, a man dressed in a long blue gown was making his harp sing, accompanied by his harmonious voice.

"Here is the Thracian priest," said Deiphobe as she indicated the man to Aeneas. "And here are the descendants of Teucer, a hero born in better times than those we are living today."

She pointed to another man. "That is Dardanus," she said. "He is the founder of Troy, escorted by his companions. Look upon their spears and the ghost chariots next to them. Their delight in weapons and horses, which they tasted while living, followed them even in their descent to the Underworld."

Aeneas took a step toward the founder of the city he had loved so dearly, but the Sibyl quickly grabbed his arm.

"We're not here for him, Trojan," she said.

She dragged the hero away, and the beach turned into another field of tall, soft grass. On either side of the path they followed, more souls were enjoying a feast on the grass and singing in chorus, their voices harmoniously joining with the gentle rumble of the clear river nearby.

Aeneas was moving slowly behind the Sibyl, unable to look away from these heroes and other ancestors. Here was a group of warriors who had perished while fighting for their homeland. A little farther on were priests who had rigorously observed the rites for their entire lives. There were also pious poets, whose voices were worthy of Apollo's own, and who sang stories of their people and praised the feats of the heroes who had built their nations.

Deiphobe nodded from a distance to those who noticed them, but she hurriedly pulled the Trojan along by the hand. Elysium was a magnificent place, and it was easy to lose oneself in its splendors, but they had to keep going on their path without wasting a moment. It had been hours now since Samuel and Angeline had left them to get into Tartarus, and Deiphobe was worried they would never escape from the prison.

However, she also knew the Yfel were resourceful, and they would have never sent the sorcerer into Tartarus without knowing he could get out. That was why she was eager to move forward. Deiphobe feared that Samuel had fallen into a trap, and she was now the only one able to protect Aeneas. She knew the sorcerer could not follow them into Elysium—his soul was much too dark to be allowed inside—but she preferred not to linger any longer than necessary. One never knew what tricks the Yfel had up their sleeve.

Aeneas was a powerful hero who knew how to defend himself, but without the Lorekeeper he would not be able to hold his own against the forces of Yfel.

A moan echoed from the horizon, so faint that Aeneas did not seem to hear it, but Deiphobe's hair prickled. She knew what this moan meant, even thought it did not belong to the legend, and the idea that they were now hunted by a nightmarish nymph made her hasten her pace even more.

Deiphobe dragged Aeneas through the crowd of shadows, and she finally spotted the one she had been searching for: the poet Musaeus, who had forged his reputation in the public places of Athens. She would have recognized his curly blond hair and androgynous appearance anywhere. The Sibyl hurried to the poet as fast as she could, as thunder rolled in the distance.

"Tell me, blissful soul," said Deiphobe when they came close to Musaeus, "you who are most gracious among the poets, which place does Anchises have for his own?"

As she spoke, the Sybil did everything in her power to keep calm. "It is for his sake that we came here," she added, "and for his sake that we crossed the vast rivers of Erebus."

The poet turned his angelic face to Deiphobe, and looked at her with gentle, half-closed eyes. Evidently this place was like a drug for him, and left him in a constant state of lethargy. His lack of urgency made Deiphobe want to smack him across the face, but she managed to contain herself.

"We have no fixed dwelling," said the poet, pronouncing each syllable with exaggerated care. "We lie on the soft-swelling shores ..." He paused to gesture toward the riverbanks with a languid movement of the hand. "... And we live among the meadows fresh with streams."

He looked at Aeneas and Deiphobe in turn, waiting for them to thank him for his answer, which he probably deemed perfectly acceptable. Just before Deiphobe lost her patience and strangled him, Musaeus turned his back to them and walked away toward a small hill, signaling for them to follow his steps. As soon as they reached the top of the hill, the poet raised a finger to the opposite side, where they saw a boulder as large as a house.

"You will find the object of your quest over there," he said.

Then, without another word, Musaeus returned to his people, walking with a step that looked more like a strange dance.

Deiphobe followed the poet with her eyes for a few seconds, intrigued by his bizarre gait, but her curiosity quickly turned to anguish when she noticed the storm floating over the Fields of Elysium. The presence of dark clouds in this peaceful place was unprecedented, and when the Sibyl saw the spectral nymph hovering between the blinding flashes of lightning, she understood they were in real danger.

"Melinoe," murmured Deiphobe with a trembling voice.

Before Aeneas had a chance to follow her gaze and see the incoming storm in the distance, the Sibyl grabbed him by the elbow and led him to the foot of the hill, where he would find his father.

As she glanced one last time over her shoulder, the poor woman prayed for a miracle, because she was certain the avenging nymph would be upon them before Aeneas could finish his conversation with Anchises.

28

Angeline had been pushing and tugging on the bars of her cage for over an hour, but they obstinately refused to break.

As she sat panting in the center of the cage, her face glistening with sweat, Angeline decided to adopt a new tactic. If she could not move the bars, maybe she could slip between them. The space between each metal rod was rather narrow, but with a bit of luck—and a few contortions—she might be able to do it.

Angeline took a deep breath and walked over to the bars. She slid her right shoulder between two of them. Her shoulder squeezed through without any problem.

That's a promising start, she thought.

The next step turned out to be a little harder. First, she snuck her hips between the two rusty bars, grinding her teeth when she thought of her beautiful white toga rubbing against the dirty metal. Then she twisted her body in every possible way, moving forward a hairsbreadth at a time, until her right leg finally made it out of the cage.

It's not easy, but I will make it out, thought Angeline.

Careful to stand as straight as she could, Angeline slipped a little farther between the bars. Once again, she managed to move a few whiskers forward, taking short breaths from time to time to keep as little air as possible in her lungs. After a few more seconds, she paused to evaluate her progress. Realizing she still had a long way to go, she quickly tucked her belly in and tried one more time.

This time, Angeline did not move forward at all. Something prevented her from going any farther. She pushed as hard as she could with her arms, but in vain.

Angeline shot a look over her shoulder and saw her wings stuck inside the cage. She cursed under her breath, then pushed the air from her lungs and pinched her lips. On the verge of passing out, she shook her shoulders, pulled on the bars and pushed with her legs, again and again, wiggling her body any way she could, searching for the right angle that would allow her to squeeze her wings through, but alas, nothing worked.

After a short while, black dots blurred her vision and she released the tension in her muscles and took a much-deserved breath of fresh air.

It was a lost cause. She would never fit between the bars.

Even worse, she was now stuck in this awkward position.

Cursing her weakness for honey sandwiches and blackberry-jam cakes, Angeline wiggled her cheeks and twisted like a fish between the rusty bars, now trying to get back inside the cage. A few seconds later, the metal let go of her and she found herself lying on the cage floor again.

When she raised her head to adjust her crown, Angeline saw a shadow appear at the cave entrance. Her throat clenched when she recognized the Yfel sorcerer. The presence of Virtus's sworn enemy tied her stomach in a knot, and she quickly picked up her sword.

"I thought you would never wake up," said the sorcerer as he walked closer to Angeline.

"Where am I?" she asked, raising her sword before her.

The sorcerer walked up to the cage. Despite the purple glow still coming from Angeline's crown and weapon, his face remained hidden in the shadow of his hood. However, his fetid breath almost made her faint.

"You will be glad to learn we are no longer in Tartarus," answered the sorcerer. "For now, that's all you need to know."

His voice was hoarse and grating, like a bone-chilling winter wind blowing over a barren plain. Angeline had never been alone with the Yfel's sorcerer before, and she hoped she would never have the occasion to do so again. This man was evil incarnate. His soul was so dark that she understood perfectly why the Furies had dragged him into Tartarus with so much enthusiasm a few hours earlier.

"How did you get out of Tartarus?" she asked in a voice as defiant as she could muster.

The sorcerer remained quiet for a few seconds, and pushed at the cage with a finger, rocking it. Angeline looked daggers at him as she waved her arms trying to keep her balance. She was terrified by this wicked man, but would not give him the satisfaction of seeing her fear.

"Poor little dumb fairy," said the sorcerer. "You're exactly like the Lorekeeper you're vainly trying to protect. You think you know more than anyone else about the war between Yfel and Virtus, but deep down you are completely ignorant of what's really going on."

Angeline pinched her nose and waved her hand before her face.

"Was it with your stinky breath and feeble name-calling that you managed to get out of Tartarus? The demons couldn't take having you in the same room as them, is that it?"

The sorcerer burst out laughing. "I have to admit it's much more fun chatting with you than with that dumbass Samuel, little fata. At least you accept your defeat with a sense of humor."

"I'm not accepting anything!" Angeline shot back, pointing her sword at the sorcerer. "Samuel will find us, and when he gets here you're going to be sorry!"

Once again, the sorcerer laughed harshly. Being ridiculed like this was almost unbearable for the fata, but she was doing everything in her power to remain calm. She did not know the extent of the sorcerer's power, and a direct confrontation with their enemy could easily turn sour. The best she could do for now was to gain some time, and trust that Samuel would find a way to help her.

"Don't kid yourself," said the sorcerer when he finally stopped laughing. "At this very moment, Samuel must be having a little conversation with Sarpedon, and believe me, that is not the sort of meeting that warms the heart. If you think I'm a bad and sinister man, I assure you I'm nothing but a lamb compared to that guy. Sarpedon has a completely twisted mind, and since Samuel is a unique soul, I wouldn't be surprised if the warden-in-chief of Tartarus decided to pay special attention to your dumb Lorekeeper." The sorcerer paused for a moment, and then pushed again on the cage to make it swing at the end of its chain. "I assure you, little fata, that Samuel will never get out of Tartarus," he said. "He will rot for all eternity in there, with madness as his only companion."

"If you got out of there, Samuel can also do it," replied Angeline as she grabbed hold of the bars to stay on her feet, looking her enemy in the eyes.

It was no longer fear she had in her eyes now; it was anger. This man was so evil it filled her with rage and vengeance. Caution advised her to remain calm, but her fingertips sparkled with hundred-year-old energy, and her blade flickered like a purple flame.

The sorcerer moved a few steps back from the cage, remained still for a moment, then dug his hand into his black robe.

"Maybe you are right," he said. "Maybe Samuel can convince Sarpedon to let him out. In any case, it's not important. It's too late now to save this legend anyway."

He pulled his hand from his robe, and Angeline let the tip of her sword fall to the metal floor when she saw the golden bough between his fingers.

"Aeneas is probably already dead," the sorcerer said. "Even if Samuel were to find us, the legend has already changed. You have lost, dumbass."

Angeline had her purple eyes locked on the sacred branch, a bewildered look on her face. The consequences of what the sorcerer had done were catastrophic. How had she not thought that their enemy only needed to desecrate the ritual demanded by Persephone to sign Aeneas's death sentence?

"Melinoe," she whispered in a shaky voice, as if the name burned her lips.

The sorcerer stepped up to Angeline's cage. With a lightning-fast gesture, he pulled the sword from his robe and slid the tip of the blade between two rusty bars. Angeline immediately stepped to the back of the cage, her eyes on the sharp blade less than an inch from her face.

"Precisely," said the sorcerer in a triumphant tone. "The nymph Melinoe is already on the hunt for Aeneas, and let me tell you she is just as frightening as the stories tell. The Trojan and the old crone with him have no chance against her."

The sorcerer wiggled his sword between the bars, forcing Angeline to move to her left and lean forward to avoid the blade. He then raised the golden bough before his hood and turned it between the thumb and index finger of his gloved hand. "I admit I never quite understood why the gods were so obsessed with these stupid rituals," continued the sorcerer. "Isn't it enough that they ask men to fight among themselves in their names? Why do they have to torture us poor humans with idiotic rules? And you, little fata, why are you so bent on protecting these narcissistic beings?"

Angeline remained silent and defied the sorcerer with her look.

"You think I am wicked, don't you?" said the sorcerer. "You think I'm evil made flesh. However, the gods you protect are much more vicious than I could ever be. You think it's fair to sentence a hero to die just because he forgot to put a stupid branch on an altar before continuing his journey? You don't think that kind of punishment is a little excessive?"

"It's not our place to judge the gods," answered Angeline.

The sorcerer shook the sword, and Angeline had to duck again to avoid getting cut to pieces.

"And there lies Virtus's mistake," he said, laughing as he watched the fata wriggle and dance. "Judging the gods is precisely our role. The gods have been abusing the men and women of this world for far too long, and I intend to put a stop to it."

"Samuel will—"

"Your Lorekeeper is nothing but a coward," the sorcerer cut in. "He has always refused to fight me, even when we were young, but I promise you that if Samuel does make it out of Tartarus and find us, I will not let him get away this time. He's going to taste my—"

The sorcerer never had a chance to finish his thought, and it was only by a miracle that Angeline dove to her right in time to avoid the blade, which suddenly jerked forward. A second later, Angeline knocked her head on the cage's ceiling, and before she realized what was going on, her metal prison fell to the ground, the sorcerer's blade still stuck between the bars.

It was only when she managed to get to her feet that she saw the sorcerer lying on the ground, next to the cage. She also saw the golden bough, a few inches from her. Before the sorcerer realized the sacred branch had slipped through his fingers, Angeline pressed against the bars. Her face twisted by effort, she stretched her arm as far as she could, wiggling her fingers, and finally grabbed one of the leaves between her index and middle finger. Delicately, she pulled the bough toward her until she was able to seize it. Without wasting a second, she pulled the sacred branch into the cage, and hid it as best she could behind her.

A little farther away, the sorcerer raised his head. Picking up his sword, he jumped to his feet without noticing that the bough was gone.

"I must admit, I underestimated you," he said toward the cave's entrance.

Angeline swept the cavern with her eyes, but could not see anyone else.

Then she understood who he was talking to, and a smile widened on her lips.

Samuel took the Helm of Darkness from his head. "It's not the first time you have underestimated me," he said. "You're not the only one who knows the secrets of Tartarus."

The sorcerer slowly walked forward, his sword held straight up in front of him. Behind his enemy, Samuel saw the tiny cage and Angeline locked inside. Seeing her like this, a prisoner between rusty bars, he regretted trying only to knock out the sorcerer with the hilt of his weapon. On top of having completely failed to do so, he had put Angeline's life in danger when the cage had come free of the chain. However, as evil as the Yfel sorcerer was, Samuel had not been able to kill him. Even after he had sneaked into the cave without the sorcerer noticing his presence, Samuel had not been able to take a man's life.

Maybe one day he would regret his decision, but he thought his compassion was one of the things that made him different from his enemy.

"I should have known Sarpedon's reputation was overblown," said the sorcerer in a chilling voice. "But don't worry, Samuel, I have no intention of disappointing you as well."

As soon as he said these words, the sorcerer raised his sword and pounced on Samuel. The young man turned to his right, dodged the attack, and then struck the sorcerer between the shoulder blades with his elbow. His enemy staggered to the cave wall, where he had to rest his hand to get his balance back.

"All right," said Samuel, "but I must warn you: if you think I'm scared of you, as you pretend, you're the one who may be disappointed."

Before the sorcerer could turn and strike again, Samuel pushed him flat against the stone wall with his foot. The sorcerer cried out in anger and collapsed to the ground.

"Show him what you can do, Samuel!" yelled Angeline.

"Are you all right?" asked Samuel, glancing at her.

"Yes, I'm okay," answered Angeline. "Watch out!"

Samuel took a step back to avoid a projectile of Yfel energy. It was not the first time he had fought the sorcerer, who was so predictable it was almost pathetic. Samuel had deliberately turned his eyes away from him, knowing the sorcerer would seize the occasion to send a spell his way. Now that it was done, and his enemy was vulnerable to a new strike, Samuel leapt toward the sorcerer. A second later, he hit the sorcerer with a right hook to the head. The sorcerer fell to the ground again and let go of his sword.

"Your little magic tricks don't work on me anymore," said Samuel. "You should give up and tell us what the Yfel plans to do, before things really take a turn for the worse."

The sorcerer got up on one knee. Before he answered, he spit blood on the ground.

"If you think you can force me to do anything," replied the sorcerer, "you're sorely mistaken, dumbass!"

Without any warning, the sorcerer produced a light so bright it blinded Samuel for a second, which was enough to allow his enemy to pick up his sword again and jump to his feet. When Samuel opened his eyes, the sorcerer pounced on him, his sword high above his head.

Samuel raised his own weapon and parried the sorcerer's strike, but he tripped on a rock, let go of his sword, and fell heavily to the ground. The sorcerer took advantage of his fall to jump on him, and Samuel had barely enough time to grab his wrists and stop his momentum, the sorcerer's blade less than an inch from his neck.

"There's no point in resisting," said the sorcerer as he leaned with all his weight on the weapon. "You're only delaying the inevitable."

"That's what you think," replied Samuel as he pushed with all his might against the arms of his enemy, "but I'm going to teach you something that could be useful …"

Samuel hit the sorcerer in the ribs with his knee. Taken by surprise, his enemy loosened his grip on his weapon, and Samuel seized the opportunity to push with all his strength to his left. The two foes rolled several yards, until Samuel jumped to his feet again.

"You talk way too much," he said, picking up his sword with lightning-fast movements.

The sorcerer turned on his back, but before he could stand up, Samuel kicked his weapon away and angled his own sword under the chin of his enemy.

"But since it's so hard for you to hold your tongue," said Samuel, "I'm going to give you a chance to speak. Tell me which goddess you are trying to kill."

The sorcerer tried to pull himself up a little, but Samuel leaned harder on his sword.

"I know you found the secret to the gods' immortality," added Samuel, "and I know you intend to use it to kill one of them. Tell me which, and I will let you live."

The sorcerer stayed still for a moment, his face hidden by the shadow of the hood. Samuel felt his icy gaze on him, and heard his hoarse breathing whistling through his teeth.

Then the sorcerer burst out laughing, and anger grew in Samuel's guts.

"Let me live?" asked the sorcerer. "Come on, Samuel, we both know you are not capable of killing me. If you'd had the guts to do it, you wouldn't have tried to merely knock me out with the pommel of your sword earlier. That was an opportunity you'll never get again, I can promise you that."

Samuel looked straight into the darkness floating inside the sorcerer's hood. His enemy had called his bluff. Samuel had no intention of killing him.

"Maybe he can't kill you," yelled Angeline, still locked in the cage, "but I assure you, I know particularly efficient ways to loosen tongues. Get me out of here, Samuel, and I promise he will not appreciate the next fifteen minutes!"

Samuel raised his chin, but kept his eyes locked on the sorcerer lying before him.

"It seems you have a decision to make, dumbass!" said the sorcerer.

"Shut up," answered Samuel.

The sorcerer replied with a laugh that echoed across the small cave.

Samuel could not move a muscle, his gaze still on his enemy. He hated to admit it, but the sorcerer was right: he had a decision to make. For the first time since he became the Lorekeeper, his foe was at his mercy. It was a unique occasion to learn what the Yfel really had planned, but Samuel had no idea how to force the information out of the sorcerer. He might have spent a bit of time in the dungeons of Tartarus, but he was not a seasoned torturer.

Angeline had offered to do it, but to free her, Samuel had to step away from the sorcerer. His enemy would surely take the opportunity to jump back to his feet and try to turn the tables. Samuel could not let their enemy off the hook so easily. If he could not obtain the answers they wanted, then he had to make sure, once and for all, that the sorcerer could not do any more harm.

Samuel pushed the tip of his blade a little closer to the sorcerer's throat, forcing him to lift his chin.

"If you were in my position, you would have already sliced my throat," he said.

"Without hesitation," said the sorcerer defiantly.

Contrasting emotions tangled in Samuel's mind. The sorcerer was his enemy, but he still felt a certain amount of compassion toward this man lying at his feet. Samuel was convinced he had not chosen to be the Yfel's sorcerer, just as Samuel had not asked to become the Lorekeeper. As frightening as he was, the sorcerer was first and foremost a human being—an unfortunate soul placed in a situation he could not control.

Still, the sorcerer was also a man with a mission, and the aim of this mission was nothing less than changing the world Samuel lived in. The Yfel was trying to kill a god, and the consequences for Earth's history were as unpredictable as they were catastrophic. Samuel could not close his eyes to such an attack against his world and remain with his arms crossed over his chest. He had to do everything in his power to thwart the Yfel's plan, even if it required actions he never thought he would be capable of doing.

And then there was another feeling trying to make itself heard in this whirlpool of emotion in Samuel's mind. It was a curious sense of familiarity, as if a part of Samuel's soul knew the man at the end of his sword was not a stranger. Angeline had repeated many times that the sorcerer could be anyone from his own world. Was this the reason for his hesitation? Did he fear hurting someone close to him, someone he cared about?

"So, what's it going to be?" asked the sorcerer with scorn in his voice. "I don't have all day."

Something in the sorcerer's tone reminded him of someone he regularly encountered when he was on Earth, when he was only Samuel, an ordinary young man attending high school and—Samuel opened his eyes wide. It was not the sorcerer's voice that had evoked this familiarity, but rather the insult he had used.

"Danny…?"

Time froze around Samuel. His limbs became numb, and his breath turned to stone in his lungs.

"It about time you got it, dumbass," said the sorcerer.

Samuel's legs wavered for a moment, and he had to take a step back to keep his balance. The sorcerer took the opportunity to pull himself to a sitting position. He leaned against the stone wall behind him.

"But ... how..." mumbled Samuel. "How is it possible? I thought that ..."

Reality hit him like a herd of buffalos. He knew the sorcerer, and although he was not someone with whom he had a lot of affinity, he was nevertheless a young man, who he saw almost every day, who had friends and family, and probably dreams and ambitions as well.

The sorcerer raised his hands to his head and, after a slight hesitation, he pulled back the hood. What Samuel saw made his heart jump to his throat, and he had to sit on a rock to keep his stomach where it was.

"By all the gods," said Samuel, "what have they done to you?"

Danny's face was unrecognizable. His skin was colorless and cracked like the bark of an old tree. His cheeks, forehead and chin were covered in black scars, and his eyes were as dark as the abyss. His nose was pulled back grotesquely, dragging the upper lip after it and revealing rotten teeth, between which whistled a laborious breathing. Danny's white and patchy hair fell alongside his face, and gave him the look of a hundred-year-old man.

"Not all of us are so lucky as to be chosen by the white dice," said Danny. "My powers did not come to me without any effort, like yours. My training was long and painful, as you can see."

Samuel was speechless. Danny was the sorcerer. How was that possible? When he had left Earth for Metverold, Patrick had told Samuel he had given the black dice to his younger brother.

"Samuel!" shouted Angeline. "This man isn't the same person you knew. Don't forget he is the Yfel's sorcerer. Stay on your guard."

Samuel briefly glanced at Angeline, but it was enough time for the sorcerer to jump to his feet and pick up his sword. Before Samuel had a chance to defend himself, Danny had disarmed him and now pointed his own blade under the Lorekeeper's chin.

"You should have listened to the little dumbass," he said.

The cold, metallic bite of the sword sent a chill down Samuel's spine. His throat clenched, and his vision blurred as if he was in a nightmare he was not able to escape. His muscles were as stiff as the ropes of an old ship, and his heart beat like thunder.

He was going to die here, in Hell.

Slowly he looked up at Danny. His enemy would not hesitate much longer. He would not show the same pity Samuel had shown him a moment earlier. Any second now, the sorcerer would cut the Lorekeeper's throat, and everything would fade to darkness.

However, Danny remained still, and held Samuel's gaze. For what seemed like endless seconds, he looked at the young man at the end of his sword. Then the blackness in the sorcerer's eyes vanished, and for the first time Danny looked at Samuel's face with the eyes the Yfel had stolen from him. It only lasted for a heartbeat, before darkness covered the pupils again, but it was enough for Samuel to note a subtle change in the sorcerer's face.

A few seconds later, Danny pulled the hood back over his head, hiding his horrible face again in the shadows. Then he lowered his weapon and stepped back toward the cave entrance.

"Next time I find you in my way I will not be so merciful, dumbass," said the sorcerer, before turning and vanishing into the darkness.

Despite Angeline's shouts to chase his enemy, Samuel did not move. He had truly thought his time had come; that the sorcerer would seize this unique occasion to get rid of his enemy—but he was still breathing. Something deep inside Danny had stayed his hand and prevented him from doing what could not be undone.

Despite all the horrors he had endured to become the Yfel sorcerer, a part of Danny was still human, even if it was buried in the deepest parts of his soul.

29

"Hurry up, Samuel!" yelled Angeline. "You have to get me out of here."

Samuel's legs were still shaking when he stood back up. For a moment, he really thought his time had come, but something strange had happened, and the sorcerer had decided to let him live.

"Samuel!" shouted Angeline with more insistence.

The young man lowered his eyes to the fata, still a prisoner of the cage on the ground.

"Are you all right?" he asked.

"I think so," answered Angeline. "Well, nothing's broken, that's the important thing."

Samuel knelt next to the cage and checked the padlock.

"I've already tried to unlock it with some Virtus energy," said Angeline, "but all it got me was a jolt in the fingertips. The sorcerer has cast a spell on the padlock with the Yfel's energy."

Samuel examined the lock more closely. He had never tried to pick a lock before, and he doubted he could succeed on an enchanted one. He opted for a more traditional method, and grabbed his sword from the ground behind him.

"I suggest you move back a little," he said to Angeline. "There might be some sparks."

Angeline looked at him worriedly, but she quickly moved to the back of the cage. Samuel straightened and took hold of his sword with two hands. Since the blade still glowed with Virtus's energy, he hoped to obtain the same result he got with Aristaeus's skull, during his last adventure. The explosion had been particularly violent, but the skull had also been much bigger than the padlock. In theory, the explosion should not be as powerful this time.

At least, he hoped not.

Angeline curled into a ball on the floor. Samuel took a deep breath, raised his weapon over his head and struck the padlock as hard as he could. A detonation echoed in the cave, and thousands of purple and green sparks flew in all directions, but fortunately the shock of both energies colliding only produced a small explosion. Nevertheless, it was big enough to open the padlock. A few seconds later, Angeline soared out of the cage holding the golden bough in her hands.

"Why couldn't I make the padlock explode when I tried to touch it with Virtus's energy?" she asked.

"I don't have the slightest idea," answered Samuel. "Maybe it was too dangerous to do it with your hands, and Virtus's energy wanted to protect you?"

"Or maybe you're getting more decisive results because of the link you share with the sorcerer."

Angeline's last remark had been said in a tone that wavered between an accusation and a question, and Samuel thought that sooner or later he would have to explain to the fata who Danny was.

"Is that the golden bough?" he asked, to change the subject.

"Yes. The sorcerer stole it and we have to give it back to Persephone in a hurry, or Aeneas will be in serious trouble."

Samuel was not sure he understood exactly why the bough was so important, but Angeline did not give him the opportunity to ask more questions. Instead, she hurried out of the cave, and Samuel followed her.

The small cave they emerged from stood at the foot of a hill, lost in the middle of a deserted scarlet plain. A forest of giant trees, as dark as the water of the Acheron, stood on the western side of the plain, and to the south the red grass stretched endlessly, until the landscape fused with the blazing horizon. To the east, an ash-gray marsh threatened to spread its thick fog over the plain.

When Samuel walked over to Angeline, she was looking worriedly in all directions at once, while her wings buzzed.

"By all the gods of the Underworld," she said. "I don't know where to go! I don't know where Persephone's palace is."

"This way," said Samuel as he started toward the murky swamp. "The palace is on the other side of this marsh."

Angeline looked at him in shock, then flew after him.

"How do you know where it is?" she asked.

"Because I followed the sorcerer to get here."

Angeline was still looking at him with bewildered eyes.

"After I got out of Tartarus," Samuel explained, "I went back to King Minos's court, and then I followed the road leading to Elysium. The path brought me to a white palace, which I thought must be Persephone's."

Angeline nodded.

"When I got close to the palace," continued Samuel, "I saw the sorcerer walking away. That's when I put the Helm of Darkness on my head to become invisible, and I followed him here."

Angeline's face suddenly darkened, and she moved in front of Samuel, both fists on her hips.

"Why didn't you stop him?" she asked. "He had stolen the golden bough, and you let him get away with it! Aeneas may be dead already."

"I wanted him to lead me to you, Angeline. It was out of the question that I abandon you in the Underworld. Following the sorcerer was the only way I could find you."

Angeline's features suddenly softened. Slowly, she came closer to Samuel's face and put a delicate hand on his cheek.

"I'm sorry I got so angry," she said. "Please don't think I am not grateful, because, I assure you, I had no desire to spend the rest of my life in this horrible place. Thank you for rescuing me, Samuel."

Samuel held Angeline's gaze for a moment, then lowered his eyes to the golden bough between his fingers.

"It's okay," he said. "You would have done the same thing for me. Come, we have to bring this branch back to the goddess's altar, right?"

Angeline nodded, and they both darted across the murky swamp.

"By the way, how did you get out of Tartarus?" asked Angeline as the first fingers of fog wrapped around them.

"It's quite a story," replied Samuel. "Unfortunately, it will have to wait, because first I'd like you to explain to me why it's so important we bring the golden bough back to Persephone. Is Aeneas really in danger just because the ritual was not respected to the end, like the Yfel sorcerer said?"

"Indeed he is, but it's more complicated than that. You see, Hell must remain forbidden to the living. Can you imagine what would happen if anyone could just walk in here without any restrictions? It would be total chaos. Everyone would try to rescue their loved ones, and it would upset the natural order of things. That's why the gods have put many hurdles in the way, as well as several guardians."

"Like Charon and Cerberus?"

"Yes," said Angeline. "They are the most famous guardians of Pluto's kingdom, but there are other, subtler, mechanisms, like the ritual to Persephone. Contrary to what the sorcerer believes, the ritual was not put in place by the goddess on a whim. It's the ultimate barrier protecting Elysium. It's there in case the previous guardians fail in their tasks, and let impure souls reach the white palace. Only a living soul who had been previously granted the golden bough by the gods can accomplish the ritual, and therefore only the worthy can access Elysium before their death."

Samuel ducked to avoid the branches of a dead tree, and hopped over a puddle of thick mud.

"Elysium is a heavenly place," added Angeline, "where violence does not exist. If a living person could access this place to attack a soul, acting by vengeance or envy, it would be the end of this region of the Underworld. And if Elysium stopped existing, the souls of those who hadn't sinned during their lives would suffer the same torments as those who had. If that were the case, what's to keep anyone from murdering whoever they wanted, or stealing whatever they desired? This is why the ritual exists and why it's important to respect it. The ritual protects this promise of a better afterlife, to keep people from descending into lawlessness."

"I see. And what happens when the offering is removed from the altar?" asked Samuel.

"Persephone sends Melinoe to kill the intruder," answered Angeline, a bit hesitantly. "She is a terrifying nymph, nicknamed the Bringer of Nightmares and Madness. If she gets her hands on Aeneas before we can place the bough back on Persephone's altar, she will subject him to torments that would make the cruelest demons tremble in fear."

"In that case, we don't have a second to lose," said Samuel, quickening his pace.

Deiphobe hastily guided Aeneas among the souls lounging on the shores of the River Lethe. The poet Musaeus had indicated in which direction they would find the venerable Anchises, but for the moment, the Sibyl had no intention of leading the Trojan to his father. Constantly moving was the best option right now.

When she peeked over her shoulder, she saw the ominous storm clouds pursuing them, as well as the silhouette of the horrible nymph Melinoe, sometimes clear, sometimes blurry, like images in a bad dream. Until now, Deiphobe had been able to keep a distance between them and the nightmarish nymph, but she doubted she would be able to do so for much longer. Sooner or later, Persephone's assassin would catch up to them.

But what else could she do? There was nowhere they could hide, nor any way to lose Melinoe. Their only hope lay in Angeline and Samuel accomplishing the ritual in their name to enter Elysium, and Deiphobe did not even know if their two companions were still alive.

Thunder ripped through the sky over Elysium, and the souls on the idyllic riverbank looked up in surprise. Aeneas suddenly stopped and looked up at the flashes of lightning slashing the distant horizon.

"Priestess of Apollo, what is the meaning of the storm unleashing its fury over there?" he asked.

Turning, Deiphobe saw the storm was now closer than ever, and her heart raced faster. In her entire life, she had never been more terrified than she was at this moment. Still, she did her best to hide the fear in her voice. "Pious Aeneas, now is not the time to stop," Deiphobe told him. "This storm that you see has been sent after us by your enemies, and should these clouds cast their dark shadows over our heads, we will be forever doomed. Come, let's not stay here any longer, and pray the gods that the lightning and thunder pursuing us be blown toward other skies."

Samuel and Angeline were gasping for air. Well, Samuel was. Angeline had abandoned the idea of following him a few moments ago, and had decided to take her usual place on his shoulder—without asking for his permission, of course.

Fortunately, the outline of Persephone's palace stood against the horizon, and with renewed energy Samuel hurried down the hill toward the white wall. A few minutes later, with his face drenched in sweat and lungs burning in pain, he came to the fountain of invisible water, as well as the altar of immaculate marble. Without thinking twice, Samuel rushed to the altar, his arm stretched out before him to place the golden bough on the marble as fast as possible.

"Wait!" yelled Angeline. "Not so fast!"

Samuel stopped just before he dropped the sacred branch on the white stone.

"We have to observe the entire ritual," continued Angeline. "For Melinoe to abandon her hunt, we have to execute every rite owed to Persephone."

In the following minutes, Angeline dictated the instructions that Samuel followed as fast as he could. First he took off his armor and hastily purified his body with the cool water—after asking Angeline to turn around, of course. He then recited a prayer to the queen of Hell, careful to point out that he and Angeline were companions of Aeneas and Deiphobe, and that the offering was done in their name as well.

When he was done, Samuel placed the golden bough on the altar.

"And now what do we do?" he asked, putting his armor back on.

"We wait and pray we're not too late," answered Angeline.

Deiphobe was kneeling behind a boulder, her hands joined under her chin and her eyes closed. Despite the prayers she uttered aloud, a stormy wind whipped at her face, and furious thunder shook the ground. Next to her, Aeneas had his sword in his hand, and stood ready to face the dangers hiding in the storm. He did not know he had no hope of defeating Melinoe.

Lightning struck so close that an explosion shook the rocks in front of Deiphobe. The soul of an unfortunate bystander shrieked in terror, and Aeneas screamed to the priestess, but she kept her hands together and her eyes shut, for she feared that the mere vision of Melinoe would steal her mind.

The wind's ferocity cranked up a notch, and a sudden bone-chilling rain drenched Aeneas and Deiphobe, while the ground shook relentlessly and the air became ice cold. The nymph, carrier of nightmares and madness, was close to them now. A few more minutes and they would be swept into insanity.

Then the wind abruptly fell, the rain stopped and everything became quiet again.

Deiphobe remained crouched behind the boulder a moment longer, then carefully opened her eyes. Cautiously, she stretched her neck out and got back to her feet. The sky was a bright blue again, without a single cloud to spoil its azure light, and the green grass danced under a warm and pleasant breeze.

Melinoe had miraculously disappeared, and Elysium was once again a calm and serene place.

"Priestess, can you explain to me what just happened?" asked Aeneas, his sword still in hand.

With a smile on her lips, Deiphobe stepped up to him and put a comforting hand on his shoulder.

"It would seem, Prince of Troy, that unknown allies have come to our aid," she answered. "Now, let us find your father, the venerable Anchises."

30

Samuel and Angeline hurried to join the crowd of shadows lazing once more under the warm sun of Elysium, whose rays comforted Samuel's heart. After a trip into the depths of Tartarus, feeling the warmth of the day on his skin was particularly soothing. He knew he was still in the Underworld, but the illusion of being back on the surface was sufficient to make him momentarily forget the last few hours he had just been through.

Angeline soared above the crowd, and she guided Samuel to the place where Aeneas was to be reunited with his father. They quickly passed before the poet Musaeus—who did not care for them one bit—and then went over a small hill. After walking along a river of stunning clarity, they went across a field of emerald grass. When they came to the top of a gentle slope, Samuel saw Deiphobe and Aeneas, still looking for Anchises.

Samuel walked down the hill without hurrying, so he wouldn't be noticed by the Trojan hero. When he was less than thirty feet from Aeneas, his eyes met Deiphobe's. She smiled subtly at him and gave the barest nod. Samuel interpreted the gesture as a sign of gratitude, and smiled back at her. At that moment, Aeneas located his father Anchises and ran to him, his eyes brightened by tears. The hero threw himself into Anchises's arms, and Samuel could hear their muffled laughter and joyful tears.

"Here you are at last," said Anchises, taking a step back to admire his son. "I thought this moment would never come to pass. If you only knew how I counted the days until I could gaze on your face again, my son. What lands have you crossed, what seas have you mastered, to reach this place? How many perils tested your might, my child? How I dreaded this moment would never come, but here you stand before me, safe and sound."

Aeneas seized his father by the shoulders and embraced him again, the words whispered by his heart suddenly stuck in his throat. After a moment of silence, the hero composed himself and spoke to Anchises in a voice marked by emotion: "It was your melancholic image, Father, that drove me to pass the threshold of the Underworld. The times you visited me in dreams gave me the courage to face the dangers of Pluto's kingdom."

Anchises passed his arm over Aeneas's shoulder and pulled him away. Deiphobe walked after them, followed by Angeline and Samuel. Samuel did not think the sorcerer could enter Elysium—if his enemy was still in the Underworld—but he preferred not to lose sight of Aeneas.

Anchises led his son along a path of white sand, to the top of a hill overshadowing a small vale. The clear river Samuel had followed earlier flowed at the bottom of the valley, toward a forest of majestic trees.

"Tell me: what are these woods I see in the distance?" asked Aeneas. "And this river, where the souls seem to gather by the thousands, what is it called? What is this place where countless nations flutter like bees under the serene summer light?"

Anchises looked upon his son's face, and Aeneas smiled back at him. He then took the hero's hand and guided him down to the bottom of the vale, toward the river calmly flowing through the center.

"The shadows you see here," answered Anchises, "are the souls of those whom the Fates owe a second incarnation, and who drink for peace and long forgetfulness from the River Lethe. Long have I desired to show you this crowd before us, and number all the generations of your children, so that you may rejoice with me in finding Italy."

"What is he talking about?" whispered Samuel to Angeline. "I don't understand any of those metaphors."

Angeline signaled him to stay quiet and listen.

"O my father, must we think there are souls who can climb back to the upper air, and who can aspire to slip again among the thick bonds of flesh?" Aeneas asked Anchises. "Where does it come from, this sad longing to see the light of day again and leave this place of marvel that is Elysium?"

Anchises turned to his son and gently caressed his face with a gesture full of fatherly love.

"I will tell you everything, my son, do not worry. I will not hold you in suspense any longer."

As he led his son toward the River Lethe, Anchises explained how the souls of the deceased were processed in Pluto's kingdom, and how they could one day aspire to see the light of the sun again.

"First of all, know that heaven and Earth, the liquid fields, and the shining orb of the moon, as well as the titanic star that is the sun, are all inhabited and animated by a spiritual truth. The spirit that spreads in the world's members sways the entire mass, and as it mingles, it transforms this vast frame that is our universe. From this spirit comes the races of men and beasts, and the life of winged things, and all the monstrous forms that Ocean breeds under his glittering floor. Those seeds of life have a fiery force, a divine fire they owe to their celestial origin. But this flame is numbed by the taint of the body. It is dulled by our doomed flesh. Hence, it is how the souls know fear, desire, pain and joy, and so our souls no longer make out the light of the heaven, locked as they are in the darkness of their prison-house. And even on this final day, when the last ray of life is gone, the woeful souls are not rid of the evil, of all their bodily stains.

Their vices, hardened by the years, are rooted in marvelous depths.

"Therefore, they are schooled in punishment, and pay all the forfeit of a lifelong ill. Some are hung and stretched to the light wind, and some have the taint of guilt washed out of their blood in the dreary deep, while others are cleansed in the eternal flames. Each of us suffers his own punishment. Few of us are brought to the vast Elysian fields, and called to occupy this happy land forever. It is only after long days that time finally erases the ancient scars and leaves untainted the ethereal sense of the soul, this pure spiritual flame. Then, when the wheel of a thousand years has come full round, a god summons the souls to the shores of the River Lethe, so that they may see the celestial vault again, after having lost all memory of their passage in this place."

When Anchises finished his explanation, he led Aeneas and Deiphobe across the crowd pressing on the shores of the Lethe, followed at a distance by Samuel and Angeline.

"I'm not entirely sure I understood what Anchises was talking about," whispered Samuel.

"He was referring to reincarnation," Angeline told him. "According to the Romans, the souls are, at their most basic level, pure and untainted. It's only once they are in our body that they become soiled by our sins. After our death, our soul has to be purified by different ordeals, until it becomes divine and pure again. Once it is clean, our soul can come back to Earth, after drinking water from the Lethe, which will make it forget its previous lives and its time in Hell."

Angeline's attention was drawn by Aeneas and Anchises. Samuel followed her gaze, and saw the old man climb on a rock in the middle of the crowd and pull his son up after him.

"You see that man over there?" asked Anchises. "The one leaning on a blunt spear? He holds the nearest place allotted in our groves. He shall rise first under the rays of the sun with Italian blood mingled with our own. He's name is Silvius, of

Alban race, and he is the last child that your wife Lavinia will nurture at the end of your life, and whom she will raise in a woodland. From him, in Alba the Long shall our house have dominion."

Samuel shot a questioning look at Angeline.

"Alba is a town that once stood close to Rome," she said.

Anchises then swept the rest of the crowd with his eyes, and pointed at a gigantic man who was pushing his way to the river with the help of his large shields. He was followed by two men of equally imposing size.

"See, over there," said Anchises as he indicated the three men. "Here comes the one who shall renew your name, Silvius Aeneas, along with Capys and Procas, glory of the Trojan race. See what strength they display! You see in them founders of cities: Nomentum, Gabii and Fidena."

"More ancient cities?" asked Samuel.

Angeline nodded. "They are towns that will eventually be a part of the Roman Empire," she said.

Again, Anchises looked over the crowd. He seemed to be searching for a particular soul, and when he found it, his eyes shimmered in pride, and he quickly pointed him out to Aeneas.

"Here comes the one who will grow the glory of your lineage, my son. His name is Romulus, son of the god Mars. By his augury shall the illustrious city called Rome see the light of day. The empire of Rome shall have no equal other than Olympus, and shall gird about seven fortresses with a single wall."

Samuel stretched his neck to spot the one Anchises was pointing out. When he saw Romulus, he could hardly believe he had the founder of Rome in front of him; the founder of a city that would give birth to an empire that would change the face of the world. Unlike Aeneas, Romulus was short, potbellied and covered in dirt.

"*That's* Romulus?" asked Samuel.

"Yes," answered Angeline. "Let's just say that Rome's beginnings were not as glorious as the rest of its story."

On the small boulder, Anchises passed an arm over Aeneas's shoulders, then swept the crowd with the other hand.

"Now turn your eyes and look upon this nation, your Romans, who will come from your blood. Here is Caesar and all of Iulus's posterity, and there is this man who was so often promised to you, Caesar Augustus, son of a god, who shall again establish the age of gold in Latium. He shall push the boundaries of his empire farther than the Garamants and the Indians, to the land that lies beyond the Zodiac sign."

Once again, Samuel tried to see the legendary character pointed out by Anchises. Angeline gently tugged on his armor to let him know he should remain discreet, but Samuel was not about to let a chance to see Julius Caesar pass. He followed Aeneas's gaze toward a group of souls to his right, but was unable to see who exactly the old man was referring to. He was about to turn his eyes to Aeneas again, when he saw a familiar face in the crowd. Seeing this man with his brown beard and piercing eyes made his heart jump in his chest, and it was only by a miracle that he managed to keep his joy in check.

"He won't recognize you," whispered Angeline. "His soul hasn't lived the adventures waiting for him yet."

At the same time, Anchises saw the man in question and pointed him out to his son Aeneas.

"Here comes proud Brutus of Troy, who shall be exiled from his lands," said Anchises to his son. "Like you, he shall face many dangers and survive a most perilous journey, before reaching a land where he will establish a nation that will bear his name. See how tall he stands, and how he will honor his ancestors with his deeds."

Anchises continued to list the descendants of his son, but Samuel was no longer listening. His eyes were locked on the shadow of his friend Brutus. How he would have loved to talk to him and tell the stories of his latest adventure. He wondered if Corineus was also somewhere around, but could not spot the warrior's huge silhouette.

"I think we can let them continue their discussion in peace," whispered Angeline. "We have a lot to talk about, you and I. Let's take this opportunity to do it, while Anchises presents each of his descendants to Aeneas."

Samuel and Angeline walked a little away from Anchises and Aeneas, but made sure to stay in range to keep an eye on them. After they found a quiet spot to chat, Samuel sat on the silky grass, and Angeline sat facing him.

"There are so many things we need to discuss that I don't know where to start," said Samuel.

"Why don't you start by telling me how you escaped Tartarus?" suggested Angeline.

Samuel nodded and began telling the story of his meeting with Nona, one of the three Parcae. As soon as he started telling how the youngest of the three sisters had come to talk with him, Angeline opened her eyes wide with amazement, and hung on each word.

"Usually Lorekeepers have no contact with the Parcae," she said when Samuel finished his tale. "To tell you the truth, I think no one has laid eyes on one of them for many centuries. If Nona made a point of coming see you, it has to be because these are dire times."

"That's more or less what Nona seemed to be saying. She mentioned the Yfel was trying to kill a god, and that even she and her sisters could not foresee the consequences should they succeed."

Angeline flew above Samuel and circled his head a few times.

"And you say she gave you a golden thread that you took back to Tartarus?" she asked.

"Yes."

"What did you do with it?"

"When I came to my senses, I was a prisoner of Sarpedon, Minos and Rhadamanthus's brother. He did not want to hear a word of my story, but when I showed him the golden thread, he immediately freed me."

Angeline stopped before Samuel and shot him a stunned look. "He freed you? Just like that? Just because you showed him a golden thread?"

"It's wasn't only a golden thread. Just before I left Tartarus, Sarpedon explained to me that after his death, a long time ago, the Parcae offered him to be the head warden of Tartarus. In exchange, the day would come when they would give him what his heart desired the most."

"And it was this golden thread?" asked Angeline.

"In truth, it was more than a golden thread. It was the life thread of his one true love, a man named Miletos. It's because of him Sarpedon always fought with his brothers and had to go into exile."

"And what is he going to do with this thread of life now?"

"I have no clue, but in his eyes it was a priceless treasure. As soon as Sarpedon saw the golden thread, he took the chains off me, and that's what really matters."

Angeline did a few more circles around Samuel, then landed in front of him and leaned on his knee.

"All right," she said. "So Sarpedon was blown away by the thread of life belonging to his love and, to thank you, he let you go. Then what did he do?"

Samuel told Angeline about his meeting with the poor Tantalus. When he told her the man had told the sorcerer how to kill a god, Angeline almost passed out in the grass, but when Samuel added that this secret was the ambrosia, she seemed to pull herself back together.

"So Tantalus never truly served his son for dinner to the gods?" she asked.

"No. He claims it's a story invented by Zeus to hide the truth."

"And this truth is that gods can be poisoned if they drink ambrosia mixed with human blood?"

"Yes," answered Samuel. "To be honest, I was expecting something a little more complicated. How can we hope to stop the sorcerer from mixing a few drops of his own blood to a god's drink?"

"Don't worry, Samuel, it's not as simple as you think. You see, in Greek mythology, ambrosia is a mysterious beverage. No one knows its composition, not even the gods. It is delivered daily directly to Olympus by gigantic doves, and no one knows where they come from. If the sorcerer wants to poison a god, I don't know how he will be able to get his hand on some ambrosia."

"Aren't there any legends that would give him access to ambrosia?"

"There are a few, but they are known only by a handful of people, and access to the divine food is always very well guarded. The gods of Olympus are extremely protective of their ambrosia, and even the Yfel would not dare to steal some directly under the nose of a god. To deny a god his food is a crime punishable by death."

Samuel thought of Tantalus, sentenced to an eternity of constant temptation. "Or worse," he muttered.

"So the sorcerer never had the intention of freeing anyone from Tartarus?" Angeline asked.

Samuel shook his head. "No, he only wanted to learn Tantalus's secret," he said. "I think he knew we were following him, and he was hoping to lose us in this dark place."

"Which brings me to another question," said Angeline. "How did you get out of there? I thought the doors could only be opened by Tisiphone."

"I escaped the same way the sorcerer did, when he kidnapped you," replied Samuel.

"I was unconscious! I don't have the slightest idea how I got outside the impenetrable walls of Tartarus."

Samuel explained how Sarpedon, after their discussion with Tantalus, had revealed to Samuel how to get out of the prison.

"You remember the river that runs around Tartarus?" he asked.

"The Cocytus?"

"Yes. When we crossed the bridge over it, you told me it drew its water from the tears of Tartarus's prisoners."

"That's what they say, yes," said Angeline. "Don't tell me you—"

"To get out of Tartarus, one only has to follow the tears. Sarpedon told me most cells are equipped with piping too small for a man to squeeze through, but there are a couple of exceptions, like Tantalus's cell."

"I'm not following you."

"As part of his punishment, Tantalus must stand in a pond he can never reach to quench his thirst. This pond is fed by the tears he sheds, and it's directly linked to the Cocytus through an underground pipe."

"And that pipe is large enough for a man to squeeze through," said Angeline.

"Exactly. That's how I got out of Tartarus."

Angeline was stunned. There *was* a way to get out of Tartarus. "Wait a minute," she said suddenly. "If there is a way to escape right beneath Tantalus, why isn't he escaping?"

"I asked myself the same question," replied Samuel. "I don't think he knows the tunnel even exists. He was barely conscious of our presence in the cell. The only things that interest him are the apples before his nose and the water under his chin. Plus, most of the time, one of the Furies keeps him company, just to taunt him some more."

Angeline's tiny body shivered.

"I had forgotten about them," she said. "I really hate those creatures. You can count yourself lucky Sarpedon can control them. If he had left you in their hands, you could have said goodbye to your mental health."

Samuel and Angeline remained silent for a few moments, each trying to get rid of the memories of their frightening journey in Tartarus. Even though Samuel had previously dominated his fears, it did not change the fact that his short stay in the gloomy halls of the Titans' prison would leave a deep scar in his memory.

"So, it turns out you do know the sorcerer," said Angeline after a little while.

"Yes. His name is Danny."

"He's a friend of yours back on Earth?"

"Quite the opposite. Danny and I ... let's just say we don't see things the same way."

"What do you mean?" asked Angeline.

"Me, I'm more the 'live and let live' type of guy. All I want to do is mind my own business and not bother anyone, but Danny is the complete opposite. He constantly tries to pick a fight with everyone, especially those smaller than he is, which is pretty much every student at our school."

"He seems like a real rainbow of joy."

"I don't know what his problem is," said Samuel. "No one has ever done anything to him, for all I know. It seems he's always angry, for no reason at all, and lately it's like he's getting mad by just looking at me."

"It's probably because he knew you were the Lorekeeper from the very beginning."

Samuel looked into Angeline's eyes. "That is also pretty strange, because Danny should not be the sorcerer. It's impossible."

"But you saw him, didn't you?"

"Yes, but he's not the one in possession of the black dice."

Angeline shook her head and pinched her nose.

"Wait a minute," she said. "What do you mean, he's not in possession of the black dice? Of course he has them; otherwise, he wouldn't be the sorcerer."

"I don't know how he became the sorcerer, but the black dice were not bought by him. There is this guy Patrick, who my sister is seeing. When he saw the white dice on my desk, he told me he had bought the black ones at the same hobby store I did. At first I thought he was the sorcerer, but then he told me he had given the dice to his younger brother, Simon."

Angeline looked at Samuel with troubled eyes, trying to understand what he was getting at.

"You remember our first adventure?" asked Samuel.

"Of course."

"I was brought to Metverold the day after I'd bought the dice, and the black ones had still been in the store. Between the moment I bought the dice and the time I was carried to Metverold, someone bought the black dice and became the sorcerer. If Patrick did buy the dice, how did they end up in Danny's hands on the first night? Also, why would he say he gave them to his younger brother now, more than two months after our first adventure?"

"Maybe he lied to you," suggested Angeline. "And we don't even know if the sorcerer is always the same person. Maybe Patrick, Simon and Danny are each the sorcerer at one time or another."

Samuel shot a look at Angeline that made her cheeks turn red.

"What? It's possible," she said.

"Don't be foolish," said Samuel. "I doubt Danny would accept to work with anyone. No, there has to be another explanation."

"Well, no matter the reasons that make Danny the sorcerer, it doesn't change the fact that he now knows the secret of the gods' immortality," said Angeline. "Maybe we saved this legend, but once again let our enemy get what he wanted."

"All we need to do now is find a way to get some ambrosia before he does," said Samuel.

31

In the hour that followed, Anchises pointed out to Aeneas the heroes that would figure among his descendants, and Samuel saw the faces of Pompey, Nuna and Augustus, who would later become the first real emperor of Rome. He also saw the good and just Numitor, King Servius Tullius, and some of the families destined to play an important role in Rome's history: the Decius, the Druscus and the Torquatus, to name a few.

When Anchises finally reached the end of his long list and presented the last of his descendants—a man named Marcellus—to Aeneas, Samuel hoped that they could finally get out of the Underworld, but instead of shutting up, the voluble Anchises sat in the grass and went into a detailed description of the wars Aeneas and the Romans would wage against their enemies.

As soon as the old man started talking again, Angeline sighed deeply, threw her arms to the sky, and let herself fall back in the tall grass.

After a time that seemed to stretch over several lifespans, Anchises finally ended his tale and stood up, quickly followed by Aeneas. The two men embraced each other enthusiastically, expressing once again all the love they had for one another. Anchises seized his son by the shoulders and looked into his eyes.

"You understand now why it is important you continue on your journey, my son," he said. "A great nation will be born from your blood—a nation that will change the face of the world."

"I understand," said Aeneas.

"Now you must find the light of the sun again, my son, the last prince of Troy. Keep in your memory the faces of those who will follow you to the upper air, and stand strong before the perils that await you."

"Thank you, Father," said Aeneas. "Thank you for showing me my destiny, and for indicating the road that is mine."

Deiphobe walked over to the two men, signaling to Samuel and Angeline to follow behind. The end of their adventure was approaching, and Samuel could not wait to feel the wind on his skin and the warmth of the true sun on his face. Still being careful not to get noticed by Aeneas, he squeezed through the souls, followed closely by Angeline.

Anchises guided his son and the Sibyl along the River Lethe for about ten minutes. Everywhere around them, the shadows of the deceased sang, danced and wrestled, patiently waiting for the gods to call them up to the world of the living again.

Soon Aeneas and his companions came to a road that climbed along a steep cliff. Carefully, the old man went up the path, helped by Aeneas and followed by Deiphobe. Samuel and Angeline lingered at a safe distance, and then stepped onto the path as well.

The road wound along the cliff for a few hundred yards, before it disappeared into a tunnel in the middle of the stone wall. As soon as Deiphobe, Aeneas and Anchises vanished inside the passage, Samuel and Angeline hurried up the path after them, so they would not lose their trail. When Samuel entered the tunnel, he saw a bright white light farther ahead, with the shadows of the three people he was following outlined against it. A few seconds later, their silhouettes were swallowed by the light. Samuel immediately moved forward in the tunnel, followed by Angeline flying just above his head.

When they reached the end of the tunnel, the white light was so intense that they had to shield their eyes with the backs of their hands to keep moving forward. A few moments later, the light vanished and they found themselves in a beautiful cave.

The vault of the cave was about thirty feet from the ground, and was completely covered with a type of gemstone Samuel had never seen before. The stones looked like diamonds, but rather than merely reflecting the light, they seem to be producing it. This white light illuminated the cavern with such clarity that Samuel rubbed his eyes a few times to be sure of what he was seeing.

On his left was an arch almost ten feet high, which seemed to be made of a kind of organic material, its color somewhere between beige and hazelnut. Several faces were carved around the opening, and at the top of the arch was the bust of a man with a short beard, wearing a strange crown on his head. Across from this door, on Samuel's right, was a second archway, identical to the first except that it was white. At the top of this second arch was another bust of a man with a short beard, but this time without anything on his head.

Samuel took a few steps into the cave, but Aeneas, Deiphobe and Anchises had disappeared.

"Finally we're here," whispered Angeline as she passed in front of Samuel. "The exit from Pluto's kingdom! There were times I thought we would never get here."

"Where are the others?" asked Samuel.

"They are already back on the surface," replied Angeline. "At least, Aeneas and Deiphobe are. I imagine Anchises has returned to the shadows on the shore of the River Lethe."

Samuel walked to the center of the room. He examined the door to his left, then the one to his right. Both held darkness beyond their thresholds.

"Why are there two exits?" he asked.

"It's very simple," answered Angeline. "They are the twin portals of Sleep. The one to your left is the Gate of Horn, through which the real shadows can easily exit. Across from it, to your right, is the Gate of Ivory, through which the ghostly illusions are sent to the surface."

"Of course," replied Samuel. "Why do things the easy way?"

Angeline burst out laughing.

"Come on, let's get the hell out of here," Samuel said. He turned to the Gate of Horn and took a few steps, but then he realized Angeline was moving toward the Gate of Ivory instead.

"Where are you going?" he asked.

"Through there," answered the fata, pointing at the white gate. "This is the door Aeneas and Deiphobe used to get out."

"I thought it was the gate of ghostly illusions?"

"Uh … yes, but it's still through this gate that Aeneas leaves Hell, according to the legend," said Angeline.

"Why? Isn't it more logical to leave through the gate of real shadows?"

Angeline flew closer to Samuel and planted her fists on her hips.

"Are you really going to debate me on which door to use, when we are a hairsbreadth from getting out of Hell?"

"Okay, all right!" said Samuel. "There's no need to get angry. Let's use the Gate of Ivory. After all, you're the one who knows how this legend ends."

"And don't you forget it!"

Angeline turned her back to him and darted for the Gate of Ivory. Samuel glanced one last time at the Gate of Horn, and then followed the fata. However, she abruptly stopped, and he almost walked right into her.

"By the gods, now you've put a doubt in my mind!" yelled Angeline, looking at Samuel with angry eyes.

"I'm sorry, but you have to admit the Gate of Horn seems like a logical choice. We are not ghostly illusions. We are real."

"I know. You're right. Still, the legend is clear: Aeneas and Deiphobe leave Hell through the Gates of Ivory."

Angeline went to the Gate of Horn and inspected the arch running around the opening. She came back to Samuel. Exasperated, she let her arms fall along her sides, lowered her eyes to the ground and sighed deeply.

"I don't know anymore," she said. "Maybe you're right after all. Maybe we should leave through the gate of real shadows, since we are not characters of this legend."

"True, but according to that logic, we should use the door of ghostly illusions because we are not supposed to be here."

Samuel observed the Gate of Ivory more closely, then turned and did the same to the Gate of Horn. What would happen if they used the wrong door? Would they be sent into another world? Would they be reincarnated in the body of a newborn, after losing all memories of their previous life?

"Oh, the hell with it," said Angeline suddenly. "I'm leaving this way!"

Before giving Samuel a chance to protest, she darted for the Gate of Ivory, plunged into the darkness and immediately vanished.

Samuel stayed still for a moment, but decided to follow Angeline. After all, he had to make a decision, and Angeline knew more than he did about this legend.

He carefully walked over to the arch, his eyes locked on the bust of the man above the gate. Once he stood under it, he paused and stretched his hand before him. When the tip of his finger passed the gate and touched the blackness, a painless electric shock climbed along his arms and up the back of his neck.

Samuel took a deep breath, stepped forward and crossed the cold darkness under the Gate of Ivory.

A wan light floated above Samuel, so far away it was barely visible.

The suffocating darkness around him seeped into every pore of his skin, into his eyes, mouth, ears and nose. Samuel tried to shake his head to get rid of the smothering darkness, but he did not have a physical body anymore. He was just a conscience, suspended at the bottom of a black ocean.

Above him, the light gained a little in intensity, but it remained out of reach. He was unable to move toward it. Without muscles to transform his intentions into actions, it was impossible to move forward, turn, or even take a breath of fresh air. He was completely at the mercy of the forces of this mysterious place.

The white light was becoming brighter now. Samuel realized he was floating toward it, his conscience soaring rapidly out of the dark depths. The light soon transformed to a luminous stain oscillating above the surface of this black sea. Samuel rose closer to the surface, but not fast enough for his liking. The desire to take a breath of oxygen became stronger, and this natural desire rapidly occupied all his thoughts. Even if he did not have any lungs, he felt the pressure against the back of his throat and the burning in his chest, while even the thought of being denied fresh air was enough to make him lose control of his mind.

Then, at the very moment he thought he was going to pass out, Samuel broke the surface of the dark ocean, and the light shrouded him in its warmth.

Samuel opened his eyes and sprang up, breathing in as much air as he could. His lungs were ablaze in his chest, and his mouth seemed as dry as an African desert.

"Welcome back to the land of the living," said a rasping voice.

Samuel raised his eyes and saw Deiphobe leaning over him, sitting on the throne of stone inside the Chamber of a Hundred

Doors. Turning his head, he saw Angeline smiling at him, her face a few inches from his own.

"For a moment, I thought you had picked the Gate of Horn," she said.

Samuel's tongue was so dry he was unable to answer that he had never been happier to be wrong.

"You were fortunate to make the right choice," added Deiphobe, standing up from her seat. "You have no desire to know the fate that awaited you if you had chosen the Gate of Horn."

Samuel and Angeline turned to the Sibyl, but she abruptly left the room through the tunnel leading to the heart of her lair.

"How did I get here?" asked Samuel.

"That is one of the great mysteries of death, life and the constant cycle of souls, my dear Samuel," replied Angeline, stroking his cheek. "I think we came back through one of these doors, but I'm not entirely sure."

"Maybe, in a way, it's better we don't remember too much of it," added the young man. "So far, the doors of this room give me no desire to open them."

Samuel got to his feet and walked out of the Chamber of a Hundred Doors, followed by Angeline. They joined the Sibyl, who was reviving the fire in the hearth. As the flames rose, Deiphobe turned to Samuel.

"Would you mind helping me out and hanging this kettle over the fire?" she asked.

Samuel, who was still having some difficulty standing up, obeyed her without saying a word. Deiphobe added thyme, parsley and sage to the cauldron, and asked Samuel to fill it with cool water. When that was done, she placed a jointed rabbit in the broth, and grated a bit of salt over the kettle.

"Where is Aeneas?" asked Samuel. The syllables scratched the back of his throat as he uttered them.

"He has already returned to his people," answered Deiphobe.

She poured some of the cool water into a copper goblet, sprinkled a bit of brown powder over it and handed it to Samuel.

"Here, drink this," said the old woman. "It will calm the fire in your throat and give you back a bit of energy."

Samuel took the goblet and cautiously brought it to his lips. The smell reminded him of the flu medicines his mother had forced him to take when he was younger. He turned to Angeline, who nodded, and then closed his eyes and emptied the goblet into his mouth. The beverage spread over his tongue and down his throat like a soothing balm, and the dryness of his mouth immediately vanished, replaced by a feeling of freshness.

"What is it?" asked Samuel. "It's quite remarkable."

"Water with a bit of crushed mint," replied Deiphobe, with a look that made him feel like an idiot. "It's particularly effective against bad breath. When one comes back from the Realm of the Dead, one's body tends to bring back unpleasant smells."

Samuel subtly lowered his head and sniffed his own body. He immediately grimaced, quickly lifted his nose, and did his best to keep his stomach calm.

"So, we won, right?" Samuel asked to change the subject, hoping no one would get too close to him. "We protected Aeneas."

"Yes, we succeeded," answered Angeline, smiling at him.

"But barely," added Deiphobe. "For a while, I thought we were doomed. You took some time to get the golden bough back on Persephone's altar. A few minutes longer and the nymph Melinoe would have shrouded Aeneas and me in her storm."

Angeline shot a stern look at the Sibyl and crossed her arms over her chest in defiance.

"You're not the one who had to climb down to the darkest pits of Tartarus!" she said.

Deiphobe calmly walked over to Angeline.

"And what makes you think I've never been down there?" asked the Sibyl. "You're not the only one to take risks on the account of Virtus, little fata. We all have our role to play in this war against the Yfel."

Angeline held Deiphobe's gaze for a moment, then raised her chin and turned away. Samuel tried to loosen the tension in the room.

"The important thing is that the legend is intact," he said. "Aeneas will continue on his path toward his destiny."

"Yes, of course," answered Deiphobe, "but you did not prevent the sorcerer from getting what he wanted. Now he knows how to kill a god."

"Maybe," said Angeline without turning back, "but it won't be easy for him. It's not like he can just walk into a market and buy a bottle of ambrosia."

"Don't underestimate the Yfel," replied Deiphobe. "They are more resourceful than you can imagine."

"Are they now?" said Angeline, suddenly turning around. "Well, we have Samuel! He is the bravest Lorekeeper I've ever had under my care, and the Yfel doesn't stand a chance against him!"

Pride filled Samuel's heart when he heard Angeline talk about him this way. Since he had become the Lorekeeper, there had been a few moments when his courage had failed him, and those moments had haunted him ever since his first adventure on Metverold. But after surviving a journey through Hell and hearing the words of the fata looking after him, he took some comfort in knowing the moments were now behind him. After all, he had just faced the horrors of Tartarus and he was still breathing. What could possibly scare him from now on?

"We may have saved this legend and won this battle, but Deiphobe is right," said Samuel. "The Yfel is winning the war. The sorcerer is now closer to his goal than he was before setting foot in the Underworld."

"And according to what Angeline told me while you were unconscious, the sorcerer isn't a stranger to you," said Deiphobe.

The images of Danny's disfigured face floated into Samuel's mind.

"He's a student attending the same school I do," said Samuel, "but I still don't understand how he can be the sorcerer. I'm convinced he doesn't have the black dice."

"And yet he's the one you saw," said Deiphobe.

"Yes … well, I think …" Samuel stammered. "Yes, I'm positive it was Danny, but his face was so horrible. He was completely different from the Danny I know in my world. His eyes were so black and sinister, they almost seemed inhuman."

Deiphobe turned to the pot over the fire, and stirred the broth with a wooden spoon. "The Yfel have that effect on those chosen to be the sorcerers," she said without turning around. "Just like Virtus, the Yfel energy coursing in their veins generates changes in their minds, but also in their physical bodies."

"What do you mean, 'like Virtus'?" asked Samuel. "My appearance hasn't changed since I became the Lorekeeper."

"Maybe not the way you look, but your body certainly has experienced some kind of changes."

Deiphobe turned to Samuel, brought the spoon to her lips, and sipped loudly. After a quick pause to check the broth's seasoning, she spoke again.

"Did you ever get seriously injured during your adventures?" she asked. "Were you ever struck by a blow so powerful you should have been writhing in pain for days?"

Samuel reflected for a moment on what Deiphobe was asking. He thought of his first adventure again, when the sorcerer had struck him with a spell that should have been deadly. Was it really Angeline's potion that had saved him? Had his body fought back the effects of the spell to buy some time for the fata to cure him? And then there had been the giant's slap that had sent him flying several yards during his adventure on Albion. He remembered how he had thought his shoulder would be shattered into pieces, but he had nothing more than a good bruise.

"I … I can regenerate myself?" asked Samuel timidly.

Deiphobe burst out laughing. "I wouldn't go that far," she said. "Let's just say you are more resilient than you look."

Samuel turned to Angeline, who had her fists on her hips and was glaring at Deiphobe.

"Angeline? Is Deiphobe telling the truth? Why didn't you ever mention this?"

"Because I didn't want you to rush headlong into dangerous situations, that's why!" answered the fata sharply. "I've been doing this job for a long time, and I've seen my share Lorekeepers get hurt unnecessarily because they thought they were invincible. But what do I know? Who am I to decide what I should or shouldn't tell you? After all, I'm only a 'little fata'!"

Deiphobe raised her eyebrows at Angeline, held her gaze for a moment, then pushed aside the fata's insinuations with a wave of her hand and tended to her broth again.

"I'm sorry I've hidden a few details from you, Samuel," said Angeline "You have to understand it was for your own good. You may be more resilient here than you are in your own world, but you are still mortal. Promise me you will remain cautious, all right?"

"I promise," replied Samuel, hardly believing what Deiphobe had just told him.

"You know, there is a question that's been running through my mind ever since our encounter with the sorcerer," said Angeline. "Why didn't he kill you when he had the chance?"

"I have to admit that for a little while, I really thought I was done for," replied Samuel. "Then Danny looked straight into my eyes and I saw something strange in his. For a brief second, the blackness veiling his eyes vanished, and I have a feeling he saw the Samuel he knew before him. I think he hesitated because, for only a breath, we were Danny and Samuel again, not the Yfel sorcerer and the Lorekeeper."

"In that case, maybe your friend isn't completely lost yet," said Deiphobe. "If he was able to seize his own will and let you live, the Yfel's hold on his mind isn't complete."

"You mean Danny is acting against his will?" asked Samuel.

"Not exactly," answered the Sibyl. "It's more like he doesn't know what he wants anymore. The Yfel is trying to dictate what he needs to do by making him think it's his own desire."

Samuel suddenly felt something warm against his hip. Inside the small leather pouch, the dice were demanding his attention. Samuel quickly untied the pouch, as well as the Helm of Darkness.

"I'll make sure this gets back to Apollo," said Deiphobe as she took the onyx crown. "We certainly wouldn't want this artifact to fall into the wrong hands in your world."

"Will you thank him for me?" asked Samuel. "Without the Helm of Darkness I doubt I could have surprised the sorcerer and freed Angeline."

Samuel emptied the small pouch onto the table. The ivory dice bounced around a few times, and cast scarlet stains on the wooden surface.

"Looks like I have to get back home," said Samuel.

"But we still have so much to talk about!" said Angeline.

"One cannot object to the will of the Parcae," Deiphobe cut in.

Once again, Angeline narrowed her eyes at the Sibyl.

Samuel stood and walked over to the oak cabinet, where he had stored his clothes upon his arrival on Metverold. He carried them into the tunnel leading to the Chamber of a Hundred Doors and changed. When he started to undo the scabbard at his side, images of the two vampires waiting for him came back to his mind. Curiously, he almost smiled thinking about those two. He had just battled harpies, hellish demons, a three-headed dog, a couple of enraged Furies, and a hundred-armed giant. Suddenly, the two little strigois did not seem as frightening.

When he came back to the Sibyl's kitchen, Samuel handed his armor to Deiphobe, but he kept the sword with him.

"If you guys don't mind, I'm going to keep this with me," he said. "There are two vampires waiting for me back on Earth, and I wouldn't want to disappoint them."

"Okay," replied Angeline, "but be careful."

On the table, the dice shone with a light so bright that Samuel had to turn away when he picked them up.

"What do you intend to do with the sorcerer?" asked Angeline.

"Danny? I haven't really thought about it."

"Just stay on your guard," Angeline said. "The Yfel has to be protecting him. The vampires are only one of many tricks they can use to eliminate you."

"I'll be careful, Angeline, don't worry about me."

The fata smiled timidly. Then she jumped onto his shoulder and embraced him with her tiny arms.

"I really am proud of you," she whispered.

"I know," replied Samuel. "And I am also proud of you, Unshakable Angeline."

The fata let go of his neck and flew over to Deiphobe.

"I guess I'll see you soon," said Samuel.

Angeline nodded, and then buried her face in the Sibyl's robe.

Samuel smiled at the Sibyl, who smiled back and waved at him. He then lowered his eyes to the dice in his hand. The moment had come for him to go back home. Without waiting any longer, he cast the dice on the wooden table. Right away, the light flowed across the surface of the table and dripped on the stone floor, and then spread to the walls and across the ceiling. In an instant, the scarlet light had completely engulfed the room, and now pulsed to the beat of Samuel's heart.

"Say hi to Cathasach for me!" he yelled to Angeline, a moment before his vision blurred and the room started spinning around him. The crackling of the fire under Deiphobe's kettle and Angeline's reply melted into the sound of several musical instruments, and the colors fused to form a surreal kaleidoscope.

The swirl around Samuel accelerated, and then everything went black.

The Lorekeeper had left Metverold.

32

Before he even opened his eyes, Samuel was assaulted by the stench of rot and dry dust. It was the smell of a tomb sealed for many centuries, a forgotten cemetery, or an ancient burial chamber.

It was the stench of a vampire.

Samuel suddenly opened his eyes, and his heart jumped in his chest. The horrible face of a strigoi was leaning over him, and the monster was trying to dig its fangs into Samuel's exposed jugular.

Samuel screamed at the top of his lungs, clenched his fingers around the pommel of his sword, and plunged the blade into the left side of the vampire, where its withered heart had to be. The strigoi opened its black eyes wide when it realized Samuel was conscious, but did not react fast enough, and a breath later it vanished in a cloud of green smoke.

Without wasting a second, Samuel rolled on the gravel and jumped to his feet, ready to face the last of the three vampires. He spotted the monster a few feet in front of him. The vampire had its eyes locked on Samuel's sword, and was visibly surprised to see its prey now armed.

"Come on!" yelled Samuel. "If you think I'm scared of you, you'll see how wrong you are. Compared to the place I've just been, you're about as frightening as a wildflower."

The strigoi let out a sinister growl, but remained at a prudent distance from Samuel. After a second of hesitation, it took a few steps to its right, and Samuel followed it to keep facing the vampire.

The strigoi stopped after a few feet, and remained still for a moment. Then, without warning, the monster pounced on Samuel. The young man tried to move to his left to dodge the attack, but he was not as fast in this world as he was on Metverold. The vampire hit Samuel with its shoulder and sent him flying. The sword flew from Samuel's hand and plunged into the ground a dozen feet away.

Before Samuel could get it back, the strigoi jumped in front of him and lunged again. Samuel had just enough time to grab the monster's wrists to avoid the claws trying to slash his face, but the vampire was too strong for the young man, and in an instant, Samuel found himself on the ground, his back pinned against the gravel and the vampire on top of him.

Samuel tried to hit the vampire with his knees, but his strikes were badly lacking in strength. Still grabbing the monster's wrists, he did everything in his power to keep the vampire's fangs away from his neck, but he was quickly getting tired. Samuel had to get out of this position.

Samuel tried to hit the monster again, with his heels this time, but in vain. The vampire continued to push its head forward and was getting closer to Samuel's throat. At the exact moment the vampire pushed forward to finally satisfy its thirst for blood, the monster suddenly stopped. Then it disappeared in a cloud of green smoke.

Samuel closed his eyes, held his breath, and chased away with his hands the particles floating close to his face. When he got his senses back and opened his eyes, he saw Clara extending a hand to help him up. In her other hand, she held the sword Samuel had brought back from Metverold.

"I can't leave you alone for even a minute, can I?" she asked with a smile.

Still in shock, Samuel took her hand. Clara pulled him to his feet with surprising strength.

"C—Clara?" he managed to mumble. "What are you doing here?"

"I'm sure you have a ton of questions," answered Clara, "but I don't think we should linger around here much longer. It's a little too isolated to my liking. You never know what sort of monstrosity might be lurking in the area."

Without giving Samuel a chance to get his full senses back or add anything, Clara turned and walked away, glancing left and right. When she passed under a street lamp, she did her best to hide the sword along her body, and then she walked toward the street.

"Samuel!" she shouted, when she looked back and realized he still had not moved a muscle.

The shout pulled Samuel out of his stupor, and he hurried to catch up.

They walked in silence to Samuel's home. In the distance, they heard the murmurs of the Fourth of July crowd lingering in the park after the fireworks. Samuel hoped with all his heart his parents, Shantel and Patrick were not home yet, so he could talk in peace with Clara.

The question was: talk about what, exactly?

As they approached the house, dozens of questions bounced around Samuel's mind, and he had no idea which one to choose to start a conversation. Should he talk about his role as the Lorekeeper, about Metverold, or about the way Clara had not showed a single hint of fear upon seeing a vampire?

"I think I should begin by giving this back to you," said Clara, handing the sword to him, pommel first.

"Thanks."

He laid the sword at his feet and let his eyes linger on the steps' rough surface for a moment.

"I know who you are, Samuel," said Clara after a couple of minutes. "I know you are the Lorekeeper, so we can drop the charade now, both of us."

Samuel had dreamed of this moment for months now. He had wished a thousand times to be able to tell Clara his stories. He wanted so much to make the young woman understand he was not like the others, and that if he sometimes he looked strange it was for a good reason. Now that this moment had arrived, Samuel was unable to say a single word, and even less capable of looking Clara in the eyes.

"I know about Metverold," added Clara. "To tell you the truth, it's where I come from."

This declaration pushed Samuel out of his state of shock, and he quickly turned to the young woman. As soon as he met her wide, green eyes, his heart melted, and his face turned scarlet.

"You ... you come from Metverold?" he asked. "How is that possible?"

"It's a long story that really doesn't matter for now. I only want you to know I understand what you are feeling, and ... and you can trust me, Samuel. We are both on the same team."

"Virtus sent you here?"

Clara nodded and raised her eyes to the stars.

"Yes. A long time ago, the Parcae sent me here, to Earth."

"Why did they do that?"

"Because I asked them to. I wanted ... I wanted a change of air, and to discover new worlds. I'd had enough of always reliving the same stories, over and over."

She turned to Samuel again.

"Sometimes ignorance is bliss, Samuel. As soon as I became aware of the forces like Yfel and Virtus, and realized the world of Metverold was only a world of legends, I understood my existence began and ended with the stories I was part of. After a while, I wanted to get out of that endless cycle."

"You're a character of legend?" asked Samuel, hardly believing what he was hearing.

"I *was* a character," replied Clara. "These days, I'm just Clara."

Samuel burned to ask her what legend she had belonged to in the past, but he held his tongue, worried she would see it as an invasion of her private life, or would bring back memories she preferred to forget. He thought that if the right moment ever came, she would tell him all about it.

"I assure you, the legends I was part of aren't that important," said Clara, who had probably read the questions in his expression. "What's more, I'm not the same person I was."

"I ... I didn't mean anything by it," whispered Samuel.

Samuel remembered Angeline's words, and what she had mentioned a few times during their conversations. She had said agents of the Yfel and Virtus were on Earth. Some of them were here to measure the impact of any changes in the legends, while others were here to ...

"You're here to keep an eye on me, aren't you?" asked Samuel.

Clara nodded once again.

"And from what I can tell, you're lucky I'm here," she said.

Blood rushed to Samuel's cheeks once again.

"I could have gotten out of that jam by myself," he said, looking away.

Clara started laughing and gently punched his shoulder.

"I won't say a word to anyone, don't worry," she said. "But you can stop playing 'who is tougher' with me, Samuel. We both know you don't have the same powers here as you do on Metverold."

"What about you? Do you have any special powers?"

Once again, Clara's laughter echoed in the warm summer night, and Samuel could not help but smile.

"No, unfortunately, but I know how to defend myself with a weapon."

Samuel recalled how Clara had fought during the live-action role-playing game, and the ease with which she had bested her foes.

"Let's just say I have many years of experience," she said.

"Then it's not very fair," said Samuel. "How come the vampires have powers and we don't?"

"It all depends on your point of view. Their powers aren't anything special. For a vampire, it's normal to have superior strength and move faster than a human. It's part of who they are. In any case, it didn't really help them. We don't always need special powers to succeed, Samuel."

Samuel still had a hard time believing Clara was part of Virtus, just like him.

"You know I went to Metverold, when you came here the first time, right?"

Clara nodded.

"I wanted so badly to ask where you had been," she said.

"I was in Britain, fighting the giants of Albion."

In the minutes that followed, Samuel told Clara of his adventures. He described how he had fought the Saxons, met the young Merlin and saved the red dragon of the Britons. He told her in detail how he had battled with the giants of Albion, as well as his meeting with the giant Aristaeus. And finally he told her about his latest adventure in the Underworld, with Aeneas, the last prince of Troy.

"I'm impressed, Samuel!" said Clara when he was done with his tales. "You descended into Hell and you're not that shaken by it? Maybe I underestimated you."

Once again, blood flowed to Samuel's face, but he did not mind it this time. He was floating on a cloud. Finally he could tell someone about his adventures.

And not just anyone, but Clara!

For a long time now, she had been the one he wanted to confide in, to impress with his tales and feats, and now she was looking at him with eyes brimming with admiration.

They stayed silent for a moment, watching the stars above them. Samuel was wrestling with the desire to pass his arm over the young woman's shoulder, but he did not want to ruin this magical moment.

"You know who the Yfel sorcerer is?" asked Clara after a moment.

"Yes. It's Danny."

Clara's eyes widened.

"The bully at school?"

Samuel nodded.

"I thought he didn't want anything to do with role-playing games and trivial stuff like a pair of dice," she said.

"I know. It's really strange. Plus, I know who has the dice, and it's not Danny." Samuel told Clara how Patrick had mentioned giving the dice to his younger brother, Simon.

"And you're certain that Simon still has the dice?" asked Clara.

"I think so, but there's only one way to be sure. Tomorrow I'll try to buy them from him."

"Still, stay on your guard. This is all very strange. I should come with you."

Samuel turned to her, a smile on his lips.

"I just fought a bunch of monsters in Hell. I think I can defend myself against a stuttering boy."

"Okay, fine."

She looked at Samuel with a gaze that melted his heart. Samuel held her gaze for a moment, but turned away before doing something foolish.

"Well, I think I should get back home," announced Clara.

"Where is that exactly—your home?"

"Don't think I'm going to tell you that! I still have to keep some mystery about myself, don't I?"

Samuel smiled as he got up, and then he helped Clara do the same.

"And between you and me," added Clara, "I suggest you take a shower before your parents get home. You stink like an old tomb."

Before Samuel could say anything, she walked away.

With a heart as light as a feather, Samuel picked up the sword, unlocked the door and climbed upstairs. He jumped into the shower and vigorously scrubbed every inch of his body, making sure to remove any trace of his last adventure on Metverold.

When he was done, his parents were still not home, and he slipped into bed.

As sleep gradually shrouded his tired mind, he thought of Clara, and the way she looked at him now, and all the things he wanted to tell her, but could not find the courage to say.

The next morning, the sun was already high in the sky when Samuel opened his eyes. At the slightest movement, his aching muscles reminded him of the trials he had endured on his last adventure. Fortunately, he had not brought back any apparent wounds he would have a hard time explaining to his parents.

As if on cue, his father knocked on the door.

"Samuel, are you up? Can I come in?"

"Just a minute."

Samuel put on shorts and t-shirt, and then opened the door for his father. Mr. Osmond looked at his son for a moment. He was holding a bronze sword—the blade he had used to threaten Shantel's new boyfriend. He walked over to the bed and sat down.

"I can explain—" Samuel said.

Samuel's father raised a hand.

"Listen, Samuel," he said. "I know that teenage years can be … troubling for a young man your age."

Samuel rolled his eyes. "It has nothing to do with adolescence, Dad."

"Please let me finish."

Samuel closed his mouth and fell back into the chair at his desk. Sleep was still clinging to his mind, his muscles were complaining about being dragged out of bed and his stomach cried out for attention. Samuel had no desire to have a little father-and-son talk. What he wanted was to go downstairs and grab a bowl a cereal, and then contact Simon Underwood to see if he still had the dice.

"As I was saying," continued his father, "I know you are experiencing many changes right now. You're slowly getting past the age of playing games, and are becoming an adult. And it's okay. At your age I was in the same situation you are, believe me."

Samuel bit his lip to hold back a laugh.

"But it doesn't excuse you from owning a weapon like this, Samuel." Mr. Osmond raised the sword before him in a rather clumsy fashion, which was too much for Samuel, and he let out a guffaw.

"You think it's funny, perhaps?" asked his father.

"I'm sorry," answered Samuel. "It's just that I doubt that when you were my age you had access to such realistic toys."

Samuel's father turned the bronze blade of the Trojan sword in his hand.

"You really want me to believe this sword is not genuine?"

"Seriously, Dad? How do you think I could have gotten my hands on a real weapon?"

"I don't know," answered Mr. Osmond. "They sell all kinds of things at the role-playing conventions you attend, don't they?"

"Yes, but they're all replicas. They don't have the right to sell real swords to kids, for heaven's sake."

Samuel's father passed a finger along the blade. Fortunately, thought Samuel, this sword seen some use, and had lost most of its bite. It was probably no sharper than a letter opener.

"If this is really a toy, I'm going to discuss with your mother the games you and Lucien play together. Maybe they're too dangerous for you guys."

"No they're not," said Samuel, laughing. "You don't get it. This sword is a replica to hang on a wall. Nothing more. We use weapons of foam in our battles. We're not complete idiots."

Once again, Samuel's father studied the bronze sword, this time with less conviction. Samuel read the confusion on his face: Mr. Osmond hesitated between believing his son and grounding him. Samuel decided to strike again.

"Patrick is also a live-action role player," he said. "I thought he was part of a new scenario, with Lucien and me. It's a scenario that enters our daily lives. He said a codeword, and I thought he was one of my enemies. I swear I didn't really want to harm him. I did apologize to him, more than once."

Mr. Osmond raised his eyes to his son. Samuel knew everything was on the line at this very moment. If his father believed he was telling the truth, then maybe he would be allowed to get out of the house today. However, if he thought Samuel was lying, then he wouldn't be able to contact Simon to check if he still had the black dice.

After a moment, Samuel's father got up and walked to the door. "In any case," he said, "your mother and I think you're too old to be confined to your room. You're free to go out, but on the condition you mow the lawn for the entire summer, and that you help your mother with the housecleaning on Saturday mornings."

"No problem."

"And I'm taking this sword," added Samuel's father. "Replica or not, it's much too dangerous."

Samuel wanted to protest, but he thought he would be better off accepting his father's condition for now. Plus, the sword he had brought back from his latest adventure was hidden under the mattress.

"One more thing," added Mr. Osmond as he was walking out. "From now on, would you mind not mixing the real world with the imaginary one?"

"That's what I keep trying to do," replied Samuel with a smile.

"Very well. Your mother has breakfast ready. Don't make her wait."

Despite his stomach's protests, Samuel waited a few moments before following him Lucien friend answered after a few seconds.

"Samuel! How are you doing?"

"I'm all right."

"You missed quite a party last night," said Lucien enthusiastically. "You should have seen the—"

"Yeah, I know," Samuel broke in. "Listen, Lucien, we can talk about it later, but something important has come up. Can you meet me at the Brigantine again, around two?"

"Okay. Why?"

"I found the black dice I told you about."

"Really?"

"Yes. You remember Patrick, my sister's new boyfriend?"

"Yeah."

"He's the one who bought them, but he gave the dice to his younger brother."

"To Simon?"

"Yes. Do you have his number?"

"Of course."

"Could you give him a call and ask him to join us as well? Tell him I want to buy the dice for my collection."

"And what if he asks me how much you are prepared to offer? What do I tell him?"

"Just tell him I want them, and he won't waste his time."

After he hung up, Samuel went down to the sumptuous breakfast waiting for him: scrambled eggs, bacon and waffles. Samuel guessed his mother regretted making him miss last night's festivities. He made a mental note to let her know he did not blame her. To be honest, he was glad he had been able to leave for Metverold in relative peace. He did not dare imagine what would have happened if the dice had called for his attention in the midst of the Fourth of July crowd.

As he sat down, his phone vibrated, and a text message from Lucien informed him Simon had agreed to meet with them at the Brigantine in a little over three hours. Samuel quickly devoured almost all the food in front of him, and then hurried outside to mow the lawn, like his father had asked him to. Samuel wanted to do it as soon as possible and show his willingness to make amends.

When he was done, he went upstairs to wash his face and change his clothes, and then he left the house and made his way to the meeting place. He chose a table outside the restaurant, since the sun was still shining in the sky. The owner recognized him and waved, and Samuel ordered a Coca-Cola. A few minutes later, Lucien joined him and ordered a plate of nachos for the two of them.

"Do you want them without jalapeños or the 'El Diablo' version?" asked Lucien. "It says it's a real descent into Hell on the menu, but they always exaggerate these descriptions. It's never as hot as they pretend it is."

"I think I'm going to stick with my Coca-Cola," replied Samuel. "You told Simon two o'clock, right?"

"Yes. He should be here any time now."

The waiter brought Lucien his plate of nachos—the El Diablo version—and the young man attacked them. On the first bite, he coughed violently and downed his glass of water to put out the fire burning his trachea.

"Okay, maybe this time, they were right." He raised blurred, tearful eyes at Samuel, then looked past his shoulder. "Here comes Simon now."

Samuel turned to follow Lucien's gaze.

"Holy shit!" Lucien said. "What happened to him?"

Simon quickly squeezed through the tables on the terrace, his head down and his eyes to the ground. When he got to Samuel and Lucien's table, he let himself fall into a chair. He remained there for a moment, his body jerking from time to time with muffled sobs.

"Simon?" asked Samuel. "What happened to you?"

The boy raised his head. He was a little younger than Lucien and Samuel, with a round face and short blond hair. The sun made his eyes shine with a striking blue, and tears rolled down his red cheeks. Samuel noticed a small trail of blood under the boy's nose, as well as the beginning of a bruised eye. Simon's polo shirt and black shorts had probably been clean and impeccable when he left home, but his clothes were now wet and torn.

"I–I was … I was attacked," he managed to say between two sobs.

"Where?" asked Lucien.

"O-over there," replied Simon, pointing to a building farther down the street.

Samuel turned and saw a dark alley next to the building.

"Do you still have the dice with you?" he asked.

Simon shook his head.

"Who attacked you?" asked Samuel.

"D-Danny. H-he … he stole my bag and m-m-my pocket money."

The world started swirling around Samuel. He understood now why Danny had been the sorcerer from the start, even if he did not have the dice in his possession. Angeline had often mentioned that time did not flow the same way on Metverold as it did on Earth. Nothing prevented a sorcerer coming from another time to be in the same legend as Samuel.

Danny was not yet the sorcerer in this world, but he was going to be, sooner or later. It was only a question of time before he cast the dice and was carried to Metverold for the first time.

Samuel raised his hand to signal the waiter to bring Simon something to drink, and then he offered a sip of his own Coke.

"Everything's going to be fine," he said.

Simon nodded, but Samuel had said the words mostly to bolster his own courage. The sorcerer may have eluded him on Metverold, but Samuel now knew his secret. He now had a card up his sleeve as well. All he had to do was to get the dice back before Danny became the sorcerer, and the Yfel plan would crumble to dust.

And now that he had Clara for an ally, he was convinced he would succeed.

Samuel swept the street with his eyes, his heart filled with hope. Danny had said they would be waging a war worthy of the gods, and Samuel completely agreed.

The Yfel had won the first couple of battles in this war, but now it was Samuel's turn to go on the attack.

THE END

ABOUT THE AUTHOR

Thank you for reading *The Last Prince of Troy*, the third volume in the *Tales of the Lorekeepers* series. I hope this new adventure with Samuel and Angeline was as enjoyable for you as the first one.

Please do not hesitate to send me your comments at info@martinrouillard.com. I promise to reply as quickly as I can! You can also follow me on social media, where I post about many topics, including writing and self-publishing, as well as my travels and my favorite movies and video games.

Don't forget to join Samuel on his next adventure in the next volume, coming soon!

If you are thinking about writing your own book and need a hand getting started or completing your masterpiece, please let me know. It will be my pleasure to help you with your project. Please visit my website for more information about the coaching and consultation services I offer.

www.martinrouillard.com

Made in the USA
Monee, IL
28 August 2021